Tone of Voice

Kaia Sønderby

TONE OF VOICE

Copyright © 2018 by Kaia Sønderby

Cover illustration © by Tia Rambaran

Set in LaTeX using the Baskervald ADF typeface

Published by The Kraken Collective

ISBN 978-91-985297-1-5

To my nieces, Lyric and Autumn, with all my love.

Acknowledgements

First and foremost, as always, I would like to thank my husband. For putting up with vagaries of an autistic writer wife, for comforting me even if it's three o'clock in the morning, for nearly a decade of the sort of understanding I'd only dreamed of, and of course, for believing in me, always, no matter how unworthy I may feel.

To Tia Rambaran for her truly stunning cover art. It was an amazing journey from my original thoughts to your final art, and I am so honored to have it gracing my work.

To Claudie Arseneault and RoAnna Sylver, for their invaluable input. An especial thanks to RoAnna, who has championed *Failure to Communicate* from its earliest days, bringing Xandri and the crew of the *Carpathia* to the attention of those who needed it.

And of course, to my readers. I cannot express how much your words have meant to me over the course of this past year. Here is, I hope, to many more to come.

A (Very) Brief Guide to the Peoples of the Alliance and Beyond

Written by Xandri Corelel in the year 4278 AE by human reckoning

Sanavila As a species, one of three co-founders of the Starsystem Alliance (the other two are not known and believed extinct). Resemble a cross between classic Earth conceptions of "Gray" aliens and what one might term elves. Their silvery-blue skin, and the long wing-like flaps that develop, hanging from their arms, in adulthood, led humans to nickname them "angels." Somewhat flat-faced, with a humanoid body free of mammalian characteristics such as breasts.

Ongkoarrat Longtime members of the Alliance. Resemble a cross between a wombat and a sloth bear, but bulky and massive, averaging two and a half meters in length. Like marsupials, Ongkoarrat have pouches in which they carry their young. Known especially for their technical prowess and somewhat grumpy demeanors.

Nafta Little is known about the Nafta, except that they get everywhere (earning them the nickname "space pigeons") and don't seem to speak Alliance Trade Common very well. They have a similar appearance to Earth mustelids, with features that remind of otters, weasels, or ferrets; however, adults top out at an average of a meter long, and their teeth can shear through bone.

Shar Resemble extremely large Earth iguanas. Shar were uplifted and as such, have not evolved many adaptations to sapient life, and are rarely seen on starships. Their front forelimbs have developed elbows that allow them to prop the front of their bodies up to examine specimens or play games, the latter of which they have developed many, which have been adopted by other species.

Nīpa Humans would likely consider them to closely resemble large, bipedal rats. Both the male and the female of the species have horns on their faces, however. The Nīpa have lived in diaspora ever since the destruction of their home planet by Zechak. They, like the Ongkoarrat, are known for their technical prowess, and are popular choices for individuals looking to have their own starships made.

Kowari Sometimes called "space kangaroos" (but never to their faces). Indeed resemble kangaroos to a degree, with plush faces more reminiscent of red pandas. Can store fat in their tails and not need to eat for several days, and have marsupial-like pouches for their young, with muscles that can hold the pouch closed in water. Traditionally explorers and adventures. As their own language does not have words, per se, they tend to adopt the names of other species' most famous explorers, inventors, and adventurers.

Humans That's us. Just your bog-standard hairless ape. Other species continue to be astonished by our ability to reproduce; we are rivaled only by the Nafta for our sheer ability to be ubiquitous across the known universe.

Psitticans If a parrot was a bipedal, secondarily-flightless sapient, it would be a Psittican. They come in three subspecies, dubbed Macaw, Amazon, and Conure. So far only the Macaws, the largest of the three, have participated in Alliance activities away from their home world. Expressing themselves with ruffled feathers and sometimes inappropriate senses of humor, they nevertheless charm almost everyone they meet.

Anmerilli The universe's little practical joke: Despite the sheer un-likelihood of it, the Anmerilli closely resemble humans. They have strong foreheads, ridged cheeks, and have kept their tails, and are internally quite different, but appear human-like outwardly. A stubborn, reticent people with a tendency towards xenophobia.

Felera A mysterious race of large cats that somewhat resemble tigers, lions, or leopards. Almost nothing is known about them, except that they are extremely rare, and sometimes bond with another individual, frequently humans. One interesting data point: Regardless of their own ideas of gender, Felera, with few exceptions, take on the gender expression of their bonded.

Zechak Occasionally referred to with the slur "orcs." They are extremely large, with males that can top three meters in height. With their pig-like features, tusks, and bulky builds, they are intimidating figures. Hostile to the Alliance. Hostile to everyone, really.

Won-Tak The Won-Tak would like you to mind your own damn business. No one on the crew of the Carpathia has actually met one. Yet.

Chapter One

Xandri

As soon as I heard the click of claws on stone, I knew it was gonna be one of those days.

Deep breaths, Xandri. Deep breaths. I inhaled, tipping my head back, basking in the sunlight and slightly cool air coming down through the opening in my ceiling. I tried to breathe in calm, succeeding only marginally. Then Marbles, my African grey parrot, gave herself a small shake to catch my attention.

"Right," I said. "Right."

I stepped out of the beam of direct sunlight and deposited Marbles atop her cage, where she ambled across her perch to join my other parrot, a pineapple green-cheeked conure called Cake. Cake immediately began preening Marbles' tail feathers. Behind me, the clicking of claws grew louder.

"Try to behave, you two," I hissed at my birds, then spun to face my guest.

I hadn't actually invited senior *attoaong* Mrrchki, but that never stopped her. She ambled into my cave as if she was really as slow as her great, cinnamon-furred bulk would imply. Though the Ongkoar-rat might *look* like a six-legged cross between a sloth and a bear, it was foolish to think of them as either. They were intelligent and perceptive and Mrrchki, much to my dismay, was also nosy. Yes, it was her job to train me, but after six standard months, you'd think she could trust me at least a little.

"They'll be here soon," she said, lifting her muzzle in what I'd come to recognize as a disapproving look.

"I know," I replied, doing my best to hold in my temper. "I'm ready."

Mrrchki let out a rumble like rocks in a grinder. "Shouldn't you put your pets away? We wouldn't want them to disturb the meeting."

"They won't."

I gritted my teeth. Her rumbles might remind me of Aki, another Ongkoarrat and one of my best friends, but Mrrchki was nothing like Aki. Sickness, a longing for the only place I'd ever thought of as home, coiled in my stomach and I fought to keep it at bay. I had a job to do. I couldn't do this right now, couldn't fall into another spell of doubt and self-pity. *You've had plenty enough of those as it is, Xan.*

"I still question the wisdom of this match." *Click-scrape-click* went Mrrchki's claws as she trundled farther into my home. "These two could not be more opposite if they were actively trying. If you want my opinion—"

I don't.

"—Kirchak really might be better suited to…a different life."

"I appreciate your wisdom, *attoaong*," I said, "but I think this match will work."

Thank God most Ongkoarrat were shit at reading human body language, because I had a hunch I wasn't hiding my *lack* of appreciation all that well. Not that I was always great at hiding what I really felt, anyway. I'd learned a lot over the years, and a lot of people never guessed I was autistic, but I slipped sometimes.

Slipped, huh? Is that what we're calling it? snarked a voice at the back of my mind. I tried to shake it off, but it clung, sinking in teeth like a vicious dog. *Was it a 'slip,' then, that lost you your job with the* Carpathia *? That almost destroyed an alliance and started a war?* I gritted my teeth until it hurt, until the muscles in my jaw and neck ached, and refused to listen. I could *not* let these doubts interfere with my position as *attoaong*.

Very loosely translated, *attoaong* meant 'people-matcher.' As a species with a social structure wildly different from the norm among sapients, the Ongkoarrat relied on their *attoaongs* to match those best suited to forming all kinds of partnerships. For the moment, I worked only with couples, matching mainly those who were looking to reproduce; I wouldn't be allowed to match large groups until I'd been an *attoaong* for some years.

Though perhaps Mrrchki's lack of trust came more from what she euphemistically called "The Incident," than anything to do with the Cochinga mission. I'd thought I'd understood what I was getting into when I came to be an *attoaong*, I really had. I had thought of the Ongkoarrat as having high numbers of asexual and aromatic individuals—terms that worked for humans but, I was now pretty sure, did *not* really describe the Ongkoarrat—and my job was to match them.

Reading into the history, it had all seemed so logical: The high tendencies towards—well, whatever terms would suit them—had created a crisis some generations ago, and they had found themselves low on replacement population. So, to avoid extinction, it became law that every individual—barring those who were what we might, among humans, describe as sex-repulsed—must have young. Some wanted to anyway, and those matches were the easiest. Others took a lot more work, but it had made so much sense laid out in plain terms.

"Xandri?"

I swallowed. "Yes, *attoaong*?"

"Is there a problem? When Akcharrch brought you, she assured me—"

"There's no problem," I said quickly. "I was just—just making sure I'd gone through everything I need to before the meeting begins."

I twisted as if to inspect my cave for anything I might have missed, though what I needed—two stout, eggshell-shaped chairs—was already there. Yet I went over it all carefully anyway. Mrrchki hated it if my cave was untidy when a pairing showed up.

Not that it ever was that untidy. I was normally a fairly messy person, but I found it hard to spread my clutter here, and not just due to the size of my cavern. My books sat on stone shelves carved into the walls; my bed was an import, with the finest mattress I'd ever slept on; I had a desk where I kept a high tech computer and all of my other electronics; and of course, there were Cake's and Marbles' cages. Yet compared to my relatively small quarters aboard the *Carpathia*, it didn't feel like home.

"Seems like I'm good," I said, with as much false cheer as I could muster. "And Kirchak will be here any minute, so..." I began pacing pointedly towards the cave opening.

"Perhaps I should stay," Mrrchki said, moseying along beside me. "There is bound to be at least some difficulty with this match. And after Brretrit and Ahrsandr..."

And there was the crux of it, surely. Once faced with the reality of my job, I had felt a certain...discomfort, setting up mating pairs with people who weren't much into the actual mating part. Yet whenever I brought the topic up, my charges just stared at me. To them, it was a duty, one they knew from childhood that they would have to undertake someday, and they all gazed at me blankly when I asked if they were *really* sure. Maybe I shouldn't have done it at all. I was human, and they were not, and it wasn't for me to try to change their ways. But then there was Brretrit and Ahrsandr…

"Oh, I wouldn't dream of taking up your time, *attoaong.* I'm sure we'll be fine here, and I know how to contact you if I need any help."

That would be an extremely cold day in hell. Despite my doubts, Mrrchki's instruction had been invaluable so far, but at the same time, her unwillingness to trust me grated. In six standard months I'd already made eleven successful matches, with only two failures to my name—and technically Brretrit and Ahrsandr were *not* on that short list. *Of course she doesn't trust you,* came that voice again. *She knows what happened on Cochinga. She knows how you screwed up. She's just waiting for the other shoe to drop.* I bit down hard on my lip, because it would be hella weird to suddenly start screaming "Shut up! And that metaphor makes no sense! Ongkoarrat don't wear shoes!"

Mrrchki snorted. I snapped out of my reverie as we stepped through the entrance to my cave. An Ongkoarrat raced up the path to my cavern, and let me tell you, you never quite understood the word 'galumphing' until you saw an Ongkoarrat—especially one like Kirchak—run. It was the most ungainly, graceless gait you could imagine, and it carried them over the ground at an alarming rate. Kirchak, who worked as a messenger, was even faster than usual. For a moment I thought he would crash right into me, he was moving so fast.

At the last second he dug his claws in and dropped his rear end, skidding to a halt a mere meter before me. Dust clouded out around him and quickly settled in his lightly coffee-toned fur. He gazed up at me, his muzzle open in an Ongkoarrat grin; an expression I hadn't known existed until I met Kirchak.

"I'm not late, I hope," he said, without even so much as a wheeze. His voice was a bit higher pitched than your average *ongko*—what humans recognized as male, though Ongkoarrat had no real concept of gender—giving the impression of youth. I knew he was older than me, though.

"Not at all," I replied, brightening. "Well, *attoaong,* Prrchik will probably arrive soon as well, so I think we'd best get started."

Mrrchki eyed Kirchak with dismay. "Very well. I'll leave you to it. Though I *will* be checking in on you from time to time, to make certain all is going smoothly."

"Of course, *attoaong,*" I said.

I waited until she was heading down the path, towards her own cavern, before aiming an irritated, cross-eyed glare at her back. Kirchak chuffed. Mrrchki paused and glanced back at us, so I did my best to look innocent. Kirchak and I waited until she turned and had gone a considerable distance down the path. We exchanged glances, partners in crime, and turned to head into my cave, both of us smothering laughter like a couple of school kids dealing with their least favorite teacher.

Kirchak butted his head against my hand, so I let it slide down his neck and onto the soft fur of his back. As we headed back into my cave he talked, chatting merrily about his latest trip, a visit with the People of the Sweet Spring. Even for a messenger Kirchak was gregarious, but I liked it. The taciturn nature of most Ongkoarrat left me feeling a bit lonely, left me pining for life aboard *Carpathia,* but Kirchak helped me take my mind off it.

"—but my favorite thing is that every time I go, I see something new," he carried on as he clambered into his seat. "For people without mountains to work with, they make some *amazing* structures, Xandri, truly."

"I did hear something about it," I said, turning to hide a grin. "It's sort of like a green house, isn't it? Except not exactly, because it's more about correcting their soil problems. Tea?"

"Oh, no, no thank you, I'm quite all right. It's a bit warm for tea, anyway, don't you think? How very unseasonal, to be this warm—"

"Kirchak."

The Ongkoarrat froze, mouth hanging open mid-speech.

"Relax," I said, approaching the table. "There's no reason to be nervous."

"Nervous? I'm not nervous, no, not at all, what makes you think I'm—"

"You're babbling."

Yet another thing I hadn't known Ongkoarrat did. Kirchak sighed and slumped down in his egg-shell chair, folding four of his six limbs against his body. I patted his furry shoulder in reassurance. Though in certain ways we were polar opposites, Kirchak and I had one huge thing in common: among our respective species, we were both considered atypical. Which was part of why I'd ignored Mrrchki when she told me not to bother trying to partner Kirchak. My time spent with Kirchak made me believe he'd like a life-match. Why deny him, just because he was a bit strange? And besides, two of my eleven matches had been rare life-matches; I had a feeling Kirchak and Prrchik would be the third.

"Hello?" A new voice, accompanied by the tap of claws, drifted into my cave.

"Hello?" Marbles echoed back.

"Behave," I hissed at my bird, then called, "Hi, Prrchik. Come on in."

Click-click-click. Prrchik rambled into view, her wheat-gold fur dark in the dimmer lighting of the cave. She was bigger than Kirchak by a decent margin, she being a bit larger—and he a bit smaller—than the Ongkoarrat average of two and a half meters in length. But I didn't think that would matter. My plans for this relationship went far deeper than the surface.

"Greetings, *attoaong*," she said, in a voice surprisingly soft and demure for an Ongkoarrat. "Greetings, Kirchak."

Kirchak gave his great head a shake, and rumbled a greeting in return. Fighting a smile again, I gestured for Prrchik to take the opposite chair. With remarkable delicacy for her size, she climbed into the chair and settled herself, her clawed limbs coming to rest daintily one atop the other. Kirchak gazed at her with the Ongkoarrat equivalent of abject adoration. Something like fifty percent of the Ongkoarrat population did not experience what others might view as romantic love, but it had been clear from early on that Kirchak most definitely *did*. I hid a tiny, smug smile, knowing I'd been right.

"Kirchak, this is Prrchik," I said. "She's an astrophysicist and an aerospace engineer." One of the best on the planet, in fact. "Prrchik, meet Kirchak. He's the head messenger for the People of the Great Rock."

Prrchik's dark eyes brightened. "Are you really?"

"Oh, yes. I just returned from visiting Sweet Spring, in fact."

"Ah! I've heard about their latest project. I understand it's quite the feat of engineering…"

Kirchak seemed to pick up on the longing in her voice as much as I did, because he launched into a description of what he'd seen at Sweet Spring.

I hung back, letting him talk. It had taken time with Prrchik, despite her honest desire to find a match, because she was quiet even for an Ongkoarrat, and for a while I hadn't been certain I would succeed in finding someone who suited her. She seemed to only be interested in talking about engineering—and then suddenly it clicked. I'd realized she talked most about foreign engineering projects, all kinds of them, and always there was that wistful wish to see them with her own eyes. Prrchik was interested in the world, but for some reason she wouldn't go and see it herself.

"—and the pumps are quite enormous," Kirchak was saying, his nervousness gone.

"Did you know, they used similar technology to the recycling pumps on starships," Prrchik said.

"Fascinating! You know how they work, then?"

Kirchak, on the other hand, was openly and enthusiastically curious about *everything*. He wanted to travel everywhere, space included, and learn as much as he could. That was why I thought they might make a good match. On the surface they couldn't be more different, but inside they shared a longing for adventure and exploration. I smiled as they both rocked forward in their chairs, each fascinated by what the other had to say. Maybe they wouldn't be a life-match in the end, but they'd be good for one another either way, I was sure of it.

Sure, are you? Like you were sure on Cochinga? Like you were sure that Marco Antilles was your friend? I shivered and pressed my back against the worked-smooth stone wall. I didn't want to think about this. It made me miss the *Carpathia* so much. Captain Chui, Kiri, Aki, the Psittacans…*Diver*…

Oddly, the fact that I'd been exchanging holo-mails with Diver these last six months just made me miss him more. Through the entire ordeal on Cochinga, Diver had been there to protect me. Fuck, if it hadn't been for him, I might never have gotten to the point where I found out that Marco had been playing me; I would've broken down before then. *Don't, Xan. Don't think about this. You have a job to do.*

But Kirchak and Prrchik were largely doing my job for me, and it was difficult not to wonder what Diver was up to right now...

Chapter Two

Diver

"—awaiting word from MP Corelellia on the Pandora situation. Meanwhile, experts from numerous star systems agree that people like this young Ms. Corelel could be a danger to society if—"

Clank. Crash. I grinned as the podcaster hit the floor and went silent. *Experts, feh. Experts my street rat ass.* There were no fucking experts anymore, not on people like Xandri.

"Hey!" came the dismayed chorus from the rest of R&D.

I left my station to retrieve my multi-wrench. Surprisingly good projectile, that, if you knew how to huck it right. I bent, grabbed the wrench and gave it a twirl before tucking it through a loop on my belt. The podcaster I gathered up and set back on the table. A few bits had come off, but nothing major.

"I'll fix it later," I called to R&D at large. "Ain't in the mood to listen to that shit."

"That's important stuff," Mack said, raising his head from the service droid he was retuning. "We had someone like that living onboard, man. Can you imagine what would've happened if she'd gone off?"

"Yeah," I drawled, "because on a ship with one-hundred and eighty ex-soldiers who don't see enough combat, the one you should really be scared of is the woman who's barely fifty kilos soaking wet."

"People aren't always what they seem, you know. Maybe—"

"Mack," Kae hissed, "enough. Unless you want your head to be the next target."

Mack glanced at the broken podcaster, then ducked back down behind the service droid. Kae shot me an uncertain look before returning to her work. So I was a bit cranky, so what? I didn't like people talking shit about my friends. Maybe some of that loyalty my old gang had cultivated had stuck around after all. Or maybe because I'd been there, because I'd seen what happened, because I knew Xandri had been a fucking sacrifice to protect the ass of bureaucracy , it made it harder to swallow the bullshit coming off the podcasts these days.

I went back to my station, where my latest project sat, partially invisible beneath a stream of ruddy red light. *Okay, fine, maybe it's more like vaguely semi-transparent.* Metamaterials weren't exactly on the easy end of the science spectrum and I was trying to synth these to match the scales from a beastie we'd met more than half a year ago. Technically this sorta thing was Science's job, not mine, but they'd asked for another set of hands on the problem and I'd volunteered. Wasn't that much else for me to do just now, aside from the usual projects.

With a thought I accessed the analysis program in my HUD. As data scrolled across the HUD, I shoved my hands through my hair and resisted the urge to scream. *Why the fuck does it keep doing that?* The program insisted my synth matched the originals perfectly. I'd have to talk to Kiri, have her see if something had gone tits up with the code.

Ping. The soft chime echoed inside my head.

"Diver," I said into the comm channel as I opened it.

"*Good morning, Mr. Diver,*" Captain Chui's brisk voice came through, sub-vocalized.

"*No such thing, cap'n,*" I retorted, switching to sub-vocalization too. "*Need me for something?*"

"*I need you in my office.*"

I hesitated, wondering if I *really* had to spend the time. I'd been thinking of taking the afternoon to record a new holo-mail for Xandri. Was my turn.

"*Five minutes ago, Mr. Diver. This is an order, not a request.*"

"*Yes, ma'am.*"

"*Good. Chui—*"

"*Captain,*" I blurted out, 'cause I was a fucking niddle-brain like that sometimes, "*what's this 'Pandora' stuff they been yapping about on the podcasts?*"

To my surprise, she drew in a sharp breath. "*Never,*" she warned, "*say that in front of Xandri. Office. Now, Mr. Diver. Chui out.*"

I drew back. One thing I kinda hated about the HUD, I couldn't pull it away and stare at it incredulously, like you could with all sorts of ancient communication devices.

My holo-mail would have to wait. Muttering under my breath, I grabbed a rag and scrubbed at my hands, even though I hadn't been working with anything greasy today. I tossed the rag on my work table, jabbed off the light, and shoved the synthed scales into a container, marked for transport to Science. Maybe they could figure it out. I wouldn't live long enough to if I didn't haul my ass up to Captain Chui's office *now*.

Strange. First Officer Magellan wasn't waiting outside when I arrived. I gave the door access a slap. The door slid open and I stepped inside, a greeting dying on my lips as I took in the scene.

Wasn't surprised to see Kiriit Ayabara, both my good friend and my archnemesis, or people like Aki and Christa Baranka, acting Head of Xeno-liaisons. Well, not that surprised. It was a bit of an odd mix, but what got me was the man in military getup, sitting in a chair slightly apart from the rest. I knew him too. Oh, I knew him all right. Too bad I didn't have my gun. My multi-wrench would have to do.

"Diver," Captain Chui said calmly, "stand down."

"But Captain, he—"

"Stand. Down."

I dropped my hand, but I didn't stop glaring at the man. Last I'd seen him, he was being escorted off the ship after Xandri left.

"Have a seat, Mr. Diver," Captain Chui went on. "Major Douglas is here to talk to us."

"Great, 'cause his last visit was such a fucking blast," I muttered, dropping into the chair next to Kiri.

She reached over to poke my shoulder and sub-vocalized, "*I miss happy-go-lucky Diver. Haven't seen him since Xandri left.*"

"*Don't be ridiculous. Nothing's changed.*"

She rolled her eyes but said nothing more, turning her head to focus on Captain Chui. I noticed the dark look she flashed Major Douglas on the way. *Not the only one who misses our fireball, I guess.* Which I really had to stop thinking about. I was just frustrated with the job, that was all, but people kept acting like I was some lovesick brooding romance novel hero. Like I wasn't allowed to miss a good friend or something.

I folded my arms and slouched in my chair, glaring at Major Douglas. He shifted uncomfortably in his own chair, his poker-straight shoulders twitching; considering a two-and-a-half meter long sapient with six legs and long claws was also giving him the death glare, I kinda understood. Not that I sympathized. The fucker deserved it.

"So, Major," Captain Chui said, with a certain exaggerated patience. "How can we help you today?"

Major Douglas cleared his throat and shifted again. "Well…the AFC has requested my help in contacting you about a job. During a recent trading expedition to Song, it was discovered that the Hands and Voices have been developing…interesting new technology. Do you know that they cultivate all types of corals?"

Perking up, I threw out, "Yeah, they even got a type to grow up onto land and form buildings for traders to stay in, right?"

Everyone in the room stared at me. I shrugged. *So I know some shit, big deal.* And yeah, I'd learned it from Xandri. In one of my holo-mails, I'd asked her—in a sudden fit of unbridled curiosity—to tell me some of the weird and wonderful things she knew. The coral farming on Song had been one of the topics she'd returned with. It was fucking stellar, cultivating coral like that. Or maybe it had just been the addictive way Xandri talked about it, her eyes bright like suns and her hands moving, every gesture an expression of excitement.

"That is correct," Major Douglas said stiffly. "It has come to the Alliance's attention that the Hands and Voices are attempting to cultivate coral that can withstand vacuum, with the eventual goal of being able to *grow* starships."

Fuck.

Captain Chui deigned to raise an eyebrow slightly. "Fascinating, Major. I fail to see what that has to do with us. That level of technology—if you want it, you'd have to convince the Hands and Voices to take Member status. Surely the AFC doesn't need *our* help for that."

Oh, ouch. I grinned as Major Douglas flinched back. Xandri might have taken the fall for the near fuck up on Cochinga, but everyone in this room knew that the responsibility lay with the Alliance First Contact Division. They'd been the ones who'd hired Marco Antilles without knowing his background, and they'd been the ones who didn't do thorough enough background checks on all the soldiers he'd recommended to them. Probably they were still busy picking all the Last Hope for Humanity plants out of their proverbial teeth.

"How close are they to success?" Kiri asked into the silence.

"At this juncture, their coral can withstand vacuum, but is slow to develop. It will be some time before they stand a chance at growing ships, but that the technology is feasible at all puts them in greater danger."

"So you believe the Zechak may try to take it for themselves?" Captain Chui asked.

"Perhaps, perhaps not. A bigger risk is that they will attempt to ensure that *we* do not get it. As Song currently has a Non-Member status, we can protect them from the Zechak, but we cannot go to war over any actions they might take. Now would be the time for the Zechak to make a move."

"And what about the LHFH?" I put in, mostly to make the Major squirm a bit more. "Any sign of them?"

Captain Chui shot me a sharp look. I grinned at her.

"It seems they've retreated to lick their wounds," Major Douglas replied, with some of his former pomp.

"You still haven't answered my question, Major," Captain Chui said. "What does any of that have to do with us?"

He took a deep breath. "The AFC has already spoken with the Grand Matriarch. She has stated that she is *only* willing to negotiate with one Xandri Corelel. You wouldn't happen to have any idea why she would demand to speak to Ms. Corelel?"

Captain Chui paused, her fingers steepled beneath her chin, her lips pursed and her eyes gleaming. *Holy shit. Are we getting Xandri back?* I glanced at Major Douglas. His forehead crinkled and his lips drew in, a sour-as-fuck look if ever I saw one. He'd been the one to report to Captain Chui when orders came down for Xandri to be fired. He was the one who'd delivered the threat that *Carpathia* wouldn't be allowed to continue operating if Xandri stayed. This had to be going up his self-important ass sideways.

"Well," Captain Chui said, after letting Douglas squirm for a good full minute, "you may not believe this, considering your previous assessment of Ms. Corelel's competence," Douglas flinched again, "but the changes I suggested to the AFC four years ago did not come from me. The ideas were Ms. Corelel's."

"There's no mention of that on the documentation."

"True. She requested that her name be withheld. She had her reasons, Major, and no, I will not explain them to you. Clearly, the Grand Matriarch or one of her people have figured out that Ms. Corelel was responsible for the changes, and realizes she is their best hope for getting a fair deal out of this. As we already know, the Voices and Hands do not back down easily."

I couldn't hold back a snort. That was one hell of a fucking understatement if ever I heard one. Early attempts to make contact with the Hands and Voices had been disastrous. Creatures that hid under water didn't play by landlubber rules. Efforts to pry them out of their hiding spots hadn't gone well either. After the dozenth submarine had been disabled and returned, with a sort of ironic gentleness, to the water's surface, the AFC had largely given up.

Until Xandri gave them the key piece they were missing... The new membership tiers, the more complex, nuanced way of handling negotiations—I'd been there when she brought them to the table to woo the Psittacans, seen the first successes for myself. Hadn't realized, though, that she had chosen to hide her part in the changes. *Wonder what possessed her to do that...*

"Then I see we have no choice," Major Douglas said with a sigh. "Despite the danger she presents—"

I snapped to attention. "*Xandri?* She's the least dangerous person alive. I mean, she'd rather run screaming from a spider than stomp on it, for fuck's sake."

"She held Councilor Nish mar'Odrea at gunpoint and threatened to—"

"Stun him," Kiri interrupted with a snort. "Had it been any one of us, we would've threatened to shove it up his ass, then fire."

Major Douglas looked appalled.

"Meanwhile," Christa spoke up quietly, "Diver, Kiri and I have been doing some research into Ancient Earth records on the matter. To be honest, Major, as a trained anthropologist I'm disgusted. The evidence indicates that people like Ms. Corelel—people with neurodivergences—were far more often the victims of violent crimes rather than the perpetrators."

"You should see the list of autistic people killed by their own family members," I drawled. "Really sends a shiver down the old spine."

Unable to find a coherent response for that, Douglas drew himself up and said, in his most self-righteous tone, "Do you always allow your crew to speak out of turn, Captain?"

" 'Theirs not to reason why,' " Captain Chui murmured. "That was how we once spoke of soldiers on Ancient Earth. It might make for good killers, but it makes for lousy thinkers. I prefer thinkers on my crew, so if they choose to speak their mind, they're allowed to do so.

"Now *I* am going to speak my mind, Major, and I suggest you listen. If the AFC is serious about the success of this mission, then I will do what I can to enlist Ms. Corelel's aid. However, *you* do not make the rules for my ship. If Ms. Corelel does return to us, she *is staying*. Do *not* try to argue with me, Major," Captain Chui added. "Because I could toss you out the nearest airlock and there isn't a single person on this ship that would ever admit they saw anything.

"Assuming she agrees, we will be doing this her way. More than likely she'll be unwilling to work with the AFC, thus this will have to be considered *Carpathia's* mission. Outside of combat, Ms. Corelel will be in charge. I refuse to compromise on this matter, so I suggest you be certain this is what you want before you agree."

And now we'd see just how important this mission really was. Probably not quite as life or death as the last one, seeing as that had involved a god damned *graser*, of all things. But if brass believed it *had* to happen one way or another...

Major Douglas rubbed his hands over his face. Technically, since a lot of operations on *Carpathia* were only barely legal, Captain Chui shouldn't have a leg to stand on with her demands. We survived on the sufferance of parliament because we were damn useful, but if they really wanted us gone, that would be it. So we were all waiting, watching intently, to see what Douglas would say. He opened his mouth, as if preparing for one more protest.

Then his face crumpled in defeat and he dropped his hands with a sigh. "Very well, Captain. We'll do it your way."

"Lovely," Captain Chui smiled, for all the world like Major Douglas was her favorite friend. "Aki, would you start readying *Mr. Spock* for the trip? And you, Mr. Diver, please pack your things."

I blinked. "Me? Um, sorry, ma'am, but why me?"

"You *have* been in contact with her for the past six months, have you not? Who better for the job of retrieving her?"

Aki chuffed. "She's got you there, boyo."

"And as R&D have informed me that you've been a bit…off temper, since she left, I thought a short vacation might do you some good," Captain Chui added with the hint of a smug smile.

Fuck. I'm being taunted by my own Captain and *a six-legged walking carpet.* But still…seeing Xandri again ought to be fun. She knew all sorts of weird shit and lit up when she talked, like a lighthouse beam cutting through the fog. And, okay, fine, I'd considered a little something else once or twice, but I only did casual and I didn't think Xandri played that way. So there was no fucking reason for everyone to look at me like that.

"So, now that that's settled," Captain Chui said, which told me this was an order, not a request, "let's get started. Kiri, head up to the bridge and get Lieutenant Zubairi to devise a route that will take us to a position a few days out from Karrckchak. Preferably one with a sizeable space station en route."

"Ma'am?"

"Ms. Corelel's birthday was last month. And there was that business with her hair that needed taking care of. Dismissed." She folded her hands atop her desk and turned to Douglas. "Now, Major, we have a few more details to iron out."

Chapter Three

Diver

"I'm not really surprised, considering the news out of Cochinga these days," Aki said as the group of us headed to the nearest grav-tube.

At the same time, Kiri nudged me hard with her elbow. "You've been in contact with her the whole time and you didn't mention it?"

"Ow! Damnit, woman, you're violent," I complained, half joking, as I rubbed my ribs. "There's news out of Cochinga?"

"Don't you listen to the podcasts?"

"Not anymore," I muttered, remembering the podcaster I still had to fix.

"Hmmm." The sound came through Aki's throat like a low rumble of thunder. "Well, ex-Councilor Nish mar'Odrea has been put on trial for high treason. Against the entirety of Cochinga. With him in custody, several more World Council members have stepped forward to voice their support of the temporary membership. The Alliance no longer needs to uphold their agreement to be rid of Xandri."

"You're trying to dodge my question," Kiri grumbled.

"So they've found proof that mar'Odrea conspired with Antilles?" I asked, ignoring Kiri for the moment.

"We did," Christa put in, gesturing between herself and Kiri. "We helped them dig it up. Where *have* you been these past months?"

"Moping," Kiri said.

"*Working*," I grated out. I glowered down at her. She flashed a bright smile in return. "Look, I didn't know you *weren't* in contact with her."

Kiri's voice dropped, low and wistful. "She's never contacted me."

"Uh...I kinda...contacted her first," I admitted, rubbing the back of my neck.

Kiri gazed up at me with raised eyebrows and Aki let out another chuff. No way to talk myself out of this one, so I just tried to ignore them. They wouldn't get it. *Then again,* I thought, glancing briefly at Kiri, *maybe* she *would.* I'd never quite understood why Kiri hadn't made a move—far as I could tell, she wouldn't mind something more than casual with our fireball—but maybe her reasons weren't that different. Maybe we both actually *liked* talking to Xandri.

"You all really miss her that much, huh?"

I half turned and caught sight of Christa, moving at a slower, sulkier pace behind us. She'd wrapped her arms around herself, like she could shield herself from things changing. If—*when*—Xandri returned, her position as acting Head of Xeno-liaisons would be gone.

"*We* actually bothered to get to know her," Kiri retorted.

Christa held up her hands. "Look, I get it. I think. I've lost friends from here too, one way or another. I just...don't know if she'll be willing to return."

"She'll return," Aki said. "The fact that the Alliance has given the AFC carte blanche to give in to our demands indicates they believe that this technology is useful, and that possessing it places the Hands and Voices in danger. Xandri won't be able to refuse if she knows people might lose their lives."

Which seemed pretty manipulative, but it was also true. And probably part of the reason Christa had been swallowing her pride lately and helping us with our research. This was our job, after all. I'd signed up with the *Carpathia* for a lot of reasons, and not just because I'd have free rein in developing cool gadgets. I'd dug the idea of making a difference in the universe; you had to, to make it aboard the *Carpathia.* So we'd all do what needed doing, even Christa.

"Why only send Diver, though?" Christa wondered. "Why not send the team? She'll be coming back to us."

"One glimpse of you and she'll bolt," Aki said. "Right now, she doesn't trust most people—and neither would you, after what happened on Cochinga."

"Not to mention the media's out for her blood," I said.

"Just so," Aki paused at the grav-tube and gave her head a shake. "Growing starships out of coral. Even *my* people would never think of doing that."

"Well, no one's perfect," I quipped.

She gave me a look I knew all too well. "Seems *someone* is back in a good mood." Then she launched herself into the grav-tube, surprisingly graceful for something that big with that many legs.

We all stood at the edge of the grav-tube, watching Aki swim through zero g like it wasn't a thing. Christa, I noted, watched with the fascination of your typical anthropologist, and I kinda wondered if she ever realized how much she and Xandri had in common. *Better not mention it. I like my head on my shoulders, where it belongs.*

Christa gave her own head a shake. "And people say a bipedal body plan is the most advantageous one."

"Don't know about you two," Kiri said, "but I sure as hell can't knit a sweater *and* program a computer at the same time."

Christa chuckled softly. "No indeed," she said. "Well, I'd better get to work. I'd like to pull up all the files we have on the Hands and Voices so they're ready when Xandri gets back."

"So you think she'll agree, then?" I asked.

"Are you kidding? Sapient whale and squid symbiotes, and coral that may one day grow into starships? She'll agree."

Occurred to me, as Christa flashed us a grin and stepped into the tube, that maybe her opinion of Xan had changed somewhat. Or maybe it was just that whole thing good scientists did, where they understood each other. I mean, I was a non-organics kinda guy for the most part, but I understood. Even I wanted to see how these corals worked.

As I lifted my foot to step into the grav-tube, I heard a hydraulic hiss from down the hall. Glancing back, I saw Major Douglas emerge from the captain's office. Suddenly Kiri grabbed my arm and hauled me into the tube, which was not a good fucking way to enter one of those babies. I swore and grabbed a railing along the side, pulling myself straight. Once I'd retrieved a general sense of 'down,' I turned to glare.

"What the fuck was that about?"

She shook her head and pressed a finger to her lips. As we made our way down, I noticed she was listening to something only she could hear, so I waited. Eventually, my HUD pinged to let me know someone—Kiri, I figured—was signaling my private comm channel.

"*That was Captain Chui,*" she sub-vocalized to me, after I opened the comm. "*She's suspicious. She feels Major Douglas gave in to her demands too easily.*"

"*Guess they really want this technology.*"

"*Maybe. But Captain Chui doesn't trust it, and after last time, I don't blame her. The push to get us to go along, to get us to convince the Hands and Voices to take Membership status... the Captain wants me to do some poking around, see if I can find anything.*"

"*Xandri's coming home and the Captain is back to being paranoid as hell. Things are finally returning to normal.*" I grinned. "*You need any help with your poking, you let me know.*"

She grinned in turn, wide and devious. "*Oh don't worry. I will.*"

Laughing, I watched her grab hold of the bar above the exit and swing herself out. An idea came to me then. Instead of heading for my quarters—I had at least a few days before we reached our destination—I opened my comm.

"*Carpathia?*"

"Here, Diver," the ship's AI responded, in her soft, chiming voice.

"Know where the Psittacans are?"

"Hydroponics. I can call ahead if you wish, let them know you need them for something."

I grabbed the bar above my head and heaved, shooting myself up towards the Hydro-Rec deck. "Nah. Wanna surprise 'em with the news."

"And no one thought to tell me? I am devastated."

"Oh, come on, *Carpathia*, you probably knew even before Captain Chui did," I said as I swung myself onto Hydro-Rec. "Nothing gets past you."

"Far be it from me to deny it." Her tone held the implication of a shrug, though she had no body to shrug with. "And might I say, Diver, it's lovely to have your shameless flatterer side back. I quite missed it."

I was still laughing when I passed through the lock into Hydroponics.

"Tomorrow?" I repeated, glancing from Kirchak to Prrchik and back again.

Prrchik gazed back shyly. "If it's all right with you, *attoaong.*"

Kirchak stared at me hopefully and I had to fight back a sigh. While I was pleased they were getting on so well, tomorrow was a little soon. Most of the time I waited anywhere from several days to a week before bringing a match together again, as per Mrrchki's instruction. While I wasn't certain I agreed with her on that, I *did* prefer to have a little time off. Yet these two were, in some ways, like Brretrit and Ahrsandr, always wanting to talk to each other. The only difference was the constant moon-eyed looks they sent back and forth. *On the bright side, it shouldn't take long for the first stages of bonding to be finished.*

"How about the day after tomorrow?" I suggested. "I already have a pair scheduled for tomorrow."

"That would be wonderful," Prrchik said. "Thank you, *attoaong.*"

"Thank you," Kirchak echoed brightly.

I stood in the mouth of the cave and watched them go. They walked side by side down the trail, still talking. Kirchak lightly bumped his shoulder against Prrchik's, as if they had been friends for years instead of days.

"See," he said, in what sounded like he *thought* was a whisper, "I told you. She's so much more reasonable than Mrrchki."

"But then, if she wasn't, there'd be *two* Mrrchki's," Prrchik responded with a little shudder, "and the very thought is enough to give anyone nightmares."

Kirchak's heavy chuffs—and Prrchik's softer ones—brought a small smile to my face. Since they were too absorbed in each other to notice me, I turned and headed back inside. As I flopped down on my bed, a headache threatening between my temples, Marbles and Cake fluttered down off their play tree to join me. I reached out with both hands, scritching feathery heads.

"Go home?" Cake chirped.

A pang went through my heart. "I'm sorry, boy. We can't go home. Not yet."

He tipped his head to one side, the picture of studied curiosity. The pang changed, morphing to a feeling as if my heart was plummeting straight for the core of the planet. The *Carpathia* had been the only steady home Cake and Marbles had ever known, and the first one I'd had in a decade. *At least we're not back on Wraith, moving from one shit neighborhood to the next.* I didn't miss spending my days trying to stay one step ahead of all the people I'd wrangled money from.

Laying there, staring up at the ceiling that had been smoothed until it hardly looked like stone, at the skylight carefully cut into it, everything felt wrong. *I want to go home, too.* At the same time, the thought terrified me. Here at least I was safe; parliament couldn't reach me, the AFC couldn't reach me, the media couldn't reach me. *But I...I can't reach anyone else...*

I rose slowly so I wouldn't frighten my birds. A cluck of the tongue later, I had one perched on each hand. I brought them back to their cages and deposited them inside, making sure the doors were secured. It was time for a walk, I decided, and much though I loved Cake and Marbles, I needed to be alone. Completely.

Outside, I took a deep breath of clean, fresh air and gazed into the tree-filled valley below. The People of the Great Rock had taken their name millennia ago, before the species developed any words for 'mountain;' they had chosen not to change it. So my new home was part of a large complex of caves carved into the belly of an enormous mountain range, which afforded me one hell of a view. Beyond the valley I could see Trade Town—the Ongkoarrat were highly pragmatic in their naming systems—and beyond that, the telltale glimmering sheen of water.

Something flapped above me and I tilted my head back, catching sight of one of the four-winged bird-like creatures that inhabited Karrckchak. Like Ancient Earth birds—like their counterparts on many planets—they came in a wide range of species.

"I don't get it," I muttered to myself, plopping down in the dust of the path. "I should be happy here. It's perfect for me."

So much to explore, so many new things to study. I had plenty of privacy and space, and despite my job as *attoaong*, plenty of time to do all the studying I wanted. I didn't have to smile, hardly had to watch my tone, almost never had to worry about anyone staring when I stimmed, and yet...and yet...

"I'm lonely." I brought my legs up against my chest and rested arms and head atop them. "What gives, experts? I thought I wasn't supposed to get lonely."

I wished, not for the first time, that I knew someone else like me, someone I could talk to, compare notes with. Though just then, I wished I had *anyone* to talk to, whether they were like me or not. I hadn't received a new holo-mail from Diver yet. *Soon, maybe. I'd like that.*

I sighed. There wasn't much use in sitting here, feeling sorry for myself. I rose and reached for my wristlet, activating the scanner. Then I took a deep, steadying breath and pushed my shoulders back, lifting my chin. *No more self-pity. Let's do some of that studying.* Maybe I could even get some video footage of a reacher to send to Diver. The thought made me grin, and I tried not to think about how much I wanted to be there to see his reaction.

Chapter Four

Diver

Maybe 'cause of its name, I'd figured Trade Town for a bit of a backwoods, shanty-town kinda place. As I stepped—alone—into the swirling crowd streaming out of the customs office, I was forced to reassess.

Trade Town spread out around me, as noisy and crowded as any top tier space station. I clutched the handle of my luggage, grateful for my height as I tried to get my bearings. *Looks like the main part of town is that way…* Fuck me, this place was huge and confusing. As I eased my way into the flow of sapient traffic, I wished Aki had come with me. Instead she'd stayed back to run a few systems checks on *Mr. Spock*, after which point she planned to make contact with her people.

"Don't you want to see Xandri?" I'd asked, after she'd explained her plan to me.

"Of course I do. But Captain Chui and I already discussed this. We have no idea what Xandri's state of mind is right now. Better to start with one of us and see how she reacts."

"And that has to be me?"

"During our mission on Cochinga, you were there to protect her—particularly, her emotional state—more than once. Captain Chui suspects, and I agree, that she considers you synonymous with safety, and will be more willing to listen to you."

A man's got his pride, and mine fluffed up like a pleased cat at her words, though I tried not to let it show. "All right. I'll give it my damnedest."

So here I was. *C'mon, Diver, man, you've navigated shittier streets than these by far.* And this place had been designed by Ongkoarrat, who tended towards a highly pragmatic and logical mindset. I set off, tugging my luggage—heavy as hell thanks to the addition of Xan's birthday presents—behind me and whistling. The tune was largely drowned out by the crowd—humans, Kowari, a few Shar, some Sanavila, surprisingly few Ongkoarrat.

A short distance from customs, maybe a street or two at most, the town opened up into one of the largest plazas I'd ever seen. I paused to take it in, noticing the tidy, even rows of stalls lined up like soldiers across the length of the plaza. *Market square.* A bit reluctantly, I turned up information processing on my HUD. A veritable whiplash of data cracked in front of my vision, but on the bright side, I now knew where I could find lodgings.

Rubbing a hand across my eyes—which never fucking helped— I started off again, angling to the left. As I turned, my HUD went off, alerting me to an all-too-familiar signal. Startled, I came to a halt again, and got an earful of Kowari swears for my trouble.

"That's not even anatomically possible," I shouted after the agitated Kowari. "For either me *or* you!"

My eyes, however, were following the tag on my HUD. Fucking irony, man; I know I'd come looking for Xandri, but I hadn't expected to just randomly run into her in the market.

Look, no one would ever call her a beauty. Not that I found her hard on the eyes or anything, she just didn't stand out much in a crowd. She must've been spending time out in the sun lately, because her ashy hair was lighter than usual, and the faintly goldish tone of her skin had picked up a bit of faint brownish. *She's been eating properly, too.* I could tell, despite her baggy clothes, because her cheekbones weren't sticking out sharply from the narrow oval of her face.

Then she turned her head and caught sight of me; the crowd parted with convenient timing, as if the universe had decided I needed a bit more melodrama in my life. Something hard to define flickered across her face, twitching her thin lips.

Then her face changed, lighting up as brilliantly and miraculously as a sun being born. Her mouth curved into a grin, her eyes turned the color of a spring sky, and a glow of joy radiated from every pore. And then I just couldn't tear my gaze off her. In that moment there was something so beautiful about her, it hurt.

Color me surprised; she dropped the basket she was holding and came at me at a run. Without thinking I let go of my luggage and opened my arms. I was kinda just teasing, since she didn't really do much of the whole hug thing. So I was in for yet another shock when she collided with me like a starship shot outta slingspace and wrapped her arms around me. On instinct I swept her up, holding tight, as something else crashed into me: The realization of just how damned much I'd missed her.

As I lifted her right off her feet, the tips of her fingers slid into the hair at the nape of my neck, and suddenly I was afraid that my body—particular parts of it, at least—was ready to sit up and take notice. But fuck it all, I didn't want to let go, so I decided to hold her as long as she'd let me.

Xandri

What the hell are you doing?

I had to hand it to my brain, it asked the important questions. What the hell *was* I doing? I mean, on an absolute scale, I was browsing the market for some goods I needed, which was fine. But I was pretty sure that didn't involve clinging to Diver like a limpet.

Yet I didn't let go. I held on, inhaling metal and grease and soap, indulging in the fantasies I'd often had of letting my fingers linger in his hair. My heart beat a steady cadence—*he's here, Diver's here, he's here.* And maybe somewhere deep inside I was afraid that if I let him go, he'd vanish into thin air. Certainly it seemed like he'd *appeared* from thin air. Finding Diver in the marketplace was the last thing I'd expected.

His breath tickled warm against my ear as he murmured, "Good to see you too, fireball."

Oh, Sweet Mother Universe. His voice, the warm and velvety tone of it, sent tingles all down my body. I became suddenly aware of just how good he felt against me. Strong muscle moved with every small shift he made, and I finally let go, fiery heat flooding my cheeks. Diver grinned.

I swallowed hard. He looked so good. The sunlight struck bronze into his loosely curling fawn-colored hair and the red-brown of his skin. His green eyes seemed to glow with amusement, and some other emotion I couldn't put a name to. *Oh, there's a surprise, an emotion I don't recognize. Next thing you know, someone'll discover that water is wet.* And since "socially inept" was practically my middle name, I blurted out the first thing that came to mind.

"What are you doing here?"

"Ouch!" Diver slapped a hand against his chest as if I'd wounded him. "I know you don't much care for surprises, but I was kinda hoping I'd be on the list of good ones."

"Oh, I—I'm glad to see you," I said hastily. "I just wasn't expecting to."

"Well, I admit, I was *planning* to call ahead, but it seems the universe had other ideas. Don't you want to retrieve your basket?"

"Oh, damn!"

I whirled, hoping my basket hadn't been crushed. Now that Diver wasn't holding me anymore, I was back to being aware of the crush and noise of the crowd, and I wound my arms around myself as I tried to catch sight of my basket. Diver grabbed hold of his luggage, pressed a hand against my back, and nudged me gently forward, steering me through the crowd until we'd reached my basket.

"Sometimes it's useful, being so tall," he said with another grin.

I swept the basket up and settled it on my arm. "Thanks. Carrying groceries home without it is a bitch."

"I'm happy to do some lugging for you, if you'd like. Soon as I find some lodgings."

"Um...well." I stared down into the empty basket. "I uh, I have an air mattress you can use, up at my place. If you want. I mean, it's not as comfortable, but it is a lot cheaper than lodgings here. The locals never saw a visitor they didn't want to take advantage of, you know."

The noise of the market swelled to fill in the silence that descended upon us. I lifted my head to find Diver staring at me. His eyes, so intense, seemed to be searching my face for something. I took a deep breath, trying not to turn so red.

"I'm sorry," I said. "I shouldn't have—I mean, if that was too—"

"Relax, Xan. I was just surprised, is all. Figured you wouldn't want me that much in your you space, you know?"

"Oh. Well, my cave is really big. I have a *lot* of me space, more than I know what to do with. And I don't *mind* if—if it's you."

I quickly looked down at my basket again. *Way to say too much, Xan. What are you, a teenager?* Though to be fair, I hadn't had this sort of experience during my teenage years. The relationships I'd had had all come after leaving home, and calling them relationships at all was a bit of a joke. So I really ought to give myself a bit of credit, seeing as I didn't have the faintest clue what I was doing.

And then Diver said, "Wait. Your *cave?*"

I laughed and launched into an explanation as we headed to the grocers' section of the market. Talking about the cave system offered a distraction, so I didn't hold back, describing the way the Ongkoarrat had carved their very civilization into nature, working with it rather than against it. Caves that had been turned into "apartment buildings" were a common approach, and despite being part of a mountain, my home had all the amenities you could find in a more "modern" living arrangement.

"The bath is particularly impressive," I said, as I set my basket down on the edge of a stall carrying a variety of dried meat. "They carved it right into the rock, and it's enormous."

"Sounds like you've been living it up," Diver teased.

I rolled my eyes. "Trust me, after a long day of trying to get two taciturn creatures to want a relationship together, *anyone* would need a hot bath."

"Yeah, but a huge tub like that and no one to share it with? What a shame."

I focused hard on choosing what I wanted, loading it into the basket while I hummed tunelessly—and nervously—beneath my breath. Diver chuckled, a low, rumbling sound, and he stood so close that I felt the vibration of it down my neck. Swallowing hard, I set my basket on the scale and brought my wristlet down on the prongs sticking out of the payment machine. A second later it beeped, indicating the withdrawal of credits from my account.

I'd barely lifted my basket when Diver grabbed my arm and shoved me behind him. I let out a breathless squeak, blinking in surprise. *What the fuck!* I grabbed his arm and peered around him, and that's when I saw what the problem was.

"Don't worry, Xan," Diver said, reaching for a gun that, by law, wouldn't be there. Though if I knew Diver, he'd gotten at least a knife past customs. "I've got it."

"Diver—"

"Fucking hell, what is an *orc* doing—"

"Diver!" I hissed, as the Zechak in question glanced at us. "It's all right!"

I tugged on his arm, backing him away from the Zechak. She shrugged and turned back to her shopping. I'd seen her in Trade Town a few times; the first time I'd been just as badly startled as Diver. Now I slid an arm around him and steered him towards the next booth I wanted. Diver kept glancing back and forth between me and the Zechak. Fortunately, she seemed to be used to it, and merely ignored us. They were an intimidating people, the Zechak, with the female of the species being at least two and a half meters tall—the males reached up to three—and their broad, tusked faces could look hostile even when they were trying to be friendly.

No doubt Diver was not the first to be startled, nor would he be the last.

"It's all right," I repeated. "There are several Zechak refugee settlements across Karrckchak."

"Would've been nice of someone had warned me about that!"

"It isn't spoken of off-planet. The Alliance doesn't know."

Diver swore rather colorfully. *Wow, he's even chosen some of the same swears I used when I found out.* A lot of people thought the Ongkoarrat a bit xenophobic. The money they'd made from selling the slingspace drive had gone to jaw-dropping planetary defenses and *no one*—not even God Himself—got onto Karrckchak without prior approval. It allowed them to keep careful track of just who they let go planetside and, more importantly, let them stop certain people from mucking about in their society. Which was useful when you were keeping the kind of secrets the Ongkoarrat were.

"Look," I said quietly, leaning in close so Diver would hear me over the din of the market—and trying to ignore the thrill at being so near him, "that you were allowed to come here is a sign of great trust. Whoever vouched for you believed you could handle this. Otherwise you wouldn't be here now."

"Zechak, though." Diver shook his head. "Don't they—I mean, aren't the Ongkoarrat worried about them causing trouble?"

"No more so than the average citizen. They're here because they wanted to get away from Zechak society. They were lucky to escape, and even luckier that they have a place to hide."

He gazed at me, something soft and pensive in his eyes. "You always knew, didn't you? That some of 'em weren't so bad, I mean."

I shrugged. "I always *suspected.* There had to be differences among them; hive minds aren't capable of sapience. But if it's any consolation, it kinda turned my world upside down, too."

Diver drew in a deep breath and let it out slowly. I felt some of the tension ease from his body and let him go, albeit a bit reluctantly. To my delight, he slung an arm casually around my shoulders, allowing me to continue sheltering beneath his height. With him walking beside me, no one bumped into me or shoved past me, and I barely had to worry about brushing against anyone.

"All right," Diver said with a sigh. "All right. This is all fucking space-fried, but I'll try to deal."

"Good. I'd hate for you to pull a knife on my favorite green grocer."

"What makes you think I have a knife?"

I shot him a knowing look.

"Clever fireball." He leaned down to murmur the words, his mouth so close that his lips brushed over my ear. I prayed he didn't hear my sharp intake of breath. "Yes, I have a knife. Rules of the street; never leave home without a weapon."

"Trust me, Diver. This is as far from the streets as it's possible to get."

He swept his gaze over the hulking figure of Golach, the Zechak green grocer who carried the best tomatoes, and muttered, "Yeah, starting to get that."

Chapter Five

If anyone or anything was space-fried, it was me.

Inviting him to stay with me? What was I thinking? Not that I didn't want him to stay. The problem was, I wanted it *too* much. A little self-honesty—and Sweet Mother Universe but I hated that about me—forced me to admit that I'd already been a bit head over heels for Diver before leaving the *Carpathia*. The months we'd spent sending holo-mails back and forth hadn't helped. If anything, it had only deepened my feelings.

"This is really stellar and all," Diver said, interrupting my thoughts, "and I really hate to sound like less than a badass, but are we there yet?"

I laughed. "We're almost there. And don't worry about the badass thing, your secret is safe with me."

Despite his complaining, whenever I glanced at Diver, I caught him taking in the scenery with wide, appreciative eyes. Due to the nature of the trees here, which closely echoed Ancient Earth conifers, Great Rock was the closest either of us would ever come to seeing an Earthen mountain range. And the way the trail swept up into the mountains left one's jaw on the floor. Despite it being made of dirt, there was a sophistication to the way it wound through the trees, which had been carefully cultivated to grow to different heights. The end effect was a pattern of trees that echoed a railing. It even grew and shrank to match the dips and swells of the path.

"And to think," I said, "a lot of people figure the Ongkoarrat have no artists."

Diver snorted. "People always think scientists can't be artists."

I turned my head to smile at him, remembering a few of his more artistic projects. In particular, my mind fluttered back to one of my earliest memories of him, when he showed me a small, perfectly formed mechanical hummingbird he had made—a beautiful melding of science and art. As if he knew exactly what moment I was thinking of, he flashed me a grin in turn.

Diver fell into silence again, but I didn't mind. I liked listening to the sounds of the forest all around me, and anyway, we were almost there. The path evened out beneath my feet as the land plateaued, and waiting for us was my cave, the entrance a smooth arch in the mountainside. As we passed below the entryway, I pointed up, drawing Diver's attention to the cleverly carved slot where the door hid away. He whistled in clear appreciation for the seamless way it blended.

"Damn," Diver remarked. "*Damn*. This is way more space than we get on *Carpathia*."

"It's a bit much for me," I admitted. "Marbles, Cake, we have a visitor! Cages open."

The cages beeped and electronics buzzed as the cage doors opened. Cake crawled out slowly, grasping the cage bars with beak and claws and pulling himself up to the top. To my surprise—and, quite clearly, Diver's—Marbles came winging out of her cage, aiming straight for him. I had enough time to snatch the grocery basket from his hands before she collided with his shoulder.

"Ow. Damnit, bird." Diver complained, rubbing his shoulder where he could reach it beneath her claws. "Don't you know that force is supposed to be equal to mass times acceleration?"

"First rule of zoology," I told him, hiding a smile behind my hand. "Animals don't give a rat's ass about the laws of physics."

"Yeah? What's the second rule?"

Marbles made an odd sound in her throat. My eyes widened and I moved forward to grab her, but I was too late. With a small heave she regurgitated part of her lunch onto Diver's T-shirt. He yelped in surprise and disgust, and glared. Marbles warbled something unintelligible and fluttered back to her play tree, taking shelter behind Cake. Which looked absurd, since Cake was about half her size.

I smiled ruefully. "Rule number two just landed on your shoulder."

"Ugh!" Diver shook his hands and stared at me, at a loss. "That's disgusting."

"If it's any comfort, it was meant as a show of affection."

His stare turned into a glower. My smile stretched, wide and awkward. I took the basket into the small chamber that had been set aside as a kitchen and set it on the table, then returned to the main room. I found Diver stripping off his shirt, revealing bare bronze skin and the whipcord muscle of his back. Swallowing hard, I turned away and looked for something to do while he rummaged in his luggage for a clean shirt.

In the end, I retrieved the air mattress and spread it out on the floor. The gel inside squished as I flattened it the best I could. *Odd to think these things supposedly used to be filled with* actual *air,* I thought as I set up the air canister and plugged it in. *What a silly idea.* Air hissed as I turned the nozzle on the canister, and poured into the mattress. As soon as it contacted the gel, the gel turned to foam and the mattress started to rise.

"And to think," Diver muttered behind me, "I brought the damn feather-brains some millet, too."

I straightened to find him watching me. Self-conscious, I reached up and tucked a wayward strand of hair behind my ear.

"You know," he drawled, "you could've stared a little. I wouldn't mind."

Ears burning, I blurted out, "Like your ego needs the fluffing."

"Ha! That's my fireball. Now, presents."

"Wait. What? Presents?"

"Well, yeah." Diver grinned. "It was your birthday not that long ago, right? You're, what, thirty-three now?" When I nodded, he gestured at the bed. "Take a seat. Promised a few people you'd open these right away. Don't like to break my promises."

My mind whirled. *Presents? For me?* I'd gotten birthday cake my last few years on *Carpathia,* but before that I hadn't had a present in a standard decade. Hell, that I'd gotten cake had startled the fuck out of me, because I hadn't told anyone when my birthday was. I wanted people to forget that, by the modern definition of humanity—propped up by centuries of life-ex treatment—I was still painfully young.

I settled on the bed, hands shaking, as Diver withdrew a brightly wrapped package from his luggage. The golden paper glimmered even in the cave lights, making it look like a treasure.

"From Kiri," he explained, as he set the package on my lap.

An almost painful warmth built in my chest as I ran my fingertips across the paper. I took a deep breath, fighting back the sudden urge to cry. I didn't want to look like a child. I didn't want Diver to think my emotions were strange or out of place. I didn't want him to view me the way my parents always had, but it was so hard, keeping those tears at bay, because this one package meant more to me than I could ever express.

With another deep breath, I began to tear the wrapping away.

Diver

It hurt like hell to watch her. She tried to hide it, but to me it was clear as daylight. Her hands shook as she stripped away the paper. Perhaps she thought I didn't notice the way she set it carefully aside, giving it a pat, but I did. And I wondered, not for the first time, what the hell she'd been through, why she tried so hard not to let people see what she was really feeling. Why something as simple as a present made her shake like a leaf in a stiff breeze.

With a bit of struggle, Xandri opened the long white box and pulled out a bundle of deeply wine-red cloth. Her eyes widened and brightened as she shook out the hoodie with its wide cowl neck that could be pulled up to partially hide the face, its long sleeves with thumbholes, and Velcro that could hold the kangaroo pouch shut.

"Oh!" she breathed. "Oh wow!"

"Kiri said she wasn't sure about the asymmetry," I said, gesturing to the hemline like I had a fucking clue in hell; I didn't, "but she said you'd been looking to make your wardrobe a little more fashionable, so..."

"Oh, no, it's *perfect*!"

She pulled it over her head, and promptly got slightly buried in all that neckline, the deep hood flopping over to partially cover her head. *Fuck me, she's adorable.* She laughed as she straightened the hoodie, shifting the cowl so it sat comfortably on her shoulders and sweeping the hood back. Xandri gazed up at me, eyes bright and coy beneath a veil of long lashes, hands—covered in too long sleeves—clasped beneath her chin, and suddenly 'adorable' wasn't the word running through my mind anymore.

"You have to tell Kiri I love it," she said.

"Tell her yourself, fireball. You could send her a holo-mail, you know. She misses you."

It was a bit disingenuous of me; sue me. But I didn't think for a second she hadn't noticed that I'd avoided truly answering her about why I was here, and I wasn't ready to blurt it all out yet. I wanted her back on the *Carpathia*, but I wanted her to be happy, too. *Fuck, I just plain want her, which is a problem all on its own.* I turned to retrieve the next present, because she kept looking at me in a way that made my blood burn, and I didn't know if she meant to do it or not.

"From Aki," I said, handing her a small package in plain brown paper.

"Whoa," she said as she unwrapped a thin, plastic bar. Noticing my look, she explained, "Credit for Vertebrates. Biggest hardcopy bookstore chain in the known universe."

"Vertebrates? Really?"

She grinned.

Groaning at the pun, I leaned over and retrieved Captain Chui's present. Not that it'd be much of a surprise, since the rich aroma of coffee drifted out through the packaging.

Xandri let out a soft, sweet moan that set my blood on fire. As she took the present from me, her eyelashes fluttered in bliss and her lips parted in this absurdly kissable kinda way. *Diver, man, knock it off.* I focused on her hands—still trembling slightly—as she tore the paper away. She inhaled deeply and let it out in a happy sigh. Captain Chui had spared no expense; you'd be hard-pressed to find a more expensive coffee in all the universe.

"Oh, that's simply stellar," Xandri cooed. "I can get pretty good coffee here, but nothing like this."

I chuckled. "Looks like I'm gonna be replaced already."

"Nonsense. A good cup of coffee is most satisfying with either a good book or a good conversation."

"Well, I might be able to provide one or the other."

She smiled at me and I had to look away from the brightness of it. Fortunately, I had one more present to retrieve. A slight lump of not-terribly-badass nerves grew in my throat as I hauled the large, heavy-as-fuck package from my luggage. Instead of handing it to her, I set it on the bed with a sizable *whump*. Xandri stared down at it.

"Wow, Diver," she said. "I appreciate the brick and all, but you might've noticed I'm surrounded by rocks..."

I stared at her, startled. She stared back, a look of horror dawning on her face.

"I'm *so* sorry, I didn't mean—"

With a laugh, I knelt down in front of the bed and caught her hands in mine. "You're allowed to make jokes, fireball. I know what they are."

The smile she gave me was so fragile. *Who did this to you, Xan? Who made you terrified of every word that comes out of your mouth?* I wanted to blame it on the Anmerilli and the Alliance, but she'd been like this before. When she'd first come aboard the *Carpathia*, frighteningly thin, wearing oversized threadbare clothes and bruises of exhaustion beneath her eyes, she'd been as close-lipped as anyone I'd ever met. Over time she'd relaxed, especially around me. Now she was on high alert again.

"Open it," I urged.

Relaxing a little, she tore into the paper, stripping it away from the heavy duo of books. I watched her eyes take in the title—*Axion's Field Guide to the Universe*—and go very wide. She turned her head to stare at me and for once I couldn't quite read her expression.

"I know it's only the first two volumes," I said quickly. "I mean, there's *how* many of the things? But it comes with files so you can upload it onto your—oof!"

I wrapped my arms around her as she collided with me, cradling her as I hit the stone floor. She let out a squeak, as if shocked by her own actions, and immediately moved to break away from me. I tightened my hold on her and murmured some sort of nonsense in her ear, something to let her know it was all right, and felt her relax into my embrace. *Oh yeah, you're totally a tough guy, Diver. Real tough.* Why did she turn me to marshmallow like this?

Xandri sat up, her cheeks flushed, and said, "Thank you, Diver. They're *perfect*, absolutely perfect."

Experimentally, I set a hand on her waist. "Thought they might be up your alley."

Her hand rested over mine and I wondered if she'd pull me away, but she didn't. She gazed down at me with this expression that drove me wild; mouth quirked slightly on one side, eyes bright and beckoning beneath low swept lashes. Fuck, did she know she could do that?

"You thought right," she said.

I bit back a groan of disappointment as she rose and reached a hand down to me. Warm fingers closed around mine and though I didn't actually need the help, I let her give me a boost as I climbed to my feet. She dropped my hand and turned back to her new books immediately, running her fingertips over the glossy cover of the first volume.

"The Axion family has been researching the universe for centuries," Xandri said, practically cooing. "They've compiled *generations* of knowledge into these field guides."

"Yeah." I rubbed the back of my neck. "I saw them when we were shopping. Sign mentioned this was the latest update. Gifts aren't a real big skill of mine, but Kiri swore up, down and backwards that I couldn't fail with these."

"She wasn't wrong," Xandri murmured, still stroking the book cover. "So...how is everyone, anyway?"

"About how you'd expect, I guess. Not really the same without you, though. Hey, you know, there's news out of Cochinga."

She turned to me, eyes intent, and I explained what I'd learned. Working together, Kiri and Christa had turned up evidence that Nish mar'Odrea had been working with Marco Antilles to sabotage the alliance. He'd known who Antilles really was, what he was really up to, and yet Nish mar'Odrea had still exposed his people to the dangers of Zechak and the LHFH. His people were, unsurprisingly, not amused. I watched Xandri closely as I spoke, wondering if she'd realize what this meant for her. With mar'Odrea out of the picture, the Alliance didn't have to bow to his wishes anymore.

Instead, when I finished, she asked, "And what of Marco? What happened to him?"

"What?" I stared at her.

"Marco. What—"

"I heard what you said. I just don't get it. Why should you give a shit what happened to him? He betrayed you, Xan."

She bit her lip and looked away. *Damnit. Why the hell should she care?* But she did. That was the thing about Xandri; she fucking cared, even when she shouldn't. I didn't get the shit about people like her not having empathy. Far as I was concerned, she had way too damn much of it, and it was going to get her in some real, serious trouble someday, worse even than this business with Antilles.

"Look, Christa sent in some report to the Alliance, and Antilles ended up in a facility usually used for soldiers with PTSD. Okay?"

I reached for the first volume of the *Field Guide.* "So, we got some time to look at this, or you gotta work?"

She shook her head. "I have today and tomorrow off. It took some doing, convincing Prrchik and Kirchak to give me a couple days before they showed up again," she broke into a grin, "but I managed. So I can show you around a little, too."

She brightened visibly at the prospect. Satisfied that her mind was off Antilles, at least for the moment, I carried the book to the table and set it down. Xandri disappeared into the kitchen, carrying her prize, and came out a moment later with a set of mugs and a bowl of sugar. Watching her, I wondered how the hell I was gonna break the news to her. The fact that she hadn't asked if she could come back when she heard about mar'Odrea... Did that mean she didn't *want* to come back?

The smell of roasting coffee started to linger in the air as Xandri returned a second time with a pot of cream and a small plate of chocolate-covered biscuits. I dropped into a chair with a contented sigh. I might not be cooling my heels on a nice tropical beach somewhere, but I thought this might turn out to be a pretty nice vacation.

Chapter Six

Xandri

In the end, I reveled in showing Diver all there was to see of Great Rock.

At first I was hesitant, stumbling to a halt every time I found myself carrying on at length about anything. But whenever I didn't tell Diver as much as he wanted to hear—which was often—he pestered me with questions until I gave in, spilling every detail I knew. By the end of the second day of his visit I stopped trying to restrain myself, and he never once seemed annoyed by my propensity to dump everything I knew on his head.

He even brought a guest to dinner the second night, which would've been more amusing if it hadn't been a *sarrktrr*—or a leaper, if one translated to Alliance Trade Common. Sure, it might *look* like a small, six-legged lizard, but that's what it wanted you to think. As soon as I spotted it, nestled in the palm of Diver's gloved hand, I groaned.

"What? Thought it was kinda cute."

"You don't even know what it is," I retorted. "It could be poisonous!"

"Hence, the gloves."

"Get it out of here right now, before it—shit!"

With a soft *whoosh* like a flame bursting into life, the *sarrktrr* leapt out of Diver's hand. Flaps of greenish skin unfurled between its six limbs as it glided away. Unfortunately for us, it didn't decide to glide straight out. It made a cunning looping movement over our heads and twisted in the air, changing direction to head for the bird cages. I scrambled after it, waving my hands to chase it away.

"Why is it glowing?"

"It basically has its own combustion engine," I panted, as I missed another grab for it.

"Well, surely it can't keep that up long."

I shot Diver a glare. "Shut up and get the net from the kitchen before this has to get violent."

Because the little fucker could keep it up longer than you'd expect, thanks to the hypergolic substance that allowed it to flit around in the first place. And if it decided to land and take off again, it might just set a thing or two on fire. *Guess dinner's gonna be late tonight,* I complained to myself.

Sometime later, after much flailing, shouting, and running, we managed to net the *sarrktrr.* I folded up the net and thrust it at Diver, making him take it out. Then I flopped down in a chair, panting. Diver returned a few moments later and dropped into the chair opposite me, breathing pretty hard himself. I propped my head in my hand and looked at him, just looked. He gazed back.

"What? *What?*"

"Third rule of zoology," I told him. "Just because it looks cute doesn't mean it can't light your house on fire."

"Hey, *you* pointed one out to me yesterday and *you* told me it was called a leaper. You didn't mention it had a combustion engine strapped to its ass!"

"Chest," I corrected. "And I'm pretty sure it's only called a leaper because 'small, annoying, fire-starting explosion-lizard' is a bit of mouthful in any language."

A grin started to curl the corners of his mouth. I looked away, trying not to let it catch, but before I knew it I was giggling. *Now that he mentions it, I* did *point out a leaper last night.* But I'd still been in 'don't tell everything' mode and had left the more dangerous aspects of the creature out. *Guess that'll teach me.* At least this time it hadn't landed on anything. When I'd made the mistake of bringing one home myself, I'd lost a blanket to it.

"Let's eat something, yeah, fireball?" Diver suggested, still a bit breathless. "Don't know about you, but I've worked up an appetite."

I had another appointment with Kirchak and Prrchik the next day, but Diver didn't seem to mind. He took up the role of watching Marbles and Cake, keeping them preoccupied while I worked. Which was good, because Kirchak and Prrchik arrived with an unpleasant surprise.

At first, when they ambled in with Mrrchki between them, I could only stare. Mrrchki's short ears pressed back against her skull, and her mouth was partway open, a decidedly stormy expression. I swallowed thickly as I stepped forward to greet them. Prrchik looked somewhat subdued and repentant, but Kirchak greeted me with a tongue-lolling grin, with nary a sign of contriteness.

"Your match," Mrrchki said flatly, "has been sneaking out to see each other."

"Really? That's great!"

She reared her head back and stared at me in horror.

"Uh, I mean…Bad! Very bad!" I shook a finger at Kirchak and Prrchik, though I doubted it looked very convincing. "No—no more of—of that."

Ugh, this again. I'd had the same problem with Brretrit and Ahrsandr. They *liked* each other. They *wanted* to spend time together. It felt so weird, denying two people who enjoyed each other's company the ability to see each other, simply because it was tradition. *Goes to show that even the Ongkoarrat aren't perfect.* I smiled at Mrrchki, keeping my lips carefully down over my teeth; though smiling wasn't a threat display among the Ongkoarrat as it could be amongst, say, the Kowari, too broad a grin was a clear sign of disrespect. Aki would have understood that I didn't mean it that way, but Mrrchki had one hell of a stick up her furry ass.

"Don't let it happen again," she growled at me.

"Of course not, *attoaong*," I said.

She shot me a suspicious look, which she also turned on Diver for a moment before she made to leave. I followed her, ostensibly to be polite; in truth, I wanted to make sure she actually left. When I returned, I found my two wayward charges sitting near Diver. Prrchik was her usual polite self, but Kirchak leaned in close, studying Diver without reservation. I had to admire Diver's ability to not look unnerved.

"Forgive us, *attoaong*," Prrchik said. "We did not mean to get you in trouble. It's just…"

"Prrchik showed me the stars," Kirchak explained with a quick loll of his tongue. "The constellations. I've never been able to pick them out before."

"He still can't," Prrchik said with a mischievous little chuff.

"Well, no, but it was still fun." He grunted as Prrchik gave him a small nudge and added, "But of course we apologize."

I waved a hand. "I'm your *attoaong*, not your keeper. Just try not to get caught next time. Kirchak—"

"You didn't tell us you had a match, *attoaong*," Kirchak said.

"What? Uh, no, Diver's my—"

"Match. It's clear in the way you're looking at him, and the way he—"

"We're *friends*," I cut in, cheeks burning.

"But…friends can be matches too," Kirchak returned, regarding me with ears lowered in puzzlement.

Which I knew, of course. *Attoaongs* matched for every kind of relationship, from deepest friendships to well-respected colleagues. And Life Matches, rare though they were, were hardly restricted to romantic pairings. They could happen between two individuals, or amongst twenty; what mattered was the deep, abiding love that kept a Life Match together far beyond the duration of a standard match. But as much as I found my heart aching with pleasure at the thought of Diver always being by my side, I couldn't let such a vulnerability show, not here, not now.

"It doesn't matter, because humans don't do this whole…thing. Now come on, let's get started."

"Yes you do," Kirchak persisted. "Honestly, you're the only other species in the known universe more obsessed with matchmaking than ours."

"Yes, but…" I bit back a growl of exasperation. "What I meant was that we don't do it the same way the Ongkoarrat do."

"Clearly not, or you'd have better success."

I turned away, throwing my hands up in surrender. Diver had watched the whole exchange with raised eyebrows. Now he ducked his head, trying to hide a grin, but I'd already caught him. *Focus on the job, Xan.* It was supposed to be up to me, after all, to declare when Prrchik and Kirchak were ready for mating. Admittedly that felt a bit obtrusive to me, even after six months. I couldn't help but feel that it really *ought* to be their decision. But the Ongkoarrat had been doing things this way so long that they would simply wait until they died if I didn't give permission.

I hung back and observed as Prrchik and Kirchak settled in their chairs to talk. I couldn't stop a smile from curving my lips as

I watched them. Just because I didn't fully agree with the system didn't mean I wasn't happy when it worked. Seeing Kirchak and Prrchik taking such joy in each other made my work worthwhile. Oddly, in some ways they reminded me of Brretrit and Ahrsandr. There had been no romance between those two, but like Prrchick and Kirchak, they had loved to talk to each other, and had bonded deeply with surprising ease.

"*Surely being my match wouldn't be that bad,*" Diver subvocalized, drawing my attention away from my charges.

Still running on exasperation, I gave his arm a pinch and blurted out, "*You are* not *putting me on the spot like that right now. I'll have Captain Chui teach me to kick your ass if you keep it up.*"

"*Ow,*" Diver grumbled, rubbing his arm. "*You're spending too much time with Kiri.*"

"*Well, stop goofing off. I have work to do,*" I said primly.

"*And a fine job you're doing,*" he replied, his tone more serious now.

Satisfied—and only feeling a slight dance of butterflies in my stomach—I turned my attention back to Prrchick and Kirchak, who were chuffing together over some joke I'd missed. Yet I found myself hyperaware of Diver's presence next to me. Especially when he leaned over to murmur in my ear his breath warm and tickly against his my cheek and neck.

"For the record, *I* don't think it would be that bad."

The *sarrktrr* wasn't our only run in with dangerous wildlife. It seemed the local fauna was determined to give Diver a less than warm welcome.

On Diver's fifth day planetside, I took him for a hike along the heavily wooded trails of Great Rock. During my time here, I had used the scanner on my wristlet to map out the area so I'd never get lost. Now I led Diver to my favorite place on the mountainside. We'd packed a cooler with lunch, which I'd conceded to letting him carry after he stared at me reprovingly for five minutes straight. As if I was in as bad shape as I'd been when I first arrived on the *Carpathia.*

"I admit," he said, as we made our way through a field of purple *grrka,* which swayed gently in a slight breeze, "I hadn't taken you for the hiking type. Too much the spacer, you know?"

I shrugged. "I'm happy as long as I have freedom, actually."

He gave me a searching, sideways glance. I looked away. If he pried, I'd... well, I didn't know what I would do.

Instead, he reached a hand out and caught my elbow, steadying me as we climbed out of the *grrka* field and up a steep embankment. His touch warmed me through the thin cotton of my sleeve and I had to swallow against a suddenly dry mouth and throat. *Fuck my life.* Being around him this much made everything I felt stronger and stronger. As his hand slid up my arm briefly, tingles ran through me. To distract myself from longing as he let go, I looked around for something to point out to him.

The shade the trees casted made it a trickier prospect, but I knew what to look for. Moving on the balls of my feet, I picked my way over forest deadfall and the occasional tree root, keeping an eye to my scanner. It saw what I could not, sending back heat signatures, some big, some small.

"Ah!" I changed directions, giving Diver a nudge so he'd follow. "Quietly. You need to see this."

"Not more explosion-lizards, I hope," he responded, keeping his voice low.

I shook my head. "Not during the day. And they don't tend to live in woods this thick."

"That was a joke, Xan."

Oh. Right. I shrugged and continued moving onwards, eyes on the spot lit on my holo-display. As I neared it, I slowed further, my gaze low. I pointed towards the forest floor, near the edge of the lowest branches of a tree. When Diver glanced at me, I raised a finger and mouthed the word 'watch.' We both stood there, barely breathing, watching that tree.

The creature that came scampering out looked a bit like a six-legged guinea pig, though it had a less opportunistic diet. It could even 'pop' like a guinea pig, leaping straight into the air in joy. I pressed my lips together tight as tiny babies scuttled out of the tree's protection, too. *Damn, they're young.* They still struggled to coordinate their six stubby legs, which resulted in a fair bit of stumbling and bumbling, and siblings crashing into and running over one another all willy-nilly. Beside me, Diver shook with silent laughter.

Slowly, oh-so-slowly, I raised my arm and pointed the scanner at them. My heart thrummed with excitement; this was the first chance I was getting to record the babies. Some footage of them would make my catalogue more complete. *Maybe I can even send it to the Axion family!* The Ongkoarrat had yet to allow them planetside to study the species living here, but if I could gather enough information for them that they could make a case for the usefulness of it...

And then one of the babies tried to leap like its mother, missed its cue coming down, and crashed into one of its siblings. Thus ensued a furry, many-legged domino effect. As the last baby tumbled onto its side, their mom turned to snort at them in consternation. It was too much. I burst out laughing; beside me, so did Diver. The creatures, startled by our noise, dashed away into the undergrowth.

"That," Diver wheezed, "was absurd."

"Nature often is," I agreed, trying to stifle my laughter. "But damnit all...I wanted to get more footage of them. I wonder if they left anything behind under there..."

"Probably just the usual animal leavings. Shit and stuff."

"Hey, shit can give us valuable knowledge."

"If that were true, we'd get more use out of politicians."

"I said shit, not bullshit."

Diver chuckled. I started to turn, a smile slipping onto my lips; it dropped away again when I saw what stood behind him. He sobered quickly when he caught a glimpse of my expression and came, moving very carefully, to stand beside me. As he turned to face the creature, his eyes widened.

"What is that?"

It had a name in the local tongue, but I'd taken to referring to it as a dire bear. Of course, it was like unto a bear the way a candle was like unto a sun. Because bears didn't have six long, strong legs or heads big enough to bite you in two. They didn't loom above you like giants, their great backs like gently rolling hills. And they sure as fuck didn't have long saber teeth on both their upper and lower jaws. I took a step back.

"Run!" I hissed.

"No chance that's what it's called, is there?"

I was all for snarking in the face of death, but running seemed the better option. I grabbed Diver's arm and tugged; together we stumbled out of the clearing, moving as fast as we could. Normally I'd advise against running from predators—it just made most of them view you as lunch—but the sheer size and territorial nature of the dire bear made running one's only chance at survival. I was no championship runner but at the moment I was boogying like a Psittacan in a rainforest.

"Go, go, go!" I shouted, shoving at Diver's back. "There, down that slope, quickly!"

I glanced back. The dire bear loped along after us, mouth open, tongue lolling, saliva gathering on its saber teeth. If it hadn't been so fucking huge, it would've caught us by now.

We skittered down the slope, deadfall and tiny stones sliding out from under our feet. I almost fell, but Diver caught me, one strong arm looping around me to keep me upright. As we reached the bottom of the hill, he shoved me in front of him. I stumbled but kept going, my heart slamming like a jackhammer against my ribs, my lungs and throat already burning with a desperate need for air.

I wound my way through the trees, forcing myself not to look back. Just when I thought it might catch us, we burst out of the trees, into a large, clear valley. The ground seemed to drop away beneath us as it dipped, creating a bowl shape in the midst of the mountains. I staggered partway down the slope and skidded to a halt, throwing out an arm to catch Diver.

"What?" he panted. "Shouldn't...shouldn't we keep...running?"

I shook my head and leaned over, bracing my hands on my knees. "It...won't follow. Highly...territorial. Won't...leave its territory..."

"Oh. Oh good."

Diver let out a sighing wheeze, dropped the cooler, and flopped to the ground. *Yeah, good idea.* I dropped too, still breathing hard. Warm sun beat down on me, but happily there was a cool mountain breeze to counter it. Fuck, I hated running into predators these days. Particularly the big ones. Without my guns—in particular, without their stun feature—researching macrofauna had gotten a bit hairier than usual. Which was saying something.

"You know," Diver said, "a man could get the feeling this planet don't like him."

I turned my head to look at him; moss-like grass tickled my cheek. "Dire bears don't like anyone."

"Oh, see, and here I thought it wanted to give me a big hug."

"All the more reason to run," I grumbled.

Diver looked at me, and for a long moment we just stared at each other, silent. No idea who cracked first, him or me, but then we were laughing like a pair of hyenas hopped up on giddy. I laughed until my ribs hurt and my lungs started to burn again, until tears threatened to spill down my cheeks.

"Fuck," Diver wheezed, propping himself up on his elbows. "Holy fuck. You okay, Xan?"

"Outside of getting chased by a giant six-legged bear-like creature with fangs? I'm stellar."

I managed to sit up, even though I ached all over. On the bright side, the dire bear had chased us straight to our destination. I loved this valley, the way it took a rounded scoop out of the mountain range and covered it in a carpet of green. At the bottom huddled a stand of trees; water peered out between the branches, a lake that glimmered like a mirror beneath the sun. Wildflowers dotted the valley slopes, clusters of purple or yellow or white. I drew my knees up to my chest and let out a satisfied sigh.

"I can see why you like this place so much," Diver murmured.

Something in his voice made me look at him, but I couldn't tell by looking if something was bothering him. *Maybe I imagined it...* Lord knew it happened sometimes. I'd worked for years to combat the difficulties my autism gave me, but sometimes I still misinterpreted what I heard or saw. And it was so hard, much of the time, to trust myself. If I hadn't dismissed certain things about Marco, hadn't been so worried that it was only the difficulties of perception my autism could cause, would I even be here now?

"Well," I said, trying to keep my tone light, "if I have to be exiled, at least I get to do it in a place with dire bears and explosion-lizards."

"You *would* consider that a plus," he teased.

I couldn't help smiling. Diver's presence did that to me. Not even bothering to hold my smile back, I reached for the cooler and dragged it towards us. A quick depression of the button later, the lid slid back and the entire cooler let out a soft hiss as it released cold air into the warm afternoon.

We sat in companionable silence, eating sandwiches and drinking lemonade. I watched the small glade down below, keeping my eyes peeled for signs of movement. Four-winged birds fluttered up out of the copse occasionally, their wings working in paddling conjunction as they took off. Diver watched too, squinting, his lips pursed in that way he did when he was getting a new idea. For all he liked to claim he was a non-organics kind of guy, his ideas often came from the natural world. Watching it happen fascinated me.

"You're staring."

I flushed. "I'm *observing*."

"Uh huh. Well, Little Miss Scientist—whoa. What's that?"

I followed his gaze back to the copse and grinned. A reacher—a great reacher, in fact—had stepped out from the shade of the trees. It lifted its head, its enormous rack of antlers tilted backward as it snuffled the lowest branches. To anyone who didn't know better, it looked mostly like an Ancient Earth deer.

"Hold on..." Diver frowned. "One, two, three, four...It only has four legs." He gazed at me in consternation. "That's not possible."

"Watch," I said simply, raising and lowering one shoulder in a half shrug.

Diver turned back to stare at the reacher. As we watched, the creature's entire body posture shifted in some subtle way, and its antlers unfurled, moving more like tentacles than something stiff and solid. The reacher reared back slightly, coiling its head appendages around a much higher branch and hauling it down. As it began stripping away leaves with the beak-like structure at the front of its muzzle, Diver turned to gaze at me, open-mouthed.

"It's called a reacher," I said, stifling a giggle. "All vertebrates here have a hexapodal body plan, but not all six limbs are *legs*, necessarily."

"Fucking weird-ass universe," he said, shaking his head. A short pause, then he added, "Don't you want to see more of it?"

I blinked at the abrupt change of subject. "Of course!"

"Well...what if I told you that you can come back? To the *Carpathia*, I mean."

I froze. When he'd told me about Nish mar'Odrea's treason charges, I'd wondered. I'd wondered, but I hadn't dare to ask, in case I was still being held responsible for the AFC's fuck-up. Even though I tried to hide away here, I knew what was going on in the media. I knew people were talking about me, questioning my very right to exist. I didn't listen to it; if I did, *I* would start questioning my right to exist.

"I thought...I thought the *Carpathia* would be disbanded if I stayed on..." I said quietly.

"Yeah, but that was before."

"Before?"

Diver grinned, looking pleased. "Before Major Douglas came aboard, absolutely *begging* for your help. The AFC can't—"

"No!"

I didn't remember getting to my feet. Diver stared at me in surprise and I gazed back, my heart hammering and my throat threatening to close with panic. *Not again. I won't be their scapegoat again.* I took a step back, shaking my head. Diver lifted a hand, reaching out slowly, as if I were as much a wild animal as the reacher among the trees below. I took another step back.

"Xan..."

"No. Just...no."

"Just let me explain—"

But I didn't want to hear it. I turned and ran, ignoring Diver calling after me. Fuck Major Douglas and fuck the AFC and fuck *everything.* I had so many doubts left over from Cochinga, but one thing I knew for sure: I would *not* be used again.

Chapter Seven

That coulda gone better. I rubbed a hand over my face and dragged it back through my hair, trying not to let myself get too frustrated. Guess I shouldn't have assumed she'd be as pleased as I was by the AFC falling on their collective face. Or maybe I'd just approached it all wrong. Fuck if I knew.

I considered running after her; after all, there were giant, six-legged saber tooth bears in those woods. But Xandri knew this place better than I did, and anyway, I didn't want to scare her into making a mistake. So I sat for a little while, my eyes on the creature she'd called a reacher, and wondered how the hell I was gonna fix this. Didn't really blame her for being twitchy after what she'd been through, but damnit, I wanted her to come back. And I thought she wanted to herself, despite her reaction.

Eventually I packed up the cooler and rose. The reacher had left. I turned back the way we'd come and pinged my HUD for the map Xan had given me of the area. The signature from her wristlet showed up on my map, too; she was moving fast. At least I knew she was safe.

I picked my way back to her cave more slowly, giving us both some time to think. Really, thinking about it, I'd been completely rust-brained about the whole thing. *Shoulda mentioned the Hands and Voices first. That woulda got her listening.* Fuck, I even *knew* that. Been too addled by all the blood flowing to the wrong head lately, that was all. Either I had to get over it, or I had to put my big boy pants on and accept that I had a thing for her so I might start thinking clearly.

I really hated having to put my big boy pants on.

By the time I reached the cave, I was pretty sure I was gonna skip the pants and move on from this shit, cause it was taking up way too much of my brain, and what the hell would come of it anyway? But Xandri had a way of unhinging all my good sense.

Music—Ancient Earth stuff, which was most of what she listened to—drifted out of the cave entrance. I stepped lightly as I entered, trying to figure out how best to approach so I wouldn't freak her out. At the end of the short hall I reached the main room and paused, leaning against the wall and fighting a grin. *Well, that's a side of her I ain't never seen before.*

She was dancing, bloody dancing, and with her *parrots*, no less. The two birds perched atop their cages, bobbing and swaying to the music with surprisingly perfect rhythm. *Or maybe not so surprising, considering their ability to mimic.* Xandri danced with a little—okay, a lot—less skill, waving her body around with abandon. Occasionally she flapped her arms or shifted from foot to foot, and the birds mimicked her motions.

Damn, but it looked like fun. Xandri moved and swirled, letting go of every bit of restraint that she normally had, and maybe she looked a bit absurd, but the way she just didn't give a fuck appealed to me. This was the woman I saw in the holo-mails, in the moments where she let down her guard and just let herself be her.

God, so different from the waif of that first day. So different from the tiny slip of nothing who had told me, tight-lipped, that she couldn't have a HUD, who had flashed the tiniest smile of appreciation when I didn't ask her why. Who had lit up with delight when I showed her my mechanical hummingbird and laughed at my goofy behavior, only to quickly stifle her joy. Who had tried to pull away when I tried to reach out. *This is why we need her. She can help people, protect them… understand them.*

Oh, fuck it. On the big boy pants went.

I waited, watched. Let the song she was listening to drift out its last few notes. Let her stand for a moment, catching her breath and praising her birds in a warm, cooing tone I'd never heard her use before. Then the next song started up, and I crossed the room in a few quick strides. I caught her around the waist and swung her into a spin before she could protest, and I hoped she wouldn't protest, because then I'd have to let her go, and my big boy pants forced me to admit that I didn't want to.

Xandri

My heart slammed into my ribs and my brain started gibbering:

Oh Jesus mother fuck what the shit is even fucking hell—because it was eloquent like that sometimes. I sucked in a breath, maybe to scream, maybe to…hell if I knew. I just knew that when a strong arm wrapped around me in the midst of those oh-so-private moments, I almost burst out of my skin with shock and humiliation.

Then Diver—I knew it was Diver, I smelled the faint tang of metal and oil that always clung to him—swung me into a spin. I drifted away from him like an unraveling ball of yarn, and when he pulled me back I crashed into him, stepping on his toes in the process. I had to admire his aplomb as he gently set me back on my feet and swept me into another turn, his arm around my waist again.

"W-what are you doing?"

"Getting in on the fun," he responded with a grin. "This is some old music you got here, fireball."

"The birds like it. And so do I."

"Oh, I like this one, too. Great for dancing."

He swung me around again, and even though I kept fumbling, kept missing a reach for his hands and tripping all over myself, he didn't stop. I had to laugh, I just *had* to. Because I'd never seen him act quite like this. He was always happy-go-lucky, but as we spun and twirled around the cave, he pulled goofy faces, his eyes glittering with laughter. I forgot about my usual restraint and joined in, forgetting everything as I played along with his silliness.

I didn't realize that I was gazing up at him in a decidedly flirtatious way until the music stopped and he came to a halt, staring down at me. *I wonder where he learned to dance so well…* Both of us were breathing heavily; each exhalation carried the faint lilt of my laughter. Then his hands came up to cup my face and all my laughter disappeared.

"Xandri…"

I swallowed thickly and moved a step back, slowly, reluctantly. "Uh…look. I'm sorry about running off like that."

"What?" He started at me in confusion for a moment, then gave himself a shake and stepped back as well. "No, um…I didn't handle it very well. I know it's a sensitive subject. Maybe if I explain…"

"Yeah, sure. Sure."

Just like that, we were in safer territory again. Though I didn't want to think about what it said about my life, that I considered "possible run in with the AFC" to be *safer* territory.

"See, it's to do with the Hands and Voices," Diver said, taking a seat on my bed.

My brain switched from "oh dear god, relationship stuff" to "science!" so fast it nearly gave me whiplash. I dropped into a seat at the table and leaned forward eagerly. "Wait, wait, hold on. Are you saying we—the *Carpathia*, I mean—we finally have a mission on Song? We have a reason to go?"

His mouth curled into a smug little smile at my use of the word "we," but I ignored it. Ever since those days when Captain Chui had pulled me off the streets, giving me access to information about plants all across the universe, I'd longed to visit Song. I wanted— *needed*—to see it with my own eyes. From an anthropological standpoint, the Hands and Voices were fascinating; from a zoological standpoint, the things they did with coral were astonishing; and from my own, personal autistic standpoint, meeting other sapients that defied typical ideas of what sapience meant was exhilarating.

"What's the catch?" I had to ask.

"Amazingly enough, there ain't one. I know, shocked me too. See, roughly 'round two weeks ago, Major Douglas came aboard the *Carpathia*, and lemme tell you, he was lucky he got a word out before we spaced his ass. Turns out, the Alliance is after some new technology the Hands and Voices have created. They're cultivating coral that can withstand vacuum."

"Whoa."

"My thoughts exactly. Apparently their endgame is to grow their own starships. Naturally, the Alliance is interested. Only the Hands and Voices aren't playing ball."

I snorted. "No surprise there. They've never really forgiven the Alliance for the whole submarine thing."

"Yeah, well," Diver said, "there's only one way they'll agree to talk. Seems they sussed out that you had something to do with a certain change in the Alliance's policies, sometime back." Here he paused to raise his eyebrows at me, and I gazed down at my hands, repentant. "They'll negotiate, but *only* with you. Can you believe it? The Alliance is so desperate, they've even agreed to let you run the whole mission. It's your way or the spaceways."

I frowned. "They want this technology that badly?"

"C'mon, Xan." Diver rose from the bed and crossed to me. He knelt before me, catching my hands in his. "Who cares *why* the Alliance wants it? I mean, it's obvious why, growing starships'd be hella useful. But this is your chance. To visit Song, yeah, but... it's your chance to come home."

"Go home?" Cake inquired from his perch atop the cage.

My heart thrummed. *Home.* It wasn't that I didn't like it here. But the idea of being aboard the *Carpathia* again, of seeing everything the universe had to offer—it took my breath away. Despite my fear of what would happen, longing pulled at my heart. *And it's not just about going home...* There were people I missed, people I wanted to see again. Damnit, this would be easier if I was as antisocial as people always said I was.

"What—what about the Zechak? The LHFH?"

"At the moment, this whole thing is classified," Diver said. "We should be long gone before they even get the first whiff of it."

And yet the Alliance clearly felt that this was urgent, which made me wonder. Sure, they'd wanted the Hands and Voices to take Membership status, but that was before I introduced a tier of Non-Membership that allowed for trading. Now that nebula pearls could be freely traded, the Alliance was less concerned about Membership status for Song. After all, how did you get something that large—even the smallest Voices were slightly larger than Ancient Earth killer whales—on a starship and bring it to parliament when it's very nature meant it needed to live in water?

So maybe the Alliance would insist that nobody outside their sphere knew about this, and the Hands and Voices were safe from attack, but their urgency left me leery. And if Song *was* in some kind of danger and I just ignored it, I'd never forgive myself. Maybe I was being paranoid; on the other hand, life—and Captain Chui—had taught me that paranoia could be useful. And hell, I really, really wanted to see Song, paranoia or no, so shouldn't that be enough of a reason?

"I won't work with the AFC," I said firmly.

"Captain Chui kinda already had that figured," Diver responded. "She made it clear to the major that what you say, goes. You won't have to go anywhere near the AFC."

I let out a breath. "Okay. I guess—I guess we're going home, guys."

Diver shot to his feet, grinning in triumph. Torn between exasperation and amusement, I held up a hand.

"Don't jump the gun. I've still got things I need to clear up before I can leave."

"We can help you with that."

I quirked an eyebrow. "We?"

"Oh, uh..." He rubbed the back of his neck. "Look, just...later, when you're trying to decide who to take your anger out on over this, try to remember that I was following orders and *none* of this was my idea, okay?"

Fuck.

I almost ended up mad at Diver anyway, though mostly because it wouldn't be wise to get angry at Akcharrch. She was faster than me and outweighed me by god only knew how much, and anyway she was one of my best friends.

I still wasn't entirely pleased when she wandered into my cave, though I probably should've guessed that she was the one who'd brought Diver. And when she walked up to me and butted her head against my hand, I bit back my annoyance. With Aki here, things could get done much quicker. As I'd seen on the first day here, her no-nonsense handling of Mrrchki made everything easier.

"Still don't get why you left me with *her*," I grumbled, as we waited for Mrrchki to arrive.

"The People of the Great Rock are mine," Aki replied, her furry shoulders rolling in the Ongkoarrat equivalent of a shrug.

I frowned at her.

"And I knew it would do my people good to have a more unconventional *attoaong* for a while," she added after a moment. "Mrrchki does her job well enough, but is very much a traditionalist. Now that the People of the Great Rock have seen what you do, they'll want more flexibility from *attoaongs* in the future."

"How could you possibly know I'd be 'unconventional?'"

Aki stared at me and Diver stifled a bit of laughter beneath his hand. I glanced back and forth between them, confused. *What did I say this time?*

I didn't get a chance to find out. The click and scrape of claws on stone alerted us to the presence of several visitors. Mrrchki entered first, a purposeful set to her usual trundle. Prrchik and Kirchak followed behind her, exchanging mischievous glances with each other. When Mrrchki whipped her head around to look at them, they gazed back at her with sober expressions. Well, they were learning fast.

"Akcharrch," Mrrchki said, her lips pulling back off her teeth in clear displeasure. "A pleasure to see you again."

Aki let out a rock-grinder rumble low in her throat. "It is always good to come home, *attoaong.*"

"Perhaps this time you will stay and make a match?"

"Nothing has changed since last time, I'm afraid, *attoaong.*"

Even with their rumbling voices, the passive-aggressive subtext in their speech was startlingly clear. I exchanged a glance with Diver, who looked as uncomfortable and bewildered as I felt. I'd known from the first day that these two didn't get along, but the hostility in my cave was rapidly growing palpable. For the first time in a while, I found myself reaching into the pocket of my cargo pants for the strip of satin ribbon along the top. Rubbing my fingertips along the smooth surface helped to ease the sudden besieged feeling growing in my stomach.

"I see," Mrrchki said. "Am I to understand you're here to take away my apprentice?"

"I wouldn't do so unless it was necessary, and I will be forever grateful for the care you've taken of her."

Mrrchki's curl-lipped expression changed to something almost like amusement. "You were right. One must keep an eye on her or she doesn't eat."

I sputtered. Diver covered up another laugh. Aki craned her head around and flashed me a rare, tongue-lolling grin. Damn it all, why hadn't I seen that? Looking back on it now, on all the times Mrrchki had insisted on instructing me during lunch, or insisted I arrange a number of match meetings over dinner, I should've seen the ploy. Aki might not *like* her *attoaong,* but clearly she'd had more than one agenda when it came to giving me into Mrrchki's care.

"I will take over your other match for you," Mrrchki said, switching her attention to me, "as it is quite early on in the process. However, this match has something to ask you."

She inclined her large head regally, and Prrchik and Kirchak stepped towards me. They came with heads bowed, walking side by side, in step with one another. Recognizing this moment for what it was, I rose from my chair and regarded them with a deep incline of my head, my eyes sweeping briefly closed. Whatever other criticisms Mrrchki had of my methods, she regarded me with approval now.

"*Attoaong*," Prrchik began.

"We come before you to request permission to enter into the Match Ceremony," Kirchak continued.

"We value endlessly everything you've done for us, and ask that you grant us this one last favor."

"Your approval," Kirchak finished.

Against all ceremony, I reached out to them, my wonderful, unconventional match. Both of them brought their heads up to butt against my hands. I rubbed my palms across their soft facial fur, pleased when neither of them protested. *Things may have gone awful on Cochinga, but I've earned* their *trust.* And clearly the trust of the Hands and Voices, which was why I knew I had to go; I couldn't let them down.

"Of course," I said. "Nothing would make me happier than to see you two Matched."

"Nothing would give us more honor," Prrchik said, "than for you to oversee our Ceremony."

Tears pricked at the back of my eyes. "I'm the one who's honored." They weren't the right words, but I didn't care.

For all I was glad to be going home, a mixture of nerves and sadness roiled in my belly. I genuinely liked being here, being an *attoaong* for the People of the Great Rock. If I hadn't come, I'd never have met sweet Prrchik and delightful Kirchak. I'd never have seen an explosion-lizard or a reacher or a dire bear with my own eyes. And I couldn't help excitement at the thought that soon, I'd be seeing Song with my own eyes, too.

I watched Prrchik and Kirchak leave, and I realized I didn't care if my way of doing things didn't suit Mrrchki. It had suited Prrchik and Kirchak, and that seemed to me the most important thing. I didn't want to disrespect anyone's traditions, but traditions weren't one-size-fits-all, so maybe going against them this time really had been the right thing to do.

"That was gracefully done," Mrrchki said, surprising me.

"Thank you, *attoaong*."

She sighed. "I may not fully agree with—or even entirely understand—your methods, but I can't deny that they've worked. Come what may, you will always be an *attoaong* to the People of the Great Rock."

"Oh, I...thank you," I repeated. "That means a lot to me. And I'm sorry I gave you so much trouble."

"Considering you came under Akcharrch's charge, you gave me much less trouble than I expected. Now, shall we discuss the final details over lunch?"

"An excellent idea, *attoaong*," Aki agreed.

I bit back a sigh and ignored Diver's grin. *Might as well get myself used to it again. It'll be just as bad if not worse aboard the* Carpathia. Oddly enough, that brought a smile to my face. Yes, I was worried. There was simply no denying it. But Sweet Mother Universe, I was finally going home!

Chapter Eight

Later, as the sun began to set, while Diver was keeping Prrchik and Kirchak entertained with stories of the *Carpathia* crew's escapades, I nodded to Aki and then headed outside. Even as day darkened into evening, the air remained warm and pleasant. I sucked in a deep breath and tipped my head back, watching a small murmuration of tiny, four-winged birds pass through. The scrape of claws on stone sounded behind me, followed by the gentle pad of Ongkoarrat feet on dirt.

"Something you wanted?" Aki asked, stopping beside me.

"Only if you're willing," I replied. "I just… it's pretty clear you don't like Mrrchki for some reason. Something deep. And that makes me think that my being 'unconventional' wasn't the only reason you chose Great Rock. I suspect you could have gotten me a place just about anywhere, couldn't you?"

Aki sighed and dropped into a sitting position. "I forget sometimes how perceptive you are. Yes, Xandri-pup. There was something here I wanted you to witness, something I hoped might help change things."

"Does it have to do with Brretrit and Ahrsandr?"

"Who?"

"One of my matches. They… they came to me for a mate matching but something was off." I squirmed a little. These were Aki's people, her species. I didn't want her to think I disrespected them, or her. "Look, among humans, your system would be a sort of— breeding program. And that's ugly to us.

"I was trying not to act like I know better; they're your people, and this is your way. But I couldn't stop myself from asking, to make sure the couples I was assisting were sure they were okay with mating. And Brretrit and Ahrsandr were *not*. I could tell right away."

"So what did you do?" Aki asked.

"I gave them some chances to express their discomfort and after a while, they trusted me." I thrust a hand in my pocket, rubbing my fingers along the satiny ribbon for comfort. "They were lonely, Aki. They came to Mrrchki looking for a companionship match but she—she convinced them otherwise. Got them to agree to a mating match, even though they're both, well, what we call sex-repulsed among humans. They were going to forgo their dispensations and mate because they were *lonely*.

"I... convinced them otherwise. Mrrchki was pretty furious with me when they became a companionship match but it was what *they* wanted. I guess I just couldn't sit by when they were so clearly unhappy."

Aki let out another heavy sigh and nudged my free hand with her nose. "You did the right thing, Xandri-pup. As I thought you might."

"So you knew?"

"How could I not? Mrrchki is not, by any means, a bad *attoaong*, but it's a high-status position, and she likes that status a bit too much. Brretrit and Ahrsandr would have made for a very high-status mating match indeed."

It hit me all at once and I turned my head to stare at her. "So would you."

"Yes, so would I—if I weren't sex-repulsed, as you put it." Her unflinching honesty made me bite my lip. "That is part of the animosity you saw between Mrrchki and I. She is rather displeased with my unwillingness to give in and mate. I have worried for a long time that she may have been pushing others to give up their dispensations, but none of the other junior *attoaongs* ever saw anything wrong with what she was doing. That's part of why I needed you here. I knew you would see it."

A spark of anger flared inside me. "Well, then, I'm sorry, Aki. I know she's one of your people, but abusing her power like that is wrong, plain and simple."

"Does this mean you'd be willing to speak if I decide to take this to the Council of *Attoaongs*? It would be many, many people. My hope is that Brretrit and Ahrsandr will bring the situation to light themselves, but if not..."

I considered that for a long moment, my fingers working over and over on that thin strip of satin. Then I nodded. "It scares me a little, to be in front of so many people and try to speak with authority, but if you need me, I'll do my best."

Aki made a soft rumbling sound in her throat, a bit like a cat's purr but far deeper, and leaned against my leg. Hardly thinking of it, I buried my fingers in her fur. Whatever else Aki felt, she seemed to like that, for she continued her gentle purrlike sounds as we stood there, both of us gazing at the darkening sky. Then a thought occurred to me. I looked down at my companion.

"But Aki…you aren't lonely, are you? Or longing for a family? I mean, if you wanted children of your own, surely a way could be found. None of us would ever want to keep you from something that would make you happy."

Aki lifted her head to look at me. "And if I were to tell you that I *am* happy? That I consider myself utterly surrounded by family— almost more than I can bear, sometimes. And I have plenty of children. All the co-pilots I teach, and Captain Chui's chosen misfits like you and Diver *are* my children. What do you think of that?"

Without thought, I threw my arms around her to hug her tight. Only when I'd already done it did I realize the gesture might not be welcome. Yet before I could pull back, Aki wrapped a foreleg around me and returned the embrace. Her claws stroked through my hair gently. Gladness swelled in my chest. Aki was one of my first friends aboard the *Carpathia* and so dear to me. I pressed my cheek against her soft, warm fur and sighed.

"If you're happy," I told her, "then that's all I need to know."

Diver

We stayed for the ceremony, of course. I watched from the sidelines, listening with eyes half-closed to the rising and falling cadence of Xandri's voice as she spoke the words. Forgotten how much I liked her voice. It had all these odd little fluctuations of tone, up and down, high and low, bright and dark, as if it had been crafted together from multiple voices. Prrchik's and Kirchak's answering rumbles added a basso counterpoint, almost musical.

After, they—and Mrrchki, to my surprise—accompanied us to Trade Town. Had to admit, it was useful having someone to help carry the luggage. Prrchik and Kirchak hauled the suitcases while Xandri and I each carried a birdcage with a somewhat sedative-addled parrot inside. Akcharrch parted company with us to head to Control and get our liftoff confirmed, while Mrrchki helped us ease our way through customs. We reached *Mr. Spock* no more than half an hour after arriving in Trade Town.

"Well," Xandri said, as she paused at the bottom of the ramp, "I guess this is it..."

Morning sunlight gleamed off *Mr. Spock's* curving, metallic hull. Xandri stood beneath the glow, her chin raised. I saw the way she shook, and I knew she was fighting some inner battle. She couldn't hide it from me, the war between fear and excitement that raged within her. Remembering that I had my big boy pants on, I laid a hand on her shoulder, letting my fingertips brush her collarbone. She'd chosen to wear the hoodie from Kiri, and her flush looked pretty against all that red.

"Home, fireball," I reminded her. "You're going home. And don't be worrying; you and me, we'll come for a visit sometime, yeah? See if maybe they'll let us catch an explosion-lizard or two, so you and Science can observe them a bit."

Her eyes widened. "I'm not sure Captain Chui would want explosion-lizards on her ship."

"No one with any sense should want a *sarrktrr* anywhere," Prrchik remarked. "Especially not aboard a starship."

"Good thing scientists aren't necessarily known for their sense," I teased.

Prrchik chuffed. "Of course not. *Sense* does not help one discover faster than light travel. For that, one needs imagination."

Laughing softly, Xandri crouched and wrapped her arms around Prrchik. The Ongkoarrat stiffened in surprise, then chuffed again and shifted her stance to pat Xandri on the head with one three-toed paw. After a moment, Kirchak nudged his match out of the way and settled back on his haunches to wrap his uppermost limbs around Xandri.

"I'll miss you," she murmured into his fur.

"And we'll miss you," Kirchak replied. "If you have need of aid, or just a place to stay for a little while, you're always welcome with us."

"Hey," Aki called from the top of the ramp. "Xandri, if you want to take the first piloting shift, you need to get in here and set up."

Xandri straightened, brightening. She said a last good-bye to the Ongkoarrat and hurried up the ramp, carrying Marbles' cage with care. *Damnit, Aki, you really know how to push her buttons, don'tcha?* Shaking my head, I turned to say my own good-byes. I liked Prrchik and Kirchak, and I'd kinda miss 'em too.

"She *is* your match, you know," Prrchik told me. She tilted her head. "Perhaps not your only match, but yours nonetheless. One shouldn't squander that."

"Uh, thanks."

Big boy pants or no, I shoved aside the odd feeling those words left me with and headed up the ramp. *Mr. Spock's* spherical shape and relatively small size didn't leave much extra room. I took a glance at the pilot's seat, which Xandri was adjusting to fit her, then headed over to secure Cake's cage next to Marbles'. Not far from that, an extra seat was folded into the wall. Once I was certain the cage was good, I started unfolding the seat. *Fuck, why am I nervous? Xandri's been running sims for ages. She's gotta be a good pilot or Aki would never let her fly* Mr. Spock.

Still, was easy to be nervous with a pilot you'd never flown with. I kept myself busy going up and down the ramp, bringing in our luggage and stowing it, strapping it down. Then I strapped *myself* down.

"All set for liftoff," Xandri declared a short while later.

From the copilot's chair, Aki confirmed, "Clear for liftoff."

I gripped the arms of the fold-down chair, but as Xandri piloted *Mr. Spock* smoothly upward, my grip relaxed. Seeing the look of intense concentration on her face, I had to grin. *Seems we're in good hands.* I leaned my head back and closed my eyes. It'd be a while before we launched into slingspace.

During the wait, I oscillated between dozing and thinking about the surprise we had waiting for Xandri on the *Carpathia. Had* to smile at that. It had taken me most of the past six months, but I'd done it, and I couldn't wait to see her face when she saw it. Was hoping she'd light up, the way she had when she saw me at the marketplace a week ago.

"Preparing for sling." Xandri's voice broke through my thoughts and I opened my eyes.

"Clear for sling," Aki responded.

Already? I blinked at the star growing ever larger across our view port. Maybe I was seeing things, but it seemed like we were approaching at one hell of a clip.

A moment later I shot up straight, wincing as the straps dug into my shoulders. We *were* approaching the star at an alarming speed. I shot a look at Aki, but she showed no sign of worry. *What the fuck? She'd better know something I don't!* The star grew larger and larger, and Xandri showed no sign of slowing the ship. I tightened my grip on the arms of my seat again.

"Deploying grapples," Xandri called, just before I thought we'd smash into the star.

"Grapples away," Aki confirmed.

A signal went up on the view port as the grapples locked, and suddenly we were cruising parallel to the star, following its curve as our speed increased more and more. As I stared, the view port shifted, turning into a meshed riot of silvery-white and black.

Fuck. Holy fuck. We were in slingspace. We hadn't even made an entire turn around the star, and we were in fucking slingspace. Yeah, sure, it could be done, if you were enough of a shit hot pilot, but even among the Ongkoarrat, that amount of badass was rare. And yet when I glanced at Xandri, there was no sense of celebration or gloating. She went about checking readings as if that had been a perfectly normal sling.

I activated the comm on my HUD and pinged Aki's private channel. She shifted lackadaisically in her chair for a moment before opening the line.

"You could've fucking warned me!" It took some serious effort to sub-vocalize when I was that pissed.

"Oops."

"Oops? Oops!? Really, Aki?"

"Calm down, Diver. Was I upset? Did I seem worried? No, no I did not. If I wasn't worried, why should you be?"

I sighed and clutched at my hair in frustration. Damned Ongkoarrat, so fucking blasé about everything. Not that she was *wrong*, exactly—if she trusted Xandri's piloting skills, I oughta too—but fuck, who wouldn't be scared by that? Yeah, I'd known Xandri had been doing sims for a long time, and I'd even seen her load her own programs into the simulator, but I hadn't expected *that*. Who would?

"*Where did she learn that?*" I asked at last.

"*I suspect she taught herself. One of the potential benefits of self-teaching is that one isn't taught to think in terms of what is possible and what is not.*"

Scary thought. "*Is it—is it because of the…*" I hesitated.

"*Because she is autistic?*" Aki supplied. "*Perhaps. Perhaps not. But that is part of her, so no matter what, it is because she is herself. Isn't that what's important?*"

I stared at Xandri. God save me, but she intrigued me. I watched her sweep a strand of hair out of her face, tuck it behind her ear and raise her head to the view port. *Shit. Shit, shit, shit.* This was trouble in a big way, and I didn't know what to do about it.

"*Yeah,*" I responded, trying to ignore the shitstorm of feelings brewing inside me. "*That's what's important.*"

Xandri

Six months. Six standard months since the last time I'd seen the shifting hues of *Carpathia*'s opaline hull. *She's as beautiful as ever,* I'd thought as I watched her come into view. Now that I stood, waiting for *Mr. Spock's* ramp to descend, all thoughts of beauty fled my mind. I was so nervous, even the butterflies in my stomach had a serious case of nausea. What if this went wrong? What if people were disappointed to see me back? What if—

"It's all right, fireball," Diver said from beside me. "Go. It'll be fine."

I kept my eyes down as I descended, even so. My fingers tightened around the handle of Marbles' carrying cage until my knuckles ached.

As soon as I stepped off the end of the ramp, a wave of squawking, feathery Psittacans nearly brought me to the floor. I laughed and threw my head back so I wouldn't inhale a mouthful of feathers. Marbles, who was coming out of her sedative-induced calm, trilled a greeting to the five Psittacans. I'd dubbed them Psittacans because of their superficial—and somewhat less than superficial—resemblance to parrots, and now Marbles and Cake seemed to consider them to be abnormally large cousins.

"Guys, guys," I laughed, "are we going to need to have the boundaries talk again?"

I didn't actually mind, and I had a feeling they knew that. Still, they straightened. Many Kills, Day Dawns Red, Shadows Beneath Sunlight, Swifter Than Lightning, and Silence In The Night—the five all came from the same tribe, the first one we'd made contact with on our mission—my very first—to Psittaca. My eyes started to ache with the threat of nostalgic tears as I gazed at them.

"Welcome back, Xandri-bird," Many Kills said, and the others clacked their beaks in acknowledgement.

"Oh, guys, I really missed you."

"What about me?" came a familiar voice from beyond the Psittacans.

I glanced over them, and ended up grinning and flushing at the same time. "Kiri!"

Kiriit Ayabara was one of the best hackers and programmers in the universe. She was also almost painfully beautiful to look at. A slinky, silky tank top, woven in strands of gold, purple, red, green and blue—something that wouldn't look as good on someone else as it did on her—left her dark arms and shoulders mostly bare, and brought out the tones of gold in her brown hair and eyes. She'd shaved a streak of hair along the right side of her head; the rest of it hung in small, tidy locs, tipped in multi-colored beads. My gaze fell on her full mouth, curving with a smile, and I flushed as I remembered the small, quick kiss she'd given me before I'd left.

She opened her arms very slightly, offering a hug if I wanted it. To my surprise, I found I did. I set Marbles' cage down and flung myself at Kiri. She wrapped her arms around me, and I buried my nose against her neck, inhaling the scents of ylang-ylang and sandalwood. With every inch of her pressed against me, I felt that flare in my belly that I usually only ever got around Diver. *Like it's not hard enough dealing with my attraction to* one *person.*

Kiri stepped back, hands still on my shoulders, and smiled. "It's good to have you home."

"It is, indeed," interrupted yet another voice I recognized.

I swallowed. Standing beyond our huddle, waiting for us, was Captain Chui Shan Fung. She stood a mere meter fifty and a glance at the graceful bone structure of her face might give one the idea that she was a pushover. I knew better. I wasn't fooled by the carefully neutral expression in her eyes, either.

And even if she *had* been a pushover, the Kowari looming over her was *not*. An ex-heavy gunner, Magellan had a way of looking intimidating when all he was doing was standing there and breathing. Even the somewhat plush look of his face, his eyes lined with spectacle-like markings, did not dent his impressive stature. One called Kowari "space kangaroos" at one's own risk.

"Welcome back, Ms. Corelel," Captain Chui said.

"It's good to *be* back, Captain," I responded, with a nod for Magellan. The Kowari flicked his tail in what might have been amusement.

I couldn't help but peer past Captain Chui's shoulder. The docking bay was busy; maintenance crews were giving our shuttles a good, hard look-over in anticipation of our landing on Song. Aside from them, our small group and Diver and Aki hauling luggage down the ramp were the only ones in the bay. *Even my team didn't show up…* I had thought at least Xeno-liaisons would show up to greet me, out of duty if nothing else.

"Don't make that face," Captain Chui said softly. "There were others who wanted to come—*including* your team—but I asked them to refrain. I thought too many people at once would overwhelm you."

She wasn't wrong about that, so I didn't argue. And I felt a little better, knowing that the entire crew of the ship didn't hate me.

"Here we go," Diver said, setting my second suitcase down beside me. "That's everything. Mission complete, cap'n."

"Job well done, Mr. Diver," Captain Chui said dryly.

"We wanted to go," Many Kills butted in, "but the Captain wouldn't allow it."

"*I* wouldn't allow it," Aki grumbled. "Like I need my ship crowded with you feather brains."

I let out a small, happy sigh. "Yep, definitely home. So, how long before I have to see Major Douchebag and kill off the afterglow?"

Captain Chui gestured; next thing I knew, Magellan was carrying most of my bags and Kiri had Cake's cage. Since I didn't dare protest, I grabbed Marbles' cage and fell into step beside the Captain. With Diver next to me, Kiri next to him, and Magellan, Aki, and the Psittacans following behind, we started through the docking bay. I inhaled deeply; for some reason, the slightly recycled taste of the air made me grin. *Who would've thought I could miss that , of all things?*

"I've informed Major Douglas that you're not to be disturbed your first day back," Captain Chui said. "The Alliance has waited a long time already; they can wait one more day."

My eyes widened. "He can't have liked that."

"I don't much care. My concern is your well-being. If you're not ready to see him tomorrow..."

"Better to get it over with," I said.

"Better to just space the man," Kiri muttered.

Can't agree more. Though at the moment, I felt surprisingly little malice. The familiar walls of *Carpathia* surrounded me. My boots tapped faintly on the floor as we headed towards the nearest grav-tube. Everything was so *right* that even the thought of having to go for a filter rinse later couldn't bring me down. Or at least, not *much*. I flinched a little as I remembered the taste of the rinse fluid.

"We have offered to take care of him," Day Dawns Red told me. "But the Captain will not allow it."

"I think she wants to say yes, though," Many Kills added.

"Don't be absurd," Captain Chui said. "If we got rid of Major Douglas, we might have to deal with someone even *more* obnoxious."

I let the banter wash over me. Soon we were entering the nearest grav-tube, and I had to turn all my focus to keep my birds from freaking out; zero g and birds didn't mix. As I murmured and cooed, the Psittacans took their leave, heading for Hydroponics, one of the places on the ship they were most comfortable. I didn't mind; the large entourage made me feel conspicuous, and I'd noticed we were drawing stares from those we passed in the halls.

Before I knew it, we had arrived at my room, the same one I'd occupied for four years. I pressed a hand to the door lock, hoping no one would notice how I trembled, and stepped inside. Aside from my things, it was just how I'd left it. Except...*holy shit!*

On the far wall, where I used to keep Marbles' and Cake's cages, was a new structure. Cages, built of a gleaming metal with an almost pearly sheen, had been installed. Perches and toys filled both of them. I saw immediately that they could be opened onto the third cage nestled between them, where leafy plants surrounded a small fountain shaped like a Moebius strip. We'd seen those fountains on Cochinga and Diver had been hungry to understand how they worked, as there was no visible structure to form the strip.

I knew he'd figure it out eventually. Hell, I'd even teased him about building me a fountain for my birds. But I hadn't thought he'd actually go and *do* it.

"Welcome home, Xandri," Captain Chui murmured.

I whipped around to face them all so fast, Marbles squawked indignantly. But then I had no idea what to say.

"Far be it from me to brag," Diver began.

Kiri snorted.

"But the work is mostly mine."

"And the idea was mine," Captain Chui said. "Kiri was the one who picked out the perches and toys, so you could say it was a group effort."

"I...I..." Tears stung my eyes, but I wouldn't let them see me cry.

"You're welcome," Diver said brightly.

"Well, we'll leave you to get settled in," Captain Chui said.

I nodded. Then something occurred to me, and I said, "Captain? Could you make a list for me?"

One eyebrow rose slowly, a familiar expression.

"For the team I'm going to take down to Song. I'd like to bring a mix of species with me, now that I can. To represent the Alliance as it truly is. I'll need scientists, soldiers, maybe a few diplomats, so..."

Someone else might have chided me for jumping into work so soon, but Captain Chui simply nodded and took her leave, Magellan alongside her. Diver turned to leave as well, but paused at the door and glanced back at me. I couldn't read the expression in his eyes; something intense, fully focused on me. As I started to turn pink, he winked and headed out, muttering something to Aki. Only Kiri lingered behind.

"That looks good on you," she said, gesturing to the hoodie she'd given me.

"Thanks." I wrapped my arms around myself and stared at the floor, my fingertips curling and uncurling around the soft fabric. "It's perfect. Um...I was wondering..."

"Yes?"

"I uh, I need some clothes for Song. We haven't been on a planet that warm since Psittaca, and I only had a few things I could wear back then, so I thought maybe, you know—"

"Hey," Kiri interrupted gently, and I looked up. "Of course I'll help you, starshine. Come see me tomorrow, after your meeting. I'll help you take your mind off the Major, too."

Normally she would've said such a thing to tease me, but the soft sincerity in her voice left me feeling warm and calm. As soon as she left, tears started to swim in my eyes again. In a way, I was glad they'd left me alone for now. So many feelings boiled within me, and I had no idea if they were appropriate feelings; I didn't want anyone else to see them. *Do all people feel this way, or is it just because I'm autistic?*

I shook the thought to the back of my mind and turned to tend to my birds. As I bent down to retrieve Marbles' carrying cage, I shifted my thumb to open the comm line on my wristlet. There was something I had to do and I figured I might as well get it over with. Still, I hesitated a moment before sending the ping. *This is your job again, Xan. Might as well get back to doing it.* So I sent the damn ping.

"Hello?"

The voice chirped out of my wristlet as I was lifting Marbles into her new cage. I swallowed. *This* was your *choice*, I reminded myself.

"Hi, Christa."

Christa Baranka, my second-in-command in Xeno-liaisons. We didn't get along, and not just, as Aki claimed, because I had the job Christa thought belonged to her. We simply didn't mesh. After Cochinga, after I'd refused to listen to her doubts about Marco Antilles, I had no idea how things would be between us now. Maybe she hated me even more than she once had.

"Xandri?" There was no mistaking the surprise in her voice, even for me. "Captain said we weren't to contact you today."

"And you didn't. I contacted you," I pointed out. "I just wanted... to thank you."

A pause. "... *Thank* me?"

"For sending in the report on—on Antilles."

"*That's* what you want to thank me for? Aren't you angry?"

I blinked. "Angry? Why?"

"I claimed your work as my own. They think *I* wrote that report."

"Well, that was the big idea, wasn't it?" Certain Marbles was comfortable in her new home, I turned to retrieve Cake. "I figured you'd realize no one would take a report from me seriously after—after what happened—and...I guess I knew you'd understand. That you'd do the right thing by him."

Another pause followed my words, longer than the last. I held my hand out to Cake and he stepped up without instruction. As I lifted him to his new home, he pressed against my arm and gave my fingertip a small, gentle nip of affection. I blew lightly in his face and he let go. Cake was a sweetie, but give him an inch on this and he'd develop a biting habit. Not common in his type of conure, but there were always outliers.

Christa sighed. "No offense, Xandri, but you confuse me."

"If it's any consolation," I said without thinking, "you confuse me, too."

Oh, shit! I winced. I hadn't meant it to be mean, I truly hadn't, but...

"I never thought I'd say this," Christa responded with a small laugh, "but it's good to have you back."

I gazed down at my wristlet in astonishment, with no idea what to say in response. Christa signed off long before I could even consider a first syllable, let alone an entire sentence. I lifted my head to stare at Cake, who was settling onto one of his new perches with evident parrot pleasure.

"Maybe it's *not* the autism," I declared. "Maybe people are just *weird.*"

Chapter Nine

Xandri

Perhaps it was because she was, technically, all around me, but *Carpathia's* presence felt like a physical thing. Even though she hadn't said a word as I browsed the list of candidates Captain Chui had sent to me, I knew she was there. It was a bit like having someone else in the room with you, someone who sat quietly and read a book while you worked, respecting the fact that you'd granted them a right to be in your space.

As I studied each file on my wristlet's holo-display, I ran my fingers mindlessly along the satin edging of my blanket. Thanks to *Carpathia's* head chef, my mouth tasted like chocolate cake rather than rinse fluid. I had the dimmer set low, as I always did after I put Cake and Marbles to sleep. Everything was so familiar that I *had* to focus on my work or tears would threaten again, and I just didn't understand why I should want to keep crying when everything I'd read insisted people like me didn't get very emotionally attached.

I pressed my finger to the holo and swept sideways, flipping to the next file… and pausing as I saw a face I didn't recognize. Features a mix of delicacy and androgyny, large, deeply liquid brown eyes, a very full mouth, and a cap of gleaming dark hair. My brain stuttered to a halt, screaming 'man' and 'woman' at me at the same time. I glanced down at the list of gender pronouns.

"Oh dear."

"Is something wrong, Xandri?" *Carpathia* asked.

"Hullo, *Carpathia*," I replied with a wry grin. "Nothing is *wrong*, exactly. It's just that… with humans who are genderqueer or non-binary, I'm always afraid I'll get it wrong. 'Cause my brain sends a mix of signals. It tells me I'm looking at a man or a woman or both at once or neither, and I get confused. I don't want to step on anyone's toes just 'cause I've got some crossed wires in my brain." Lord knew I did enough of that as it was.

"Ah. That must be Private P'yo's file."

I glanced at the name: P'yo Jae-shin. "Yep."

"I rather like Private P'yo. Captain brought vir in shortly after you left. Vi has a real knack for keeping the heavies in line, even though vi isn't one virself. Very no-nonsense. I think you'll like vir, too."

"Well, if vi comes highly recommended by both you *and* Captain Chui, I probably *will* like vir," I said. "Which means I'll just feel even worse if I accidentally hurt vir feelings."

But nonetheless, I marked vir for the mission. Vir marksmanship scores were off the charts, and vi could handle a Gabe even though vi wasn't a heavy gunner, which was always a useful trait. And anyone who could keep heavies—inveterate goofy jokesters, the lot of them—in line was good to have around.

"Try not to worry too much for the moment," *Carpathia* said. "Let's get through the meeting with Major Douglas first."

I wrinkled my nose. "I'm going to have to pull out that version of me I used on the Cochingan World Council if I'm going to get through this, aren't I?"

"I'm afraid so."

"I don't think I like her. She made me feel like a bully."

Yeah, everything I'd said to the World Council, every bit of footage I'd shown them, was the truth. The *harsh* truth. And maybe there'd been no other solution to the problem. Sure, I'd met a few nice Zechak on Karrckchak, but that didn't change their history of imperialism and slavery, and I couldn't let them walk away with an alliance to a species that had invented a graser. Too much was at stake. That didn't mean I *liked* how I'd achieved my ends. My methods involved compromise, helping people so they got what they wanted. Which I'd done to some extent, but I'd still had to get mad. Really mad.

"Can I be honest with you, Xandri?"

"Of course," I said, surprised.

"Not that I would want you to solve *every* conflict that way, but I'm glad you did what you did. They killed some of our own, and if they hadn't agreed to sign, many more people might have died. I hope you can learn that there's a difference between being assertive and being a bully. After all, they still mostly got to have things their way."

A shiver ran down my spine. Memories crowded forward from the back of my mind, but I stubbornly refused to look at them. *Assertive? Me? That's a fucking joke.*

As if she sensed my distress, *Carpathia* changed the subject. "Well, I just wanted to stop in and see how you were doing. I've missed you."

"I missed you too, *Carpathia*." *More than you'll ever know.*

I swung myself out of the grav-tube a little before oh-eight-hundred hours and paused to straighten my uniform and check for lint. I hadn't missed the damned thing one bit. Though it had been designed to be more suited to me than the standard uniform, I still found it uncomfortable, and it had to be tidy and wrinkle-free or Magellan would give me the stink-eye.

"Hey, Xandri!"

Gah! I bit back a scream as a pair of strong arms, as wide around as tree branches it seemed, caught hold of me and scooped me up in a bear hug. *Sweet Mother Universe, no! No, no, no!* Fortunately, my assailant quickly set me down again—and I saw it was no assailant at all, but heavy gunner Private Anton Mulroney. He'd been one of my bodyguards on Cochinga, alongside...I swallowed hard. *Alongside Katya.*

"What, not gonna say hello?"

Hi, thanks for completely *violating my boundaries.* Instead, I said, "I guess...I didn't think you'd be happy to see me."

"Ah, well..." Anton rubbed the back of his neck and flashed a sheepish grin. "Won't lie, I was being a real ass when you left. But I've been doing some thinking since then, you know?"

I looked up—way up, because Anton was a helluva lot of dude—at him and managed a small smile of my own. Yeah, I didn't much care for being hugged by most people, but I didn't necessarily *mind* all the time, either. And I liked Anton. Even if he did treat me like his weirdo kid sister.

"I guess it just occurred to me," Anton went on, "that Kat wouldn't appreciate my attitude much. She was doing her job, being a damn fine soldier, and me acting like I was...I was disrespecting that. Realizing that made me snap out of it."

I tilted my head. "I can see why she liked you so much."

Anton made a small huffing noise and bowed his head, his dark cheeks developing a slight, dusky flush. *Embarrassed, huh? I didn't think that was possible.* I made a show of checking the time on my wristlet to hide my smile. I wished I could feel the same way he did about the whole thing. Maybe Katya had just been doing her job, but she was still dead because her job had involved protecting *me*. Because *I* had messed up.

"Hey, look."

I raised my head a little, but kept my eyes down.

"Antilles had most of us fooled, Xan. Even Kat. The AFC might see you as their scapegoat, but I don't. Hell, that's why I'm here. Saw the ping last night 'bout you picking me for the mission, realized what you'd be up against today and thought it might help, having a little support.

"Now," and he placed a big hand on my shoulder, steering me down the corridor, "you go in there and kick ass. I know you can; I saw you on Cochinga."

"You really came here at this hour just for that?" I asked.

"Well, uh..." He looked uncomfortable. "I was kinda in the neighborhood..." I frowned at him, and he carried on hastily, "Look, I've been doing third watch as punishment for the last week, ever since I uh, 'accidentally' dropped my lunch in Major Douglas' lap in the mess hall. Figured if I was gonna serve time for giving the bastard what he deserved, I might as well use it for something useful."

I held back a sigh and reminded myself that *Carpathia* had told me Private P'yo was good at handling guys like Anton. Not that I intended to bring along a lot of heavies, but one jokester was enough. And undoubtedly *I* was the one who Major Douglas would hate for the lunch-lap incident.

Not that he didn't hate me already.

"Good luck in there, kiddo," Anton said, patting me on the back as I paused outside of Captain Chui's door.

"Thanks. And Anton? No more accidents, please. I don't want the Major plotting my death."

"He'd have to go through us first, sweetheart."

As Anton strolled away down the corridor, I pinged the door comm to let Captain Chui know I'd arrived. A second later the door buzzed, and I placed my hand against the plate. Hydraulics hissed, the sound loud in my ears and sour on my tongue. I managed not to wrinkle my nose. It was stellar sometimes, being synesthetic, but other times it was a pain in the ass. Especially on starships, where the sounds all tasted sour or bitter or rancid. Except for the candy-like beeps of machinery up on the bridge. I'd managed to forget about that in my six months planetside.

Captain Chui sat behind her desk, just as I expected. And beside her desk, dressed to the nines in a blue and silver Alliance military dress uniform, was Major Douglas. I quirked a brow up before I could stop myself. *His dress uniform? Really? What is he hoping to accomplish with that?* He scowled at me, and I knew. Like a peacock spreading its tail feathers, he was trying to impress and intimidate me with his size, grandeur and majesty.

Humanity as a whole might leave me stymied, but certain individuals were alarmingly easy to figure out.

Hot anger burned up my throat. How petty could he be? Both *Carpathia* and the AFC had lost people on Cochinga, and we would have lost more if not for the competence of *Carpathia's* soldiers. And *I* had been the sacrificial lamb, thrown to the wolves without a second thought. Yet here I was, still willing to cooperate for the good of the universe, and he showed up in his dress uniform, covered in medals and ribbons, as if it was imperative he show his superiority?

I remembered that day now. I remembered Katya, her eyes wide and blank, a hole torn through her abdomen, shedding blood far faster than her personal nanobots could stem. Most of all, I remembered the sensation of cold that had settled on me, the ice that had run through my veins. For so much of my life I had been trained to compliance, but for the sake of Katya's memory, that her death should not have been in vain, I would give this assertiveness business a try.

"Good morning, Captain," I said with a terse nod. I turned my gaze to Douglas, not even trying to hide my cold disdain. "Major."

"Ms. Corelel." Captain Chui gestured to a chair in front of her desk. "Please sit."

I settled in the chair, sitting up straight, both feet firmly planted on the floor. A small part of me wanted badly to run my fingertips along the satin strip running down the side of my pants, but I wouldn't. Not knowing how much it would satisfied Douglas to see me fidget, how much it would confirm, in his mind, everything he believed about me. *The Hands and Voices are counting on me. I can do this.*

"Good to see you, Ms. Corelel," Major Douglas said, with that smarmy insincerity adults usually reserved for praising the clumsiness of a small child's artwork.

"I'd say the same, Major, but I'm a lousy liar."

The Major paused, drawing back in affront. From behind her desk, Captain Chui raised an eyebrow at me. I took a deep breath and plunged onward.

"I see no use in pretending we like each other; that's not what we're here for, anyway," I said. "The AFC has requested my assistance, and I've agreed. I have a few conditions, as I'm sure Captain Chui already told you I would. For one, I will not work with any individuals from the AFC. Only my own team."

"I cannot and will not stop the AFC from going planetside, Ms. Corelel. This is their job too."

"Fine. But keep them away from me."

I forced myself to hold his gaze, even though it sent pain shooting into my bones, down to the tips of my fingers and toes. A deep breath, another, and Major Douglas nodded his assent. Good. One down.

"Second, since I won't be working with them," I continued, "I will not be taking the fall for them if they screw up. Try it, and I will make sure you regret it." *Ah ha ha. As if I have any power to make this man regret anything.* "I hope that's clear, Major?"

"Crystal," he said dryly, regarding me with a narrow-eyed stare.

"Stellar. See, these aren't difficult, are they?" I smiled, knowing it was stiff and cold. "Finally, I'll have Captain Chui forward you a list of equipment we'll need for the mission. I *could* ask R&D to reproduce what I need, but it will be quicker and easier if the AFC provides them for us."

That made the Major sit up and take notice. Because this was his job and he *had* to do it, he was tolerating my attitude, but I wouldn't be surprised in the least if he took any opportunity to squash my plans with glee.

"And what equipment would that entail, Ms. Corelel?"

"I haven't constructed the entire list, but among other things we'll need High-Pressure suits—at least a dozen, possibly two dozen—and as many Barracudas as you can provide."

A smile crept across the Major's face, slow and superior, curving wide from ear to ear. "Surely, with all your knowledge of sapient species, you already know that the Hands and Voices don't allow such things on Song."

"They'll allow me to bring them."

"You sound awfully confident, Ms. Corelel, especially for someone with your... well. But if the Hands and Voices won't allow the AFC to bring HPs and Barracudas planetside, why should they allow *you*?"

I widened my eyes, trying for the very picture of innocence. "Why, Major... because they *trust* me."

His smile fled and his expression darkened. Captain Chui made the tiniest sound in her throat, quickly stifled. I didn't dare look her way, afraid the ice inside me might crack if I as much as turned my head. *Almost there, Xandri. Almost through.*

It was true, the Hands and Voices didn't allow any deep sea equipment of any kind on Song, not since the AFC had brought in submarines, an act that had practically been a declaration of war. They were a generous, pacifistic race, but they had learned distrust quickly. But if we were going to do this *my* way, we needed that equipment, and I was pretty sure that once I explained what my way was, the Grand Matriarch would agree. *Sweet Mother Universe, let me be right.*

"Very well," Major Douglas said stiffly. "I'll get what you need. However, since you will not be working with the AFC, I can't be expected to help you if the Grand Matriarch refuses you."

"She won't."

His scowl deepened. "Was there anything else?"

"Those are all my conditions. However, there is one more thing. Has there been any sign of either the Zechak or the LHFH?"

"As I already told Captain—"

"I said," I repeated, enunciating each word to penetrate that dense skull of his, "has there been any sign of either the Zechak or the LHFH?"

"No," he grumbled.

"Good. Keep it that way." I leaned back in my chair. "I believe we've covered everything. I mean, after all, I don't need to *tell* you to keep the press out of this, so yes, that should be everything. Not unreasonable, I think."

"Not in the slightest," Major Douglas said, the dry tone back in full force. "If I'm going to get what you need, however, I had best get started soon if we want it to stand a chance of reaching Song in time."

"I'll get the list sorted and sent to you as soon as I'm done here," I said, turning my gaze to Captain Chui.

Hold on, hold on. Inside I trembled, quickly losing hold of the ice inside me. I gritted my teeth and stared at the scar over Captain Chui's eye, focusing on it intently so I wouldn't break. Every second dragged, an agonizing eternity, as Major Douglas rose from his chair and cleared his throat.

"We'll talk later, Captain?"

"Of course, Major," Captain Chui said, gracing him with her tiny, unreadable smile. "Thank you so much for your cooperation."

He might be a major, and she just an ex-gunnery sergeant, but she was captain of this ship and as a military man, Douglas knew a dismissal when he heard one. I continued to sit, frozen, barely breathing, listening for the familiar hissing of the door opening and closing. Even after it closed, long minutes ticked by, in which I could only stare at the Captain.

"Is he gone?" I finally managed, in the same tone I'd been using the entire time.

She nodded.

"Oh, thank God."

I slumped in my chair as if all my bones had turned to liquid. My head throbbed and my stomach churned. *Sweet Mother Universe, what did I think I was doing?* I'd been a bare step short of antagonistic, and somehow I'd gotten away with it. Sure, Major Douglas would hate me even more now, but I'd have what I needed. But I wasn't sure I liked being assertive. It took an awful lot of energy.

A soft, unfamiliar sound caught my attention. I raised my head and found, to my shock, Captain Chui slumped over her desk, her head buried in her arms.

"Captain!" Alarm sizzled through me.

She made the sound again, a crackling, brown sort of sound, and her shoulders started to shake. I stared. I'd never seen Captain Chui like this, not once in four years. In the face of large, angry predators, xenophobic, trigger-happy aliens, and blowhard politicians, she always remained cool and stoic. Now, as she raised her head, gasping between laughs, a curl of dark hair slipped free of her perfect coif.

"God, child," she breathed. "Sometimes I really don't know what to make of you."

"Captain?"

She shook her head. "Never mind. Suffice it to say, that was very well done. It seems I've managed to teach you a thing or two after all."

"Oh. Um...well...I just really wanted to get it done with, and... come on, Captain, you saw him!" I threw up a hand. "Coming in here in his dress uniform and medals? Like I'm supposed to get down on my knees and worship his brass? Please. He's petty and foolish and—and I couldn't let him get away with it. And now the hardest part is over."

"Oh, I don't disagree about the Major, though he'll likely complain to me quite vociferously. Though...I'm not sure the worst is over for you yet, Xandri."

I frowned.

"You don't remember? The haircut I agreed to fund back on Cochinga?"

Oh, shit. Shit, shit, shit.

Chapter Ten

Xandri

"Just sit still for one more minute."

I'd already been sitting still for more than half an hour. It was hard not to fidget as Riza, the hairdresser, finished up clipping my bangs. I *hated* getting my bangs cut, hated the way little hairs fell and tickled my nose, hated the flash of scissors close to my eyes and the metallic scraping sound of them opening and closing. *At least I smell nice.* Something sort of lemony, but *better*, drifted in my hair.

"There we go," Riza said, taking a step back. "You're done."

Nervously, I raised my eyes to the mirror—and blinked in surprise. My hair had been cut much shorter in the front, though it was still long enough to curl down under my chin; and to hide my scar. A bit behind my ears, my hair got abruptly longer (so it wouldn't look "generic Ancient Earth starlet," as Kiri had put it) and still fell nearly to the small of my back. Riza had done something so it no longer looked as lank and slippery as it usually did.

"See?" Kiri said from behind me. "Even you hair isn't completely impossible."

I tugged a strand lightly, staring in amazement. "How'd you do that? Even nanobots can't do this."

"Good old fashioned hair products. Volumizer," Riza set a tub of something on the table in front of me, then a second tub, "and texturizer. Sometimes cutting edge science isn't the best solution."

I poked a finger at the tubs, as though afraid they might bite. *That was all it took? Really?* I turned in the chair, gazing at Riza, Kiri, and Captain Chui. They all watched me with varying degrees of knowing smile.

"I'll include an instructional upload for how to use them," Riza told me, as she shoved my own set of tubs into my hands. "It's not that difficult, but a little assistance couldn't hurt."

I nodded, dazed. Clutching the tubs against my chest with one hand, I reached up to touch my hair again. *It feels so different...* Between this and the new wardrobe items Kiri was helping me design, I felt like I was making some big changes. And big changes, even good ones, made me nervous. On a positive note, maybe people would start to take me a bit more seriously. Others tended to believe I didn't care about my appearance; in truth, I just didn't know what to *do* with it.

I stood up as Captain Chui made a credit transfer for the haircut. I'd *tried* to convince her to let me pay, but she was having none of it.

"It looks good on you," Kiri murmured, close to my ear. "I knew it would."

I looked up at her; for once, my cheeks only turned a little bit pink. Reacting, perhaps, to the warmth settling in my chest, I leaned in and gave her a quick, impulsive kiss on the cheek. Her skin was soft beneath my lips and it was tempting to linger, but I pulled back nonetheless. Kiri regarded me with surprise for a moment, before her expression melted into something sweetly sexy.

"You're welcome, starshine," she said.

Finished paying, Captain Chui returned to us. She eyed me for a moment, then gave a small nod. "You've got a good eye, Ms. Ayabara."

"Thank you, Captain."

"You two ready to leave?"

Kiri nodded. I took a deep breath and nodded myself, though nothing could make me ready for the chaos of a space station.

Adrisat Station was purely commercial and thus, always packed with people, like a giant shopping mall in space. I braced myself as we stepped out of the salon, where there were no walls to protect me from the noise and movement and sheer presence of people. Humans, Kowari, the occasional Ongkoarrat, groups of Nīpa and roaming hoards of Nafta; they all swirled around me, oblivious to the near panic they instilled in me.

Fingers curled tentatively through mine, dragging my attention away from the crowds. I glanced at Kiri.

"*I know I'm not Diver,*" she sub-vocalized over my channel, "*but maybe I'll do for now?*"

That time I did turn red, very red. "*What's Diver got to do with anything?*"

"*Oh, please. You already had it bad for him before you left, and he might not want to admit it to himself, but the feeling's pretty mutual for him.*"

I bit my lip and looked away. There had to be at least a hundred reasons I wanted that to be true—and a good hundred more that part of me hoped it wasn't. I had a job to do. I couldn't be distracted by wondering how Diver felt about me. And even if that wasn't the case, I wasn't sure... I shifted my shoulders uncomfortably. I wasn't sure about a lot of things.

"*Something's changed between you two since you got back. I can see it, you know,*" Kiri told me. "*I really hope you go for it. You could use some fun in your life.*"

Despite my embarrassment, I smiled a little at her words. *Maybe she's right*, whispered a voice in the back of my mind. *Maybe it couldn't hurt...* Not that I was sure Diver was really interested, but Kiri seemed to think so, and she was a good judge of—

I halted so fast, Kiri let out a small sound of surprise. One of the benefits—and at times, disadvantages—of how my brain worked was that I processed at least two streams of information at once; sometimes more. So even though I was worrying over the problem of Diver, when the flash of white caught my eye, I couldn't help but turn to look. After all, this was a sight you didn't see every day.

"Captain! Look!" I hissed. "A Felera!"

The Felera were one of the universe's mysteries. To anyone who didn't know better, they looked like Ancient Earth big cats, though we knew for a fact that they weren't, even if we didn't know precisely *what* they were. Despite the fact that no one had ever heard a Felera speak, few doubted their sapience. They traveled the spaceways as much as any other species, carrying their belongings in a set of bags draped over their backs, paying for what they needed with a chip embedded in a paw.

As if they weren't enough of enigma, every now and then a Felera would bond with a member of a species (often human, and though there were many hypotheses about why, I sometimes suspected it was simply because humans had the best, most flexible fingers for scratching) and stay beside them for life. Scientists suspected that the Felera could communicate somehow with its bond-mate, but if so, no one ever breathed a word of *how*. Of *course* I was fascinated by them.

"It's not polite to stare, Xandri," Captain Chui said quietly.

"It was staring at us first!"

Indeed, its deep blue eyes watched us, despite the people who crossed its path. Black stripes, somewhat like a tiger's, crisscrossed its snowy white fur. The resemblance to a tiger ended there: it had a more elongated face, long ears with tufts much like a lynx, and a tail like a lion's, though the tuft at the end was longer.

"Beautiful," Captain Chui murmured. "I understand how you feel, Xandri, but we really must get going. Major Douglas has already complained enough about this delay."

I sighed. Kiri tugged at my hand, and I reluctantly allowed her to pull me along. I didn't want to think about the crowd surging around me, so I glanced back at the Felera instead. It took me a moment to sort through the crowd swirling past my vision; only when a small family of Kowari slid out of my line of sight did I spot the Felera again.

It was following us, keeping to a safe distance but clearly on our trail. For a moment our eyes locked. The Felera lifted its head and its whiskered muzzle twitched, almost like a secretive smile. I smiled back.

By the time we reached the airlock back to *Carpathia*, the Felera was gone, but I had the experience of seeing it to hold onto.

Diver

Maybe I was just looking for an excuse. I stood outside Xandri's door, toying with an omni-tool. *Ain't really an excuse, right? I mean, every bit of electronics needs a checkup now and again, and her wristlet is old tech, and it hasn't been looked at in months...* I *had* to keep an eye on it, with all the new tech it carried.

Fuck, who was I kidding? That was a total excuse.

We'd both been busy since we got back, so I hadn't had much chance to see her. And if I was really gonna go through with things, I had to know it wasn't just that time together on Karrckchak. Before I started wearing my big boy pants full time, I needed to know it wasn't just me thinking with the wrong head. *Had* to know that I had a reason to feel like I was wanting something other than casual this time around, when I hadn't thought that could ever happen again.

I raised my hand and tapped the door comm.

"Yes?" Her response came through distracted.

"It's Diver. Here to check your wristlet."

A moment later, the door opened with a hiss. I stepped inside—and paused.

Xandri lay on her back with her feet propped up on the wall and her wristlet projecting three separate holo-display screens. Marbles was on the bed with her, gazing at the screens as if she, too, was reading. I noticed each screen carried different information: in the center was an enormous set of text on the Hands and Voices; to one side was a list of articles about Pandoras; and on the other, updates on the situation in parliament as they adjusted to the presence of the Anmerilli.

Xandri tipped her head back, regarding me with an expression that told me she hadn't thought it through before opening her door to me. "Uh...hey."

"Why's Cake all the way over there?" I asked, gesturing at the parrot sitting on his play tree. Figured it was better I didn't ask why she was sitting—laying?—like that.

"He's sulking. I won't let him preen my hair because I've got all that stuff in it from the hairdresser."

"Right, that was today. Can I see?"

She let out a little sigh and maneuvered into a sitting position. I tried not to grin as hair curled around her face, framing the oval shape of it in a rather appealing way. She regarded me shyly, her pale lashes dipping low over the soft, vaguely grayish blue of her eyes. There was a stillness about her, like she was holding her breath, waiting.

"It really suits you," I said, as I sauntered over and took a seat next to her. "No surprise, though. Kiri's a genius like that."

"She is," Xandri murmured in agreement.

I glanced at the holo-display again, particularly the list of articles. Shit like *Who Will be the Next Victim of Unprovoked Pandora Violence?* and *Experts Warn Against Involvement of 'Pandoras' in Society* and *Closing the Box: Is it Time to be Rid of Pandoras for Good?* Fucking hell. Reporters made me sick. I reached over, caught Xandri's hand gently in both of mine, and turned off the holo-display.

"You shouldn't be reading that shit."

"I...mostly I was rereading about the Hands and Voices. Refreshing my memory."

"Uh-huh."

She finally looked at me. "Diver, I've been ignoring all this for six months. But now I'm back, and I'm not living in some cave where I can hide from it. If this is the ammunition people are using against me, I need to know."

"All right. That's fair," I conceded. "But this stuff, Xan, you gotta know it's bullshit, it's not—"

"But what if it *is*? What if it's all true? What if—if people like me are inherently bad, inherently violent—"

I had to cut her off. "Wait a minute. You mean you don't *know*?"

She stared at me, brows furrowed in confusion. Her hands still cradled in mine, I explained the research I'd been doing, the files I'd dug up from everything leftover from Ancient Earth. As I spoke, the bits of gray faded from her eyes, like storm clouds clearing out of a spring sky. Not for the first time, I found myself baffled at the idea that she was hard to read. Hope shone from her like rays from a sun.

"You really didn't know?" I asked, when I'd finished.

She shook her head. "I was *afraid* to know. I mean, I could've looked it up but...I was scared. That it would all be true and—and that it was right to get rid of people like me."

Jesus fuck. She gazed at me, her eyes wet with tears she refused to shed, and I wanted to find every one of those fucking reporters and snap their necks with my bare hands. *Well, guess that answers what I came here to get answered.* Tentatively, I raised a hand to cup the side of her face, letting my fingers slide into her hair. Her cheek heated beneath my palm as she leaned into my touch.

"You—you weren't worried?" she asked, with a small sniffle.

"No. But I'm not the autistic one here," I said. "If it *was* me, then yeah, I might well be just as scared. But Xan, you're one of the least violent people I know."

"Most mornings, before I've had my coffee, I want to rip people's eyeballs out if they so much as look at me funny."

"Fireball, if that were a sign of uncontrolled violence, more than half the known universe would be behind bars by now."

Some of the worry eased from her eyes as she laughed. My fingers slipped through her hair as she turned her head and reached down to remove her wristlet. I let my hand fall; sure, I'd made up my mind, but slow was fine for me.

"You mentioned you wanted to give this a look."

"Ah, right. Yep. That's what I'm here for."

Marbles, who'd been remarkably silent up until then, clambered up onto Xandri's knee and chirped, "Liar."

"Marbles!" Xandri scolded. "Name-calling is rude."

"It's okay," Marbles responded.

"No, it is *not* okay, when have I ever given you the idea that that's okay? Are we going to have to have this discussion again?"

Since I had no idea how to handle this—and the damn bird was kinda right—I grabbed the wristlet and used the omni-tool to open it up. While I inspected its innards, Xandri and Marbles had what sounded alarmingly like a mother-daughter discussion of manners. At one point I glanced at them out of the corner of my eye, saw Marbles gazing up at Xandri with a tilted head and a too-innocent expression, and had to grin.

"Looks like all the physical parts are fine," I said, closing it up and turning it on. "Any software problems?"

"Not a one. Between you and Kiri, that thing is going to run for eternity."

"Good. Let me know if anything changes, yeah? I'll come fix it for you straight away."

"Thanks." She smiled slightly, gazing up at me in that way I remembered from the cave. "Um...Diver..."

"Yeah?"

"Uh...earlier, when—when we were on station, Kiri and I were talking. She mentioned...well, what I mean is..."

She bit her lip in a way I found strangely enticing and turned strawberry pink to the tips of her ears. *Well now, what have we here?* I set her wristlet down on the bed and reached out to cup her face again, catching her with both hands this time. She leaned in rather than pulling away, her eyelashes fluttering and her lips parting. I lowered my head slowly, almost shaking as I fought off the urge to drag her close and kiss her senseless. *Carefully, carefully...*

An explosion of gray feathers in my face made me jerk back in surprise. Xandri stifled a yelp and made an immediate move to scoop Marbles off her shoulder.

"Bad girl," she chided. "No shoulder bird, Marbles. No. That's it, back in your cage. It's bedtime anyway."

I stared after them as Xandri rose to bring Marbles to her cage. *I just got fucking cockblocked by a* bird. Marbles gazed back at me from Xandri's hand, looking decidedly smug despite the fact that she was being put back in her cage.

"Sorry about that," Xandri said, keeping her eyes firmly on her task. "It really has gotten late for these two. Which makes me realize that I'd better order up some dinner before *Carpathia* reports me to the Captain for not eating. Damnit."

"Right. Um…right."

"No kissy 'til you tell the truth," Marbles chattered from her cage.

Xandri turned utterly bright red. "Right, well, if you'll excuse me, I must get down to strangling my bird."

"Would you like some help with that? Because I could help."

"No, no, I don't want to impose." She shut Cake's cage and hustled over, escorting me to the door.

Damn bird. The moment was lost. But I didn't want Xandri to think it was gone for good, especially since I had a feeling I knew what she and Kiri had been talking about. So I bent down and kissed her cheek, letting my lips linger close to hers. Her breathing quickened and she started to turn her head towards me, her lips sliding more and more under mine—

"No kissy!" Marbles shrieked.

Xandri sputtered and ducked back into her room, muttering darkly at her bird. I didn't know whether to laugh, or maybe curl up in the fetal position and cry over how freakishly smart Marbles was. *Ah well. Looks like things are going somewhere.* Marbles wasn't coming with us to Song, so she couldn't get in the way there. And in the meantime, Captain had assigned me to learning the specs for Barracudas and HP suits, so I was good.

Chapter Eleven

Diver

Song floated in space like a large, richly colored sapphire. Wasn't no other way to describe it, really. The pure jewel-tone blue of it, so blue that the clouds swirling in the atmosphere looked almost iridescent in comparison. An ISTN-2 world practically dead center in the system's Goldilocks zone, larger than Ancient Earth, with more oceans and a slightly heavier gravity. Didn't sound like much, but even from the shuttle *Destination Unknown*, it looked like it might be paradise.

Next to me, Xandri pressed close to the window as we made the descent through Song's atmosphere. I waited until we passed through the thick layer of clouds, then leaned across her seat to peer out, too. She went still for a moment, a ragged breath escaping her lips; then the landscape unfolding beneath us caught her attention and she forgot about me entirely. Would've been offended, but I couldn't blame her.

"Diver, look!" she breathed. "It's amazing!"

Ocean spread out beneath us, kilometers of it, such a pure blue. Where the ocean grew shallower the water turned that breathtaking, clean tone it often had in the tropics, and even from the height of the shuttle, I saw enormous spreads of coral reef. Many of those reefs climbed their way onto land, so in some spots it looked as if small towns had grown up out of the water.

"No wonder they're leery about letting people come here," Kiri murmured from the seat behind me. "I'd be worried, too."

The farther we descended towards the planet's surface, the more Xandri shifted impatiently in her seat. She drew in a sharp breath as a town of coral spread out beneath us in a rainbow of colors. The town curved in a crescent around a large dock; smaller buildings huddled closest to the pier, spreading and growing into larger structures towards the rim. Even I had to gape, 'cause this wasn't built, it was *grown*.

"I didn't know they could keep the colors in the land coral," Xandri said. "I wonder how they kept it from losing its intracellular endosymbionts."

Kiri turned her head to stare. "*What?*"

"Well, I suppose perhaps it may not work quite like Ancient Earth coral. But even if it doesn't require symbiosis with flagellate protozoa, it has to get its color *somehow*. Maybe if I scan it..."

"Did anyone actually catch that?" The voice came from P'yo Jae-shin, who sat next to Anton in the seats in front of us.

"She means," I explained, "that the color in the coral comes from a single celled organism of some sort that lives in symbiosis with the coral."

"Why didn't she just say that?"

"Technically, she's not talking to us right now. In fact, I doubt she realizes we're here."

"If I didn't realize you were there, Diver, I couldn't ask Kiri to pinch you for me."

I ducked to the side, as far outside Kiri's reach as I could get. Unfortunately for me, that put me into Jae's reach instead, and vi delivered a sharp pinch to my bicep.

"Ow!" I rubbed my arm. "How can someone so tiny pinch so hard?"

"Practice." Jae smiled. "Now strap back in, all of you. We're almost at touch down."

I settled back in my seat, grumbling good-naturedly as I strapped myself down. Xandri turned away from the window with a reluctant sigh and strapped in as well.

The entire Alpha Team, plus Captain Chui and First Officer Magellan, traveled in *Destination Unknown*. Marla Thomas and Kirrick Chanda were with us, along with Anton and Jae, Emin Nazaryan, who'd been on the rescue team with us back on Cochinga, and a tall, golden-furred Kowari called Amelia. To my surprise, Xandri had also picked Aleevian sil masViara, a juvenile Sanavila and hardly her favorite person. We also had two members from Science and two from Diplomacy, and of course all five Psittacans and Kiri.

Beta Team rode in another shuttle and included more soldiers and the rest of Xandri's Xeno-liaisons team, as well as another pair from Science and one from Diplomacy. Between all three shuttles we also had two platoons of soldiers with us. Hadn't yet sussed out exactly what Xan was planning with all this, but I had a feeling I was getting the general idea. She'd put Christa in charge of Beta Team, and she had to have a good reason to do that

A few minutes later the shuttle set down, and Xandri was one of the first out of her straps. She squirmed anxiously, until I put a hand on her arm. Color me surprised, she settled under my touch, able to wait until the seats in front of us had cleared out before bursting to her feet. I hurried after her, telling myself I was just keeping an eye on her, even though deep down, I was as excited as she was.

Then I actually stepped outside and Song's atmosphere whacked me in the chest like a hammer. A breeze came up off the ocean, easing the heat a little, but for the first few minutes the heavier gravity settled its extra weight on my shoulders, pinning me in place. I paused, breathing deep, letting my filter-implant adjust to the new surroundings. My HUD sent back readings, telling me what, exactly, I was letting into my body.

"Fuck me," Anton complained. "I hate the planets that feel like they're trying to cook you alive."

Kiri stretched, sighing as the sun soaked into her bare limbs, and shrugged. "Could be worse. Remember Psittaca? You had to practically chew the air there."

"What I want to know," Jae cut in, "is how *she* is doing *that*?"

Jae pointed, and we all glanced at Xandri, who had immediately rushed to the nearest, pseudo-palm tree to examine it. That she wasn't too bothered by the heat didn't surprise me. She wore linen shorts and the top over her bathing suit was so thin and light, it was see-through. Nah, that wasn't the freaky part; it was the way she pranced around like the gravity didn't affect her.

"Isn't it obvious?" Kiri said, and pointed at Captain Chui, who bore a noticeable spring in her step as she headed over to retrieve our wayward fireball.

I blinked. "Heavy-worlder? But. . . "

"Not all heavy worlds are like Mei Long," Jae pointed out. "A lot of heavy-worlders have genes to combat the effects of heavy-grav. I have to say, though, this feels a little unfair."

"You'll get used to it," I assured vir. Already I was adjusting to the press of heavier gravity on my chest.

"All right, everyone," Captain Chui called, as Xandri came trotting back to us. "Line up. The Grand Matriarch has requested our presence at the dock."

Regardless of whether they had recovered from the sudden atmospheric gut punch, the *Carpathia* crew fell into formation. Alpha and Beta Teams lined up in front, with the two platoons of soldiers spread out behind us. *Wonder where Douglas and his men are.* Douglas had headed to the *Resplendence* as soon as we entered Song's orbit, but I didn't doubt the bastard would show his face soon.

Well, he kinda had to, since he had our supplies and all.

Hot sun beat down at me, and I was glad I'd worn shorts and cut the sleeves off some of my T-shirts—even if the latter move made Kiri glower at me. We'd barely been walking a minute before sweat started beading on my neck and forehead. *Fucking hell. It looks pretty, but it feels like living in an oven.* Typical. Finally somewhere I might have a chance to pursue things with Xandri, and I was probably gonna be dealing with a constant case of itchy balls from all the sweat. Real charming.

I glanced sidelong at Xandri, who walked along next to me, her eyes darting everywhere, from the trees to the town to the powdery soft, pure white sand under our feet. Mostly, I found my eyes drawn to the town. Sure, it was made out of organics, but really, a lot of technology still was, in essence. But metals and minerals and all that stuff, right now they seemed so average in comparison to freaking *coral*.

"Maybe they'll let you spend some time with their scientists," Xandri said suddenly, her tone teasing.

"Like you don't want to do that too."

"Of *course*!"

I grinned down at her. She smiled back, a bounce in her step.

As we neared the dock, passing through the edge of the town, I noticed shapes in the clear water. The closer we got, the bigger those shapes grew; by the time we were heading down the dock, towards deeper water, some of the shapes were growing alarmingly big. Like, abominable sea monster from hell big. The biggest one, drifting in the water near the back, had to be somewhere between seventy-five and ninety meters. Fucking hell.

"The Grand Matriarch," Xandri murmured, her stride lengthening.

Fucking, fucking hell. Wasn't sure I'd fully realized quite what 'Grand Matriarch' meant to the Hands and Voices, but I was about to find out.

Alpha Team took the lead, though Captain Chui and Magellan remained with us. Soon Xandri strode out in front, her sandals slapping on the smooth palm wood of the dock. Something moved in the water, rolled, showing a flipper and a grayish belly and several somethings clinging to its body. Undaunted by any of it, Xandri walked until she was mere meters from the end of the dock, then halted.

"Right," she said. "We do this *my* way."

She kicked her sandals off and, with only a hint of hesitation, stripped down to her bathing suit. If it weren't for her slender figure, she'd have looked like an Ancient Earth retro pinup in red with white polka dots, halter-style top and shorts-style bottom, the whole nine yards. I took her in, the curve of her small but well-shaped breasts and the width of her hips, grinning—until, heedless of the enormous shapes in the water, she dashed the last few meters of the dock and dove in.

"Captain?" Jae said, snapping to sharp attention.

"It's all right, Private. She knows what she's doing," Captain Chui replied. "At least, she had better."

That's funny. I didn't know my heart had taken up clogging. I breathed deep, trying to settle my racing pulse.

"She's just doing what she always does," Kiri said, stripping down to her bikini without reservations. Dazzling as always, in slinky gold with netting that made her look like a mermaid. "That Ancient Earth saying, you know? When in Rome."

"Are they out of their minds?" Emin demanded as Kiri followed Xandri into the water.

"You know," I said, as I kicked off my sneakers and stripped off my shirt, "I'm pretty sure they're the only people I know who are actually *in* them."

I cleared the end of the dock and launched myself into the water. Despite the heat of the air, the water was a perfect temperature, neither too warm nor too cold. The feel of it over my skin almost made me groan, and I realized, what the hell, this might be a mission but it was a mission in *paradise*. I was gonna enjoy this.

The water closed over my head, sweeping me down into another world, one of clear blue depths and sunshine gleaming through liquid like light through a crystal. The salinity of the water wasn't strong enough to sting my eyes, so I kept them open, gazing at the rainbow refractions spreading on the pristine seabed beneath me. I felt no fear, despite the beings in the water with me. Even the smallest was slightly larger than an Ancient Earth killer whale, but that didn't frighten me.

A splash sounded, followed shortly by another. As I let myself drift back to the surface, a shadow began to spread across the seabed, so enormous that it dwarfed everything else. I swirled in the water, turning to face her: The Grand Matriarch.

You couldn't mistake her for a blue whale for more than a few seconds. She was too large, for one thing; much too large. From the tip of her nose, down her back, over her fins and flukes, gleaming, grayish armor plates lapped over one another like broad tiles. Four yellowish-white lumps clung to her: Her Hands, the cephalopod-like creatures that had evolved in symbiosis with her species. These would be her special attendants, bonded to her as long as they lived.

I surfaced. I found that the two extra splashes had been Kiri and Diver, joining me in the water. Everyone else watched from the docks, though the rest of my Xeno-liaisons team had stripped off their footwear and sat with their feet dangling in the water. As I remained in place, treading lightly, the Grand Matriarch's head emerged partially from the water. I didn't know what struck me more, her sheer enormity, or her beauty.

"So, you have come to us at last, Xandri Corelel."

I tilted my head slightly. As symbiotes, the Hands and Voices didn't have words for 'I' or 'me,' not in the sense I was used to. They used 'we' and 'us' regardless of whether they spoke of the whole or the individual. Yet there was a slight difference to their tone, an inflection caught even by the translation-implant, that signaled which they were using at any given moment. I listened for it with care, even as the water around me vibrated slightly with the impact of her—mostly—sub-vocalized song.

"Greetings, Grand Matriarch," I said. "It is an honor to meet you."

"There is no need to be so formal with us. We hope to be friends."

"I'd like that very much."

Other Voices were joining their ruler, spreading around the dock in a half crescent, and I wondered if they were echoing the shape of the town consciously or not. Some were gray, some were blue, some were black; all had armor across their backs, and all carried Hands with them. The largest Voices bore no more than two Hands—the Grand Matriarch being a special exception—but some of the smaller Voices carried as many as a dozen small, octopus-like Hands with them.

I fought down my awe. I was here as a professional, a diplomat of an unusual sort, and I needed to do my job, not squeal like a fan girl.

"We see you have brought many others with you."

"They're here to help," I explained. "My job is to help you achieve the best outcome, and despite what some people say, I can't do that on my own.

"This is Kiri," I went on, gesturing to where Kiri floated in the water, clinging to the docks. Then I gestured at Diver. "And this is Diver. There are many of us here, so introductions might take some time."

"Time is something we have in abundance, small one."

Which wasn't entirely true, despite the long lives of the Voices, and our own life-exed lifespans. But it was protocol on Song that proper introductions must be made, and so I had to allow it.

Even though I knew it was waterproof—from experience—I checked my wristlet carefully. Satisfied, I put it on to record while the Grand Matriarch introduced her people. There were more than three dozen Voices, each with their attendant Hands, and she introduced them all by name—not *short* names either. The Grand Matriarch—whose own named shortened to Who Sings The Song That Binds The Whole—kept shortened forms of each name, at least.

My private comm channel pinged. I twitched my thumb, opening the channel carefully.

"*Are we gonna have to remember all this?*" Diver asked.

"*Hush,*" I scolded.

When it came my turn, I let everyone speak their names for themselves. By the time we'd gotten through everyone, I was starting to lose steam, the water dragging heavily at my tiring limbs.

"We appreciate your desire to adapt to our environment," the Grand Matriarch told me, "but you are yet a calf, and not a very good swimmer as our own calves are. Please, return to land. We wish to allow you time to settle in here before negotiations begin, but first there is a matter we must discuss, we and you."

"I understand."

And I knew precisely what she wanted to talk about, so far be it from me to argue. Diver climbed out first, and reached down to help Kiri and I out. As his warm, water-chapped hands closed around my arms, I flushed a little, suddenly aware of how little I was wearing. Without trouble he hauled me out of the water, setting me down close to him. Water ran in rivulets down my skin, drying quickly beneath the heat of the day—and the heat of his body, not far from mine.

Okay, Xan, job to do, remember? Focus. I turned away from Diver and settled on the edge of the dock, next to Kirrick and Christa. I'd separated my team for a good reason, but I was glad to have them all here right now.

"Grand Matriarch," I said, as I took a towel that Marla handed down the line, "I think I know what you wish to speak of. The equipment I asked for permission to bring down to Song."

"We do not feel comfortable with such devices in our home."

"I know. I wouldn't have asked if I hadn't felt it was necessary. Your job is to see to the well-being of your people, Matriarch, and right now, as the leader of this mission, my job is much the same. I have to protect all these people, and I have to see to the well-being of all of Song.

"Thus I request permission to equip my people with two items. One is a high-pressure suit for deep-sea diving." Though I must have seemed calm to anyone watching, inside I was freaking out, terrified I would stumble over one of my carefully chosen and oft-practice words. "We may or may not use them. I selected them so we might better negotiate on your level, within the parameters of your world. If you wish only to negotiate on the surface, no more need be said, but should any of us need to descend to the depths, we cannot do so without the suits.

"The second item is a weapon called a Barracuda. I know you know of it, and under other circumstances I would not think of bringing them here. However, I know it's important to your people that all songs be heard. I've created two teams, and hope to send one of them out to hear the songs of your world. They'll need protection from the creatures you call Disharmonies. As you can see, we don't come equipped with armor as you do."

The Grand Matriarch's great head dipped most of the way beneath the water as she considered my words. The water rippled with untranslated song as we waited for an answer, not a single one of us making a sound. If the Grand Matriarch refused, there would be nothing I could do, and it might limit our strategies. But even though I barely knew her, I couldn't help but feel like she'd understand.

At last her head came up again. "Very well. We will allow it under the circumstances you have described. However, should you be caught using these items for any other reasons, you will be expelled from our home."

"Grand Matriarch," Captain Chui spoke up, "if I catch even one of my people disobeying orders, they will be expelled *out the airlock* of my ship."

The Grand Matriarch made a sound that burbled and chimed through the water; a laugh, I was pretty sure. "From one Grand Matriarch to another, we hear and understand. We trust you to keep your word. Now then..." She shifted in the water, turning slightly. "Sings Brightly Beneath The Waves, come to us. We need you to show our new friends to their quarters."

A smaller Voice swam towards the docks, towing six Hands, most of them some variant of red or brown, two vaguely the color of sand. The Voice's own coloration, a brownish gray, indicated him—or perhaps her—as a shallow water Voice. I reached out my hand as Sings Brightly Beneath The Waves swam right up to the dock and pressed the slippery surface of their face against my palm.

"Hello, new friends."

"Hello, Sings Brightly Beneath The Waves," I returned. "Would you mind if myself and my people called you Bright for short?"

Bright rolled once in the water, revealing a belly with small markings that I knew would bioluminesce in the dark, and an impressive set of genitals. Which meant, from what I'd read, that he was his society's equivalent of male, for what little that was worth. The Voices' odd use of personal pronouns had left a lot of people scratching their heads for a long time. The Voices themselves had been the one to give us the final piece of the puzzle: Small markings denoted a male—the females had patterns down their entire bellies. What any of it meant beyond that was yet to be discovered.

Bright's large tongue lolled out of his mouth before he said, "If that is the best you can do for now, we don't mind. Would you like us to show you to your home while you're here?"

"We would appreciate that very much, though we must retrieve our belongings first."

Bright tilted in the water at this, gazing up at me with one large, curious eye. "You have Hands?"

"Not Hands, but things we need all the same."

"Very well. We will wait here, and when you return, we will escort you."

I thanked him and rose. The heat had done fast work on my wet skin and bathing suit, and I was able to climb back into my clothes without much trouble. *You did it, Xan. You got through the first meeting.* It was so much easier than it had been on Cochinga. There were certain expectations the Hands and Voices didn't—*couldn't*—have of me that the Anmerilli had. Feeling lighter, I stepped into my sandals and turned to look at everyone.

"We're returning to the shuttles to retrieve our belongings," I said. "Then Bright will show us to our lodgings."

"You heard her," Captain Chui added. "Move out!"

The Grand Matriarch had seen us, and clearly not felt any need to disapprove of our numbers, so there was little left to do for the day. Tomorrow we would begin in earnest.

Kiri and Diver walked with me, both to my left. Kiri had pulled her shorts back on but carried her T-shirt slung over her arm, and I made a point not to look at her, lest I start staring. Between her and Diver, my senses were a bit overloaded from attractiveness. Fortunately, my honor guard—as they were jokingly calling themselves—followed too closely for me to get a chance to act on what I was feeling, even if the idea of doing so frightened me. With P'yo Jae-shin, Anton Mulroney, Emin Nazaryan and Amelia—who looked less than happy about the whole head-to-toe fur business at the moment—shadowing us, I was almost afraid to breathe.

"So," Private P'yo said as we walked, "since we're going to be protecting you, mind explaining what a Disharmony is supposed to be?"

"I can show you." I still struggled a little to look vir in the face, but vir open body language made it easier, even if my brain kept shouting conflicting conclusions at me.

I drew up a holo-display screen from my wristlet, only stumbling once in the process. As Diver reached out to steady me, I brought up an image of a *true* sea monster. It had a head like an enormous crocodile, a mouth full of sharp teeth, a whip-like body with two sets of short but powerful fins, and a long tail ending in flukes. An image of several Alliance species beneath it gave everyone the scale of the creature: About thirty meters, or as I liked to think of it, way too fucking big for anyone's good.

"Xandri," Private P'yo began. "May I call you Xandri?"

"Of course."

"Good. Look, not that I don't appreciate your efforts here, but next time, get us bigger guns."

The other three soldiers snorted in agreement, and honestly, I couldn't blame them. The Disharmonies were the one part of this mission I *hadn't* been looking forward to.

Chapter Twelve

Xandri

We left the Psittacans at the docks with Captain Chui and Bright. The poor things weren't handling the gravity here very well. Psittaca was a lighter gravity planet, lighter even than Ancient Earth, with a thicker atmosphere and a higher oxygen content; much better for hollow-boned creatures that climbed and jumped and glided than Song was. I knew they'd adjust with time—they'd had to get used to heavier gravity since leaving Psittaca—but it would take a bit longer, and I didn't want to ask too much of them in the meantime.

During our walk to the shuttles and back, I couldn't stop looking at the town. Pinks and yellows, blues and oranges, stunning reds and deep purples, sometimes separated by color, other times blending into one another or fading in an ombre effect. Bright, eye-dazzling colors that tasted like cool sherbet on my tongue. The structures flowed one into another, so their shapes were all rounded; in some places they formed cups or spirals like seashells. I hurried to retrieve my bag, eager to see what the town looked like on the inside.

As I slung my pack over my shoulder, a hand landed on my arm. I jammed my teeth against my lip so I wouldn't scream and turned to face the owner of said hand.

Aleevian sil masViara loomed over me. I took a deep breath and gazed up into his vaguely bluish, silver face. In the early days, when humanity had first met the Sanavila, we had called them angels, for the flap structures hanging from the arms of the adults reminded us of wings, and their silvery glow made us think of the divine. *Not us. I've never seen any of them as divine.*

"You hate me," he stated bluntly. "Why'd you pick me for this mission?"

"I don't hate you, I just really dislike you," I answered with equal bluntness. Which was perhaps not what he was hoping for, but I didn't see why there ought to be a double standard. "I wanted the Hands and Voices to see the diversity of the Alliance. I know you—how you act, how you react—so you're the one I chose for my team."

He stared at me for a long moment, then said, "I really don't understand you."

"Get in line." I sighed and shrugged. "Look, Leev, I just need you to do your job, okay? You don't have to like me. Just do as I ask until the mission is done, and then you never have to speak to me again if you don't want to."

He considered me for a long moment, his head tilted slightly, his flattish nostrils flaring wide at the sides. Then he, too, shrugged.

"Well, Captain Chui seems to think you know what you're doing, so I'll leave it at that, then."

"Thanks?" I directed at his back as he walked away.

"They're all like that, you know."

I glanced at Private P'yo Jae-shin as vi joined me, setting vir bag at vir feet. Vi was tiny, roughly around the same height as Captain Chui, though with a deceptively slender build. The faint curve of vir chest vaguely implied breasts, but otherwise vi had a straight, narrow frame. Since I'd only met vir this morning, I still couldn't quite look vir in the eyes, but I could already focus on vir cheekbones when I needed to.

"I'm pretty sure it's nurture, not nature," I responded, "but to be honest, when it comes to the Sanavila, even *I* have my doubts."

Private P'yo chuckled. I hadn't meant to just say what I thought, but since vi didn't seem bothered by it, I flashed a small smile in return and turned to see where the rest of our group was.

Anton, Emin and Amelia had their bags and were heading towards us, rounding up Aleevian and Kirrick on the way. Diver was helping Marla and Kiri from the shuttle with an exaggerated gentlemanly flourish; I couldn't make out their words, but the tones of their voices sounded as if they were joking with each other. Our two scientists—Casaria siv masKania, a Sanvila biologist, and Hans Klee, our anthropologist—were arguing about something, big surprise, but at least the diplomats seemed to be getting on.

"Shall I go round up the civvies?" P'yo offered, looking pointedly at the scientists and diplomats.

I winced as Casaria raised her voice. Were she not our best damn biologist, I would've left her on the ship. "I'd appreciate that, Private."

"Call me Jae, okay, boss?"

"As long as you don't make a habit of calling me boss."

Vi grinned and marched off across the sand to gather the last wayward members of Alpha Team. Magellan was already directing Beta Team and half the troops back to the dock. As Alpha Team spread out around me, it seemed natural to fall into step between Kiri and Diver. People chattered all around me, but for once I hardly even noticed the noise. I watched the town as we neared it again, excitement coiling in my belly.

Captain Chui and the Psittacans waited for us at the closer end of the dock. Bright was there too, floating in a channel that led up the beach and into town. Coral braced the channel walls so the sand wouldn't collapse.

"Did you get what you needed?" Bright asked, lolling onto his side to gaze up at us.

"We did," I told him. "Thank you for your patience."

"Good. Now we will show you the way. Follow us."

Bright began swimming up the channel, propelled by powerful strokes of his tail. I gazed at the town as we followed. Others around me murmured, and Casaria spoke loudly, speculations on the biology of this place. I watched the buildings grow bigger, saw an arched gap in the structure ahead of us, and wondered how anyone could think of anything but its beauty right now.

"Ms. Corelel." Captain Chui's voice forced me to pay attention.

"Yes, Captain?"

"Lieutenant Zubairi contacted me while you were retrieving our things. Major Douglas and his men will be making planetfall shortly, and they'll be bringing our supplies."

"They're not staying with us here, are they?" I asked, alarmed. The path, with the channel running along next to it, carried us through coral gardens that seemed too fine for so many visitors.

"No. The next town is too far away, so they'll be setting up temporary facilities."

I let out a breath. *Good. I want them as far away from me as I can get them.* I lifted my head, watching the arch pass above us as we walked below it. Bright and his Hands swam in through a smaller entrance, following the channel into a deep pool in the midst of a large chamber. He popped his head up to regard us as we stopped; some of the soldiers didn't quite fit in the room.

"It may not seem like it, but there is enough room for all of you here," Bright told us. "We will come again in the morning so negotiations can begin."

I knelt in front of the pool. "Thank you, friends. This place… it's beautiful."

"Ah, well, we appreciate that you think so. We were involved in the making of this town, were we not?"

It took me a moment to parse what he was saying and to whom. When I noticed the Hands clinging to his sides growing brighter beneath the water, I understood. Hands had no spoken language, but they communicated in other ways, including a complex system of color changing. I had a feeling they were expressing their pleasure at the compliment.

"You should be proud," I said. "It's a work of art."

The Hands' color deepened. Bright let out a trill of song that the translator left as it was, high and cheerful, and rolled onto his belly to swim away. I wished he'd would've stayed, would've given me time to talk to him more. *But you're on Song now. With any luck, you'll get to talk to lots of Voices.* Maybe I'd even learn how to understand some of the Hands' communication methods. No one had ever been allowed close enough, long enough, to learn.

Realizing that the entire room was watching me, I stood and turned to them. My stomach clenched with fear, but I ignored it, focusing on a bright streak of yellow coral near head level. This would be one of the easiest parts.

"We had a long journey to get here," I said, "and I know many of you are still adjusting to the atmosphere. Get some rest. Tomorrow, the real work begins."

Every soldier in the crowd saluted, which felt both uplifting and intimidating at the same time. Technically, they wouldn't have a lot to do—this would be more like a vacation for them—but I doubted any of them would be off their guard completely. Truth to tell, there wasn't much reason to have them here, especially since land-based lifeforms here tended towards being small and basal, and we weren't expecting trouble according to Major Douglas but… as I'd learned from Captain Chui, better a little paranoid than a lot dead.

I stood beside the pool as people spread out to pick living quarters. The rush and press was more than I could bear, and it would be even worse in the heat. Something—no idea what—kept the inside of the building cooler than outdoors, and I didn't mind heat so much, but with all those people, pressing and bustling and...I actually shivered. *No thanks, I'll stay right here. Have to be space-fried to get into the middle of that.*

"Xandri."

"Yes, Captain?" I lifted my gaze from the pool.

"You're doing well," she said, speaking gently, but loudly enough to be heard above the hustle and din. "You've handled everything gracefully so far."

"This has been the easy part."

"I'm not so sure. I'd hate for us to get off on the wrong..." She paused, waving a hand uncertainly, then shrugged. "You know."

"Limb?" I suggested tentatively.

She smiled. "Any way you look at it, you did well. One thing I *am* curious about, I must admit. Surely the reasons you gave for our uses of HP suits and Barracudas weren't that different than what others have given..."

"Oh. I watched the vids," I explained. "They did mention that they wanted the equipment for protection, but," I bit my lip for a second, searching for the right words, "well, I made sure I pointed out how we would use the equipment not just to protect us, but the context that has for negotiations. I—I tied our song in with theirs, so to speak, so it was about the whole, not just us. If that makes sense."

I flushed as Captain Chui studied me. So it was a bit of a gamble, but I didn't think it was *that* much of one. What we knew of the Hands and Voices told us they thought of themselves almost as one being—not a hivemind, as such, but every individual was still part of a greater whole. It might be perfectly logical and sensible to most species to present only *our* need for protection, but I'd thought that for the Voices and Hands, they'd need to know how our song would harmonize with theirs.

Captain Chui was shaking her head in a way I couldn't quite decipher when Diver and Kiri reappeared, sans luggage.

"Hey, Xan," Diver said. "We found a good room for you."

"Oh! Oh, thank you."

"Go on," Captain Chui told me. "You're dismissed."

I swooped down and hefted my bag onto my shoulder, then followed Kiri and Diver down a much clearer hallway, wondering what Captain Chui's headshake had meant.

My room overlooked the ocean and was sandwiched between Anton and Emin on one side, and Jae and Amelia on the other. Diver and Kiri had their own rooms across from me, so I was surrounded by people I liked.

The Hands and Voices still hadn't figured out how to shape their coral into structures such as furniture, so all of it was imported from elsewhere. The dark wood meshed nicely with the shifting blue, purple and pink of my walls, and somewhere they'd found blankets for the bed that matched the colors of the coral. I spent a good deal of time admiring it, before settling on the bed to sip some water and eat a nutrient-bar.

Later, as the sun began to set, I got up to unpack. I had two bathing suits, the one I was wearing and another in plain blue, both chosen by Kiri. The second went into a chest at the foot of the bed, along with my clothing; happily, no one would be making me wear my uniform for this trip. I paused before reaching back into the pack to retrieve my guns. Diver had kept the pair of Atrox Mk. XIIs in good shape, but I wasn't sure I was ready to wear them again. I set them on a small table off to the side instead.

It was almost dark by the time I was satisfied. Small globes of light blinked into existence around the facility. I leaned against the sill of the wide window, my heart pounding with eagerness. I shouldn't, I knew I shouldn't, but...

I glanced over my shoulder at the closed door. Everyone would be eating dinner, expecting me to skip it because they'd gone to catch fresh fish, and I hated the texture of fish, which seemed to be the same no matter what planet it came from. Coral scraped against my palms as I pulled myself onto the windowsill and swung my legs over. A wonderful, salt-tang sea breeze rushed over me as I dropped down from the sill, landing in the powdery soft sand. A pair of moons and an abundance of stars were blinking into view above me. I stretched my hands towards that magnificent sky and sighed in unadulterated pleasure.

"Going somewhere?"

Sweet Mother Universe, I'd been getting a lot of practice in not screaming my lungs out lately. I whipped around—and found Diver behind me, his arms folded. The starlight revealed enough of his face that I could tell he didn't approve. Fuck.

"Um... down to the beach?"

"All alone. Without telling anyone."

I looked down. "There's something I want to do and—and I didn't think anyone would understand. I thought they'd think it was... weird."

Diver tilted his head, studying me. The moon shed silvery light that turned his emerald eyes to jade. I was barely breathing, but my heart beat wildly, thrashing against my ribs like a wild bird caught in a cage. *Come with me. Please, say you want to come with me.* The thought startled me. I'd wanted privacy because I didn't think others would understand, but I wanted *Diver* to understand, wanted it desperately.

"Well, let's go, then," he said at last. "Captain Chui'd kill me if I let you go alone."

I let out a yelp of thanks and started back to the beach again. Diver came with me, stretching his legs to match my excited stride. As we neared the water I paused to strip off my sandals and dug my toes into the soft sand as we walked. I avoided the small, shelled, crustacean-like creatures combing the beach, heading up onto the dock instead.

"Whoa," Diver murmured.

I nodded, grinning so hard that my face hurt. Here, without light pollution, one could see so many stars; the sky was a bowl full of them. They didn't look like jewels, as the books I read tended to describe them. No, jewels were too plain, too banal for this: they were merely rocks. This was fire and magic, real magic, as only a wizard as skilled and talented as the universe could spin. And the clear, pristine waters below reflected all those stars, so one got the feeling of staring out into the deep reaches of space.

I forgot to be unsure, to be worried that this silly whimsy of mine would make Diver think less of me. I stripped quickly, leaving everything but my bathing suit behind on the dock. Even my wristlet landed on the pile. The rustling of clothing beside me told me Diver was doing much the same; we hit the water at almost the exact same second.

My laughter peeled through the night. I stretched out, floating on my back, floating amongst the stars. *Feels like flying.*

"This is amazing," Diver murmured from close by. "Xan, I don't want to know the kinda person who'd think this was weird."

I held my hands up. All that silver-bright luminescence glittered off the water droplets running down my palms and clinging to my fingertips. I giggled and said, "Look, Diver! I'm wearing the stars!"

Fingers closed around my wrist, pulling me gently upright. I found myself gazing into Diver's eyes as he drew my hand to his mouth and kissed my starlit palm. I let myself drift closer to him.

"You wear the stars well," he murmured. "They suit you."

My cheeks burned at the compliment, but I didn't mind so much. I slid in as close as I could get and wound an arm around his neck, so we could drift amongst the stars together. I tipped my head back against his shoulder and looked up at the moon, round and full and intensely silver in the night.

"You know, I think this mission will go just fine," Diver said.

I glanced at him.

"You understand the Hands and Voices pretty well. You'll figure out what they want."

"To be honest, I think I already know. It's figuring out how to give it to them that will be the hard part."

"Well, we'll help you. No matter what else, you've got us to call on for help."

"Thanks."

He shook his head. "Nah. Thank *you.*"

"For what?"

"For giving me a chance to see the universe through your eyes," he explained. His voice was soft, his breath close to my neck. "It's one damn amazing sight."

Oh. I had no idea how to respond to that. Hell, I had no idea how to *feel* about that. Was my view of things really that different? Was that good or bad? *Diver seems to think it's a good thing*, chimed in an optimistic—for once—part of my brain.

He hadn't laughed or teased me about my errand here tonight. In fact, he understood. An impulse rose within me, and I acted on it before I could let myself think to quash it. I leaned in and pressed my mouth to Diver's. It was over so quickly I hardly felt it, and I fled immediately for the dock afterwards. But I heard Diver chuckle in appreciation, and when we climbed out of the water, he flashed me a grin and one of those strangely never cheesy winks.

Chapter Thirteen

Diver

Morning greeted us with something like birdsong, but somehow *more* annoying. Probably would've stayed in bed with my pillow over my ears if Kiri hadn't barged in to tell me I was being ordered to get some breakfast before the day began. For the first time I'd had cause to worry that Xan might be an even bigger slave driver than Captain Chui.

Thinking on it now, I had to grin. *Nah. Not Xandri.* Not the woman who'd shown me her raw, naked wonderment last night. Not the woman who set each piece of clothing she removed on the dock, stripping down to her bathing suit before fastening a floatation ring around her waist. She'd left both platoons to do as they wished; some were lounging on the beach, some were back in the town learning about the Barracudas. Both Alpha and Beta Teams were with us, but she'd given them all enough time to wake up and get ready.

"Think they'll be here soon?" Christa Baranka wondered, shading her eyes to peer out over the sun-glistening water.

As if in response to her words, a string of song trailed through the water towards us, long and loud and untranslated. I'd heard whale song before, but this… this was something more. Richer and more musical, somehow. I kinda found myself wondering if I could build an underwater vehicle, kinda like my horse or my gorilla, but more like a whale.

"Sounds like they're on their way," Xandri said. "Anyone who wants to come in the water with me, make sure you're wearing a floatation device. Anyone who'd prefer to stay dry, keep your comm channels open."

"Are you ever going to let us in on what, exactly, Beta Team is even supposed to do?" Christa pressed, though without the ire I might've expected.

"I'm hoping to have the specifics by the end of our first meeting with the Voices and Hands."

Christa pursed her lips, considering that. In the end, she nodded, apparently satisfied. *Thank fuck. Last thing we need is her making waves.* She wasn't happy, but she'd do her job, and that's what we needed.

The entire Xeno-liaisons crew prepared to get in the water. As I belted on the flotation device—which, let's face it, didn't do much for the badass image I preferred to project—I saw Emin and Anton preparing for a dip, too. Amelia sat on the edge of the dock next to Jae, who was busy slathering what looked like a five millimeter thick layer of sunscreen on every unprotected spot of vir body.

"Not gonna join us? Your people are good swimmers, right?" According to Xan, the Kowari had special muscles that sealed off their pouches, protecting the mucus membranes so they could swim safely.

Amelia blinked slowly at me. "Yes…usually. But have *you* ever tried to get saltwater out of three inches of fur?"

"But your people are explorers. Sailing your planet's seas since time immemorial," I teased.

"In *boats*. We don't generally sail boats across the ocean with the intent of falling out." She cocked her head, ears perking forward. "Do you?"

"Occasionally, but humans are weird like that."

Amelia's snuffling laughter was drowned beneath a tumult farther down on the docks. I spun—and quickly dodged to the side as five feathery bundles of hyperactivity shot down the dock and plunged into the ocean. Foamy water gushed at the impact, spraying everyone near the end of the dock, Amelia included. She growled in response, baring her teeth in a Kowari threat-smile.

"I see the Psittacans are adjusting," I remarked.

Xandri sighed and rubbed her forehead. "So they are." She waited until the initial furor died down, then snapped her fingers as loudly as she could. The Psittacans splashed around in the water, turning to face her as she jabbed a finger in the direction of the beach and said, firmly, "Shore."

Five soaked feather crests drooped.

"You can stay in the water if you want," Xandri said, her hands planted on her hips, "but you'll stay near the shore or you'll have to get out. Am I understood?"

Many Kills clacked his beak. "Our Xandri-bird is starting to speak like a leader. We'd better go, before she decides to pluck us."

Beaks clacking—as if they were perhaps not taking her one hundred percent seriously—the Psittacans headed towards the beach. Despite their enthusiasm, they *did* have trouble swimming; their wing-arms just didn't allow for the kind of range of motion they needed. Not that *they* would be likely to admit that, especially not a warrior like Many Kills.

"They're here!" Emin shouted suddenly, and we all turned to look.

Kiri, standing next to him, shook her head. "Damn. I keep forgetting just how *big* they are."

"Happily, the really big ones are filter feeders," Xandri said. "All right, everyone, we're moving out. Time to get these negotiations started."

She was trying to appear confident, as a good leader should, so I made a point of not laughing as she slipped into the water and started doggie paddling towards the incoming Hands and Voices. A few others stifled chuckles as they followed her into the water. Just like yesterday, the temperature was perfect, neither too cool or too warm; with the flotation rings, it made for a pleasant, easy swim.

Partway out to meet the Hands and Voices, I noticed smaller shapes moving through the water. For a moment, Xandri's mention of creatures called Disharmonies came back to me. Then Bright— at least, I thought it was him, they kinda looked similar—popped his nose out of the water to greet Xandri. After a short exchange I couldn't hear, Bright turned in the water and Xandri caught hold of his dorsal fin. Bright lunged forward, speeding back towards the larger Voices, and suddenly they were leaving us far behind.

"Xandri!" I hissed into her comm channel.

"It's fine!" Her voice came back half muffled by the rush of water. "They're coming to help you, too."

More Voices were moving towards us, swimming far faster than we could. In only a couple moments, one was popping its head up in front of me. *Whoa, those are big teeth!* It might've been trying a smile or something, but it looked more like it wanted to eat me. It twirled joyfully in the water, and I noted the markings on its belly. Xan had done her best to explain it to me, but speaking as a human, it was kinda hard understanding what markings had to do with gender.

Not that I wasn't used to being a bit lost on that front.

"Greetings," she sang—for her markings extended all the way down her belly. "We are Swims Strong Against The Tides. Bright tells us that you're not so good with our names, so you may call us Tides. We are here to escort you."

Trying to remember how Xandri had handled this, I reached out a hand. "I'd appreciate that very much, Tides."

Tides did a swift, agile turn in the water. I noticed three Hands clinging to her tail, and it looked for all the world like one of them raised a tentacle and waved at me. *That was either the freakiest thing ever, or the coolest.* Or both. I caught Tides' dorsal fin with both hands, stretching my body partway across her armored back. For all the armor was solid beneath me, it radiated heat.

"Hold on, friend," Tides instructed. "We were not granted our name frivolously."

Holy fuck, she wasn't kidding. She shot off through the water like a missile, sending up a spray of water and outstripping her fellows. *Hell yeah!* I laughed and leaned down low, not caring about the water spraying in my face. Tides trilled, zigzagging a little in the water. A glance behind me showed her Hands waving a few free tentacles in excitement. We closed the distance between us and Xandri and Bright, and before I knew it, the ride was over. Tides slowed to a halt before two dozen larger Voices, including the Grand Matriarch.

"Thanks, Tides," I said, as I released her fin.

"You are welcome, friend."

"Call me Diver, yeah?"

"Diver?" Her voice came out of the translator bright and pleased. "That is a good name."

Other Hands were approaching, towing the rest of the group. I swept my arms out, bringing myself to Xandri's side. Her cheeks were pink with exertion and laughter, her hair damp and her eyes bright. She turned in the water and waved as the Voices began dropping people off: Kiri, the Xeno-liaisons team, Emin and Anton. *This mission is so different from Cochinga, it ain't even funny.*

Xandri turned in the water again. "Good morning, Grand Matriarch."

"We greet you, Xandri Corelel. Do you think it well that we begin?"

"I think that is well indeed, Matriarch."

Phew. The Anmerilli had liked to start off every meeting by allowing all the World Council members to air their grievances, and I hadn't known too many sapients who did grievances like the Anmerilli. They clung to every little slight like particularly cantankerous old grannies. I couldn't really imagine the Hands and Voices having many grievances, or at least, wanting to air them out like so much dirty laundry.

"We think you already know what we want," the Grand Matriarch said. "We want—*need*—a way to be a part of your song."

"I had a feeling you'd say that."

Kirrick paddled forward. "But isn't that easy? We could set up some kind of communications devices. Between Diver and Kiri..."

"Even with the technology we have, the distance between Song and Shalien is pretty big," Kiri said. "But even so, if we worked together, the delay wouldn't be too bad."

"It doesn't matter," Xandri said. She reached out, her fingertips brushing the edge of the Grand Matriarch's enormous head. "Does it? That's not truly being a part of our song."

"We are going to build starships anyway. Should we not start to consider how we will get to space?"

I swallowed. *Fucking hell.* They wanted to go to space. How did you send creatures that big to space? Especially when they needed to be in water. And especially because I had a feeling that *I* would end up part of the effort to get them there. Xandri glanced sidelong at me at just that moment, confirming my feeling.

"Grand Matriarch, I'll be honest with you. I'm not certain we can achieve what you desire," Xandri said. "We'll do our utmost, but I can make no promises."

"We prefer it that way. Others have already tried to make us promises, knowing they could not fulfill them."

Xandri hesitated a moment, one of those rare moments where I wasn't quite sure I could read her. A touch of uncertainty lingered in her eyes, yes, but something else, something I might've described as maternal, almost. Then she lifted her chin, her expression changing, growing resolute.

"Forgive my impertinence, Grand Matriarch, but I must ask. Are you *absolutely certain* this is what you want?"

"We have talked it over for many of what you call hours. It might seem a strange decision for us, but we do not have to tell you, Xandri, that time marches on. We choose to harmonize with other songs. We are certain."

"Very well. Do you—do you think your people could choose… representatives? Among other species, we choose a number of individuals. You might say that *our* song is made of up various notes from other songs. We will need three or four notes from your song to add to ours."

"Notes." The Grand Matriarch lowered her head and, despite the gentleness of the motion, sent out a sizable ripple through the water. "Yes, I think we understand. We will discuss it further, but we are fairly certain we will agree. Now we must ask: What do you need from us to help ensure your success?"

Damn. Wish more species were this cooperative. Judging by the tiny smile on Xandri's lips, she was thinking much the same.

"We need to understand you—your environment, your song— better if we're to successfully bring you into space and, eventually, to Shalien," Xandri said. "There will be many things we'll need to look into. If I—if I make a list and show it to you by the end of the day, would that be acceptable?"

The Grand Matriarch's head came back up, sending more water rushing over us. "Yes. Yes, we believe that will do just fine."

"Press ships? *Press ships*!?"

I froze partway up onto the dock. Jae and Amelia were still there, sitting off to the side, staring at Captain Chui and Major Douglas. The two stood a bit farther down the dock, and Captain Chui should've looked like a tiny bit of nothing, wearing capris and a tank top while Douglas tried to loom over her in his uniform. *Wearing his uniform in this weather? Man's space-fried.* Not that a clear-minded individual would attempt to intimidate Captain Chui when she was that angry.

"This is supposed to be a classified mission," Captain Chui went on. "You insisted no one else knew about this, so tell me, Major, *why* are there a dozen press ships swarming around the planet like mosquitoes?"

Well, shit. I hauled myself up onto the dock and turned to help Xandri and Kiri, but Anton and Emin were ahead of me. Even so, I reached out and caught Xandri's elbow, steadying her as she climbed to her feet.

"I have no idea how it got out," Major Douglas said, "but I can assure you an investigation is already underway."

"Why is it," Kiri piped up suddenly, "that the AFC always waits until *after* someone screws up to start doing background checks?"

Major Douglas and Captain Chui turned to face us. I glanced at Xandri, concerned; she was dripping wet and wearing only a bathing suit, and I thought she'd feel too vulnerable, too exposed. For the first time since she'd arrived aboard the *Carpathia*, her Xeno-liaisons team stood around her like an honor guard, and every last one of them—including gentle, pacifistic Kirrick—looked fucking pissed. Kinda surprised Douglas didn't implode under the sheer amount of unadulterated anger being sent his way at the moment.

"Did I hear that right, Captain?" Xandri asked. "There are press ships in system?"

"Close by, in fact. *Carpathia* has instructed them not to land on Song, but you know how well the press listen."

"Almost as poorly as the AFC," Xandri said, with a pointed look at Douglas.

"Now, young lady, there's no—"

"I thought I made myself clear aboard the *Carpathia*, Major." Xandri's voice never shook, but I stood close enough to see her trembling and wondered if it was fear or anger—or both—that made her shake so. "We can't afford interference here. If you knew this was already leaked and you lied to me..."

"I didn't know," Douglas said firmly. "Trust me, Ms. Corelel, I am no happier about this than you are. I will do my utmost to aid in stopping them, but until we figure out who leaked this, there's little point in handing out blame."

A hand on my arm—Kiri, I realized—stopped me in mid-step. I shot her a look, but she just shook her head in warning. *Goddamnit! I'm supposed to just stand here and let the bastard get away with this?*

The AFC had been plenty willing to hand out blame on Cochinga. Xandri, recipient of most of said blame, went pale and wobbly at Douglas' words. Surely I was allowed to punch the guy, just this once.

"Major," Captain Chui broke in sharply, "perhaps it's best if you get your investigation underway. And see if the *Resplendence* can do anything about the problem." She turned away from him before he could answer and said, seemingly into thin air, "Lieutenant?"

"Yes, Captain?" The voice that answered was Lieutenant Khalida Zubairi, Acting Captain of *Carpathia.*

"Send out our fighters and Aki in *Mr. Spock.* Have them round up as many of the press ships as possible. Tether them to *Carpathia* and bring the reporters on board."

"*Reporters?* On board the *Carpathia?*"

"Better that than having them end up planetside. *Carpathia* will keep them in check."

Boy, would she ever, once she understood what they were doing there. Almost sad I was gonna miss that.

Douglas, seeing that no one was likely to give him the time of day anymore, turned and walked off down the dock. Amelia made a rude gesture at his back—an *incredibly* rude Kowari gesture, if I remembered correctly what Xan had told me—and I decided I liked her. And that I'd have to learn that.

"Oh, Sweet Mother Universe," Xandri groaned, running her hands over her face. "Don't we already have enough to deal with?"

"The press problem will be taken care of," Captain Chui assured her. "You worry about the rest of the mission."

"But there's *so much.* We need to understand their biology, their society, their etiquette, everything we'll need to make them comfortable both physically and emotionally on *another damn planet.* That's so much information, and that's assuming we can even find a way to give them what they want in the first place, which I'm not sure—"

"Hey." Kirrick, speaking softly, set a hand on Xandri's shoulder. "That's what you've got us for, remember?"

"Kirrick is right," Christa said. "I think I'm starting to understand this whole team thing. For now, Sho, Kimi and I will team up with our diplomats and come up with a plan for dealing with the press, just in case."

Xandri nodded slowly. "Right. That sounds good. Kirrick, Marla, I need you two to help me sort out the list for the Grand Matriarch."

"No problem," Marla said with a grin. "After Cochinga, if there's one thing Kirrick and I are good at, it's lists."

Kirrick let out a beleaguered sigh, but didn't disagree.

"Good. Okay." Xandri took a deep breath. "Kiri, would you help Diver? I know you're more a computer kind of woman, but whatever we figure out will probably require some level of computerization, anyway."

"Will do."

"What about us?" Emin asked, from his seat on the dock between Anton and Jae. "Anything we can do?"

"Up to," Anton added, "and including feeding Major Douglas to the nearest thing with large teeth."

Tempting offer. Xandri looked like she was seriously considering it, until Captain Chui cleared her throat pointedly.

"For now, there's not much you can do. There's only so much anyone can do until I get this list sorted, so you might as well take some leisure time," Xandri said. "If any of those press ships make it planetside, you'll be wrangling reporters pretty soon."

"I'd rather be wrangling the things with large teeth," Jae muttered.

"Yes, but that's mostly because we can legally shoot them," Captain Chui pointed out. She clapped her hands once. "All right, everyone, you have your orders. Time to get to work."

Easy for her to say. She wasn't the one who had to figure out how to launch a whale into space.

Chapter Fourteen

Xandri

We chose a spot on the beach; if we had to work, we might as well be comfortable. The first thing I did, as we settled in, was send Marla to speak to our scientists and diplomats. Aside from Casaria and Hans, Beta Team had their own scientists, a chemist and another biologist. I wanted lists from the scientists and diplomats, all the things *they* thought we needed to know, so there'd be much less chance of missing something.

I settled on a blanket spread on the warm sand and tried to ignore my growing feelings of being overwhelmed and panicked. Not to mention uncertain. Part of me had wanted to protest, to convince the Grand Matriarch not to go through with this. Part of me was terrified what the Alliance might do to the people of Song. I kept reminding myself that it wasn't my place to act as if I knew best. I had to trust that the Grand Matriarch knew what she was doing. *And I can probably get some special dispensations for them, at the beginning.*

"Xandri?"

I started and glanced at Kirrick. He sat next to me on the blanket, his legs folded, his dark, curly hair still damp and a bit stiff with salt water. I tried to smile.

"Sorry, Kirrick. I've got a lot on my mind."

"Understandable. So why not get it *off* your mind?" He set a holo-slate down on the blanket in front of us. "Everything will look simpler once it's organized into a list."

"You really believe that?"

"In this case? No." He smiled ruefully. "But let's pretend for now, yeah?"

Something about his laid-back acceptance of the situation made it easier to take a breath and get started. I grabbed a couple of bottles of water out of the cooler by our blanket and handed one to

Kirrick, before leaning over the holo-slate. Using a wand, Kirrick quickly set up an interactive list graphic, complete with separate sections and section headers. I had to smile a little at that.

"Very good," I told him. "Honestly, Kirrick, we'd be lost without you."

He tipped his head in appreciative acknowledgement.

We were far from alone on the beach. Many of the soldiers were hanging around; Anton and Emin had joined in a game of volleyball. Diver and Kiri had claimed another blanket nearby and were leaning together over their own holo-slate. Two of the Psittacans, Silence In The Night and Shadows Beneath Sunlight, had taken refuge under a large umbrella and were playing *dashiv*, a Shar strategy game that Psittacans in general had quite taken to.

I took a moment to spy out the rest of my feathered brood. The other three were on the docks, staring curiously into the water. I noticed three heads poking up from the sea, three equally curious Voices. Well, good. The Psittacans, given the chance, had a tendency to charm every species they met. Perhaps they'd learn a few things that could help with the effort.

Satisfied that everything was going as smoothly as I could make it—hell, *more* smoothly than *I* could make it, really—I set my mind to work.

"All right, got everything," Marla announced as she dropped down onto the blanket next to Kirrick.

I immediately reached into the cooler and produced a sandwich for her. "Good work. Honestly, I was worried you'd be at it all day."

"I would've been," she said, taking the sandwich gratefully, "but it turns out I have a bit of a knack for moving scientists along. Who knew?"

She grinned, her usual bright, infectious smile, and I grinned in turn, even though my head was beginning to ache slightly. Kirrick and I had come up with a fairly comprehensive list, and I just hoped that the information Marla brought back wouldn't complicate things too much.

"Well, let's see what you've got," Kirrick said, taking her holo-slate from her and slaving it to ours. "Whoa."

The throbbing in my head increased in tempo and intensity as the long list scrolled into existence in front of us.

"Don't worry," Marla said around a bite of sandwich. "I took down everything to make my job easier, but there's stuff here that's completely superfluous. Like this. And that. And that, too."

With a flick of a finger she cleared several items off the holo-display. Kirrick leaned in, and together they made quick work of all the doubles. Everything that seemed necessary was slid, with careful fingertips, into an open column waiting on the holo-display Kirrick and I had worked on so hard. As soon as Marla's holo-display was cleared, she shut down the slate and finished off her sandwich.

"Bengtsson? Who the hell is Bengtsson?"

"Our chemist," Marla said. "You handpicked him, remember?"

I winced. "Oh, right. Let's see… he wants to check to chemical composition of the water? Why? We can just ask the Hands and Voices for that."

"Which I mentioned, but he said that that was all well and good, but hands-on is best for learning. If there's enough of a difference in the water that we'll need to compensate for it, it's best that we understand it to the fullest." She shrugged. "It actually sounded like a decent point, so I added it."

"Hmm. Well, he's the expert. And he'll be with Beta Team, so he'll get his chance. Now let's see… "

I reached out and moved Bengtsson's idea into the column reserved for Beta Team's science tasks, then studied the rest of the list. Two of the diplomats wanted to study the Voice's song from region to region, to understand linguistic and dialectic differences. *A bit advanced for what we're trying to do now…* But it would need to be done eventually and would make translation work better, so I added it to the list and marked it as 'only if there is extra time.'

"Is this one of yours?" Marla asked, startling me out of focus.

"Huh?"

She pointed with the tip of a pinkie finger. " 'Learn how/what games they play.' That's one of yours, isn't it?"

"Oh. Yeah." I looked down. "Living beings play, and sapients play a lot. Making sure they're provided with what they need for games will be one more step towards making them comfortable, and it'll be good if they have young off-planet."

Marla grinned at me again, eyes bright with approval, and it occurred to me that of my team members, she was the one who never seemed to doubt me. I dropped my gaze back down to the sand, in time to see a pair of bare feet stop in front of our blanket.

I looked up. P'yo Jae-shin stood over us, vir face shaded by an enormous, wide and floppy-brimmed hat. Unable to help myself, I blinked a few times, like maybe I could clear the sight of that hat from my memory.

"Yes, I know. It's hideous," vi said with a sigh. "Unfortunately, I have two settings: 'pale' and 'redder than a lobster in a steam bath,' so ugly-ass hat it is. Here." Vi thrust out a hand which, I noticed with alarm, clutched a nutrient-bar.

"But I ate lunch!" I protested, holding up my empty sandwich wrapper. "Ask Kirrick. Kirrick, didn't I eat lunch?"

"She did," Kirrick said, though he didn't look up from the holo-display, so I wasn't sure that helped.

Jae shrugged. "Sorry, boss. Captain Chui gave me orders that I should give you one of these a day, sometime in mid-afternoon."

I let out a sigh of my own and took the nutrient-bar. Loathe though I was to admit it, Captain Chui had a point. A fucking disgusting, foul-tasting point, but a point nonetheless. All the heat and sun, the time spent in the water, and the heavier gravity would take its toll on me. The genetic adaptations that allowed Wraithens to cope with heavy-grav without developing a stockier build actually required some pretty strict nutrition, which I was bad enough about getting to begin with.

"If it's any consolation," Jae said, "we're all assigned one a day, though we can eat ours with any meal we choose."

"It's true," Marla assured me. "I've decided to have mine with my coffee in the morning."

"Does that help?"

Her face fell. "No."

"Oh well." I reluctantly tore open the wrapping. "Thanks, Jae."

"No problem. Or maybe I should say I'm sorry?" Vi flashed a small smile. Vi started to turn away, then turned back, reaching up to tilt vir hat back slightly. "Hey, uh, look. During my tour of duty, I spent a year with the Corps of Engineers. Spent some time doing construction on a space station, picked up a few things. I'm no scientist, but maybe I can help."

I brightened. "That would be great! I'm sure Diver and Kiri would welcome a third brain working on this one, to be honest."

Jae tilted vir head, something flickering across vir face that I couldn't read. After a moment vi smiled and saluted, the kind of joking salute usually shared between soldiers. Vi headed off to take a seat with Kiri and Diver, who did indeed seem pleased to see vir. *Good,* I thought, turning back to the holo-display and taking a tiny nibble of my nutrient-bar. *Surely, working together, we can find a way to succeed.*

We continued to work as the afternoon wore on. By the time we got everything sorted and assigned to the appropriate teams, my head was aching in earnest. I let out a groan and flopped back onto the sand, glad to be done with the first round of work.

Blue skies, with barely a cloud to be seen, spread above me. I watched something flap across the sky, wishing I had the wherewithal left to lift my wristlet and scan it. It had a rather long, flexible looking tail and a wide wingspan, and I wondered if it was as basal as some of the other land creatures. *There'll be time to find out...* Assuming, of course, all the work we had to do didn't leave me too exhausted to move.

"Tired, Ms. Corelel?"

I jackknifed upright so fast, my neck protested. Captain Chui stood in front of me, her hands on her hips, and even in her casual garb, with her hair in a ponytail, she looked formidable. Until she flashed a small smile, and everyone gathered on the beach started to laugh.

"Doesn't matter who you are," Anton said, and I glanced at him, where he sat with Kiri, Diver, Jae and Emin, "when Captain Chui says jump, you say how high."

"On the way up," Emin added.

"Good evening, Captain," I said, ignoring them.

"Good evening. How's the work going?"

"We've got a list together," Kirrick said, holding the holo-slate up to Captain Chui. "All that's left is to deliver it."

Captain Chui took the slate, examining the list on the screen instead of in holo-display. She studied it for a long moment, her lips slightly pursed, then handed it back with a nod.

"Looks good."

"Thanks, Captain," Kirrick said.

"Um, Captain?" I ventured, before she could leave.

"Yes, Xandri?"

"How goes the uh, little press problem?"

She sighed. "Not as well as I'd hoped, but it could be worse. We've managed to round up four of them, and at least two are fleeing the system. According to Lieutenant Zubairi, the *Resplendence* caught one, and two of the remaining five are incapacitated. We should be able to catch them..."

"But?" I asked, because I was pretty sure there was a but.

"But," and she smiled wearily, "one of them is giving us some trouble. Bootleg scanner jammers, from the looks of things. Normally not something that can undermine *Carpathia*, but they've got a damn tricky pilot on top of it. But we *will* catch them."

I nodded. I had all confidence that *Carpathia* would take care of the problem. Bootleg jammers were simply no match for a warship, and *Carpathia* had upgrades that weren't exactly legal. Well, mostly they were *experimental*, which wasn't the same as illegal. Technically. *Once they're out of the way, it'll be one less thing to worry about.* This was going to go so much more smoothly than Cochinga.

"Looks like everything's transferred," Diver said as he shut down the holo-slate.

"Thank you," Bright replied. He rolled onto his stomach, submerging his fin—and the chip now storing the data from the holo-slate. "We will bring it to the Grand Matriarch. You should have an answer by morning."

"Thanks, Bright," I said. "See you tomorrow, then?"

"Of course. We look forward to it."

He disappeared beneath the waves. A moment later, much farther from the dock, he breached; in the falling darkness, I could just make out the waving tentacles of his Hands. Diver chuckled and raised a hand to wave back. I watched him with a sense of warmth growing in my chest. None of the others seemed to know quite what to make of the Hands, perhaps because they couldn't speak, but Diver didn't appear to have that problem.

"Well," he said, settling an arm around my shoulders, "I'd better get you inside before Captain Chui decides to send an entire platoon to find you.”

I rolled my eyes. “We’ve only been out here a few minutes. And I’m not in danger here like I was on Cochinga.”

“I’d still prefer to get you back indoors.”

I grumbled a little, but it was half-hearted. With his arm around me and his body pressed against mine, I didn’t much care where I was going, so long as he was with me.

We walked in companionable silence, through the coral garden, lit star-like by the small globe-shaped lanterns, and into the building. A couple soldiers on watch in the central chamber grinned at us; I flushed and looked away, but didn’t slip out of Diver’s grasp. It felt too good. After a long day of sun and water and work, I leaned into the strength and warmth of his body without reservation.

“So,” I said, as I reached for the door, “how’s your own work going?”

“Frustrating,” he admitted. “Thing is, it does us little good to get them off planet if we can’t figure out the next step.”

“So you need to kind of work backward.” I hoped it seemed casual, the way I held the door open for him. Like I just wanted to continue the conversation. Which I *did*, but it might look weird.

“Which is tricky, because starships for whales? Kinda not invented yet.”

“You can do it,” I said firmly. “I know you can.”

The words came out with more intensity than I’d intended. I paused and looked down at the multi-colored floor, embarrassed. Diver took a few steps, closing the distance between us. I continued to stare at the floor, until he cupped my cheek with one hand, gently tilting my head upwards. *God, he’s so beautiful.* I could’ve stared into those so green eyes for ages. Until I noticed he was studying my face with a frown.

“What?”

“You’ve got something on your face.”

“What?” I started to reach up. “Where?”

Diver leaned down, his voice a sweet murmuring whisper. “Right…here.”

His mouth settled on mine. Oh. *Oh.* My eyes fluttered closed and my lips parted slightly, as if I couldn’t help it. I reached up, tunneling my fingers through his hair and pulling him closer. He made a soft sound, a groan of surprise and perhaps pleasure, and buried his fingers in my hair in turn, cradling the nape of my neck. His other hand trailed lightly down my back, sending sweet shivers all over my body.

I made a small sound as his tongue slid between my lips and pressed into him more, as much as I could. His hand slid beneath my shirt, brushing against my back where my bathing suit left it bare. It felt so good.

So good that I froze. It might seem an odd reaction, reacting to pleasure with fear, but this…this had never felt good before. My experiences were all fraught with pain and the terror of being left out on the streets, with no roof over my head and no food in my belly. What if pain was all there was? I didn't want to experience any of those feelings again, and I especially didn't want to experience them with Diver, but what if—

"Xandri?"

He'd stopped kissing me but was still holding me, his hand resting at the small of my back.

"I, um…uh…"

"If you don't want me to—"

"I'm tired," I blurted out. "It's not that I don't want to, totally not, but there's so much on my mind and—oh god."

"Hey…hey." Diver's hands shifted, one coming to rest on my shoulder, the other on my cheek. "We've all got a lot on our minds. Ain't nothing wrong with that. You really think I'm gonna be offended 'cause you're too tired?"

"Oh. Well, no. I guess I didn't want you to get the wrong idea."

He broke into a grin that made me flush. "Oh, trust me, fireball. I'm pretty sure I got all the right ideas."

"Oh."

"Why don't you get some rest?" he suggested. He leaned in and kissed my cheek. "We've got more work to do tomorrow."

"Right. Um, Diver?"

"Yeah?"

"Don't brag too much to Kiri. We need you alive."

He laughed as he left. I turned and flopped down on the bed, face first. My emotions roiled like a storm-tossed sea, a horrific mix of fear and uncertainty and happiness and warmth. Too much all at once. I lifted my head, brought my fingertips to my lips—and let myself smile. For just a moment, a tiny, precious moment that glowed like a spark in my heart, I let myself feel only the good and threw the bad to the back of my mind.

Chapter Fifteen

Diver

"I don't see why this couldn't wait until I finished my coffee."

I glanced at Xandri, trying not to laugh. She clutched the handle of her mug and regarded me with bleary eyes. God only knew how she'd look at me when she was fully awake. Couldn't tell, after last night, whether she'd be embarrassed or what. I just hoped that she didn't think she'd made a mistake. The way she'd frozen up last night had been a bit strange, tired or no.

"You're finishing your coffee," I pointed out, as I steered her through the building. "Trust me, fireball, this is worth it."

Her eyes darted upward towards me, and for the first time she seemed to actually register my presence. Blushed a bit, but didn't pull away. Well, that was good.

She took another sip of coffee—and almost spat it out as we stepped outside to find our entire party, soldiers and all, spread out on the beach. Xandri sent me a quizzical look, but I shook my head and led her on, down the path and onto the sand. It was one hell of a morning, already warm enough to fry an egg on the nearest flat surface, but damn, it was beautiful too. The sun blazed off the water, turning it into a large, rippling sapphire.

In truth, not our *entire* party was assembled on the beach. Five of them—the Psittacans—were in the water. Playing what looked to be some sort of version of volleyball against three young Voices and their Hands. Xandri stumbled to a halt, some of her coffee spilling; said something about the moment that she didn't even notice.

With the heavier gravity, the Psittacans couldn't jump as high as usual, but they could still jump pretty high. Using the motion of the waves, they launched themselves upwards whenever the ball came back towards them. The Voices, gathered together in as shallow water as they dared, breached slightly, bopping the ball with their noses or letting their Hands give it a surprisingly strong whap with their tentacles.

"What's that ball?" Xandri asked, her coffee forgotten. "It's not ours. How do they get it to go so far in this atmosphere? Have you gotten a look at it?"

"Not yet," I said, not even bothering to hide my grin, "but I intend to."

"This is amazing."

She started forward again, pushing her way through the gathered crowd, completely heedless. *Shit.* I hurried after her, muttering apologies to all the surprised, somewhat offended soldiers she left in her wake. She got like that, when something had her entranced like this, but she didn't actually mean to be rude. Not as far as I could tell, anyway.

Xandri kicked her sandals off mid-stride and stepped into the surf, paying no attention to the water soaking the bottom of her cargo shorts. I stopped a short distance away from the water to watch. Damn, but they put on a stellar show. With a thought I set my HUD to record, to capture this moment for later.

My HUD beeped, indicating it was picking up a signal. *Stupid thing. It's just Douglas and his soldiers, probably.* I turned down its scanning options so it wouldn't distract me from the show. Immediately something bright flashed at the corner of my vision. Fucking ow. I glanced to the side and saw nothing there. *Probably just the sun off the water.* I stepped to the side and the bright flash disappeared, allowing me a clear view.

"I should never have agreed to the Cochinga mission."

Startled, I pulled my gaze away from the show. I hadn't heard Captain Chui approach, but I guess that's why she's Captain. Her eyes were on the water, on the spectacle of Psittacans and Voices playing in the surf, and on Xandri, standing alone and watching, almost vibrating with excitement. At least, that was how she looked to me. I wondered if Captain Chui saw it too, if that's why she said what she did.

"She wasn't suited to Cochinga," she went on. "If there'd been any other choice..."

"She succeeded anyway," I pointed out.

"Which is due largely to her willpower and determination. I prefer those traits in my crew for a reason."

"And here I thought you picked us because we're all stubborn and more than a little space-fried."

Captain Chui tilted her head back to look up at me and smiled. "That too." Her gaze drifted back to the water. "It doesn't change the fact that this mission is a much better one, for her and for all of us. I think we're going to do good things here."

"Me too. If I can figure out how to get the damn whales into space."

The sidelong look she sent me contained both reproach and amusement. I shrugged. *Probably shouldn't call them whales, though. One of these days, Xan is gonna notice.* They sure *looked* like whales, but I'd already gotten one lecture about how that had to do with hydrodynamics and the bauplan necessary for water. I'd also learned the hard way not to ask why the Voices looked so much like cephalopods, then.

I glanced again at Captain Chui. Might as well ask. With another thought, I used my HUD to ping her private comm channel.

"*Yes, Mr. Diver?*"

"*Just wondering something, Captain. How's it going with the uh, problem?*"

She sighed, too gently for anyone to tell we were talking. "*The press, you mean? It seems to be under control. Eight of the twelve ships are tethered to* Carpathia. *One is docked aboard the* Resplendence. *Of those left, we're positive that two of them left the system. The third… that's the one that was giving us trouble.* Carpathia *is pretty sure it, too, left the system, but she's checking just in case.*"

"*Good.*" I hesitated a moment, then added, "*You really think Douglas didn't know there was a leak?*"

"*I don't think it's out of the realm of possibility, at least. Even so, I don't see how the leak* couldn't *have come from the AFC.*"

"*Want we should poke around, Kiri and I? Dig into their records, see if we find any underlings alerting the press or anything?*"

Captain Chui shook her head. "*The problem appears to be solved. For now, focus on your job. If anything changes, I'll let you know.*"

Fair enough. Though I might have to mention it to Kiri anyway. She loved that kinda project.

Down in the water, the game had broken up for the moment, and Xandri stood talking with Many Kills. The Psittacan was drenched; hell, all of them looked half-drowned. Both Xandri and Many were about as animated as two individuals could be, Xandri's arms flying, Many's crest rising and falling. Finally Many let out a clack with his beak, loud enough that it carried across the water, and Xandri turned to come back to us.

She stepped out of the water and trotted up the beach, picking up a light dusting of white sand on her wet feet and calves. Out here, under all this sun, you'd almost think her beautiful, not just attractive on a personal preference level, but actually beautiful. She smiled so much more, her face and eyes constantly lit by joy and wonder. Right then, she could've lit up a newborn universe, she was so bright.

"They've agreed," she said breathlessly, as she skidded to a halt in front of Captain Chui. "The Voices. We have permission to do as we've requested."

A cheer went up from Xeno-liaisons. Christa, happier than I usually saw her, stepped out of the crowd and caught Xandri around the shoulders, talking about a lightyear a minute. Xandri looked startled, but didn't have time to utter a protest before her team closed in on her, all of them chatting excitedly. I briefly considered rescuing her, but decided I didn't much feel like getting my head bitten off by overzealous xenoanthropologists.

"I guess *we* have our work cut out for us." Kiri's voice.

I turned to her. "Why can't I shake the feeling we got the shit end of the stick?"

"Because everyone else is going to be running around exploring the planet and learning more about it while we're stuck trying to get the whales into space."

"Hands and Voices," I corrected primly, in an approximation of Xandri at her most pedantic.

Kiri snorted. "Whales, Voices; either way, we're still talking around seven or eight tons a pop."

"Tell me about it," I sighed.

For Kiri and I, the day—and perhaps many days—would be about solving our part of the problem. We took a seat on the beach while Beta Team ran around like chickens with their heads cut off, preparing to leave, and Alpha Team ran around like equally headless fowl, trying to help. We didn't even have Jae's help at the moment, 'cause

Xandri remembered that vi had excellent organization skills and absconded with vir for the preparation efforts.

Won't lie, it wasn't easy, sitting there trying to work out the problem. Most of the soldiers were relaxing, the bastards, and before long a few of them waded into the water to take the game over from the drenched, exhausted Psittacans—who immediately settled in for a sun-and-sand bath to dry themselves off.

"Everyone is having more fun than us," I complained.

"Which is why we need to solve this," Kiri said. "Then we'll have time to have fun, too."

I picked up the wand and poked at the holo-display. I thought with a bit of work, we could figure out an engine configuration that could, potentially, lift eight tons plus a load of water into space. It wouldn't be the most comfortable journey, but it *could* work. The problem was figuring out how large it needed to be and how sturdy. I couldn't test it, for obvious reasons.

"What if we ran our ideas through a simulator?" Kiri suggested. "It's not perfect, but it's better than nothing."

"Do *you* have a whale-to-space simulator lying around?"

She shot me a look. "No, I do not, but I *can* modify a simulator for our purposes. Smart ass."

"That's not the only part of me that's smart."

Got a handful of sand to the face for that, which I probably deserved. Feeling a bit lighter, I turned back to the holo-display, while Kiri set her own holo-slate on her lap and started futzing with some code. A simulator probably *would* help, and if anyone could modify it properly, it was her.

I sketched out design possibilities while Kiri coded, and the day wore on. Down in the water, both humans and Voices kept switching out teams, stopping only for lunch. We ate while we worked, and Beta Team ate while they packed, and when I looked up again, they were wading into the water. A small group of Voices waited for them, to carry them off to their first destination. Lucky fucking bastards. Sure, we'd be on Song a good long while, getting everything sorted and learning everything we needed to know, but I wanted to go exploring too. Now, not later.

Sweat trickled down my neck, and into a few less than classy places. I set the holo-slate down and leaned back to take a short break, noticing Xandri standing on the shore near the water to watch the game. Sunlight glowed in her hair, painting it with streaks of near silvery white, and a gentle breeze toyed with a few strands, sweeping them around her neck and bared shoulders.

"Keep looking at her like that and people will realize there's something going on between you two," Kiri remarked.

I started. "What?"

"You're grinning. Like a damn fool, I might add."

"I am not."

"You totally are. You kissed her, didn't you?"

I sat up and grabbed my holo-slate. "Don't we have a job to do?"

"Uh huh. That's what I thought."

"Seriously, how are we going to get this done if you keep slacking off? Don't forget, we not only have to get them into space, but find a way they'll fit on a starship. Not sure a swimming pool would cut it."

She seemed content to leave the teasing for the moment, instead sitting back, her brow furrowed in thought. She pressed the wand to her lips, and hey, give me a break—she was fucking gorgeous, *of course* I noticed. Not to mention I had a real thing for women using their brains. It was sexy as hell.

Then she set the wand down and called, "Hey, starshine!"

Xandri turned.

"Come over here."

"What are you doing?" I hissed.

"I've got an idea, that's all," Kiri said. "Relax, I'm not going to tease her about your little make-out session. She's got enough on her mind."

"I've got plenty on my mind, but you're teasing *me.*"

She merely grinned and turned her gaze to Xandri, who came trotting up to us, bare feet still covered in sand. She plopped down on the blanket next to me, her bared knee pressing against mine. *Oh for fuck's sake, man, you're not fifteen anymore.* Thank god my shorts were kinda baggy. No idea why she had such an effect on me, but it didn't help matters when she pressed a hand against my thigh, bracing herself as she leaned in to study my holo-slate.

"How's it going?" she asked.

"Not great," Kiri admitted, "but I think you might be able to help."

I glanced at Kiri. What was she up to?

"The thing is, even if we can figure out how to lift them, they'll need appropriate accommodations aboard a starship, and we have *no* clue how to manage that. I was wondering if you knew of a ship that might already be partway suited—something with a deep pool or something."

Of course! Kiri, you're too brilliant for anyone's good. Team you up with Xan's damn bird and you'd take over the universe. One of my more recent discoveries about Xandri was that she had a thing for starships. Knew all about them, and could often list a rundown of their stats. If something like what we wanted already existed, then she would probably know, even if it was obscure as hell.

Xandri blinked a few times, then leaned back, bracing herself on her palms. Her teeth sank into her lower lip as she thought. I forced my gaze back to the holo-display, so she wouldn't feel pressured. We waited in silence as the moments passed. If there was something out there that was even partway ready for our needs, we'd have a huge head start.

Suddenly Xandri sat up straight. "Ah! Why didn't I think of this sooner?" With a few clever movements of her fingers, she'd drawn up a holo-display from her wristlet; a moment later the holo took on the shape of an enormous cruise starship. "The *Paraiso*. GalaCorp's flagship cruise vessel. They built more than twenty, but none of them *quite* like the *Paraiso*.

"Look here." With a flick of her fingers she zoomed in on the holo, diving the view inside the walls of the ship and gesturing to a large, hollow-looking spot. "*This* is the aquarium. Other cruise ships have pools sometimes, even large ones, but no other has ever had something like this. It's so large and deep, the passengers could go diving in it. It was built expressly so they'd feel like they were in the ocean."

I shook my head. "Wealth and privilege know no boundary of absurdity they're not willing to cross."

"Well, in this case, it's what we need," Xandri said, and I thought it a bit odd that she flushed a little. "GalaCorp went bankrupt more than twenty standard years ago, and all her ships were decommissioned. No one is using the *Paraiso*. Even better, though her cargo shuttles—the ones used for moving sea life aboard—are gone, she still has her passenger shuttles. Because of the nature of the ship, those were larger than usual, and strictly ship-to-surface. They're already made for shifting large quantities of mass."

I let out a triumphant laugh, slung an arm around her shoulders, and dragged her close. She squeaked as I planted a big, somewhat sloppy kiss on her cheek.

"This is *perfect*!"

"Well, we need permission to use it, first..."

"And Captain Chui will do everything in her power to get it for us. You know she will. It's not being used, which means it technically belongs to the Alliance—why shouldn't they give it to us?"

Kiri let out a sigh heavy with relief. "Should've thought to ask you sooner, starshine."

"Doesn't matter," I said. "We've got our next step and now—now we can finally take a break!"

"You could've taken a break before," Xandri pointed out. "Everyone else has."

"But this is one of the most important parts. Figuring this out for y—for us makes everything else that much easier."

"Well, go take your break, then. I'll contact Captain Chui, see what she has to say about it."

She smiled at both of us, one of those genuine smiles of hers. Wanted to stay there with her, but Kiri pulled the holo-slate out of my hands and urged me to my feet. As soon as I was up, I realized I'd been sitting a helluva long time. With a groan, I stretched out my legs, then followed Kiri down to the water, where a new game was forming up. I raised my brows at Aleevian, and raised them higher at Amelia, who both came crawling out of the surf soaking wet.

"*You* were playing?"

Leev glowered at me. "She dragged me along because I'm tall."

"And he *still* sucked," Amelia said, shaking herself off and dousing Leev with extra water. "Boy, you need to learn to loosen up a bit. Have some fun."

"Fun." He swiped at his dripping hair. "You have an odd idea of fun."

"I thought you hated getting water in your fur," I said to Amelia.

"I have a competitive streak. It's a known flaw," Amelia said primly. She flicked her ears at us. "You two wanna join in? Anton's running the next round, if you wanna see if he's got room."

She started up the beach, grumbling as sand caught in her damp fur. Her tail swayed, scattering a few more droplets on Aleevian. I cleared my throat hard to cover a laugh; Kiri didn't even try to stifle hers. Leev glared at both of us before storming away up the beach, his nose in the air. *Typical Leev. He's always a bit of a drip.* I didn't dare speak the pun aloud, though.

"So, you up for a game?" Kiri asked, when both Leev and Amelia were gone.

I glanced back up to the blanket we'd abandoned. Xandri stood, clearly speaking. Her eyes were on the water where the game was gathering, and maybe I was only seeing what I expected to, but there seemed to be an air of longing hanging around her. *She keeps herself apart a lot. But she needs to know that she doesn't* have *to, if she doesn't want to.* Mind made up, I turned to the water.

"Hey, Anton!" I called. "Got room for a few more?"

"Sure do! Come on in, the water's fine." He grinned at us and waved.

"I'll be right back," I told Kiri.

Up the beach I went. Xandri was just signing off with Captain Chui when I reached her.

"All right, the Captain will talk with Major Douglas soonest and they'll draft a message—why are you looking at me like that? I don't like it."

"Let's go have a little fun," I said, catching her arm and steering her towards the water.

"What? Oh no. No, Diver, this is a *bad* idea. When it comes to sports, I'm as coordinated as an ostrich on ice skates."

"I've always wanted to see an ostrich on ice skates," I assured her. "Don't worry, Xan. We've got your back."

Chapter Sixteen

Xandri

"For the record," I said, as I stripped down to my bathing suit, "I still think this is a really bad idea."

"Relax, kiddo," Anton replied. "Just have some fun. You've earned it."

He clapped me on the back, like he often did, and I braced myself so I wouldn't stagger. Out here under the sun, he looked like a giant, dark-skinned statue, big and covered in muscle, like some ancient, potent god. *It's a miracle I didn't fall right on my face,* I thought, as I set my wristlet atop my pile of clothes. Though I was starting not to mind. It was just Anton's way of expressing affection, something he did with everyone. I kind of liked being part of "everyone."

"Ready?"

I looked up. Kiri stood at the edge of the water, waiting for me. She'd pulled her 'locs into a bundle to keep them out of her way, though the beads at the tips still chimed lightly when she moved.

"No," I answered honestly.

"If you really don't want to..."

I shook my head. "I...kinda do? Only I don't think I'll be very good at it."

"Well, let's try to have some fun anyway." She held a hand out to me.

I reached out. Her fingers slid through mine, and of course I turned pink. Hand-in-hand we waded into the water to join the others: Anton, Emin, Diver, Jae and, to my surprise, Hans Klee. I lifted my free hand to shade my eyes, trying to see if I could make out which Voices awaited us in the water. *Pretty sure that's Bright...* They could be tough to tell apart, but he was one who had a dorsal stripe visible over his armor.

"Hey!" Diver called, raising his voice to carry across the water. "If we win, we want to see your lab facilities!"

Voices bobbed in the water, lowering and rising, exposing their Hands briefly. Song drifted along the waves, but whatever they were discussing, we weren't privy to it. Finally the one I thought was Bright poked his head out of water. More song carried, and I thought it might be laughter.

"We agree," he called back. "But you will not win."

That seemed to be all the prompting my team needed. They spread out. Kiri loosed my hand and took up a position out towards the side. I hesitated. Wading out far enough to have any effect at all brought the water up to chest.

The game began. I swayed and shifted on the spot, uncertain what to do. My teammates used the motion of the waves, as they'd seen the Psittacans do earlier, to boost themselves higher and reach the ball. *Oh… oh Sweet Mother Universe, what do I do!?* I tried to bob with the waves too, but mostly I just got water up my nose. Give me a gun and I could shoot a bumblebee at ten meters, but heaven forefend I could hit a ball.

And then said ball was coming right at me, arcing high in the air despite the heavier gravity. I raised my hands and stretched up onto my toes. *There's no way…I can't…*

A pair of strong arms folded around me and hoisted me into the air, what seemed like a great height. As the ball dropped towards me, I swung with both hands, smacking it as hard as I could. To my delight, it went soaring through the air, back towards the Hands and Voices. As I was set down, I turned to find Anton grinning at me.

"Nice job," he said, tousling my wet hair.

I grinned back. "Thanks!"

That quickly became our strategy. Kiri, Jae and I all found ourselves hoisted into the air time and again. Sometimes it was Anton who lifted me; other times it was Emin or Diver. Each boost filled me with a sensation like soaring, like I was a starship shooting up to the sky, and even though there was water flying everywhere, getting in my eyes and nose, I couldn't stop laughing.

At one point Emin put Kiri down a little roughly, and she stumbled into me. I went under briefly and came back up, nose and eyes full of water, coughing and laughing at the same time. Kiri grabbed my shoulder to help steady me.

"Are you all right?" she asked.

"Are you *both* all right?" Emin put in, wide-eyed. "I'm sorry, Kiri, I lost my grip..."

"Not used to men telling me *that*," she teased, making him flush.

At that moment Anton came crashing towards us, sending up water in every direction. He made a leap for the ball; I ducked, protecting my already water-punished nose. Anton smacked the ball back towards the Hands and Voices and landed, uncontrolled, back in the water, sending up a veritable tidal wave. I rubbed my nose and started to laugh as he straightened and hurried back to the game.

"Xan?"

I looked up at Kiri, my hands covering my face—and my giggles.

She broke into a grin. "I think you'll be fine."

I nodded and dropped my hands, grinning as well. And then I was shrieking and laughing as Emin caught me and hoisted me up, toward the incoming ball. I bit my lip to halt my laughter and struck the ball with all my might. It whizzed through the air, past the reaching tentacle of one of Bright's Hands, and landed in the water. My team let out a raucous cheer of triumph.

"I can't believe we lost."

I glanced at Diver. The evening was rapidly dimming towards darkness, but the glow of the globe lamps flickered golden against his skin. His fawn-colored curls showed streaks of red-gold from all his time in the sun, despite the low light and the saltwater still dampening his hair. He held the ball between his fingertips, giving it little tosses and spins as we walked.

"But they gave you the ball," I pointed out.

He brightened. "True."

"And they said they'd ask about getting us access to their labs even though we lost."

Now he practically glowed. "Also true. Which'll be good, if we want to know how to best set things up for them. Still, for a while there it looked like we might win that one."

So far, only the Psittacans had managed to win a match. Of course, I didn't mind that we'd lost; I'd actually done okay for my-self out there, which was good enough for me. But Anton, Emin

138

and Diver—and even Jae, a little—had been disappointed. *Well, they'll get more chances to win before we leave.* Even once—if—we got permission to use the *Paraiso*, there was a lot of work to be done.

"Still can't believe Klee, of all people, played too," Diver remarked.

I shrugged. "He's an anthropologist. He got a chance to play volleyball with an ocean-going symbiotic sapient species. Of course he was there."

"Good point." Diver grinned at me.

I stumbled. He quickly shifted the ball under one arm and caught my elbow, steadying me. With his hand on my arm, we stepped inside the building. Coral rasped against the soles of my bare feet, a sensation I wasn't sure I liked. Yet I focused on it anyway as we headed to my room, trying to let it distract me from the tightness growing in my chest. I wanted...Sweet Mother Universe, I wasn't entirely sure what I wanted. *No. I know. I want to be sure things will be different if it's with Diver.*

I was trembling a little by the time we reached my door. I glanced nervously at the other doors, worried that someone might emerge at any moment and see us. *They'd never stop teasing me...*

"You know," Diver said, "not that I think you mean it that way, but it does kinda sting when you act like being caught with me would be a fate worse than death."

"I don't think that!" I blurted out, horrified. "I don't at all, it's just..."

"Easy, fireball. I get it. Slow and steady, s'fine with me. Just relax a little, okay? You know I won't let anyone tease you."

How'd he...? Diver grinned. Somehow, he always knew. Maybe it really *could* be different with him. I leaned back against my door for support, stood on my toes, and reached for him. His grin melted into something sexy and warm as he leaned toward me. His free arm snaked around my waist and I buried my fingers in his hair, making up for all those daydreams I'd never had a chance to fulfill.

I sighed, sagging against the door, as his soft kisses sent delightful frissons up and down my spine. His fingers curled tightly in my shirt and his entire body tensed, but his mouth remained tender and slow, urging my lips open bit by bit. I groaned at the touch of his tongue, and the desire that spiked through me was so hot, I feared it would turn me to ash. I wanted to pull him into my room with me, to answer my questions once and for all, but caution reared its head, nearly freezing me to the spot.

"Xandri?"

I gave him another quick kiss, hoping he wouldn't notice that I'd frozen again. "Slow and steady, right?"

"Fine by me." He smiled and gave the ball a little toss. "And hey, there's still something interesting for me to do tonight."

"Lucky you," I said. "Captain Chui wants me to do a write-up on the benefits of using the *Paraiso*, just in case."

"Ah, well, don't let me keep you from *that* particular joy."

I stuck my tongue out. He waggled his eyebrows in mock lasciviousness, an expression so absurd that I *had* to laugh. My fear abating slowly, I slipped into my room. I'd change first, then do a bit of work before dinner.

Maybe it was because my nerves were still so alive, because that caution hadn't abated fully. I should've missed the soft thump that sounded from beyond my window, should've lost it in the rustling of my T-shirt as I drew it over my head, but I heard it. Felt it, almost. I froze to the spot like a frightened rabbit, *positive* that someone was out there. A fellow *Carpathia* member would've let me know they were there, and nothing native that was big enough to make that noise would come so close to the building.

I forced myself to drop my T-shirt and start humming, as if I hadn't noticed anything—or had dismissed it. Toying with a shoulder strap of my bathing suit, I padded across the room, pausing with my back to the window, my body between it and the table where my pistols sat. Hoping I looked casual, I continued to draw the strap down my arm, continued to hum, even as I reached for one of my guns.

As soon as my fingers closed around the grip I spun, already flicking the settings to a wide-angled stun. As I fired, I screamed for Diver at the top of my lungs.

Something hit the ground outside with a thump, and voices—at least two—started swearing. Mere seconds later my door burst open and Anton shot through, followed closely by Emin and Diver. I pointed wordlessly to the window. Without hesitating they went through the window. I heard more swearing and the sound of footsteps hurrying away.

"Xandri?"

I turned. Amelia, Jae and Kiri hovered in my doorway.

"Someone was at my window," I explained breathlessly. "I think I stunned one of them but—but there are others. They're making a run for it."

"We'll head them off," Jae said, gesturing to Amelia.

The two of them shot off down the hallway, Amelia quickly drawing into the lead. Only then did I notice my iron grip on my pistol and the shaking of my hands. The pounding of my heart rang in my ears. I'd been ambushed before, on Cochinga, and I'd seen people die. Not just once, but twice. The second time, my bodyguard and friend, Katya, had died taking a bullet meant for me. *No one is going to die this time,* I told myself. *It's not that kind of mission. No one will die.* But in my mind's eye I could still see the hole in Katya's abdomen and the blood rapidly pooling around her.

A light touch on my shoulder made me start. I glanced up to find Kiri watching me. She didn't say anything, and she didn't try to take my gun away. Gently she steered me towards the bed and urged me to sit. My legs gave out and I crashed hard against the mattress.

Kiri sat with me while we waited. It seemed as if an eternity passed, though I doubted it was more than few minutes. My head shot up as I heard footsteps coming down the hall. Kiri's hand covered mine, stroking lightly, easing the trembling. By the time all of them—Anton, Diver, Emin, Jae and Amelia—had entered my room, I'd set the gun back on the table. *They're safe. Everyone is safe.*

"You okay, kiddo?" Anton asked.

I nodded.

"Looks like we figured out where that final press ship went," Jae said.

"Reporters?" I squeaked. "There were *reporters* at my *window?*"

"With a camera," Diver grumbled. Noting my expression, he added, "They're with Captain Chui in the main room. She ordered us to check on you."

"You got one of 'em," Anton added. "Out like a light at the moment. There were two others. Amelia and Jae caught 'em before they got very far."

"I shouldn't have set my weapon to stun," I muttered.

I paused, wondering if I should've said that, considering the stories going around the news about people like me. But the only response I got was rueful laughter, as if they'd all been thinking the same thing.

Now that the moment had passed, I wasn't afraid anymore—but I was starting to get *pissed*. I rose, and for the first time in months, retrieved my gun belt and strapped it on around my hips. I was unaccustomed to the weight after all this time, but I'd readjust. Satisfied, I turned to regard the room.

"Let's go."

Diver and Anton flanked me, with the other four behind us, as we headed down the hall into the main room. Captain Chui and a number of soldiers had gathered there, and not a single soldier had their weapon holstered.

"Don't you think this is a bit excessive?" asked a voice I didn't recognize.

There was a man laying prone on the floor, and another sitting up beside him. The speaker was a woman, thin and willowy and probably tall. A bit of sand clung to her tall black boots—an odd choice of footgear for such a warm planet but then, she was also wearing designer jeans with a faux-distressed look and a tank top that had to be silk. She kept tossing her hair— deeply ruby red in color—back over her shoulders in agitation.

My private comm pinged and Kiri's voice came through. *"Bet you anything she dyes it."*

Which said something about how pissed she was; Kiri normally never took that kind of potshot.

"Excessive?" Captain Chui repeated in that too calm tone we all knew well. "You were caught spying on one of my crew. I think I'm being rather cordial, given the circumstances."

The woman shrugged. "We were only doing our job."

"Your job is spying on people, is it?"

"If we have to. And you have no right to detain us. Freedom of the press—"

"I don't give a shit about freedom of the press," Captain Chui retorted, voice still calm.

"And it doesn't apply here, anyway," I pointed out. Which made everyone turn to look at me, which made me want to sink through the floor, but I pressed on. "Song isn't an Alliance world. You have no rights here that you haven't been granted by the people of Song."

The woman turned to me, smiling like a shark. "You're Xandri Corelel."

Fuck.

"Which reminds me," Captain Chui cut back in, "I'll need identification for all three of you. We'll be holding you here until we decide what to do with you."

"You can't do that!"

Captain Chui looked to me.

"Technically, we can," I said, doing my best to keep from dropping my gaze to the floor. "In the morning we'll speak to the Grand Matriarch and see what she advises. If she desires it, we can hold you indefinitely, until the AFC negotiates your release."

The woman gaped.

"You came here without knowing that?" I tilted my head. "You can't be a very good reporter."

Laughter echoed throughout the room. I peered around in confusion. *What did I say?* The woman and the one conscious man both glared at me. That was when I realized what I'd said and winced. I hadn't meant it as an insult—not that they'd believe that—only as an observation. What kind of reporter decided to go to a planet without knowing how the laws worked? Or perhaps they had thought they could get away with their trespass. Reporters did, sometimes.

"Well, now that that's settled," Captain Chui said, "are you going to give me your names, or do I have to have my soldiers search you for ID? We're within our rights to do so."

The woman sighed. "I'm Ashley Betancourt, from Orion News."

Beside me, Diver stiffened.

"This is my assistant, Steven Markham, and the guy you knocked out is our cameraman, Dave Smith. Happy now?"

Captain Chui looked at Kiri. "Run them." She turned to the soldiers standing behind the reporters. "Maddox, Teke, Sherazi, Gorski, escort them back to their ship and take first watch on them. You *will* cooperate, Ms. Betancourt. Ms. Corelel is not the only member of my crew handy with a stunner."

Ashley Betancourt nodded sullenly. Maddox reached to help her up and she jerked her arm away, turning her perpetual scowl on him. Teke and Gorski hoisted Dave the Cameraman and Teke smiled viciously at Markham until he scrambled to his feet. With its usual inappropriate timing, my brain noted the tendency for tiny, vicious women among the *Carpathia* crew. Captain Chui seemed to like women after her own heart.

As Maddox escorted her towards the door, Betancourt peered back over her shoulder. "I *will* be talking to my lawyer about this."

"You do that," Captain Chui said without concern.

Betancourt's eyes drifted over all of us, lingering longest on me. Her lips curved in a vindictive smile. *I have a bad feeling about this...* I needed to look her up, find out who she was. So many reporters had covered the fallout from Cochinga, more than I could keep track of, and if she was one of them... Shit. I didn't need someone like that lurking around while I was trying to do my job.

"All right everyone, dismissed for now," Captain Chui said. "I'll be pinging some of you later for second watch. Right now, get some rest. And good work, you five," she added, nodding at my Alpha Team soldiers. "Xandri, you're with me."

Well, researching Betancourt would have to wait. I glanced at Diver. He reached over and gave my hand a brief squeeze. It was all we had time for, but it was enough. I left the group and fell into step beside Captain Chui.

"You requested my presence, ma'am?"

She sighed. "I'd like to brainstorm about how we're going to explain this to the Grand Matriarch. This mission was *supposed* to be classified, and now there are reporters on her planet."

Chapter Seventeen

Diver

Wasn't normally an early morning kinda person, but sitting on the dock, watching the sun rise slowly above Song's great oceans—a man could get used to that.

Made for good thinking, too. I had my holo-slate in my lap, loaded up with the schematics for the *Paraiso's* shuttles, and my HUD turned as far down as it would go. Of course, we wouldn't hear back for a few days yet, but I figured I might as well get started. The Alliance really seemed to want this and hell, I liked the challenge. These shuttles gave me a leg up, but I'd still need to be clever to get them to suit the Hands and Voices.

I wasn't the only one up early. The Psittacans were on the beach, taking a morning sand bath—and waiting for their new friends to arrive, no doubt. Said friends were out some distance in the water. With such clear oceans, it was easy to see them even when they were far away.

Footsteps sounded on the dock, to my surprise. I twisted around—and grinned as I caught sight of Xandri coming towards me. A slight sea breeze toyed with her hair and rippled the light, translucent material of her top, pressing it over the small curve of her breasts. Her face lit up as she saw me and her step quickened. If I was being honest with myself, that smile relieved me. The way she kept freezing up—well, maybe it was just down to inexperience, after all. Some people were like that.

"Morning," she said, dropping to sit on the end of the dock with me. "You're up early."

"Always up for you, fireball," I teased. When she gazed at me blankly, I shrugged and moved on. "Just thought it'd be a good time to get some work done on this problem. Don't get me wrong, I love *Carpathia*, but it's nice to work in the fresh air sometimes."

"Mmm," she murmured in agreement.

"What about you? Figured at the least you'd still be inside nursing your coffee."

"I'm here to meet with the Grand Matriarch."

She lifted a hand and pointed. Following the gesture with my gaze, I noticed a truly enormous shape moving through the water, making its leisurely way towards us. Had to shiver a little at the sight of her Hands, swimming freely alongside her; they were like an Ancient Earth sailor's worst nightmare, the kraken come to life. Yet you couldn't help admiring them all the same. There was something graceful about the way they swam, tentacles drifting behind them like great bridal trains.

"They're beautiful," Xandri said quietly.

She watched them with this soft glow in her eyes, this slight smile touching her lips, an expression I couldn't define with something as simple as an emotion. Words like 'joy' or 'pleasure' or 'excitement' didn't cover it. I reached out to touch her cheek. *You're what's beautiful, fireball.* But she'd never believe me if I said it.

We sat in silence as the Grand Matriarch and her Hands approached. As before, I found myself gaping at her enormity. She was *three times* the size of the largest living creature Ancient Earth had ever seen. In all our explorations of space—in all of *anyone's* explorations of space—no other creature, sapient or otherwise, could challenge her in size. And yet my little fireball wasn't intimidated at all. As the Grand Matriarch neared, Xandri leaned forward and held out a hand.

I quickly changed the settings on my HUD. The Grand Matriarch's head rose out of the water, dwarfing us and the dock, and her nose bumped against Xandri's palm. I flicked my lashes, snapping several stills of that quiet tableau. Though I doubted it was a moment I'd ever forget.

"Greetings, Xandri Corelel."

"Greetings, Grand Matriarch," Xandri replied. "I have brought news, though some of it may upset you. I'm afraid there are intruders on Song."

Water sprayed from her blowhole in a way that might've been a sigh. "We see. Please explain."

Xandri laid out everything, starting with the *Paraiso*. That, at least, seemed to please the Matriarch.

As Xandri continued to talk, describing the encounter with the reporters last night, the Matriarch's Hands reaffixed themselves to her sides. I had a feeling, though it was hard to tell, that they too were listening to Xandri's words. I kept seeing slight movements of their tentacles along the Matriarch's armored back, and I remembered what Xandri'd said about how they used sign language in part to communicate. *Are they talking to her about this?*

"So these intruders are in your custody, then?" the Grand Matriarch said when Xandri finished. "We much approve of your Grand Matriarch's choices. She is wise. Does she have advice for us?"

"Captain Chui thinks we should keep them in our custody until the mission ends or until some other solution is devised. We suspect that the leak may have come from someone lower down in the AFC—a soldier, perhaps—and are concerned that the reporters and this person are working together, so we think it best that *we* keep an eye on them instead."

Fuck. Major Douglas ain't gonna like that. Hopefully I'd be far away when he showed up to complain about it. He pushed too hard and Captain Chui was likely to go supernova on his puffed-up military ass.

"She also thinks…" Xandri hesitated. "She thinks the reporters should be allowed to wander around during the day. To see a bit of the area, maybe even—even film you a little, if you'll let them. Under supervision, of course. They'll have soldiers with them the entire time."

The water rolled and lapped as the Grand Matriarch lolled slightly to one side. A huge eye gazed up at us, dark and framed by armor.

"And how do you feel about this idea?"

"I don't like it," Xandri said baldly. "But… Captain Chui doesn't do things without reason. If she believes we should do this, then I trust her judgment."

"Me too," I added, though I didn't know if my word carried weight with the Matriarch.

"And she, we know, trusts the two of you a great deal," the Grand Matriarch said. "Very well. We will allow these reporters to see our world, though perhaps not as much of it as you will." Water gushed over her as she settled back on her belly. "This afternoon, Bright would like to show you some of the reefs. We think it would be good for your scientists to better understand the differences between our coral and what you know as coral.

"Tomorrow, you will be escorted below to our labs, so you might better understand all we will need to live adequately. Even those among us who live in the shallows do not like to be without something to do."

I damn near leapt to my feet with happiness. "Thank you, Grand Matriarch! We're honored."

"We know. Which is why we are allowing it. If we should become aware of any problems with having these reporters wander, we will let you know. In the meantime, we will discuss the matter of this ship. Perhaps we can lend some nebula pearls to speed the process of refurbishing it."

I held back a whistle as Xandri said, "That would be a very big help."

Would it ever. Xandri's addition to the Tier system had allowed for trade of nebula pearls, and they were in high demand everywhere there were sapients. Their shiny black surfaces, speckled with flecks of gold and silver and covered with swirls of red, pink, blue, green, and purple, caught the attention of every species in the known universe. Even the Ongkoarrat were interested in them, though not for decorative reasons. Since they'd only been available for about four years, their value was still enormous.

The conversation came to an end, and we sat in silence again, watching the Grand Matriarch maneuver back out into deeper waters. As she disappeared, becoming only a dark smudge on the horizon, I stood and reached a hand down to Xandri. She folded her fingers around mine absently, her attention caught by the Voices and the Psittacans. From the looks of things, the Voices were trying to teach the Psittacans to swim better.

"Sometimes I wonder," I said, as we started down the dock.

"Hmm?"

"If we're doing the right thing, I mean. Bringing them into the Alliance. They seem so innocent..."

That caught her attention. She swiveled to look at me, her brows furrowed. "Because they see the world in a different way than you do? Because they interact with it differently? Because they don't have the exact same—"

"Whoa!" I held up my hands in surrender. "Easy, fireball. Didn't mean it as an insult, I swear. It's just…well, *look* at 'em."

"I know." Xandri sighed and ran her fingers through her hair, mussing her ponytail. "It's not like the thought never crossed my mind, but…it's wrong to judge them as too innocent, simply because their expression *appears* innocent to us. They're a sapient species, shown to be shrewd in negotiations, as seen by their nebula pearl trade. They're smart, technological, and they know to be cautious about other sapients; in fact, they learned that lesson quicker than most. This is their choice to make and—and it would be wrong to try to take their choices from them."

She stared straight ahead as she spoke and, not for the first time, I got the feeling her words weren't just about the Hands and Voices. She spoke like that sometimes, like she was seeing a problem from the inside, like she'd experienced it herself. I remembered the skin-and-bones waif who'd appeared on our ship that day, and once again I wondered where she'd come from. A poor situation, certainly, but how'd she get into it? Wraith was hardly the sort of under-policed outrim backwater I'd grown up on.

I reached for her hand and she let me take it, but tension vibrated through her body. Time to throw on the charm and cheer her up.

"Well, hey, we're gonna be going deep sea diving tomorrow," I said. "And today we're gonna get a real close look at them reefs. Not just the dead stuff we're living in."

"If they work at all like coral reefs on other planets, then most of it will be dead. New coral takes up residence on the old coral when it dies."

Yup, she'll be fine. "C'mon, let's go wake everyone up and tell them."

Xandri

I took one last glance back at the beach as we waded out. Ashley Betancourt and her team—the camera guy awake now—were standing there, getting their first shots of Song. While we'd been getting our wetsuits on, Betancourt had been trying to find the perfect spot: where the breeze could stir her hair dramatically without blowing it in her face. Now she spoke into a mic-implant while gesturing at the playing Voices behind her.

"It'll be fine, starshine," Kiri said from beside me. "Captain Chui knows what she's doing. Let's go see the reefs, yeah?"

I nodded and forced myself to look away. The entirety of Alpha Team was marching into the water, including Amelia, though she wore nothing but her fur. Though it would likely be unnecessary, we all carried Barracudas. Straps held mine in place against my thigh so it wouldn't bang around while I swam. *I'm not sure about giving Hans a Barracuda*, I couldn't help thinking. Our scientists generally weren't trained to handle anything with more oomph than a small pistol.

As the water rose, I pulled my mask down over my eyes and slid the mouthpiece of the tubing under my chin. The small air recycler on my back would provide oxygen much longer than Ancient Earth tanks ever had.

The water hit chest level. A prickle of excitement grew in my chest, erasing the thought of the reporters back on land. From here I could see dorsal fins in the distance, Bright and perhaps Tides and other Voices waiting for us. I brought the tubing up, affixing it firmly over mouth and nose, and took a long, deep breath. As I sank beneath the water, I took another breath to test it. No air bubbles escaped and I had no troubling breathing. Good to go.

We followed the coral that crawled up on land to form the town; the living reef would be at the end.

"Pretty stellar down here, huh?"

I glanced to the side and saw Diver swimming beside me. *"It's beautiful. We can see everything so clearly."*

Kiri swam up on my other side. *"Look...you can even see the reef from here, a little bit."*

Indeed, it showed through the clear water, a riot of colors like sunset on the horizon. Even Casaria drew in a sharp breath of awe at the sight, though perhaps that was the biologist who was awed, not the Sanavila. And the closer we swam, the brighter the colors became, resolving into structures that resembled rocks or plants or flowers or at times a little bit of all three. Corals in layers like steps; corals in bunches like bouquets; corals spread across the ocean floor like a scrub-ridden prairie. Pink, purple, orange, red, green, blue and even some colors I found hard to put a name to.

Casaria laughed and swam ahead, swirling in the water amidst a scattering school of brightly colored fish. Song vibrated through the water, the laughter of Voices.

"*A Sanavila being undignified,*" Diver said. "*Who knew.*"

"Greetings to you, friends," Bright sang as he swam towards us through the reef, Tides beside him.

"Greetings, Bright," I returned. Speaking aloud sounded so strange underwater. "This place…it's beautiful."

"It's much more than that," Casaria cut in. "Look at some of these specimens! From a distance it looks similar to some of the corals we know from other planets, but once you get closer, it's clearly different."

"Oh, don't touch that one," Tides warned, breaking away from Bright's side to swim up next to Casaria. "It's quite the indiscriminate eater."

"Well, it wouldn't want to eat *her,*" Aleevian muttered as he swam past me. "No one wants indigestion that bad."

"I *heard* that, Aleevian sil masViara."

I swallowed a laugh and turned my attention to the nearest coral formation, watching tiny fish—different from clown fish, but just as brightly colored—peek out from something very like anemones. Beyond the formation, Jae and Anton hovered in the water together, watching a long, snake-like creature with rippling wings, somewhat like a ray's, swim past them.

"*Hey, Xan,*" Marla's voice came through the channel. "*You have got to see this thing.*"

I glanced around and spotted Marla and Kirrick a short distance away, watching something move across the ocean floor. As I swam over, I caught sight of a—a—well. I *might* have called it some kind of snail or slug, only it was larger than a young kitten, violently acid green in color, and the shell on its back curved into a high, pointy cone. A number of little tentacle-like structures surrounded its—well, I *thought* it might be its head.

"Face only a mother could love," Diver remarked, swimming up next to me. "*Is* that its face?"

"I think so. Look, you can almost kind of see it eating. See how the tentacle-things are wiggling? It's probably eating plankton."

"Gross."

"Hey, Bright?" I twisted in the water and spotted the Voice nearby, showing something to Casaria and Aleevian.

"Yes, Xandri Corelel?" He didn't look away from his task, but I had a feeling his brain might be a bit more like mine—picking up more than one frequency, so to speak, at once.

"The coral themselves... are they nocturnal?"

"The creatures? Yes. They are quite nocturnal. But... well, perhaps we should do them the honor of showing them, Tides?"

"We can do that, yes," the other Voice agreed.

"You see," Bright explained, as one of his Hands detached and settled near a coral formation, "it is vital that we be able to examine them closely at any time of day, to ensure no sickness has bled into the water. Harvester," he turned his nose slightly in the direction of the Hand, "since we will be doing this anyway, please take a sample."

Harvester raised a tentacle in what might have been acknowledgement. The Hand moved across the ocean floor, chose a formation and stopped beside it. From somewhere—I honestly wasn't sure I wanted to know *where*—Harvester drew out a small tube. The end of one tentacle split into numerous filaments as Harvester reached up for the coral.

"Now, Tides."

The female Voice swam into the middle of the reef and sang, a long note that quivered like the sound vibrations off of a struck glass. All around us the reef came into further life, filaments unfurling, flower-like corals blooming open and swaying in the water. Tiny, tiny creatures, the very root of the formations, that normally only showed themselves when darkness fell. They quivered along to Tides' song while Harvester made a quick choice, breaking off a piece of structure and stuffing it into the tube.

Tides' song died away and the coral withdrew. *Wow. There are no words...* They had manipulated coral, groomed and evolved it to a state that one normally only saw in non-organic tech. *I was right earlier. It would be wrong to take away their choices...*

"Amazing!" Casaria exclaimed. "How did you teach them to do that? Are they smarter than coral otherwise would be?"

Water bubbled around Bright as he chuckled. "No. We bred that response into their nature many generations ago. Each reef responds to a different note. Among us, Tides is the best singer for this reef.”

“And Bright is the best flatterer.”

I took in their back and forth with a silly grin on my face. *This, now* this *is what seeing a new planet ought to be like.* No politics, no conspiracies, no hunting or ambushes, just enjoying the wonders of nature. And sure, okay, some of the wonders of nature were large and wriggly and had more eyes than really seemed necessary—*what the serious fuck* is *that thing, anyway?*—but that didn’t make them less wonderful. That just made them wonderful and…looking at me. With a lot of eyes. I chose to swim away, rejoining Diver, Marla and Kirrick.

“…told you we get to go on the best adventures,” I heard Anton say as he swam by behind me, accompanied by Amelia, Emin and Jae.

“Certainly better than the last one,” Emin agreed. “Though there was this one night at a restaurant in Cochinga—”

I tuned out his voice as best I could and was relieved when it faded into the distance. I remembered that night too, the night I’d made the biggest mistake of the whole mission. I’d rather not think about that while I was supposed to be enjoying myself.

“Xandri Corelel.”

I looked at Bright.

“We would like to have coral with us on our starship, but we are not yet certain how to move it there. Growing it would take a long time. Can your scientists help us find a way?”

An interesting thought, that, but not precisely Diver’s area of expertise. I shifted in the water and spotted Casaria and Hans, trailed by Leev, who managed to look quite beleaguered even with most of his face covered. I beckoned them over, and when they reached us, I repeated Bright’s request. Behind the mask, Casaria’s eyes lit up.

“You can keep it alive in those tubes you used?” she asked.

“We can, in small amounts.”

“I’ll need to study it more myself. Take samples, examine it closely, if I’m to understand it well enough to help. Will that be all right?”

What looked like quite a conference ensued, with Bright and Tides sending song back and forth between themselves and the other Voices there, while the Hands joined in with a great deal of tentacle waving. Harvester—I thought it was Harvester, at least—was being rather emphatic about *something*, though I couldn't tell if anyone was for or against it. Finally, after long moments, the furor died down.

"We have decided we can allow it," Bright said, "but it is best if you take your samples from a smaller reef nearby for today. We have disturbed the coral here enough."

"I can escort you now, if you wish it," Tides added.

"Of course!" Casaria exclaimed.

I sighed. "Not without guards. Take Emin and Amelia with you, as well as Hans and Leev. Use your HUDs to record everything, and we'll store it with the rest of the information later. Got it?"

"Clear," Casaria agreed. "Come, Aleevian, we have much work to do."

"Do you suppose," Aleevian said, hanging back a moment as Casaria swam off, "that she's really forgotten that I'm ten Sanavin years her elder, or do you think she does that on purpose?"

"Maybe she likes you," I suggested.

He shot me a look of pure, utter disgust before swimming away. I giggled beneath my breathing tube. *This is less like a job and more like a vacation.* Yes, there was a lot of work to do, but this—drifting around in a gorgeous coral reef—didn't feel like work at all. I only hoped tomorrow's deep sea dive would go as smoothly. For that might be the most amazing experience of my career yet.

Chapter Eighteen

Diver

"Are you absolutely sure?" Jae said. "I mean, I want to see this too, but I'm no anthropologist."

I looked up. Jae had the HP suit up around vir waist. From the front it looked similar to a diving suit, but it had plating along the back. Having poked around to understand how they worked, I knew it was really fucking cool, and I couldn't wait to see it in action.

"Oh, that's quite all right," Hans said. "Perhaps there'll be another chance. For now, I'm content to spend time with our new friends."

He turned and waved cheerfully to the Voices out in the water, some of whom would escort us out to sea, others who would stay behind. A few tentacles shot into the air and waved back. *Funny, on the trip down here he seemed like such a walking stick. Guess I was wrong.* Or maybe I'd been right, and the Voices had the same effect on him as they had on nearly everyone else here. 'Cause it turned out that Voices liked having their bellies rubbed, and *Carpathia* soldiers liked rubbing bellies.

"All right. We'll be bringing back some footage, so there's that," vi said, shrugging the HP suit up over vir shoulders.

"I look forward to it."

I'd never be satisfied with footage. I had to see this with my own eyes, hell, *craved* it, like a starving man craves a steak. *All we need now is for Xandri to get here...*

Since we only had six of the twelve HP suits, our team for this trip would be small. Casaria had chosen to spend the day studying coral, and Aleevian had reluctantly gone with her to help gather samples. I'd insisted Kiri and Jae come along, since they were helping me with all the engineering. In the end, Marla and Kirrick had given up their places—not with *that* much reluctance, I'd noticed—to Emin and Anton, figuring Captain Chui would like it best if we had some soldiers with us. Spotting Captain Chui overseeing the suiting up herself, I had to agree.

My HUD pinged, alerting me to the presence of Xandri's wristlet. I turned and spotted her walking down the beach towards us. She'd caught her hair back in a braid and had her HP suit pulled up to her waist. Her hands flew as she walked and as she drew nearer, I saw her mouth moving; talking to someone, then.

"...are going well, then," I caught as she approached. "When are you leaving for the next area?"

"A few more days, I think," came Christa's voice from the wristlet. "Not more than that."

"All right. Contact me again before you leave and let me know where you're headed to, so I can keep a record."

"Got it."

"Xandri out."

"You know," I said, as Xandri paused next to me, "making Christa the leader of Beta Team was hella smart."

Xandri just stared at me. "It was the obvious choice. She's the one with the experience to do it."

I opened my mouth—then closed it again. Knew a lot of people who'd have given the job to someone else outta spite, but I guess I shouldn't be surprised that the thought never crossed Xandri's mind. It might, later, and she might even kick herself for not taking the chance when she had it, but at the time she'd made the teams, she'd been too focused on work to think of pettiness. I'd been around her long enough to realize that was how her brain ticked.

I shook my head. "C'mon. Everyone's heading down the dock. Let's go."

I offered her my arm in mock gallantry. She rolled her eyes, pulled up her suit the rest of the way, and took my arm. Chuckling, I led her down the dock to where our team waited, accompanied by Captain Chui and Amelia. Like yesterday, we all carried Barracudas, and Anton, Emin and Jae all had extra ammo with them, too.

"Sure you don't want to go?" Emin was saying to Amelia in a teasing tone. "I'd give up my suit for you."

Amelia's ears pressed back against her head. "I didn't want to put that thing on *before* it had you in it. I definitely don't want to now."

"Ouch. C'mon, Mia, that's harsh."

"It *smells.* And now it smells like it *and* you."

"Poor Mia," Xandri said, and I hoped I wasn't the only one who heard the sincerity in her voice. "I think Doctor Marsten brought some *casah* with her. That'll fix your nose right up."

Amelia's ears came up at the name of the popular Kowari tea-like drink. "Good idea."

"All right, enough teasing, all of you," Captain Chui cut in. "I want you to be careful out there. There's a lot that could go wrong on a deep sea dive. I know the Hands and Voices will be with you, but even so, if there's so much as the tiniest glitch, I want you to abort. Those are orders."

"Yes, Captain," we all chorused.

A slight smile twitched at the corners of her mouth. "And have fun, yes? But not *too* much fun."

Shallow water Voices towed us out to the continental shelf, where our official escort waited. There were three of them, mid-sized Voices, each of them somewhere between fifteen and twenty meters long. Their armor, I noted, was thicker than that of the shallow water Voices, and extended to cover their fins and most of their heads. A gray, the biggest of the three, with four Hands attached to their sides, swam across the shelf to greet us. It did one of those little pirouettes in the water, revealing a belly covered in markings.

"So you are the ones we have heard so much about," the Voice said. "We are called Sings In The Depths Of Darkness, but our friends call us Darksong."

"Greetings, Darksong," Xandri said. "I'm Xandri. This is Diver," and she pointed to each of us in turn, "Kiri, Jae, Anton and Emin. We're honored to be allowed to see your facilities."

"So we've heard," spoke another Voice, this one male and blue. "We are Delves Deep And Builds Well, but you may call us Builder. Which of you will we carry?"

"Um," Jae began slowly. "I—I don't mean to offend, but…is it safe to travel with only three of you? The Disharmonies…"

"We have reported no sightings of Disharmonies today," Darksong assured vir. "And we will be greater in number once we reach

157

the lab, so if you are uncomfortable, it is best we get started immediately."

Jae nodded. "All right. Just making sure I do my job, ma'am."

"We understand."

Satisfied, Jae signaled for us to shift Voices. I let go of my
Voice—whose name I hadn't caught—and followed Xandri. She
swam boldly up to Darksong, reaching her hand out to touch the
Voice's nose. Though not nearly as big as the Grand Matriarch,
Darksong was hardly what you'd call *small*. Yet Xandri let the water
carry her up onto Darksong's back without flinching. I followed,
settling behind her. Tentacles came creeping up Darksong's sides
and coiled around our legs.

"We will be moving swiftly, so they will help you stay aboard,"
Darksong explained. She paused a moment, as if listening to the
Hands clinging to her sides, then added, "Engineer is curious about
the stuff you wear. The plates are clearly armor, but we do not
recognize what it is made of."

"Brace yourselves," Anton muttered as he climbed aboard
Builder with Jae.

"It's a synthetic material," Xandri explained, ignoring him.
"One of the rare bits of tech humanity brought to the Alliance.
We based it on an Ancient Earth creature called a mantis shrimp.
Well, on its claws. You see, the mantis shrimp eats hard-shelled
crustaceans, and it does this by shooting out its claws at about
eighty kilometers an hour." She said it the same way a person
might talk about the adorable fluffiness of a kitten. "It needs to be
resistant to withstand that.

"There's a second material, too," she went on, "if you're interested."

"How about later?" I suggested quickly. "We ought to get moving."

"I can talk while we move," Xandri protested sullenly, but she
didn't carry on.

Emin and Kiri ended up on the remaining Voice, another male
who we eventually learned to call Swift. Then we were off, and damn
but the Voices could swim. They moved through the ocean, far
enough below the surface that the water came up to our waists, and
they seemed to almost fly. Surf flew up around us and we would've
been dragged off if it wasn't for the Hands holding us in place.

Xandri leaned back into me and I wrapped my arms around her, forgetting for a moment that we weren't alone out here. Her damp hair whipped back into my face and I felt her excitement even through the HP suit; her heart fluttered with such anticipation that the vibrations came right through the thick material. She glanced back at me, a smile lighting up her eyes and face, and I bent my head, trailing the tip of my nose against her cheek.

"Well now!" Emin exclaimed over the roar of water. "Looks like someone's getting cozy!"

Xandri froze. *Goddamnit, Emin, must you?* I knew he was just being friendly and teasing, but Xan clearly didn't know how to cope. I leaned back from her a little and glanced at Kiri, hoping for a save.

"Aw, Emin, don't brag," she drawled, giving the soldier a slight shove. "It's only because there's surprisingly little room up here. I mean, Amelia is right, you do smell a bit odd."

"Hey!"

"It's that Ancient Earth cologne he likes," Anton chimed in. "Practically bathes in the stuff, too."

"So *that's* what that is," Builder remarked. "If we do encounter Disharmonies today, you might be safe, Emin. They have quite sensitive noses."

Builder seemed quite perplexed by the laughter he got in response, but Xandri had relaxed, and that's all I cared about. She leaned back into me again, and this time I refrained from any nuzzling, though the curve of her ear was tempting. I looked away, catching Kiri's eye and mouthing a thanks in her direction. She nodded and mouthed something back, which I thought might be "take care of her."

A short time later, the Voices slowed. I took a quick glance around, trying not to be unnerved by the fact that I couldn't see the shore.

"We will descend now," Darksong said. "It will be dark most of the way, but there are lights below. Our Hands will keep you secure on our backs. The best thing to do is to wait it out and not panic."

"Right," Jae said. "Everyone, full suits."

The armor plating, which had seemed rather bulky, grew much less so as plates slid forward, covering torso and arms and legs, locking together to create a solid whole. Subtle clinking rang in my ear as plates extended over my neck and head. In front of me, Xandri's armor was doing much the same. Then the mask closed over my face, first the breathing apparatus, then the visor, clear material that locked together as firmly as the rest of it.

"Now," Anton said, his voice slightly muffled behind his mask, "I dare any one of you to look me in the eye and tell me that's not badass as hell."

"Not happening," Emin responded. "That was *definitely* badass as hell."

Jae sighed. "All right, *everyone*," vi said firmly, shooting them both looks. "If anything appears to be wrong with your suit—anything at all—signal *immediately*. If you don't, I will drag your drowned carcass back to Captain Chui and *you* can explain it to her."

"If you are all quite done?" Darksong interrupted.

At our murmured assent, the Voices submerged. I held onto Xandri, feeling her tense with excitement and uncertainty as the water rose. Air recyclers and HP suits aside, this was a little terrifying. Not that I'd admit that out loud.

At first light broke through the water, allowing us to see, but with each meter we descended, it grew slowly dimmer. Lights within our masks flared to life, providing us with illumination for a little longer. A school of fish swam right past us, fluttering by our faces, and I heard Xandri laugh beneath her mask. The fish surrounded us like a cloud of glittering silver; then they turned sharply and were gone.

Down, down we went, deeper and darker, until the only light at all came from our helmets. Might not have been manly of me, but I shivered as my range of vision narrowed to no more than a meter all around me. Beyond lay darkness, thicker and blacker than any I'd experienced before; you'd have to be adrift between the arms of the universe before it'd be this dark. Anything could be out there, anything at all, and we'd never know until it was on top of us.

Xandri shivered. I tightened my arms around her and pinged her private channel. "*The Voices will know if anything comes.*"

"*I know. But...it's so dark.*"

"*It's another world,*" I murmured. "*Just like going to a new planet, right?*"

"*Yes,*" she agreed, her voice soft and wistful. "*There's always all kinds of strange creatures deep in oceans, some of them—oh, Diver, look!*"

There were lights below, small and dim like dying coals in a campfire. They grew brighter and brighter as we approached, illumining a large area on the ocean floor. Numerous glass squares, all of differing sizes, stood together like a tiny city. It wasn't until I saw a Hand plunge a couple of tentacles through small openings in the side of one glass case that I realized what they were. *Like the chambers we used on Ancient Earth, to learn how to manipulate items in vacuum.* Except if I had to guess, *these* ones held plain air.

"Forgive us for the slow descent," Darksong said, as her Hands released us, "but it is our understanding you are not made to handle swift changes in pressure, armor or no."

"The armor holds up pretty well," Xandri said, "but it's better to be cautious."

"Are all your labs like this?" I cut in, sliding off of Darksong's back and making for the nearest case.

"All of our deep water labs, yes. Some of our work can be done in open air by our shallow water brethren, but when it cannot, we send it here."

A Hand detached from Darksong's side and followed me. Other Hands left their Voices, shooting through the water to join other members of their species at different stations. Darksong's Hand swam up to the case with me, and I got the feeling it was watching me closely as I leaned in, examining the machinery within. All of it delicate and gleaming, much of it made of some glass-like material.

"This is where we are working on the coral you have come for," Builder explained, swimming a slow circle around the case. "Darksong, will Engineer acquiesce to showing them a little of our work?"

The Hand—Engineer, I realized now—attached herself to the case with some of her tentacles and waved two free ones emphatically. Maybe it was a one-scientist-to-another kinda thing, but I didn't need to understand her sign language to know that was a yes. As all of us—me, Xandri, Jae, Kiri, Anton and Emin—gathered around one side of the case, Engineer settled on the other and slid her tentacles into the opening.

"Damn," Anton murmured. "She's really going to work with that stuff? With those tentacles? I mean, no offense, but—"

Engineer's tentacles shot across the glass square. As they slapped into the opposite panel, they spread apart into multiple filaments. Everyone—except for Jae, damn fierce little thing—shied back from the glass at the impact. Engineer turned yellow under the lights. In fact, all around us, Hands were turning some variant of yellow. Darksong swam up and gave Engineer a gentle nudge.

"You must forgive Engineer," she said. "We are a bit of a prankster."

"Well," Xandri said, a little breathless, "that's nothing compared to the trick Diver played on me my first few days aboard the *Carpathia*."

I drifted back towards the glass. "Hey, come on. I freely admit that wasn't my proudest moment, okay?"

"I've never heard about this," Kiri said. "What did he do?"

I groaned. "Can we not? Please?"

"Oh, now you have to tell us," Jae said.

Xandri turned her head to me, and somehow I knew she wouldn't tell if I really didn't want her to. *Aw, what the hell. I can tune it out anyway.* I gave a small nod and shifted my focus to Engineer, leaving Xandri to explain about the day a cleaning bot had followed her around like a puppy. Engineer was using those filaments to set up the instruments she needed, so deftly that she might as well have had fingers. I pressed as close to the glass as I could and, getting the sense she was looking at me, raised a hand and gave her a thumbs-up. A long moment later, her filaments folded into a mimicry of the gesture.

Best. Day. Ever.

With the air recyclers, we could've potentially stayed down there for hours. But despite the HP suit, it simply wasn't safe. The pressure still had effects on the body; science had solved the issues of prolonged exposure to zero-g, but the exposure to deep water pressure had proven a stickier wicket. After an hour and a half, despite my fascination with Engineer's work, my shoulders were starting to ache from the push of all that water.

As I reached up to rub ineffectually at my armored shoulder with my armored hand, Xandri reappeared at my side.

"I think it's time to call it," she said. "We've got an hour and a half of footage now, and maybe we can come out for more another day, or maybe they'll take more for us."

I nodded. "Much as I hate to agree, I'm starting to feel it down here. But damn, Xan, this was…was…"

"Completely and mind-breakingly stellar?"

I grinned. *Perfect. Today has been perfect.* Sure, genetic engineering wasn't my bailiwick, but it had been cool to watch, and now I had even more ideas for the plans of this ship for the Hands and Voices. Of course they would need facilities to continue their work. They might have scientists amongst their chosen representatives, after all.

Then a long held note of song broke through the water, sending everything around us into a flurry. Hands darted back and forth as the Voices communicated in what sounded like frantic spurts of song. Next thing I knew, the rest of the team was back with us, all three soldiers with a hand resting on their Barracudas. And as if that wasn't enough to terrify, all roughly twenty meters of Darksong came at us just as suddenly.

"We must return to the surface, and quickly," she said. "There are Disharmonies about."

"Wouldn't it be safer to stay down here?" Jae asked. "Or are they coming here?"

"They are at the surface. Normally, we would stay here. But some of your own are out on the water in one of those contraptions you call boats, and they are surrounded."

"What?" Xandri squawked. "But our people would never—" She stopped. I couldn't see her face behind the mask, but I could imagine her going pale. "Oh shit. Shit, shit, shit!"

Jae set a hand on Xandri's shoulder, meant to calm. "What is it?"

"The reporters," I said grimly. "It has to be."

"Oh, it is," Xandri said, swimming for Darksong's back. "They'd just better hope the Disharmonies *eat them* before I get there."

Chapter Nineteen

Xandri

We ascended faster than we'd descended, but we still had to take care, for the HP suits could only handle so much.

Fear, worry and anger roiled like fire in my belly and tasted like ash in my mouth. *How dare they?* They had no business being here in the first place and now they were putting both themselves and the people of Song in danger. How had they escaped from their guards? There were only a few potential answers, all of which were bound to put them on Captain Chui's shit list. *Assuming,* I thought, my mouth quirking wryly behind my mask, *they don't just plain end up as Disharmony shit.*

"How are things on the surface?" Jae shouted through the rush of water.

"Not good," Darksong said grimly. "These are very deep water Disharmonies, larger than any of us. And they have already surrounded the boat. That is how they operate; they isolate their prey, then circle around them until we must accept that the victim is lost. It is hard to break a Disharmony circle, especially when they're larger than us."

"What are they even doing here?" I asked.

"Water carries sound far. We believe they heard the boat and came to investigate."

"*Ugh,*" I complained to Diver on the private channel. "*Are these people completely space-fried?*"

"*They're reporters. You even need to ask that?*"

I gritted my teeth and pressed my hands hard against my armored thighs. Soon the darkness began to break, parted by light shining through the water. Darksong had angled her ascent so we could see the imperiled reporters; their boat looked like little more than a leaf adrift upon a lake in comparison to the dozen thirty-meter Disharmonies swirling around it. They moved in two circles, a tighter one and a looser secondary one. Maybe not sapient, but far from unintelligent.

A dozen Voices harried the outer ring. Tentacles shot out, rapping Disharmony noses, before the Voices shifted back out of range of all those sharp teeth. I swallowed hard and reached for the Barracuda strapped to my thigh. The closer we drew, the larger those horrible beasts got. And even though it was usually my way to view animals as *animals*, not terrifying vid monsters, the Disharmonies made that difficult. They were so big and so, so menacing.

The holos I'd seen could not do them justice. Like any large ocean creature, their bodies were massive football shapes, yet they moved with deadly grace. Small scutes on their heads and along their backs gave them an unusually craggy appearance, but did not seem to interfere with their hydrodynamics the slightest bit. And when one of them opened its mouth to let out a crocodile-like hiss, it revealed double rows of sharp, serrated teeth.

"Our Lord in Heaven," Anton said, "how are we going to stop those things?"

"We've got Teeth," Jae said, using the soldiers' slang for Barracuda. Vi unstrapped virs. "Let's show them they're not the only thing in this ocean that can bite."

"An excellent idea," Builder agreed.

Darksong let out a small bleat of song. "Brace yourselves, my friends."

Her bleat became a stream, a trumpet almost. The harrying Voices all made turns in the water and pointed themselves at the Disharmonies. Darksong started to fly through the water; Diver and I bent low against her back, clutching our Barracudas. Faster, and faster still, and we came up partially out of the water as Darksong rammed, full-speed, into the side of the nearest Disharmony.

It hissed, a sound that seemed to boil in the water and twisted, snapping at Darksong despite its obvious pain. I raised my Barracuda and fired; it did *not* like that. It shook its head and I noticed it drifting to one side, as if the blast had thrown off its equilibrium. Darksong clearly didn't care for the weapon's fire either, but she cared less for the Disharmonies. As we emerged more fully from the water, she drew up beside the dazed Disharmony, and her Hands went to work, harrying it with stinging slaps. Diver and I pelted it with Barracuda shots.

Finally it hissed and dove, swimming rapidly away from the danger. I glanced around and saw the outer circle was breaking up. Some Disharmonies tried to hold, but fifteen Voices plus their Hands, and us with our Barracudas, were not odds a smart predator willingly faced. And if the outer ring fell...

My triumph died as a scream split the air. In the middle of the inner ring, several Disharmonies had gotten fed up with waiting and charged the boat. The force of their impact sent the vessel reeling, one end shooting up into the air. Considering it was nothing more than a collapsible, and light at that, it was amazing it didn't go flying. I held my breath as the three occupants scrambled in the boat, trying to right it.

I told myself I didn't know them, so I couldn't possibly tell whether it was Steven or Dave who tumbled from the boat. Yet I felt nothing but guilt watching him flail in the water. The risen side of the boat dropped back with a harsh slap, sending up a furious wave that dragged the poor man under.

"Steve!" Ashley Betancourt shouted.

The boat still rocking beneath her, she threw herself against the side and reached out for her crewman.

"We have to help!" I raised my voice so Darksong would hear me over the din and chaos.

A Disharmony made right for the man in the water, skimming along the surface like a crocodile. Betancourt bellowed at it, screaming insults. She grabbed something from inside the boat and hurled it at the Disharmony. Whatever it was, it bounced off without deterring the creature, but even so, Betancourt grabbed her crewman's hands as he reached the side of the boat. *We'll get there in time. We have to, we* have *to.*

I knew I'd never forget the scream that rent the air. The pure, primal terror of it was like a shot through the gut, and the way it died off, in a piteous gurgle, was even worse. Betancourt screamed herself as she realized she was only holding half of her crewman. She let go and fell back into her remaining crewman, sobbing and shrieking. I didn't blame her. A horrified scream welled in my own throat but I swallowed it down.

This has to end. Now. I raised my Barracuda. Darksong bore down on the inner ring without hesitation, encouraged by the song ringing through water and air. A Disharmony twisted towards us, head up, mouth open, determined to preserve its prey.

I drew in my focus. Even as I told my suit's helmet and mask to withdraw, my gaze never left the gaping maw with its many, many teeth. *There,* I told myself, staring hard into that darkness. *That's the target. Put it right there.* I set my jaw, narrowed my eyes, and pulled the trigger. The Disharmony let out an unearthly squeal, a sound that raised the hairs on the back of my neck. There was a sizzle, a pop, and smoke poured from its mouth. The squeal wound down, dying to a keen, then to silence as the Disharmony went still, floating like so much driftwood on the surface of the water.

Bad enough we'd injured them and scattered their outer circle. A death was more than they would take. They broke and fled, chased by the original dozen Voices who'd been here when we arrived. No peaceful retreat for them.

Silence settled all around us, except for the lapping of water against the boat and Betancourt's quiet mewls. Part of me sympathized; I'd wanted to curl up in the fetal position and never move again a few months back, when I'd gotten a man's brain splattered all over me. Being up close and personal with someone's innards was horrifying. But an even bigger part of me was furious. There were grim expressions on the faces of my team and a spreading stain of blood in the water.

As far as I was concerned, there was blood on Ashley Betancourt's hands, too.

Slam!

The canister struck the table so hard, I was surprised neither of them broke. Despite her diminutive meter-fifty stature, Captain Chui seemed to loom over the two remaining reporters. Dave the cameraman stared at the tabletop, his eyes blank, his demeanor meek; I saw it in the downward tilt of his chin and the way his body folded in on itself. But Ashley Betancourt gazed up at Captain Chui with red-rimmed but defiant eyes, and I might've admired her if I didn't want to leap across the table and tear her fucking face off.

"You gassed my soldiers," Captain Chui said calmly.

Betancourt's gaze remained defiant. "It's not lethal."

"*You gassed my soldiers!*" Captain Chui never raised her voice, yet her words rang through the room as if spoken on loudspeaker.

I stood against the far wall between Kiri and Diver. For the first time since I'd arrived on Song, I had a hand in my pocket, rubbing my fingers over the satin lining at the top. After everything I was exhausted and overwhelmed, and the room was pretty well stuffed. The silky texture under my fingertips was all that kept me from running off and finding a place to hide.

Emin, Anton and Jae, as fellow witnesses, were with us. A ring of soldiers surrounded the table where Dave and Betancourt sat; if Captain Chui hadn't put her foot down, every soldier—minus the gassed ones—planetside would be in that room right then. They were furious on behalf of Maddox, Teke and Gorski, the three who'd been on watch when Betancourt had used the canister. *Fuck. We're all furious.* Apparently Doctor Marsten had been angry enough to start talking about keeping the reporters in comas while they were here.

"It can't hurt them."

"Actually, yeah, it can," Diver cut in. "Ain't *made* to be fatal, but there are side effects and allergies to it." When Betancourt turned to him, he smiled; a smile so brutal that it made me shiver. "Type's pretty common on the streets of many human colonized worlds. Especially the illegally made stuff. I've seen what it can do."

I glanced at him. Although no one talked about it, I'd always suspected Diver'd grown up on the streets. Ten years on the streets of Wraith were enough for me to recognize the signs.

"Fortunately for you," Captain Chui went on, "Doctor Marsten reports that Privates Maddox and Gorski, and Sergeant Teke are going to recover without ill effects. Otherwise I'd be handing you over to the authorities for use of illegal weaponry so fast, your heads wouldn't even get the chance to spin."

Betancourt snorted. "You're one to talk. Is *any* of your gear legal?"

"Technically speaking…" Diver began.

Captain Chui shot him a look and he went silent immediately, holding up his hands. There was no fucking around when she was in that mood. *None.*

"My ship, my crew, and our equipment are none of your goddamn business, Ms. Betancourt. *Nothing* here is. You're on this planet quite illegally and yet the people of Song were gracious enough to let you stay. They even let you spend time running your cameras on their planet, and this is how you repay them?

"Your actions today put lives in danger, and you're damn lucky only one was lost. Because let me tell you something, Ms. Betancourt, we're dealing with a people that want to be part of the Alliance, that want to join us, and once they do, they'll be well within their rights to bring charges against you. What do you think they'd do if you'd gotten some of their own killed?"

"But *they're* fine," Betancourt shot back. "You're all fine. I'm the only one who lost someone."

"You might as well have spaced him yourself," Captain Chui said, making Betancourt go pale. "You came here looking for a story, Ms. Betancourt, and I gave you one."

Betancourt sneered. "Whales playing on the beach? What kind of story is that?"

"One your parents would have appreciated."

Whatever bravado Betancourt had left disappeared, dying out as suddenly as if someone had switched it off. I eyed Captain Chui curiously. There was definitely a story here; maybe I should've taken the time to look up Betancourt after all. Now…now I was dead tired, my head was throbbing from exhaustion and anger and the lingering effects of fear, and I thought I might puke if I had to look at this woman much longer.

"So what are you going to do with us?" Betancourt asked, after a long, uncomfortable silence.

"Largely what I've been doing, except this time, you're staying here. Both your remaining crew and your ship will be thoroughly searched for any further surprises. And if I get word of you putting so much as a toenail out of line again, I'll have your filming privileges revoked."

My exhaustion evaporated. "You can't let them keep filming!"

Amazing how damned loud silence could be. It crowded in my ears as every set of eyes in the room turned on me. I didn't need much skill at reading body language to see the astonishment on all those faces—or the disapproval on Captain Chui's. Old instincts, far from dead, flared up, and I wanted to shrink against the wall, to bow my head in obedience and shame. In compliance. *This is about more than you, Xan. You can't just give in.* But Sweet Mother Universe, that would be so much easier.

"I *can't*?"

I swallowed hard. "You shouldn't. Even if the Grand Matriarch will still allow it, they don't deserve to be rewarded for what they've done."

"I will speak to the Grand Matriarch, Ms. Corelel. If she allows it, then I want them to continue recording." Her expression didn't change in the least, so I was startled by the gentle tone that came through on my private comm channel. *"I appreciate you standing up for what you believe in, Xandri, but in this case I* need *you to trust me."*

I bowed my head. "Very well."

"You six…you've had a long day, and you must be tired. I think it's time for you to get some rest."

"With all due respect, ma'am," Anton said, "I'm more than awake enough for ship search duty."

"Me too," Emin seconded.

After a moment of silence, Captain Chui raised an eyebrow at Jae.

"Oh, sorry, Captain. I was thinking I'd like to stay in tonight." Vi flashed a vicious smile at the reporters. "I figured first watch sounded good."

I knew she wouldn't protest; as a soldier herself, Captain Chui understood the camaraderie that developed between them all too well. Even if they needed to take some stims, they *would* participate in what punishment the reporters were getting. Part of me wanted to volunteer too, but I was losing my grip on my ability to cope. I needed to get away from all these people, all that *presence* cutting into me. I needed space and quiet.

Not caring what anyone thought—far too worn to care—I reached for Diver. He didn't hesitate to put an arm around my shoulder and lead me out of the room. I thought Kiri might follow, but when I glanced back at her, I saw that she had pulled Anton and Emin into the corner of the room and was saying something to them; at least, she must have been, though all of it was sub-vocalized as far as I could tell. *I hope she's okay. That must've been scary for her, too.*

"I'll check in with her later," Diver murmured to me, because somehow, goddamnit, he always knew.

I leaned against him without reservation as we headed back to my room. And even as we crossed the threshold and closed the door behind us, I didn't let go. Diver wrapped his arms around me and I buried my face against his chest, inhaling the scent of ocean and him. Guilt threatened to overwhelm me. I hated that I couldn't save Steven, even if those damn reporters shouldn't have been there in the first place. And I hated that I'd had to kill something to save the rest of them. The Disharmonies might be scary, but they were animals and had simply behaved as animals.

"Don't be acting like this is your fault, fireball."

I lifted my head in surprise.

"Four and a half years," Diver said, tapping the tip of my nose with a finger. "Long time to know a person, even one who hides as much of herself as you do. But you can't hide from me, Xan. You try, but I see you. Right now I see a woman who's too exhausted to be placing blame anywhere."

"I can't help it," I whispered.

"I know. And *you* know I'm right."

"Also, insufferable."

He grinned. "Yeah, but that's a given. Look, you go on and get cleaned up. Take a shower." When I opened my mouth, he put a finger beneath my chin and gently closed it again. "Ain't going anywhere. I'll be here when you get out."

That was all I needed to hear. I fled to the bathroom, eager for once to be clean of the smell of the sea. I stripped, tossing my clothes and bathing suit in a pile in the corner, and stepped beneath the hot spray of water. Then I leaned against the wall, rivulets of warmth running down my body, and tried not to think about the fact that I'd thrown myself headlong into a fight with something big enough to swallow me and not even notice.

Chapter Twenty

Diver

I dropped down on Xandri's bed and buried shaking hands in my salt-stiff hair. *Holy shit. Holy. Fucking. Shit.*

Until now, adrenaline'd kept me going. Kept me from thinking about the sheer size of those monstrosities. Kept at bay the image of Steven's guts dripping into the water as what was left of him hung from the boat. I'd been working with a paramilitary organization for years, but in this day and age, you just didn't see that kinda shit very often. Sure, people got blown to bits and stuff, but I wasn't usually on the field to see it.

But then, there was Xandri. A tiny smile broke through. She'd been like a vengeful goddess of the seas up there, hair wet from all the water spraying, Barracuda never wavering. And yet I knew she was in the shower right now, hating on herself. Mad at herself for this happening, thinking there must've been some way to stop it, if only *she* had done something different. Probably even thinking that maybe if she hadn't made mistakes on Cochinga, somehow none of this would've happened at all. *And knowing her, probably feeling guilty over killing that thing, because that's Xandri.*

A light rap on the door pulled me out of my thoughts. I rose and paused for a second, listening. Shower was still on. When I opened the door, I found Kiri waiting for me.

"You look wasted."

She flashed a wan smile. "You must be tired too; your flattery switch is off." She tipped her head vaguely in the direction of the bathroom. "How is she?"

"Funny," I said, "she was wondering the same thing about you."

"I'm sure I'll stop having nightmares eventually, after enough years of therapy."

Things might not be between us like they were for me and Xandri, but Kiri was my friend, so I opened my arms in offering. She took me up on it, clutching me almost as tight as Xandri had. Not that I minded; big boy pants forced me to admit that *I* needed the hugs as well. When she stepped back again, she looked a little less frazzled, though still tired.

"Xan's... Xan. I sent her to get clean. Hoping I can get her to rest before she thinks too much more."

Kiri nodded. "That's probably a good idea."

"So, what were you up to with Emin and Anton?"

"Whatever do you mean?" She widened her eyes. "I was just giving you and Xandri a little time alone together."

"And you were up to something."

She let out a soft laugh. "Yes, I was up to something. I gave Emin and Anton a little something to attach to Betancourt's ship's computer. Captain Chui likes her crew to think for themselves and take initiative, well... I'm *going* to find out how they knew about this mission." Her expression turned grim.

"Good," I said. "You need any help, just let me know."

"I will." Her expression changed yet again, turned soft and concerned. "Look, Diver... maybe this isn't my business but—but Xandri is my friend too. I want her to be okay. And I was just wondering: Have you had any... trouble? Like, her freezing up or anything?"

I should've told it *wasn't* any of her business, but instead I stared and sputtered, "How—how'd you...?"

"It's just a suspicion I've had for a while now. I know she often doesn't like touch because the autism causes her sensory issues but... there's something in her, something I recognize. I know you'd never hurt her but I think someone else has," Kiri said, her eyes sad. "I think someone's hurt her really bad."

I opened my mouth—and closed it. Suddenly the pieces made a bit more sense. I'd thought her freezing up was because she'd never had sex before. Society didn't tend towards the ancient hang-ups about fictitious shit like virginity anymore, but plenty of people still got nervous about taking that step in their lives. And Xan seemed like maybe that wasn't a step she'd ever been ready to take before. But looking at it now—fuck.

"If you have any idea who—"

Kiri shook her head. "I'm pretty sure it was long before she came aboard the *Carpathia*. I just—thought you should know. God, maybe I shouldn't have said anything at all, but I started remembering what she was like when she first joined us, how she'd *never* admit something was wrong, and I thought..."

I nodded. Xandri preferred to avoid conflict, and it'd been worse in the early days. She'd keep her mouth shut when people teased her, even if it hurt her feelings. I hated to think she wouldn't say something, wouldn't stop me if she wasn't in the mood or got scared, but Kiri, at least, feared it was possible. Now I knew. And I'd be on sharp lookout, because the idea of hurting Xandri like that made me sick.

In the room behind us, the shower went off.

"Guess I'd better go," Kiri said. "As much as I'd like to see her, I'm dead on my feet, and I need sleep if I'm going to give that ship's computer hell tomorrow."

"You do that. Maybe see what you can dig out of Betancourt's personal files, yeah?"

"I take it you read that article she wrote on Xandri and 'Pandoras' back after Cochinga first happened."

Oh, had I ever. That was what had made me decide, once and for all, to go digging for the truth. The article had been full of nasty fearmongering about the dangers of neurodivergence, making sweeping generalizations and unsubstantiated claims that past serial killers and dictators had all had some kind of mental illness. Honestly, for a woman supposedly from a family of journalists, it was the epitome of shitty reporting. *She ought to be ashamed. Lord knows they would be.*

I paused in turning back to the room and glanced at Kiri. "What do you know about her parents?"

She paused as well, hand on the knob of her door. "They were journalists. They had a very good reputation among xenobiologists for accurate and accessible reporting."

"Were? Had?"

"They were killed in the field. By LHFH terrorists." She opened her door. "Goodnight, Diver."

Huh. Now that just makes things even weirder. I stepped back into Xandri's room, pulling the door shut behind me, and found Xandri herself waiting for me.

She wore a long, worn-looking tunic top and was scrubbing her hair dry with a towel. I caught a flash of something under her ear, something that looked much like a scar. *Impossible. No one allows scars anymore, unless they're weirdos like Captain Chui.* Personal nanos couldn't always stop them, but medical nanos could. Even so, it wasn't a big deal, so it surprised me when Xandri abruptly dropped her hands, as if I'd seen something shameful.

"That was Kiri," I said, acting as if I hadn't seen a damn thing. I bent to pick up the towel she'd also dropped. "Think you'll like this. She gave Emin and Anton a little something that'll help her slip into Betancourt's ship's computer."

She smiled a little. "Good. If nothing else, Kiri'll leave them a surprise. Maybe some Kowari porn."

I chuckled and handed back the towel. She grabbed it, hugging it to her chest and burying the lower half of her face against it. Watching me through the tilt of her eyelashes, she twisted slowly back and forth. I'd hardly seen these repetitive movements—called 'stimming,' as I'd learned in my research—from her since we came to Song, but now... damn. Fucking damn. This shit was messing with her but good.

"Um..." she began, her gaze dipping to the floor and the twisting growing more pronounced. "Would—would you stay here? Tonight?" Her head came up, her eyes growing wide with horror at her own words. "I don't—I didn't mean like... it's just, I don't..."

I reached into the pocket of my shorts and produced a nutrient-bar. "Eat this. I'm gonna go take a quick shower, yeah?"

She wrinkled her nose, but took the nutrient-bar. Instead of heading back to my room, I took a quick shower in Xandri's bathroom, washing away the sea salt. When I returned, I found her curled up on the bed, holding the empty nutrient-bar wrapper as proof. I took it from her, leaving it in a pile on the floor with my T-shirt and towel, and slid onto the bed with her. She stared at me with large, uncertain eyes, so I scooped her into my arms and dragged her close.

She settled against me with a sigh, tucking her chin against my shoulder. Under other circumstances it would've been torture, having her pressed to my side like that, her breaths tickling my neck. But we were both exhausted, and I fell asleep easily, lulled by the beating of her heart.

Took me a long, long moment to realize the rapid thumping that'd woken me wasn't Xandri's heartbeat, but the sound of boots on the coral floor. *The fuck?* It was so comfortable in that bed, laying on my back with Xandri's head on my chest, one of her arms flung across my abdomen and her bare legs coiled around one of mine. She shifted, stretched and groaned, burying her face against me. I considered ways to get the noise to stop so we could go back to sleep.

Then someone started pounding on the door. Xandri whimpered and curled up tight. Swearing, I climbed out of bed and stomped over to answer it. Jae stood there in full armor, ammo belts crisscrossing vir chest, vir weapons at the ready.

"Captain Chui wants to see you both," vi said. "Now."

I turned to find Xandri sitting up in bed, fear starting to blaze through the blear of sleep in her eyes. My own heart was beginning to race.

"We'll be there," I said. "Give us five minutes."

I hurried back to my room for fresh clothes and when I came back, I found Xandri up and dressed, her hair thrown back in a loose ponytail. Like me, she carried her weapons and an extra belt of ammo. Together we hurried down the hallway, neither of us speaking a word. We found Captain Chui in the room she'd chosen as her base. The entirety of Alpha Team was there, plus both lieutenants, and Magellan. Xandri and I slotted ourselves between Kiri and Emin and waited.

"Any telling if they're working together?" Captain Chui asked, and for a moment I was hella confused.

Then Lieutenant Zubairi's voice responded. "I'm afraid I can't say, Captain. There have been no indications either way."

"Keep me posted, Lieutenant." Captain Chui turned to all of us. "At oh-eight-hundred this morning Lieutenant Zubairi delivered urgent and disturbing news. Zechak scout ships are near Song orbit."

Xandri stiffened.

"Worse, there are other ships. What appears to be—by their own admission—an LHFH fleet."

I stared. *A fucking fleet? Who gave those anti-alien fucks a fleet? And what the fucking hell were they doing here?*

"How many ships?" Kiri asked, voicing the question all of us were dreading the answer to.

"Lieutenant Zubairi?" Captain Chui queried.

"As far as we can tell, there are a dozen Zechak ships and—and a hundred LHFH ships," Zubairi answered. "Our estimates put LHFH fighter numbers at somewhere around two-hundred, based on the ship classes. They—oh." Her voice caught and we all waited expectantly. "I don't think they're working together. One of the LHFH ships fired on a scout. It's gone."

"What classes of ship?" Xandri asked quietly, and for a moment I thought the lieutenant wouldn't hear.

"I can't tell all of them. There's at least a dozen refitted Crystalliad-class ships, and another two dozen Harrier-class, but I don't recognize the others."

"Have *Carpathia* scan them," Captain Chui ordered. "She should be able to identify them, but if not, send us the specs. We're sending the shuttles up for the other two platoons, and then I want you to take the *Carpathia* and keep her away from the fight."

"But Captain—"

"We have only six fighters, Lieutenant. We need back up. Get a message out to the Alliance immediately but *do not* engage with those ships. Am I understood?"

"Yes, Captain. Zubairi out."

The room went deathly silent after that. *A hundred ships. They came for a slaughter.* My stomach twisted and I clenched my teeth. Fuck that. Just fuck it. Like hell we'd let those bastards come here and do harm. And I didn't have to ask to know it was what we were all thinking. Even Captain Chui, whose calm demeanor never seemed to waver, was clearly furious. She swore and slammed her fist against the table serving as her desk.

"How?" she hissed. "This was supposed to be a classified mission! Yet here we are, first reporters, now—"

Xandri drew in a sharp breath, the sound loud and startling in the quiet of the room. Something flared in her eyes, the spark of wildness and anger that had first had me calling her fireball. *What did she—uh oh.* The reporters. I made a grab for Xandri's arm, but she moved surprisingly fast. She skipped sideways, eluding me, spun on her heel and dashed out the door. Fucking fuck.

"She's going after the reporters!" I shouted over my shoulder as I sprinted after her.

Despite her size, Captain Chui kept pace with me. "Relax, Mr. Diver, I doubt she'll—"

"She hasn't had any coffee yet!"

"Shit!"

Somehow, despite our best efforts, we couldn't keep up with her. She reached the reporters' room ahead of us and when the two guards reached out to stop her, she ducked low, slipping under their arms and darting into the room. I poured on an extra burst of speed, shooting past the startled guards and into the room. Just in time, too. Xandri was reaching for Betancourt, who sat frozen in shock in her chair. I grabbed Xan around the waist and hauled her back before she could scratch the reporter's face off. Not that I'd necessarily have a problem with it, as such; but *she* would feel guilty about it later.

Okay, there was a chance she wouldn't, but I didn't wanna take the risk.

"Let me go!" Xandri howled, wriggling fiercely. "This is their fault! I know it is! Let me go, let me go!"

"Goodness," Betancourt said, regaining her composure. "She really *is* mentally unstable. And here I was beginning to think that was all a bunch of blather after all."

"Me? *I'm* mentally unstable?" Xandri shot back. "I didn't bring an LHFH fleet down on the heads of a sapient species! That was all you!"

Dave snickered. "Wow. She's delusional, too."

"Hey, I could let her go," I pointed out.

Dave blanched.

"Enough," came Captain Chui's voice, strong and firm. She stepped into the room, followed by the entire group that had attended her in her office. "Ms. Corelel, you will stand down or you will be removed. Am I understood?"

Xandri grumbled and for a moment I thought she'd disobey. Then she sighed and went limp in my arms. I released my hold carefully. When she didn't make another leap for Betancourt, I caught her shoulder and pulled her back to stand with the rest of our group. She continued to glower, her entire body vibrating with fury.

"Really, Captain Chui," Betancourt said, looking smug. "If you can't control your pet Pandora, you should—"

"You should be quiet, Ms. Betancourt."

Captain Chui's low, threatening tone would bring even the biggest of orc warriors to a halt. Ashley Betancourt sank back in her chair, looking truly frightened. Captain Chui stalked across the room and paused a meter away from the reporters, her arms folded as she gazed down at them.

"There are a hundred LHFH ships just within orbit. And Zechak scout ships, as well. It seems an awful lot of uninvited guests are crashing this *classified* mission."

Betancourt paled. "That's awful."

"I want to know how they knew to come here, Ms. Betancourt."

"It wasn't us!" Her head came up. "We didn't tell—"

"You wouldn't have to," Xandri cut in. "All they had to do is *follow* you here. You might as well have told them. Your carelessness is going to get people killed!"

"You mean the way yours did on Cochinga?"

Xandri reeled back as if she'd been struck in the face. Kiri started to take a step forward, but Jae grabbed her shoulder and held her back. I clenched my hands into fists to keep myself from taking a few threatening steps forward myself. But Captain Chui, who stood between the reporters and us, turned on Betancourt in a slow, menacing way that reminded me of those Disharmonies opening their mouths to bite.

"A woman who got a member of her own crew killed *just yesterday* should perhaps consider her choice of words more carefully," Captain Chui warned. "Especially when said woman is *this* close to being brought up on charges for endangering an entire world."

"You can't charge me with anything," Betancourt said, raising her chin. "I didn't tell anyone else about this. And even if the LHFH followed me here, that's not a crime. Not for the press."

"If the LHFH attacks—and they will—it *will* be a crime," Xandri put in, voice strong despite Betancourt's insults. "Your intentions won't matter then, and your press status won't protect you; you should know that. Article fifty-six, section eight, paragraph ten of the Alliance Charter."

We all stared, every one of us. I brought it up on my HUD, and sure enough: once I made heads and tails of the legalese, I realized it meant that Betancourt and Dave the cameraman could be held partially responsible for bringing harm upon any ISTN classified world, regardless of its Alliance membership status. Judging by the look on Betancourt's face, she knew it too—and had been hoping none of us would.

"Well, that's cleared up," Captain Chui said pleasantly. "Now—"

"Captain?" Lieutenant Zubairi's voice. "We've got a problem. A new one."

"Speak."

"The LHFH fleet destroyed three more Zechak ships. The Zechak are retreating. The LHFH...they're staying near orbit, but scattering."

"Scattering to where?"

"That's what we're trying to figure out. They've got a lot of sneaks-works on those ships; that's part of how they got in under our radar to begin with. *Carpathia* has pinned some of them, but others are slipping through our fingers."

"Keep working on it," Captain Chui said, already on the move and beckoning for us to follow. "If you're having trouble, ping Ms. Ayabara for assistance."

"Yes, ma'am."

"Which reminds me: Ms. Ayabara, tap into *Carpathia's* resources and see if you can find out who let the cat out of the bag. Mr. Diver, lend a hand."

"Yes, Captain," we answered in unison.

"Lieutenant, send me any information you get on the coordinates of those ships the moment you get it. I must go speak with the Grand Matriarch."

"Inshallah," Lieutenant Zubairi breathed. "Safe travels, Captain. Zubairi out."

Chapter Twenty-One

Xandri

"Eat it. Now."

I glared at Jae, but vi didn't even acknowledge me. With a soft growl, I took the nutrient-bar from vir and tore the wrapper violently away. I didn't want to eat; in fact, I was pretty sure if I did, it would come back up.

A hundred ships. *One hundred freaking ships.* I took a vicious bite of the nutrient-bar and glared up at the sky. How could this be happening? Everything had been going so well. I bit down again with as much vigor as before, fighting back an urge to cry in frustration and worry. *How can we possibly take on one-hundred ships?* I wanted this all to be a dream, something I could wake up from. The sting of my teeth sinking into my lip as I took another bite told me it definitely wasn't a dream.

The dock seemed to sway beneath by feet. I stared at the end of it, where Captain Chui stood explaining everything to the Grand Matriarch. Magellan—who'd been using his work as an excuse to stay indoors, hidden from the sun and heat—stood with her. Alpha Team's four soldiers stood with me like bodyguards, and I desperately wished I had Diver to lean on, but he was inside, working with Kiri.

"This worries us deeply," I heard the Grand Matriarch say. "We may be able to defend ourselves, but we are not…adept at the art of war."

"Grand Matriarch," another voice cut in, and to my surprise I recognized Darksong, "among us there are those who have long fought the Disharmonies. What are these people but more Disharmonies? We *can* fight them."

"We do not say we cannot. Only that we are unsure how."

"Then perhaps we can help," Captain Chui said. "We will do whatever it takes to fight this threat with you, if you wish it. Either way, we will not simply leave you to take your chances against them."

"They were grand help against the Disharmonies, Grand Matriarch," Darksong said. "We would be honored to fight with them again."

Water rose and fell in little hillocks around the Grand Matriarch as she shifted. A trickle of song chimed around us. I clutched the wrapper of my nutrient-bar; sure enough, the food sat in my stomach like a rock and I had to swallow hard to keep it there. *Maybe we should never have come here. Maybe I should've refused. Then the Hands and Voices would refuse to negotiate, and this would never have happened...* But it was foolish to think that. My presence—or lack thereof—couldn't keep the LHFH away when they got an idea into their heads.

I bit back a moan. A fleet. An LHFH fleet! How had they gotten it? How were we going to stop it? I forced myself to take a deep breath. It wasn't just us here. The Hands and Voices had already proven they could take care of themselves.

"It seems," the Grand Matriarch said at last, "that our warriors look forward to fighting alongside you again. So that is what we will do."

"Good. We'll set up a comm channel specifically for the planning, and ensure that you have any footage or maps that we—"

"Captain Chui!"

Thud, thud, thud. We all turned. Major Douglas strode down the dock toward us. A platoon of AFC soldiers stood at the far end of the dock, standing at attention despite the fact that they looked like they'd marched down here triple-time. All of them—Douglas included—wore full armor, like our soldiers. As soon as Douglas reached us, he came to a sharp halt and saluted Captain Chui. She returned the gesture.

"We got the news from *Resplendence* this morning," he said without preamble. "They're sending down every AFC soldier aboard. Meanwhile...I know you prefer not to work with us on this mission, but I thought a backup platoon..."

"Will not go unappreciated," Captain Chui said. If she was surprised, she didn't show it. "Thank you for acting so quickly, Major."

"We've also sent word to the Alliance, though I imagine you have as well."

"Indeed. Major…please understand, I don't speak with intent to offend. But that is an LHFH fleet up there that I had *no* idea existed. If you knew…"

Major Douglas shook his head, his expression grim. "If anyone in the Alliance knew about this, no one told *me*. And if I ever find out just *who* kept the information from me, I'll…well."

"Space them?"

"Worse. I'll hand them over to you."

That's actually pretty mean. But I was starting to feel a little better. Extra troops would help, and the Hands and Voices would be difficult to reach in the water. They could fight, yes, but if worst came to worst, they could hide. Still, worries loomed. Captain Chui had already assured me that our two other platoons were being sent straight to Beta Team, yet I wished I'd never sent them off on their own in the first place. And while three platoons were more than two, that didn't leave us with a whole lot of soldiers. Without the types of ships the LHFH had, it was difficult to know what, exactly, we'd be up against.

"Grand Matriarch," Major Douglas greeted.

"Ah. Major Douglas." Maybe it was just me, but the Grand Matriarch's voice didn't sound entirely pleased.

"I've brought some soldiers to fight with you, and there'll be more coming. As well, I brought my finest tactician, Captain Eira Rhees. She is the best in the AFC." He smiled, and for once it seemed genuine to me. "I suspect one day I'll lose her to Captain Chui, but until then, it's my sincerest hope that she can be of use to you."

"Thank you, Major. We appreciate it a great deal."

"Captain," the major went on, "any further news? Do we know what we're up against? Numbers, anything?"

Captain Chui glanced in my direction, and for a moment I wondered what the hell any of this had to do with me. *I'm not in charge, why should I—oh. Right.* I knew ships.

"They have twenty-four Harrier-class ships—or something built very like them—and they'll carry somewhere between a hundred and two -hundred ground troops apiece, depending upon the weapons and armor they're carrying," I said, drawing everyone's attention. "The other dozen ships that we've been able to recognize are decommissioned Crystalliad-class cruisers, modified, though we don't know how. A Crystalliad can potentially hold up to three-thousand personnel, though if you want to use it to land ground troops, it would be more efficient to use some of that space for heavy armor and weapons.

"We don't know yet what the other ships are," I added after a moment. "Lieutenant Zubairi and the *Carpathia* are investigating now."

"Speaking of which," Captain Chui cut in, before anyone could start to panic about the numbers. "Lieutenant Zubairi has just pinged me. Lieutenant?"

"Captain," Khalida returned. "Which do you want first, the bad news or the worse news?"

"Does the bad news sound better when compared to the worse news?"

"Not really."

"Then just tell me."

"We've received word from Sarvadot Station. They've got all hands on deck and will be launching as soon as possible, but it will still take them three days to get here."

I almost thought I heard a splash as my heart plummeted, as if it had gone straight through the dock and into the water. Three days might not seem like much, but it was a lot when you were only a few hundred troops facing possibly thousands. *There are many, many more Hands and Voices,* I reminded myself, but it didn't help. I shoved my hands into my pockets, rubbing the pads of my thumbs along the satin lining, but that didn't help either.

"Then we will simply have to manage until then," Captain Chui said calmly. "What else?"

"As far as we can tell, the LHFH is preparing to land in several spots, including a number close to your location. I'm already forwarding you the data. I don't think they've realized we've broken through some of their cloaking, just yet."

"Any word on the other ships?"

"*Carpathia* has some ideas what they might be, and has requested I send scans down to Ms. Corelel for a second opinion."

"Then do so. And continue to keep me updated on whatever other data you find. Chui out." Captain Chui regarded us all without the slightest show of fear. "Ms. Corelel, begin work immediately on identifying those ships. Privates P'yo, Nazaryan and Mulroney, you've got legwork. Get communications up and running between us and the Hands and Voices. Private Amelia, get Captain Rhees and the AFC platoon settled in. We'll meet in my office at twelve hundred hours. Dismissed."

My wristlet pinged at that very moment, letting me know the data had arrived. *And I have only about an hour to look at it.* At least it would give me something to do to take my mind off all my fears.

I must've looked like the weirdest mother duck ever as I stepped into Captain Chui's room, trailed by all five Psittacans. Captain Chui looked up from the holo-display and her quiet conversation with Captain Rhees and frowned.

"If you want them gone, ma'am," I said wearily, "you give the order."

"Along the wall," Captain Chui said with a wave of her hand, looking only slightly exasperated.

I lined up with everyone else: Anton, Emin, Jae and Amelia, Kiri and Diver, both platoon lieutenants and the AFC's lieutenant. Marla and Kirrick sat at the table near the holo-display; I'd lent them to Captain Chui as note-takers, so none of our plans could be electronically intercepted. As I pressed myself in between Kiri and Diver, both of them reached out and took my hands. I clung to them for dear life.

"I've heard about you," Captain Rhees said to the Psittacans as they lined up against the opposite wall. "Glad to have you on our side."

If it weren't for her soldier's tan, Eira Rhees would've looked like an ice goddess come to life. Her hair was white, purely white, without even the tiniest hint of yellow, and so were her eyebrows and her long eyelashes. She had blue-gray eyes and an oval face with full, soft lips. There was a time, back on Ancient Earth, when people might've said she was too beautiful to be a soldier. I had a feeling that if anyone said that to Eira Rhees' face, she'd punch them in theirs.

"Any luck with those ships, Ms. Corelel?" Captain Chui asked.

"Some, I think." I held on to Kiri and Diver to resist the urge to flap my arms against my sides. "I recognized another dozen of them as really old freighters. No armor, no weapons, useless as troop carriers. Probably carrying extra supplies—food, ammunition, that sort of thing."

"Would that be this dozen?" Captain Rhees asked. She pointed to a spot on the holo-display, which showed Song and its atmosphere. A dozen ships lurked high in orbit. "They haven't moved from that position."

I nodded. "That's them. Now they've got a big chunk of their fleet—thirty-two ships—that aren't a class I recognize, but they're built similarly to modern Hunter-class corvettes. *Carpathia*, with Ms. Ayabara's aid, is working to break in and get a look at their specs. If I'm right, then they're probably here to lay siege and fight back against any Alliance ships that come." I pointed to their locations on the holo-display. "And that would explain their positions."

"Indeed, it would," Captain Chui agreed, watching me with approval.

"We're not sure with those fifteen back there," I said, pointing now to the larger ships behind the corvettes. "They could be extra troop carriers, or they could be command ships. We're leaning towards command ships at the moment. They're no class I know, but they're big and bulky, and *Carpathia* suspects heavily armored. Command ships seems most likely. But the last five..."

I took a deep breath, released Kiri's and Diver's hands, and stepped up to the holo-display. Using my fingers, I drew glowing green-blue circles around the five remaining ships. Each one held a different position above Song, all of them a sizable distance from each other. The incoming data showed them flying low. They *could* have been drop-ships—the Harriers could fly low in the atmosphere to drop troops—but if they were, why only five? Why not just build more Harriers?

"We can't figure out what they are," I admitted. "They're small enough and light enough to be drop-ships, but...they're almost *too* small, in the case of an army this large. They could be anything— even just scout ships."

Captain Rhees studied me for a moment, then nodded. "Have you ever considered a career in the navy?"

I couldn't help it; I wrinkled my nose. "Of course not!"

"Definitely raised by Marines," Rhees said with a chuckle. "Captain Chui?"

"Right. For now, our concern is the Harriers and the Crystalliads," Captain Chui said. "Our readings tell us we have an entire dozen Harriers and four Crystalliads focused in our area, which means they must know where we are. These eight may be coming in via the water," and she pointed the ones in orbit over the ocean, "which is not the smartest idea they've ever had, but this is the LHFH we're talking about. The bigger worry is these.

"There's a large patch of jungle about six hours' march from here." Captain Chui drew another screen out of the holo-display to better highlight the jungle. "It appears they're planning to set troops down on the other side and march them through, probably figuring that will give them cover on the approach."

"Wait," Many Kills spoke out. "Captain, did you say…jungle?"

She paused, her eyes brightening and a rather wicked smile curving her lips. I felt an answering smile touch my own, and all around me there were low chuckles; the *Carpathia* crew had seen the Psittacans in action. Moreover, we'd been called in to deal with them four years ago because the earliest attempts had ended poorly. Troops went into the jungles of Psittaca, but not a single soldier emerged. We got most of them back eventually, as POWs, but the Alliance had learned the hard way not to send soldiers into Psittacan-infested jungles.

"A very good thought, Many Kills," Captain Chui said. "Nazaryan, Mulrony, P'yo and Amelia, you'll go with Ms. Corelel, the Psittacans, and two platoons to meet our new friends at this jungle."

"Me? But Captain, I should stay here! The Hands and Voices—"

"We will be fine, Xandri Corelel," came the Grand Matriarch's voice through the comm, the first time she had spoken during the meeting. "We are already making plans to meet this enemy. And you need not worry about your job. We like Hans Klee; he will act for us in your absence."

"Oh. Well…"

"I need you there, Ms. Corelel," Captain Chui told me. "No one else on this crew understands the Psittacans' signals as well as you. If they slip into their own language, even at a distance you'll be able to tell my soldiers what those sounds mean."

I nodded and held down a sigh. She was right.

"Then I'm going with her," Diver said.

"No, Mr. Diver, you are not. I've ordered Lieutenant Zubairi to send down the gorilla. We will need you to operate it when it arrives. In the meantime, you can either help Ms. Ayabara with her work, or help the Hands and Voices with their defense, but I need you here."

Diver opened his mouth to protest, so I nudged him with my elbow. Yes, I wanted him to be there with me. Hell, I didn't want to go at all. But this wasn't about us or what we wanted. It was about protecting Song. I looked at the holo-display, at the hundred ships preparing to attack. If we could get the Psittacans to the jungle in time, there was a good chance those eight ships of soldiers wouldn't get very far. *We have to at least try.* If following Captain Chui's orders would save lives, that's what I'd do.

"All right, Captain Chui," Rhees cut in, "I trust your judgment a great deal, but are you sure you want to send them? No plan survives contact with the enemy."

Captain Chui smiled. "No enemy survives contact with Psittacans in a jungle. They are excellent at improvisation, especially in jungle territory."

"Very well. I'm glad I'm not a member of the LHFH, then." Everyone chuckled a little, and Captain Rhees smiled. "Now, Captain Chui has put me in charge of planning the beachside defenses, and I'd like—"

My wristlet pinged. I considered ignoring it, but it pinged again, and when I looked I saw the incoming was from Christa. Heedless of the looks being thrown my way, I opened the comm channel.

"Christa?"

"Xandri? Oh God, Xandri, it's... it's horrible!" Christa gasped.

My heart pattered in my ears like the wings of a butterfly as it threw itself hopelessly against the glass. *No... oh no. How can something have happened already?* My hands shook. I looked up at Captain Chui, saw her grave expression. Diver's hand rested on my shoulder. I swallowed to get some moisture back into my dry mouth.

"What—what happened?"

"There was this ship. I—Xandri, I've never seen one like it before, it was smallish but not—I don't know," Christa explained, her distress increasing. "It dropped something in the water, I'm not sure what, but it looked like some sort of metal canister. Maybe about man-sized. The—the Hands and Voices here, they went to investigate. We offered to go with them, we did, but they told us not to and…oh God, Xandri, it exploded.”

Hands caught me under the arms as my knees gave out. Captain Rhees vacated her chair and Diver hustled me into it. *I think I know what those five ships are now.* The back of my mind, which wasn’t trying to absorb the shock of Christa’s words, made a note to tell *Carpathia* about this, to see if she could estimate how many of these canisters each ship could hold.

“Xandri?”

“I—I’m here,” I managed. “How many?”

“Twelve went out. Only one came back and God, she’s not in a good way. Her Hands are gone and—and there are chunks just— I’m sorry, I can’t.”

“It’s okay. It’s fine. We’ll…uh…” I didn’t know what to do. Christa was part of my team, this was my job, but I didn’t know what to do.

Diver knelt in front of me and rested a hand over one of mine. He didn’t say anything, just gazed up at me, his green eyes bright and clear of doubt. *He* believed I could figure this out, that I could handle it. How could he believe in me when I couldn’t? I sat up straighter. I wanted to show him that his belief in me wasn’t misplaced.

“Soldiers are on their way to help protect you, Christa,” I said. “For now, tell the Hands and Voices to stay away from any more of those canisters. I’ll have Captain Chui hook you up with Doctor Marsten and Hans and—and they can assist you with first aid for that Voice until her people get there to help. Okay?”

“Right. Got it,” Christa said, sounding slightly calmer. “Xandri…we’re going to get these bastards, right?”

I glanced up, saw the determined looks on the faces of my fellow *Carpathia* members. “Yeah. They’re going to wish they never heard of Song or the *Carpathia* by the time we’re through. Xandri out.”

“All right, let’s move,” Captain Chui said, before I got a chance to draw another breath. “Ms. Corelel, get packing. Private P’yo, alert the platoons. I want you all ready to march in half an hour.” She spun. “Mr. Diver, you’re working with Ms. Ayabara right now. The moment we get the smallest piece of information on these things, I want you to analyze it. Tell me how they work and how to stop them.” Finally, she turned to the table. “Marla, fetch me that reporter and her goddamn camera.

“This has just become a warzone.”

Chapter Twenty-Two

Xandri

I threw one change of clothes, a comb, several nutrient-bars, a canteen, a small med-kit, and as much extra ammo as I could manage in a backpack and was ready to go. Four years on a ship with soldiers and I knew how to pack light.

Of course, once I finished, I had plenty of time to think about Christa's news. Eleven Voices and goodness only knew how many Hands were dead, and another Voice was in critical condition. The LHFH had some kind of weapon they could drop from low in the atmosphere, something with one hell of a payload, and we didn't know how it triggered. Motion-detecting? Manual? Timer? *And now I have to go off, leave the Voices and Hands to figure this out for themselves.* They could, I knew they could, especially with Diver's help, but I was also very, very good at feeling guilty.

Mother hadn't done guilt-trips so much as package guilt-cruise deals.

I strapped my gunbelt into place. Both pistols sat low on my thighs, which was the most comfortable way for me to reach down and draw them. I focused on the way they moved against my legs as I shouldered my bag and headed down the hall. *A warzone*, whispered that treacherous voice at the back of my mind. *This paradise is about to be torn apart.* I shivered in spite of the heat.

Outside, I felt like I might choke in the hot air. *At least I* brought *pants and boots.* Even if having to wear them was a pain.

"Hey, bo—Xandri." Jae came trotting up to me as if vi wasn't head-to-toe armor. "Come on. Time to get you suited up."

I blinked. "I *am* suited up."

"Nope, sorry. Captain wants you armored. No risks."

"Me? I'm not going to be on the front lines."

"No risks," vi repeated firmly, and steered me over to where Emin, Anton and Amelia waited.

At least they were quick and efficient about it. I had to dart back inside for a moment to change into the smart-fab fatigues. Once I returned, my Alpha Team soldiers got me into the light weight, flexible but strong armor. The largest piece protected my chest and neck, but there were pieces for my thighs and upper arms, as well. The helmet was a fold-up, like on the HP suit, so at least *part* of me wasn't baking in the sun.

"Well, well, well," came a familiar drawl, and I spun to find Diver watching me. "Look at you. All Amazon'd up."

"I feel ridiculous."

"You look hot."

"I am," I agreed. "It's like a billion degrees in this thing. Celsius."

Diver got a look on his face, like he was trying very hard not to laugh. No one *else* tried not to laugh. *Okay, what the hell did I say this time? He said I look hot and I—oh.* I flushed. It occurred to me then that there were a lot of other people outside, mainly the two platoons who would be going with us. The Psittacans were down on the dock, saying farewell to their friends, so at least they weren't watching this too.

Diver strode up to me and put his hands on my shoulders. "Look, Xan, I'm really sorry."

"Huh? For wh—"

His kiss caught me off guard. What caught me off guard even more was that there were more than eighty people watching us and I didn't care. He made to pull back quickly, just a small, chaste kiss, but I kissed him back with the full array of emotions pinging through my system—fear, desperation, need—and for a moment, everything was okay. For a moment I could forget that we were less than a hundred soldiers off to face hundreds, possibly thousands, and that the LHFH was waiting to destroy everything we were working for.

Diver drew back and leaned his forehead against mine. "It's gonna be okay, Xan. We're gonna beat them. So you come back to me safe, got it?"

I nodded, still light-headed from the kiss.

"Hey, lovebirds, that's quite enough!" I didn't know where the bellow came from, but it sounded like it had to be a gunnery sergeant. "It's time to move, move, move!"

I broke away from Diver and swooped to grab my bag. Then suddenly Anton had me by one arm and Jae had me by another, and they were pulling me in among the surging rows of soldiers. I glanced back once, saw Diver and Kiri standing together, watching me go. And even though I wished that they could be with me, or that I could stay with them, I knew that what we were doing now was important.

For the first time since my return to *Carpathia*, I had reason to be grateful for all the hiking I'd done around the Great Rock. I'd been afraid I wouldn't be able to keep up with the soldiers at all, but the terrain was fairly flat, and though I wasn't much of a jogger, I managed well enough. We took several short breaks, and there were also spans when we marched rather than jogged.

During the first break, I hung near the back, resting my hands on my knees and panting. Sweat soaked my hair and trickled down my back. *Why does it have to be* so *hot?* Normally I dealt well with heat, despite growing up in the temperate climate of Wraith. In fact, I took to warmer climates better than most people I knew, but that damn armor. Even though it had gone lightly colored to protect from the sun, I was still boiling.

"Hey."

I glanced up through loose, damp strands of hair and saw a soldier standing over me, looking fresh as a fucking daisy. A quick look at his collar told me he was a corporal. He watched me with large, cat-tilted eyes, only the tiniest bit of sweat tracking down his skin as he tried—but failed—to hide a smirk of amusement. I straightened, tossing my hair back.

"Didn't anyone teach you how to use the environmental controls?" he asked.

I blinked. *Oh… right.* I knew that. Some armor had automatic EC, but Captain Chui didn't like it. It tended towards faultiness. Diver told me it was planned obsolescence, that the companies that designed it *made* it that way. And Captain Chui had spent all her years in the military lobbying for auto-EC armor to be military made, like most other armor was, but parliament didn't seem that concerned about it. After all, what we already had worked just fine.

"I um…I forgot," I admitted, as I turned on the EC. "We kinda…were in a hurry."

He laughed. "Yeah, and you were a bit busy there at the end."

My cheeks burned even as the rest of me slowly cooled a few degrees.

"Hey, I'm not blaming you. Just figured I'd check in. Captain Chui will have all our hides if we don't bring you back in one piece."

"She'll space us *all* if we don't come back in one piece," I said with a tentative smile. "Thanks, Corporal."

The environmental controls helped cool me down a bit, which made the trek easier. Even so, six hours was a long time, and we couldn't afford to waste a second. We kept moving as the sun climbed higher in the sky. The gunnery sergeant assigned to each platoon called out when we should rest, when we should march, when we should jog, and when we should drink. We took ten minutes for lunch—which, of course, consisted of nutrient-bars—and then we were moving again.

I focused on putting one foot in front of the other; focused quite intensely, in fact. I didn't want to think about all the fears crowding up my mind. I did keep an eye on the Psittacans, but they seemed to be getting on just fine. And I kept wishing that Diver was here with me, or maybe Kiri. Maybe both. *I hope they'll be okay.* Maybe this would feel a bit easier if I could be certain they were safe.

It took me a while to realize that the dark line slowly drawing along the horizon was the jungle we'd come looking for. I only noticed when the Psittacans started chatting excitedly to one another. They spoke without using their translators, and it occurred to me then that they could easily sound like local fauna. Especially to people who didn't *know* the local fauna. *And the LHFH isn't very good about getting to know alien life. Hmm…*

By the time we reached the edge of the jungle, I had an idea. I watched the troops fall into place, separating out into fire teams, then squads, each grouped with their proper platoon. Only my four Alpha Team soldiers and the Psittacans stood apart. I took a deep breath and approached one of the gunnery sergeants. *Why'd it have to be a Kowari?* They always got cranky in full armor, since it meant restrictive garments on their tails and ears.

"Um…" I began. "Gunnery Sergeant, uh…"

"Jemison," she told me, looking down at me from an impressive two meters twenty. "You're the one in charge of the Psittacans, yes?"

The idea of anyone being "in charge" of the Psittacans was more than a little absurd, but I bit my tongue on that. "Yes, ma'am. I was thinking... maybe we should just let them use their own language? I know what a lot of their signals mean, for this sort of thing, at least. The LHFH doesn't know much about them at all, and will likely mistake their calls for local fauna. I thought there might be less risk of drawing attention to ourselves that way..."

She studied me for a moment, and I thought maybe I'd over-stepped. Then she nodded. "It's not a bad plan. Do you know what their own plans are?"

"No, ma'am. But when it comes to jungles, it's best to let Psittacans do what they do best. I'll make sure they know to tell us the real important bits, though."

"You do that. Go see where they want us."

Her tone was brusque, but at least she didn't bare her teeth at me. I gave a small nod and turned to trudge over to the Psittacans. It came as no surprise that they wanted us in the jungle itself. That was the sort of warfare they knew best.

With the approval of both lieutenants, I gave the Psittacans the lead as we marched beneath the trees. Both smart-fab and armor shifted immediately, taking on the dark greens and browns and light sun-dappling of the environment. Only one of the Psittacans—Silence In The Night—blended down here, but they, I knew, would do a lot of their work up in the canopy.

"This," Many Kills said at last, coming to a stop in a semi-clearing, "will do as a base. Not prime for Psittacans, but best for the rest of you." He looked up and carried on, talking mainly to his fellow Psittacans. "We will set up rigs first, yes? To lift them into the trees."

"Best place," Day Dawns Red agreed. "Tailless bald monkeys never learned to look up." Her crest came up partway, a clear signal of embarrassment, and she glanced over her wing at us. "No offense."

The chuckles in the clearing seemed to relieve her.

There wasn't much else to do but let them go about their business. I sat against the boll of a sizeable tree, with Emin, Anton, Jae and Amelia, as the Psittacans made quick work of setting up rigging. They raced up into the trees, claws gouging into bark and wings flapping wildly as they ran up the trunks, causing every soldier in the clearing to stare in amazement. As the Psittacans disappeared into the foliage, my entourage turned their stares on me.

"Did you know they could do that?" Anton demanded.

"What, WAIR? Of course I knew they could do that."

Jae raised an eyebrow. "Ware?"

"WAIR. Wing-assisted incline running. It's common among anything with feathers covering a significant portion of their bodies," I explained. "Many Ancient Earth birds can do it. Even chickens."

Emin shook his head. "Fucking aliens, man. They're weird."

"But I just said that even chickens—"

"*Anyway*," Jae put in sharply, cutting off my pedantry. "What did they mean by rigs?"

"They'll set it up so we can get into the trees easily. Then they'll probably—oh." I paused as a vine rope slithered down next to me.

Many Kills and Shadows Beneath Sunlight came down from the trees, their wings fluttering to slow their drop and soften their landing. Once again they drew stares.

"We will need someone to test it," Sunlight declared.

"I'll do it," Anton offered. "Got bones like a dinosaur, so it shouldn't hurt too much if you drop me."

Perhaps it was nerves getting to me, because I couldn't help blurting out, "Actually, dinosaurs had hollow bones. But they were filled with struts, like Psittacan and bird bones, so..."

I trailed off as Sunlight's crest flicked in a Psittacan eye roll and sank against the tree trunk, embarrassed. As Sunlight began instructing Anton in putting on the rigging, Many Kills wandered over to me and crouched. His legs folded beneath him, making him look as if he was brooding a rather large egg. To my surprise, he pinged my private comm channel. Psittacans almost never bothered with privacy; probably something to do with growing up without walls.

"*Nervous, Xandri-bird?*" he sub-vocalized.

"*What gave it away?*" I returned wryly.

His beak clacked. "*All will be well. We have big plans for this little jungle. No one will get past us.*"

"*So...so you realize you'll have to kill, right? I know you prefer to take prisoners, but the LHFH...*"

"*Are xenophobic bastards who would rather die than surrender, yes, and will kill us without even half of a second thought. We are prepared.*" Many cocked his head to one side to study me. "*And you, Xandri-bird? You don't like to kill. Though... it is my guess that you have done so before.*"

I stared at him, and suddenly I was glad he'd chosen to make this conversation private. I pressed shaking hands against my thighs. *I don't want to talk about this. Not now. Not ever.* And how could Many even know that? It was one of the things that no one, not even Captain Chui, knew about me. She didn't know about the knife, the blood, the feeling of triumph and all the regret I'd never once felt.

"*Among my people, we kill for two reasons,*" Many went on. "*To feed ourselves, and to destroy an existential threat. Don't worry, Xandri-bird. I will tell the others to watch for your shots. We will finish your work for you.*"

"All set," Sunlight announced, before I could respond. "All right, Anton, you just cut this rope here..."

A second later Anton shot up into the branches, howling the whole way. Sunlight and Many gazed up after him, their crests slicked most of the way back, with only the ends sticking out straight. I'd pinned that one down to something like chagrin, a bit the way a cat got when it accidentally fell off something: unable to decide whether it was more upset and embarrassed because it had fallen in the first place, or because someone had seen it do so.

"Perhaps we should have warned him?" Sunshine suggested tentatively.

"I'm all right," Anton called down. "Think my heart's still down there somewhere, but I'm all right."

"Then let us continue! There is much to be done!" Many declared.

I glanced into the darkness of the jungle. Much to be done, yes. And we had no idea how long we'd have to do it.

The Psittacans worked tirelessly. Within an hour, they had us all rigged up and had disappeared deeper into the jungle to set up traps. There was little for any of us to do. While the watchers stayed vigilant, Anton, Emin, Jae and Amelia roped me into a game of *shasinki*. I didn't know Emin and Jae well enough, but Anton and Amelia were open books, so I won about half the hands we played. I never failed to beat Amelia, who had a habit of twitching her ears whenever her hand was good.

Darkness came earlier beneath the canopy than it otherwise would. At the behest of our gunnery sergeants we ate a quick meal, then slid our visors into position for night vision. By then, I was beginning to wonder. What was the LHFH planning? To come under the cover of darkness? I didn't like the idea of fighting at night, but it would be the more foolish choice for them to make. The idea of being out here in the forest, with Silence In The Night searching for me, gave me the cold shivers.

The lieutenants were settling down to discuss watch hours when it happened. A call went up in the night, raucous and ear-piercing. Several calls answered. If I hadn't known better, I'd have thought it was simply a flock of local bird-like creatures, calling to each other to 'check in' before bed. But I happened to know those cries.

"*Lieutenants,*" I sub-vocalized into the private channel meant for all the troops.

"*That was the Psittacans?*" someone asked in returned.

"*It was. The enemy is coming.*"

With that, I cut the anchor on my rig and it hauled me, swiftly and soundlessly, up into the branches above.

Chapter Twenty-Three

Diver

"But Captain, there's no sign of any soldiers out there right now!"

I looked up from my holo-slate, wondering if Captain Chui was, even now, contemplating smacking Casaria. She'd been furious when she had to send out troops to bring the biologist back to shore, and Captain Chui furious was scary as fuck. Far scarier than Casaria, who was trying that look-down-the-nose trick Sanavila liked so damn much. Aleevian mainly looked relieved to be safely back on dry land.

"I don't care who or what is or is not out there," Captain Chui returned, dangerously soft-voiced. "I gave you an order, and you disobeyed."

"But—"

"Enough!" Captain Chui shot Casaria a look of disgust, then turned to Leev. "On the other hand, sil mas Viara, I understand they found *you* halfway back to shore."

"I work as Aki's copilot, ma'am. I've learned to obey orders, regardless of whether or not they suit my preferences."

Casaria glared at him. Didn't really blame her, he was a real smug bastard. *But in this case, he's also right.* I turned back to the holo-slate. Kiri, sitting across from me, was caught up in a bit of hacking she didn't need me for, so I was going over my plans. Or trying. Kept catching myself thinking about Xandri, worrying, wondering if she was okay. Things were just starting out between us, and now...

Well, fuck it. Had my big boy pants on, might as well accept what I was feeling. Sure, I didn't know what I was gonna *do* about it; all I knew was that I wanted her in my life, and so that was that. Being stuck here, not knowing what was happening to her *and* not having much to do, it was making me space-fried. *At least the gorilla ought to touch down shortly.* I'd want to give it a look, make sure everything was operational.

"And what about tomorrow?" Casaria was saying. "If there's still no attack tomorrow, I don't see why we shouldn't—"

"Did you listen to a single word I just said?" Captain Chui snapped. "You're not going back out there until it's safe. End of story."

"And anyway," Leev added in a mutter, "there's no way in hell I'm going back out there with you right now."

Captain Chui sighed. "That's enough out of both of you. Dismissed! And don't make me have to put guards on you, Casaria; I *need* my goddamn soldiers right now."

It looked like Casaria might protest, which made me wonder, because I was pretty sure she'd been with us even longer than Xandri. But Leev grabbed her arm and, ignoring her snappish insults, dragged her out of the room. *Gotta give him some credit for that. Takes balls, messing with an angry woman.* At least, it did aboard the *Carpathia.* Captain Chui liked 'em on the vicious side.

"Scientists," Captain Chui groaned, turning to face the window.

I cleared my throat. "*We're* scientists."

"But not Sanavila, so you actually have *some* sense."

Her words came out distracted as she gazed out onto the beach. I sat up straight and peered past her, out the window. Helluva lot of bustle on the beach, that was for sure. The remaining platoon, under Captain Rhees' instruction, was building some kind of trap. Looked like trip wires. They used driftwood, bleached as white as the sand, and hammered it down into the ground near the edge of the water. The wire was clear, so it would all blend. Anyone who tried to come at us from the water would be hard-pressed to avoid those.

Ping! The sound startled us all, even Captain Chui, though she hid it better. Kiri, on the other hand, yelped and looked up, dazed. Wondered if she'd heard any of what'd gone down with Casaria and Leev. She'd been working hard, her focus now on those LHFH ships and their sneaks-works. And I knew once she'd gotten all that clear, she'd be back to nosing about those reporters' ship, without a thought to her own well-being. In that way, she reminded me of Xan.

"Chui," Captain Chui said, answering the ping.

"No sign of enemy troops yet," came Rhees' voice, "but we've got...well, one of your shuttles swung by, dropped something off at the edge of our perimeter."

"Is it big, made of metal, and looks somewhat like it was built by a mad scientist?"

"I...yes, actually."

"Mr. Diver," Captain Chui said over her shoulder to me, "looks like your gorilla has arrived. Go have a look."

"Aye, aye, cap'n," I joked, relieved to have something to do with my hands.

"He should keep an eye out on the way," Rhees warned. "There's a lot going on out here. The soldiers will warn him if he gets too close to something."

As if I couldn't navigate my way around traps. But I didn't say a word, just closed up my holo-slate, locked it down, and left the office. Glanced back over my shoulder once, to see Kiri's attention back on her work. As I made my way through the corridor, towards the exit, I pinged Captain Chui's private comm channel and waited. I was just stepping outside when she got back to me.

"*Yes, Mr. Diver?*"

"You're gonna keep an eye on her, right? Make sure she don't run herself ragged?"

"*What an absurd question. Of course I will. Now get to work.*"

If she'd had a receiver to slam, she would have. I grinned. *Right. Never question the caretaking abilities of an ex-gunnery sergeant.*

Even though everything looked good, I still spent some time rubbing the gorilla down with oil and a rag, until the metal gleamed like silver chrome. Was about as elegant as this monster would ever look.

In shape, it did vaguely resemble an Ancient Earth gorilla; even moved in a similar way. But the head didn't have mouth and eyes, it had weapons, small guns with a surprising amount of oomph. Larger guns stood in two rows of two on the heavily armored chest, with a few extra surprises at the shoulders. Despite its bulk, the gorilla moved fast, and it didn't *need* guns to take people down. I could control the arms, smashing and throwing like a real gorilla would. Once I armored myself up, I could fit into the hollow in its back.

All because one day I decided military designs for armored vehicles were boring as fuck.

Can't use it to distract you all day. I sighed, tossed the rag aside, and swiped my hands clean on my shorts. *Maybe I should go check on Kiri.* I'd been outside for hours now. Wouldn't be long before the sun started to set. Last I knew, the LHFHers were still out above the water and hadn't made any move to do anything. Certainly they hadn't shown up while I'd been at work.

I retrieved the rag, tossing it idly from hand to hand as I strode carefully across the beach. Captain Rhees stood near the entrance with the entire platoon; debriefing, probably. And then suddenly someone was running up the beach, leaping to avoid the hidden traps. Even though the figure was a blur, I recognized Marla. She'd been in track and field once, according to Xan. *Coulda probably made a career of it, too, from the looks of things.* She reminded me a bit of the *carouas* back on Cochinga, fleet and lithe.

"Captain!" she called as she ran. "Captain Rhees, we've got trouble!"

The soldiers came to attention like dominoes in reverse, the lieutenant in charge of the platoon straightening first, with all the others following sharply after. I sped up. If we were gonna have soldiers landing, I wanted to be there to punch them in the face. With the gorilla.

"Easy, Ms. Thomas," Captain Rhees said, as Marla skidded to a halt. "Just take a deep breath and tell me what's going on."

"I was on the docks, talking to Bright," Marla explained, only slightly out of breath. "Boats. The LHFH has been dropping boats. Collapsible pod boats, mainly, that they dropped from the Crystalliads. Mostly of them are small but—apparently they were using the Harriers to construct a larger one they could drop from a safer distance. The Hands and Voices intend to go after them, and they're asking for our help."

Captain Rhees didn't hesitate. "Captain Chui? I need you outside immediately."

"On my way," Captain Chui replied through the comm.

She might as well have teleported, she got there so fucking fast. Magellan had come with her, and at Captain Rhees' request, Marla repeated her news. Captain Chui's expression never changed, but I'd been on the *Carpathia* some time now. I could see it in her eyes, the gears turning away.

"Interesting," Magellan said. "They waited for us."

"Yes." Marla nodded. "In fact, Bright said that Darksong and Engineer suggested Diver be among the people you send."

That got an awful lot of raised eyebrows in my direction.

"Makes sense," I pointed out. "I know tech, especially weapons. That's probably why they're waiting; they want to know exactly what they're up against before they charge."

Captain Chui shook her head. "I really must stop underestimating them. All right, Mr. Diver, suit up."

"Captain," Marla blurted out, "I want to go too."

"Ms. Thomas, you're not a soldier. I can't allow—"

"Please, Captain. Kirrick can stay and run messages. I...we've wanted to come to Song for such a long time. Am I supposed to just sit around and do nothing while it's under attack?"

Captain Chui tilted her head slightly, reminding me of the Psittacans. Wasn't like Marla—or any of us, really—to speak out of turn to the captain. Orders were orders, to be questioned only if someone felt there was something *wrong* with said orders. But Marla's desire, I could understand it, and I kinda thought Captain Chui did as well. This meant something to all of us.

"Very well. But you're to stay near the back of the fight, am I understood?"

Marla nodded. Captain Chui dismissed us both, and we headed inside. While we climbed into HP suits, a dozen other soldiers filed in to put on wetsuits and armor. *Don't know if this'll be enough...* But we had the Hands and Voices. They had a reputation for being able to deal with boats. I had to wonder what the LHFH was playing at, bringing boats down here. Or were they so damned prejudiced, they didn't believe the stories? Sorta scary, how likely that was.

Once in suit, I grabbed my guns and hooked my Barracuda to my belt. Still wished I had a good place for a knife or two. Never underestimate the value of a melee weapon.

"We're going to need as many here as you can spare," I heard Captain Chui say as I headed back outside. "I doubt the Hands and Voices intend to let them make landfall, but if any significant portion of troops slips past, we'll be completely overwhelmed."

On the other end of the comm, Major Douglas snorted. "The day Captain Chui Shan Fung is completely overwhelmed is the day Zechak join the AFC. But I'll send what I can. I want to keep the ground between here and the jungle covered, too."

"Understood. Chui out."

She shook a hand at me, a hurry-along gesture, and I headed down to the dock, following the footsteps of the other soldiers to avoid the traps. Voices awaited us in the water, all of them in the range of Darksong's size. The soldiers—all from the AFC—lingered uncertainly on the dock. I commanded my armor to unfold into place and jumped right in.

Something moved in the water as I went under, and a rather large head collided with me, forcing me back to the surface.

"Hello, Diver," greeted a familiar voice.

"Darksong!"

"Come. And tell your fellows to hurry. It grows dark and we must be on the move."

"You heard her," Marla hollered from up on the docks. "Let's move it, people!"

Someone missed their calling as a sergeant, I thought, as Marla dove in. Considering we were both technically civvies, and soldiers hated being shown up by civvies, they were soon following us into the water. I reached up, grasping Darksong's dorsal fin and hauling myself onto her back. Tentacles crept up to wrap around my legs, and I had to smirk a little when several soldiers yelped as they received similar treatment. When I glanced over my shoulder to check the Hands, all of them had raised one tentacle, folding the filaments into the thumbs-up gesture I'd taught Engineer.

Despite the urgency of the situation, I grinned and flashed a thumbs-up in return.

The second we were ready, the Voices took off, skimming rapidly through the water. I leaned low against Darksong's back. Water splashed up around me, speckling my visor; above, the sun was sinking towards the horizon. *Don't like the look of that one bit.* I turned on the light on my HP suit. Out here, without a kilometer or so of water on top of me, the light was much brighter, spilling across the water ahead of us.

Soon the sound of gun fire reached my ears. I closed my eyes, listened. Big fucking guns, from the sound of it, but they'd still need a lot of ammo to damage larger Voices with them.

Shapes loomed in the dusk light. Boats. And in the water, Voices, several dozen of them, circling the boats in much the same way that the Disharmonies had circled the reporters. Excitement and a slight twinge of worry set my pulse racing. I sat up straight and commanded my visor to zoom, trying to get a better look at the LHFHers' weapons. *Hmm…those look a bit like Gabes, but they ain't actually Gabes…*

"What do you see, friend Diver?" Darksong asked.

"Most of what they got—that I can see, mind you, they might got something hidden—won't hurt you easily. You should still take care, but it won't pierce your armor without difficulty. You see them big guns though? Tell everyone to steer clear of them."

Song carried through the water around us, loud and piercing in the falling night. Startled LHFH soldiers whipped around in their boats, looking for the source, a few of them firing aimlessly. I pulled out one of my pistols, a heavy—and heavily modified—Scorpion Mk. XX. The other soldiers were pulling their weapons too, and even Marla drew hers. Adjusting my HUD for targeting, I took aim and fired back.

"Tell 'em to stay clear of the biggest boat!" I shouted over renewed yelling and increased gunfire. "Odds are good their heaviest hitting stuff is there."

While Darksong sang more orders, something began to happen. I hadn't noticed anything going on *beneath* the water, being so focused on the surface. Us non-ocean dwellers, we all focused on the surface—until something sent one of the smallest boats shooting about two meters into the air. It careened in mid-air, listing to the side and spilling its passengers into the ocean. And another boat followed quickly after. A short glanced showed me dark, large shapes disappearing back into the depths.

"In the water!" Marla shouted, aiming for the men and women now paddling frantically towards other boats.

A smaller Voice darted through the fray, allowing its Hands to grab and haul in one of the soldiers. A chirp of gleeful song rang out as the Hands slung the soldier forward and the Voice caught him in its teeth. I winced at the crunching sound of the soldier's armor collapsing beneath the pressure of a bite four and a half tons strong. Assuming there was anything left to find of that one, they'd be identifying him by his nanos.

I funneled all my focus into shooting, while around me the world became a blur of screaming and shots fired and boats shunted into the air. Smaller Voices and their Hands made careful forays into the heat of battle to grab the soldiers our shots missed. Darksong squealed triumphant song as one of those soldiers came flying our way. Her Hands grabbed the soldier, swathing him in tentacles. The soldier screamed as his helmet was torn away, and kept screaming until tentacles covered his entire face, muffling him. I shuddered. *Scratch that whole 'innocence' thing.*

The body hit the water with a faint splash.

Darksong and the other Voices kept moving, kept circling, all the while. Some Hands caught soldiers and dragged them along; others dragged them under the water, down into the depths. And all the while it grew darker, grew harder to see. I swore, adjusted my HUD again and took aim, but missed. *Why ain't they leaving? We've given 'em hell!* But I knew. If Xandri was here, she'd point out that xenophobic, brainwashed zealots like this wouldn't let a little thing like death stop them.

Rat-tat-tat-tat. The sound rang out in the night, and despite the speed of it, I *knew* it wasn't a Gabe. It was bigger, hella bigger, probably mounted on the largest ship at the middle of all this, the one we hadn't gotten near yet. *There's one…no, at least two, from the sound of it.* Maybe more. And that boat was no flimsy collapsible. Even strikes from breaching Voices wouldn't take it down easy. *Shit. Shit!*

Wasn't a panicking type of guy, normally, but it was a hard urge to fight. Especially when a stream of song was cut off and faded into a whimper of pain. To watch a Voice—such a large and powerful being—struggle to swim away, trailing blood in the water; the sight just pulled the courage right outta my guts.

"Fall back!" Marla shouted, before any of our own soldiers could get the idea. They started echoing her immediately.

"She's right," I told Darksong. "Tell them to fall back. This strategy ain't gonna work on that thing."

Damnit. Fucking damn it all to hell. I kept firing while Darksong and the others swam a distance from the boats, until we were too far for it to do any good. I slammed my pistol back into the holster, frustrated.

"What is that thing?" Marla called to me.

"In exact terms? No idea. But we gotta find a way to get rid of it."

Darksong and her fellows had been singing back and forth the whole time. Now, she spoke to me. "Would you be willing to help us distract the soldiers on the large boat?"

"We can try our damnedest." I twisted towards the AFC soldiers. "You guys hear that? They need a distraction."

"Then that's what we'll give them," someone answered.

The Voices closed in again, just enough for us to fire. It didn't matter if we hit a fucking thing; we just had to keep the fuckers on the boat dancing. Smaller Voices darted around to distract the crews of the few remaining small boats. Before long, someone started screaming bloody murder.

"What is it? *What is it!?*"

Darksong completed half a circle and slowed. And that's when I saw what 'it' was. My jaw damn near hit the sea bottom and for a moment, I forgot to fire. Primordial fear rose in my throat at the sight of the Grand Matriarch shooting through the water, headed straight for the boat. *Oh shit, oh shit. Fucking hell, I'm glad I'm down here. Shit.*

"Shoot it!" someone shrieked. "Shoot! Shoot!"

Good fucking luck with that. She came low in the water, her Hands clinging to her underbelly—at least, that was my best guess—only her armor exposed. The resumed *rat-tat-tat* of the guns broke through my shock, and I started firing again, aiming as best I could at the soldiers manning the turret gun. Bullets struck the water; a few struck the Matriarch's armor, but didn't seem to do much.

The boom as she collided with the boat was so loud, I was amazed the damn thing didn't shatter to pieces. It rocked wildly to one side, down towards the water. The crew screamed and scrambled; some of them fell in. I held my breath, wondering if the boat would right itself—and tentacles shot up out of the water beneath it, winding around rigging and struts, anywhere they could grab. I couldn't see it, but I could imagine their Voices diving deeper, using the strength of their swimming to drag the boat under. And under it went, the water burbling and bubbling around it, desperate LHFHers trying to get away. For a moment, I felt sorry for them. Then I remembered Christa's breathless report, and the feeling died.

The terror of being dragged into the depths to a watery grave was too primal for even the worst fanaticism to overcome. The few small boats that were left started to turn, started to speed away, their crews working frantically, all thoughts of combat washed from their minds.

"We shouldn't let them go," I told Darksong, speaking up over the din of celebratory song.

"They are retreating. It is not our way to kill those who have surrendered."

"And I respect that, but retreat and surrender aren't the same thing. Especially not for these—"

"Diver! In the air!" Marla shouted.

I looked up. Several Harriers loomed above us, large enough to blot out patches of stars. They weren't retreating, just sort of drifting up there in a way that set my stomach boiling with nerves. My fingers tightened around the grip of my pistol. *Something tells me they ain't planning to give the boat thing another shot...*

Chapter Twenty-Four

Xandri

We waited, all of us silent. I'd gotten myself fairly comfortable in the wedge formed where branch met trunk and sat as still as I could, listening. Another cry from the Psittacans, one I didn't know the translation for; I did, however, recognize that they were communicating with each other, not us. Then came a deep-throated *skraw* sound that I *did* know: It meant that Silence In The Night was in place.

"*Are we really sure about this?*" someone spoke over the comm, much to my annoyance.

"*Uh, Dan, I don't think—*"

"*No, I'm serious here. I know Captain Chui thinks highly of the girl and the birds, but putting them in charge of this entire mission?*"

"*Dan...*"

"*Especially after what happened on Cochinga. Bran Halifax was a friend of mine, you know, and as far as I'm concerned, it's her fault he's—*"

"*Boys,*" cut in a new voice: Gunnery Sergeant Jemison, "*even if this was a private channel—and by now I'm sure it's gotten into your thick skull, Private Marten, that it is not—now is hardly the time for tea and a chitchat. Be quiet!*"

"*Yes, Gunny,*" they replied in unison.

Dead, I thought, finishing Private Marten's sentence. *It's my fault his friend is dead.* I pressed up hard against the tree trunk, wishing I had room to draw my legs against my chest. I felt a sudden, pressing need to be as small as possible. No matter how good the Psittacans were, no matter that we had the advantage of a high position, there were a lot of soldiers out there; people were going to die tonight, even some of our own. Would they blame me for that, too?

A hand landed on my shoulder, heavy enough that I felt it through the armor. I glanced up and found Anton watching me.

"Ignore them. They're wrong," he whispered. He who had more reason than most to be angry at my mistakes on Cochinga. "And once the Psittacans get to work, those guys'll be eating crow."

"Thanks, Anton," I murmured with a tentative smile. My night vision showed him grinning in return.

A shrill cry, a screech somewhere between a movie-monster roar and nails down a blackboard, shattered the momentary quiet. Branches rustled faintly as a number of soldiers jumped. And then that low sound was drowned out by gunfire, and screaming, *horrible* screaming. There was such terror in that sound, sharp-edged terror that cut through me like a hot knife. It occurred to me then that we had let these people walk into their very worst nightmare, and for a moment I couldn't move for the guilt.

For once, the voice at the back of my mind had all the sense. *If their worst nightmare is the people they want to oppress and kill fighting back against them, then* they *are the ones with the problem.* I shook loose of the guilt. I'd rather no one got killed at all, but if the LHFHers didn't want to wind up dead, they could just as well have not attacked Song.

"*Any ideas what's going on, Corelel?*" Jemison asked.

"*Judging by the screams? Nothing pretty. They'll—*" I paused. Many Kills and I had worked a bit of this sort of thing out, and now I recognized his voice screeching a familiar pattern. "*The LHFHers are on the move. Many and the others will do their best to herd them in our direction while taking more out. Their traps should help with that, too.*"

"*Good. Let me know if you learn anything more.*"

I wished desperately for my sound dampeners. Instead, I gripped an Atrox tight, digging at it with the tips of my fingers. The sounds grew louder. A heavy crash somewhere off to the west was probably some kind of trap triggering. More screams. Sweet Mother Universe, I wanted to run. It was like being assaulted from all sides by knives. *But I will not break. I* will *protect Song, no matter what.*

The first LHFH soldiers appeared in our semi-clearing, obviously panicked. In the darkness, several of them got tangled up in a trip-wire and went down; several more, right behind the first, tripped over them. I couldn't help myself; as our own soldiers shot them, I winced. *Damnit, Xan, you're in a paramilitary organization.*

You've got to stop with the squeamishness. But I didn't see any way it could ever seem right, killing another living sapient. Necessary and right, I reminded myself, could not always be the same thing.

"*Xandri-bird,*" Many Kills contacted me suddenly, "*Sunlight and Dawn are heading your way with two platoons. Many have scattered, many have died, but there were thousands to begin with, and still thousands to deal with.*"

"*Soldiers, coming our way, two platoons worth,*" I repeated, even though the others had likely heard. "*Thanks, Many.*"

My heart raced. It seemed to take forever for the soldiers to arrive; it also seemed to take no time at all. They came less panicked, more alert, especially when they saw their dead fellows. Even though I knew the plan was to stay safely in the trees, I worried. The plan couldn't survive intact. Yes, right now the LHFHers were looking around at eye level, but eventually they'd have to catch on.

"*Open fire,*" both lieutenants commanded at once, and their gunnies repeated the order.

I was the only one shooting to stun, but it didn't matter. Projectiles rained down on the LHFHers. Some of them ducked. A few of them noticed us and fired back. Many more of them died. I noticed movement to one side and shifted, catching sight of an LHFHer making a run for it. Almost, I let him go. Out of pity, I stunned him. Sunlight appeared, leaping out of the darkness; she caught his shoulder with one clawed foot and opened his throat with the other before he even hit the ground.

"*Cease fire! Reload!*"

On the ground, only Sunlight and Dawn moved. They used their feet to turn over bodies, checking for soldiers who had survived being shot or who I had stunned. I looked away, and didn't look up again, even when that familiar touch settled on my shoulder, and my private channel pinged.

"*You know,*" Anton said, "*I'm starting to get what Diver means when he says reading you is easy. You ain't really got the heart for killing.*"

"*I'll do it if I end up with no other choice. But…no. I don't like it one bit. I'd much rather we could take them as prisoners, but I know—*" A warning cry cut me off.

"*Xandri-bird, there's at least a company coming your way. We will try to cut down their numbers as much as possible.*"

My heart sank. A company? That was twice our numbers! "*Gunnery Sergeant Jemison...*"

"*I heard, Corelel. Everyone, get ready!*"

Sweat poured down my back. I shifted my pistol to my left hand long enough to wipe my sweaty palm on a bit of bared smart-fab. *Any minute now. Any minute... Oh, Sweet Mother Universe...*

Someone must've warned them. As they burst into the clearing where we waited, they aimed up. Only the dark—difficult to penetrate even with night vision—kept us safe; they couldn't see well enough to hit us. Leaves and twigs rained down around us, which didn't help *our* aim much either. Yet it was chaos down there, and up here we could at least take our time. Far more of our shots connected than theirs.

I didn't know if it was something to do with the autism, or just a knack I had, but I *noticed* things. Odd things, things others often missed. This time, I found my gaze drawn to one soldier, hidden beneath the shade of a tree, outside the range of my stunner. Something about the way he moved, hunched over, his hands at work on something, alerted me. I fiddled with the settings on my visor, using a trick Kiri had taught me to put all of its targeting capacity into zooming in.

The soldier stepped from behind the tree, lifting something metallic and cube-like in shape. Shock held me speechless for a moment, then I blurted out, "That's experimental tech! He shouldn't have that!"

I didn't think; there wasn't time. Gripping the rope vine rigging me up, I launched myself out of the tree. Anton and Jae both made a grab for me, but I was already swinging through the air. I twisted, lifting my legs so I wouldn't hit anyone else, wouldn't lose the speed of my swing. The soldier caught sight of me a second too late. Before he could dodge, I slammed into him, knocking him off his feet.

I let go, remembering just in time to roll with the fall. Even so, the landing hurt like fuck. Aching and bruised, I shot up onto my hands and knees, looking around frantically for the device. *Where is it? Where, where, where—ah!* I pounced. A boot caught me in the side, an unintentional glance rather than a kick. I gritted my teeth and ignored it, closing my fingers around the boxy bit of tech.

"*Corelel!*" Gunnery Sergeant Jemison bellowed—and let me tell you, sub-vocalized bellowing was a trick only gunnies seemed to know. *"What in the everloving fuck do you think you're doing?"*

No time to answer. I scrambled to my feet. The back of my brain screamed in terror, knowing I could be shot at any second, but I ignored it and hurled the device as far away from me as I possibly could.

It wasn't quite far enough.

Whump! The sound wave radiated out from the device. It felt as if the very air around me was being shaken by a violent quake. A swath of LHFH troops were thrown back. The trees shook from the force, shedding a number of our soldiers; were it not for the rigging, the fall might have been enough to kill them, or seriously injure them. I had just enough time to notice, with a small spark of pleasure, that I'd gotten the grenade far enough away that most of our soldiers remained in the trees, before something crashed into me.

I wheezed as the air was knocked out of me. Hands grabbed my shoulders and shoved me down, into the shelter of a tree trunk. I looked up, dazed, into Anton's angry, visor-shielded face. Beyond him I noticed our soldiers descending from the trees in a much more controlled manner than the LHFHers had intended.

"Stay here!" Anton growled. "I mean it, Xandri."

I didn't protest. I huddled there as our soldiers took advantage of the damage the grenade had done, shooting down the LHFHers trying to straggle back to their feet. *There's so many of them...*

But there were still traps, and we had the Psittacans. Swifter Than Lightning had joined Dawn and Sunlight, picking off soldiers at the edge of the group. Some of ours remained in the trees, enough to help pick off even more. Even so, I saw two *Carpathia* soldiers go down in short order, riddled by too many shots for their armor to protect them. I dug my teeth into my lip to hold back a cry and took aim, able to stun one of the LHFHers who'd done the deed.

I tried to keep my wits about me even with the chaos swirling around me. A few more LHFH soldiers trickled in, only to be cut down by Sunlight. Another of our soldiers went down. At one point someone grabbed me from behind and I swung around, stunning them square in the chest on instinct. Maybe I should've stopped to wonder why they hadn't just shot me, but there wasn't time.

I recognized the fourth soldier who went down.

Even with her back to me, even with the armor obscuring the color of her fur, even with only night vision to aid me, I knew it was Amelia. A scream caught in my throat. Forgetting everything I'd been told, I shot to my feet, darting out of cover. Shots whizzed past me as I hurried to Amelia's side, praying she wasn't hit too badly. If she could recover, if her personal 'bots could do enough to save her...

"Corelel!" Gunnery Sergeant Jemison roared.

Part of my mind noticed that instead of shooting, a group of LHFHers was coming towards me. Most of my focus was on Amelia, who rolled over with a wheezing groan. For a moment my heart lifted with hope. The sheer number of bullet holes and the blood leaking out of them dashed that hope immediately.

In a fury, I turned my attention on the approaching group of soldiers, who slipped in and out of the shelter of trees, trying not to be shot as they came for me. I grabbed my second Atrox and flipped the stun setting on both pistols to the highest it would go. Holding them out in front of me, I waited, judging the distance— and pulled the triggers. The force scattered them like bowling pins, throwing them to the ground and into tree trunks.

"You're not the only ones with experimental tech," I said.

"Xandri..."

Surprised, I looked down at Amelia.

"Get...get off...the battlefield," she wheezed.

"But I..."

She bared her teeth. "Now!"

I went, stumbling my way back into cover. The shooting resumed. *Why...why would they stop shooting while I was out there?* I suddenly remembered the one who'd tried to grab me, and my stomach clenched. Oh God, if they recognized me, if they knew who I was... *Don't think about that now. No time.*

It felt like it would never end. The only thing that kept me from curling up and crying was the fact that our soldiers were so superior. The LHFH may have gotten their hands on some good tech, but they didn't have enough training to use it all properly. And none of them had heavy gunners. Our soldiers switched back and forth; whenever they were reloading their rams, our heavies opened fire with their Gabes, and vice versa.

A squawk behind me made me twist around. It was easy to forget that the battle was raging elsewhere, not just in our little alley. One of the Psittacans—Lightning or Sunlight, judging by the appearance of their yellow feathers in my night vision—huddled in the growth, favoring a wing-arm against their side. I made swift adjustments to my pistol settings and shot the soldier aiming for my friend.

The Psittican's crest came up all the way. The front feather tipped forward just a bit, marking him as Lightning.

"Over here!" I hissed.

I leaned out from behind my cover, taking aim into the jungle to ward off anyone who might take a shot at him. *You bastards are* not *taking another one of my friends!* For the first time in my years aboard the *Carpathia*, I was tempted to change my pistol to kill settings. But I kept it to stun, and the other Psittacans emerged every time a soldier went down, to finish the job. By the time Lightning reached me, the Gabes were roaring again.

"*It's not that bad,*" Lightning insisted, as soon as we were both crouched in the shelter of my tree.

"*Let me see,*" I demanded.

Inspecting his wing distracted me from the noise. A strip of feathers was gone, and whatever they'd used had been an energy weapon, judging from the thin burn on his flesh. When I poked it carefully, Lightning snapped his beak at me. His crest came up— then immediately went down in embarrassment.

"*I can still fight. I can use it, I was just stunned.*"

"*Be careful. If it gives you any trouble at all, get under cover and stay there.*"

Lightning reached for me suddenly, his beak opening in surprise. Injured, his reflexes were slowed. He couldn't quite grab me before someone caught my shoulder and yanked me out of the shelter of the tree. I stumbled, struggling to get my feet under me as Lightning let out a raucous warning cry. *Oh, no. No, no, no. One kidnapping a standard is my fucking limit.* I twisted like an angry cat and jammed the muzzle of my pistol against the first armored surface I found.

A hand grabbed my wrist before I could fire and twisted so hard, I screamed. Pain shot down my arm and it took every ounce of willpower not to drop my gun. Then suddenly the pain eased as the soldier went down in a heap.

I turned, rubbing my arm. There stood Jae—I knew it was vir because not many of our soldiers were that tiny. I opened my mouth to thank vir, but gunfire drowned out my words. Jae grunted and half spun, before going down in a heap. My heart stuttered and I forgot I was on a battlefield, that people were shooting, that someone was trying to kidnap me. *No. No, not vir too!* Heedless, I started toward the place where vi'd fallen.

"Mother fucking ow!" Jae popped back up, rolling vir injured shoulder. "When I find out who—Xandri, down!"

I hit the deck. Shots arced over my head and Psittacan war cries filled the air. As did the screams of the dying. I waited it out, my arm and wrist still throbbing beneath armor and wristlet. God, how I wanted it to be over, all of it, the entire fight. I was no soldier. What had Captain Chui been thinking, sending me out here?

"All right, c'mon," Jae said, beckoning me over. "And stop wandering off!"

"I didn't wander off," I complained as I hurried back to the tree. "Someone else wandered me!"

"I can vouch for that," Lightning put in.

"Well, guess I'd better stay and make sure no one 'wanders' you again."

I glanced at vir shoulder. Despite vir bravado, the wound looked bad. Vi slumped against the tree trunk with vir ram propped on vir knees, and I settled next to vir, like some kind of watch, as if we were keeping lookout. A pseudo-anthropologist/pseudo-diplomat and two injured warriors. *Some line of defense we make.*

It was the longest night of my life. I thought it would never end. All the gunfire filled the air with smoke and vile smell, and as the sun began to climb above the horizon, shedding reddish-orange light beneath the canopy, I began to grasp the Christian image of Hell. At first I didn't even notice how much the gunfire had lessened, I was so exhausted and overwrought. When I began to realize the noise was fading, I slumped against the tree.

I started awake when a hand came down on my shoulder. *Shit. Did I really fall asleep?* I blinked up through my grimy visor and saw Emin and Anton looming above me. Glancing to my side, I saw Jae and Lightning dozing too, though Jae's eyes came open almost immediately. When I first tried to speak, only a croak came out.

"You three all right?" Anton asked.

"They—they're injured," I said, raising a weary hand to point at my companions.

Jae groaned. "Tattletale."

"Anyone real bad?"

Emin had already knelt to inspect Jae. Now that there was some light, I could see that vir personal 'bots had been working for hours. And that the wound must've been pretty brutal to begin with. There was still a huge hole in vir shoulder; the reddish-pink flesh surrounding the wound indicated what the 'bots had managed to patch up. A tiny glisten of white bone showed through, and I shuddered to think of what it had looked like when vi first got it.

"You'll live," Emin declared after a moment.

"Lucky me."

"We got word from Lieutenant Zubairi while you three were out," Anton said, reaching down to help me up. I didn't even think to protest. "The Harriers all lifted a couple hours ago. Both Crystalliads and two Harriers returned to orbit, but the rest are fleeing the system. Estimates put it at something like five-, maybe six-hundred solders that got away."

I looked around. Everywhere my gaze landed, there were piles of LHFH soldiers. And yet, several hundred of them had gotten away from us. *At least they got back in their ships instead of heading for base*, I reminded myself wearily. I let my helmet retract and ran my fingers through hair left grimy and stiff from sweat, all the while turning slowly to inspect the carnage. I froze when I saw the *Carpathia* soldiers laid out on the ground, saw Gunnery Sergeant Jemison crouch to close the first set of unseeing eyes.

Anton gripped my elbow as I stumbled over. I heard the rustle of Jae following, heard the Psittacans chattering as Lightning rejoined them, but all of it reached me vaguely, as if needing to penetrate my sound dampeners.

Jemison rose as I approached, her ears forward. "Only eight," she said. "*Only eight.* I've been at my job more than half my life and

I've never seen anything like it. Nothing short of a miracle."

Eight dead. That didn't seem like a miracle to *me*. I looked down at Amelia's unmoving form and wished—absurdly—that I'd let her win more hands last night.

"And even though Captain Chui will probably skin me for it, we have you to thank, at least in part, Ms. Corelel."

"Hmm?" I couldn't drag my eyes away.

"If the impact from that thing you grabbed had hit us square on, we'd all have come down from the trees unprepared. Would've been sitting ducks. How'd you know what that was, anyway?"

"A good question," someone nearby muttered. "Even better: Why wouldn't the LHFH shoot her?"

I did my best to ignore that. "I'm friends with Diver from R&D. He showed me that earlier this year, in a holo-mail. It's experimental Alliance tech." I frowned. "It's strange enough that they'd have it at all, but... the Alliance isn't developing it for military use. We have better choices for that sort of thing. It's bizarre."

"Oh, they had experimental Alliance tech *and* they refused to shoot her," came the mutter again. "That doesn't sound suspicious at all."

"Private Marten, enough!" Gunnery Sergeant Jemison snapped.

But I was at my wits end and turned on Private Marten. "I don't know why they wouldn't shoot me, *or* why they tried to kidnap me several times during the night, but I'm pretty sure I don't want to know the answer."

"Hey, look, I just find it a little weird, that's all," Marten replied with a smirk. "You seemed pretty reluctant to shoot to kill."

"She never shoots to kill, you asshole," Anton growled.

"Well, I've heard—"

"Fuck you *and* what you've heard," I snapped, losing my grasp on what little cope I had left. "You want to talk shit about me, go ahead, but do it somewhere else. Let the dead rest in peace."

I spun away and dropped to my knees near the last body in the row, reaching to close the soldier's eyes. My hand froze as I recognized the face I was reaching for. It was the corporal from yesterday—was it really only yesterday? The one who had reminded me of my environment controls and teased me gently about Diver.

I'd never gotten the chance to learn his name.

Chapter Twenty-Five

Diver

No matter how I adjusted my HUD, no matter the settings I changed or the way I hooked it into the HP suit's own rig, I couldn't make out what the Harriers were up to. And I didn't like that one fucking bit.

"I think we should leave," I told Darksong.

"And let them slip by us to reach the shore? We think not."

"Look, it ain't that I want to argue with you, but what're we even gonna do from down here? You got some anti-starship weapons you ain't been letting on about?"

Water gushed out of her blowhole in a sigh. It wasn't that I didn't understand—I wanted to stop these bastards as much as she did—but we weren't equipped for this. No matter how much I looked around, no matter how hard I wracked my brains, I couldn't see a good way to fight back. Especially without the faintest idea what they were planning.

"Very well," Darksong conceded. "We suppose we have no other choice but to sound the retreat. But we must begin forming a new idea—"

A shrieking, drawn-out whistle pierced the air, a sound like a demon rising triumphantly out of Hell. *Fuck!* The hairs on the back of my neck and all along my arms stood at attention. I looked up and my heart damn near stopped.

What light we had gleamed off the chromed casing of a sleek, barrel-shaped canister. It had to be roughly the size of me, maybe even a little bigger. I should've taken that time to get a read on it, see what info—if any—my HUD could pick up. But the damn thing was moving fast, heading straight towards the middle of a group of Voices on the other side of the battle wreckage. Before I could think to do much of anything, it hit the water.

And exploded.

Shrill, agonized song went up all around us. Darksong let out a very long bleat herself and fought the roll and drag of water as the explosion pushed it away. Debris washed over us; I ducked my head, bringing my arms up over it in an effort to protect it. Someone was screaming, several someone's in fact. With my ears ringing from the explosion, all of it sounded distant, like it could've been happening half a world away.

But it wasn't. I clung to Darksong, holding on until the water settled. When it did, I slowly lifted my head, afraid of what I would see. First thing I caught sight of was fresh blood in the water.

"The wounded!" Darksong was already calling to her fellows. "Get us away immediately for treatment!"

Wounded? Someone survived that? My stomach rolled worse than the waves. Bits of fin and flesh littered the water. I swallowed back bile at the sight of dismembered tentacles floating past. Other Voices were moving quickly through the death-littered ocean, and I saw two others, badly injured, adrift at the edges of the blast radius. The weak movement of a flipper told me that at least one was still living. The other Voices surrounded their injured fellows, using their size and strength to hold them in place as they swam off.

"We must scatter," Darksong continued. "We cannot let them catch us grouped together like that again."

"We should flee." And it was only 'cause I was a street-raised badass with a reputation longer than I was tall that my voice didn't shake. Much.

"Did you get any readings on the device?"

"No."

"Then some of us must stay. Where is the Grand Matriarch?"

"We are here, Darksong," came the Matriarch's voice from somewhere below.

"We must leave, Grand Matriarch," Darksong said.

"We would much rather stay with our people. This song belongs to us as well as to us."

"We put us in charge of this mission, Grand Matriarch, and as our adviser in this, we insist that we leave immediately, and take as many of us with us as possible."

My head spun. Goddamnit all, but I couldn't pick up on that nuance Xan had mentioned that would clue me in to just who the fuck they were actually talking about when they got started with all those 'we's and 'us'es.

Another whistling sound broke my concentration. Voices scattered in all directions as a second canister came down, and this time I had enough wits to try to get a read off it. It plummeted through the sky too fast for me to lock on, and I swore under my breath as it hit the water. This time, instead of exploding, it dipped low and then bobbed back to the surface. Not sure any single one of us drew a breath for a long time, as we waited to see what would happen.

When nothing did, Darksong sang out, "Go, Grand Matriarch! We must go, and take as many of us with us as possible. We few will stay and see if there is more to be learned."

"Very well."

A long, loud, trumpet-like note of song carried through the water and soon the Grand Matriarch and many others had fled the area. I watched the canister, but it did nothing but bob along with the waves. A bit of debris left over from one of the boats collided with it with a *clank*, but still nothing happened. *So it's not impact of any kind that sets it off. Manual? Motion control?* Once again, I adjusted the settings on my HUD.

All I got back were surface readings. A little bit about what the canister shell was composed of, and that was it. Frowning, I reached up and tapped my visor. *That can't be right...* I tweaked the visor settings and still came up empty. Confused, I commanded my HUD to link directly into the visor. Just a little bit of prodding here, a tiny bit of finagling there, and together the two would have enough power to—

"Agh! Fuck!"

I cringed back, throwing an arm up to shield my face as something unbearably bright flashed across my vision. Noise screeched in my ears. Swearing up a storm, I hurried to turn my HUD settings as low as they'd go.

"Diver?"

"Ow! Jesus fucking...ow!"

"Diver!" Darksong's voice again, but alarmed this time.

"I'm—I'm all right," I managed. "Or I will be. Man, fucking thing has some sort of shields or something protecting it." I raised the visor and rubbed my smarting eyeballs. "We need some way to hack it."

Darksong didn't answer, but I didn't really notice. She was busy talking to her people, and I was busy trying to figure out what it would take. *If Kiri and I work together...* But the problem was, though she and *Carpathia* were almost through with the sneaksworks, there were still entire systems to hack. Fuck only knew where we'd find what we needed to reach these things.

In the middle of my silent deliberations, something caught me around the waist, and I won't lie, it scared the shit out of me. I was already reaching for my guns when I realized it was tentacles. Not Darksong's Hands, though. Another Voice had come up next to us and it was their Hands who were pulling me from Darksong's back.

"What's going on?" I demanded.

"We have been talking, and we agree. There is no time left," Darksong explained. "These things have been dropped all over Song, and there are likely more to come. We must understand how they work, and... we have a hypothesis about how to defeat them."

"Well, what is it? We'll head back to shore, see what we can—"

"There have been more reports of deaths," Darksong interrupted. "We are out of time, friend Diver. Stars will take you back to shore."

"What? No!" I struggled, but the tentacles pulled me inexorably off Darksong's back. "C'mon, Darksong, there's another way! There's gotta be! Just—just give me a few hours, something!"

"We are dying! Our children are dying!" She turned a half circle in the water and stared at me with one large, dark eye. "This is not a thing we can allow to continue. Surely you understand?"

Yeah, I understand. I understood, but I fucking hated it. I continued to struggle as Stars' Hands lifted me clear and brought me down on the slightly smaller Voice's back. But it was useless to struggle so much. What could I do, except delay this for a few minutes? I couldn't offer an alternative, something that would stop the killing quickly. I clenched my hands in helpless frustration and wished, desperately, for a stroke of brilliance.

None came. I craned my neck around as Stars swam off, trying to get some last glimpse of Darksong, praying she'd change her mind. Something seemed to be going on between her Hands, what looked like some kind of argument, but I knew that wouldn't stop her. Three other Voices had taken up position surrounding the canister. As Darksong shrilled to them, I looked away. *Can't watch this. I can't.*

Stars had carried us a good distance away before the canister exploded. The sound of it, the force breaking it apart, was drowned out by long, mourning notes of Voice song. I buried my face in my hands. *I'm sorry, Xandri. I didn't know how to stop it.* I didn't cry. I wasn't a crier; you didn't make it as a street-kid if you couldn't hold in the tears. But my chest ached like hell, as if all those years of unshed tears had lodged like a hard ball between my ribs.

When Stars slowed and began circling back, I reluctantly lifted my head. I heaved at the sight of the carnage in the water. Bits and pieces, some of which were all that was left of Darksong and her Hands. And something dark moving through the water towards us, dark and long, trailing tentacles.

"Engineer!" Somehow, I knew it was her. I flailed a bit as I tried to get to her. "Eng—let me go, damn you! Now!"

The tentacles loosened enough to allow me to slip into the water, but that was all. A stillness settled over everything, the kind of internal stillness that the lapping of the waves couldn't break. I reached out, barely breathing as Engineer swam towards me. Maybe it was all the time I spent with Xandri, but despite the huge difference in body language, I could see her grief clearly. When one of her tentacles finally slipped into my hand, I saw it was blacker than the night sky. She wrapped her tentacles around me, nuzzling in close, and if she could have whimpered and sobbed, she would have.

"It's all right," I crooned, even though it was anything but. "I've got you. It's gonna be fine."

Tentacles hauled me in against Stars' side. They slid down around me, contacting with Engineer. Her color lightened a tiny bit, but whether it was mood or conversation, I couldn't tell. Questions flooded my brain, but I waited, biting my tongue so I wouldn't ask. Didn't seem right to pry when Engineer had just lost her entire family. I stroked the alternating slippery-bumpy surface of her skin, hoping it would comfort her.

"Good work," Stars said at last. "We have brought us information. We were chosen to stay behind to report back, and we have done so with great bravery." Notes of song echoed the sentiment.

"We now have a distance on these devices, and a way to destroy them. We must contact the Lone Verses immediately."

I didn't know what the Lone Verses were, and I didn't rightly give a fuck. Engineer's coloration had gone completely dark again. I had no idea what to do but hold her, so I did. I refused to let Stars' Hands pull me back up. Instead I had them tug me along through the water next to Stars and held tight to Engineer the entire way back to shore.

"Diver!"

I groaned. Instinct told me that I'd only been asleep for maybe three or four hours. Even once we'd gotten back to shore, there had been things to do. We'd lost one AFC soldier, which had to be reported Major Douglas, and of course Captain Chui and Captain Rhees needed to hear everything, too. Marla, wan and tired, had claimed the responsibility for herself, leaving me to help Engineer. I'd done what I could, but the best option had been leaving her amid a bunch of other Hands, who had separated themselves from their Voices for a time.

By the time I'd crawled into bed, I felt like I could sleep for a month. And yet here I was, being woken up too damn soon.

"Diver, it's Engineer! She needs you!"

That woke me up. I moved to get out of bed so fast, I tangled up in the sheets and ended up on the floor.

"You didn't see that," I said, raising my head to see Kiri in the doorway. "It never happened."

She managed a tired smile. "Your secret is safe with me. Bright came up just a few minutes ago. Engineer is in a bad way, and neither the Hands nor Voices know what to do. They were hoping maybe..."

"Not sure what I could do that they can't." I tossed the sheets aside and stood, glancing around for a T-shirt.

"You might be surprised. You have a real knack for helping out sad female sapients with unusual modes of communication."

I paused, T-shirt in hand, and stared at her. *Xandri...* God, I'd been so fucking exhausted last night, I'd barely had time to won-der about her. *Surely if something bad happened, I would've been told immediately, right?* Shit, I didn't think I could take more bad news. Losing Darksong last night—hell, even losing the Hands and Voices I didn't know, it fucking blew. But Kiri didn't *look* as torn up as I thought she would, if Xandri...

"Captain Chui heard from the jungle team a little while ago," Kiri said. "There were a few casualties—including Amelia—but surprisingly few. Xandri is...unhurt. But probably not okay."

I nodded and pulled my T-shirt on. "Guess that'll have to be good enough for now. I'd better get going."

This was the hardest damn part of the paramilitary aspect of *Carpathia's* crew. Shit like this happened sometimes. You lost people, people you considered friends—people like Amelia. And then you didn't even have five fucking minutes to mourn, because there was inevitably something else you *needed* to do. Amelia was gone; weren't shit I could do to help her now. But Engineer needed me, and her, maybe I could help her.

Kiri held out something wrapped in glittering silver plastic, and for once I understood how Xandri felt. I grabbed the nutrient-bar anyway and tore it open, taking large bites as I hurried down the hall. Knowing that Xandri was safe allowed me to focus my urgency on poor Engineer.

The sun was partway up the horizon, giving me a pretty clear view once I stepped outside. Out in the water were dark shapes, including the Grand Matriarch. Maybe it had something to do with this 'Lone Verse' business. And Ashley Betancourt was on the beach too, with her cameraman at her side. She was focused on the same thing I was after, it seemed: All the Hands floating in the shallows.

I downed the last of my nutrient-bar and started to run. Engineer floated in the middle of a ring of fellow Hands, unmoving. Her skin had gone corpse gray over the course of the night, and terror made my heart race. *She was uninjured. She can't be dead!* I flew past Betancourt and Dave and straight into the ocean. Water splashed up all around me as I hurried out to Engineer. I was up to my neck before I reached her.

"Engineer!" I held out a hand, grasped one of her tentacles. It moved feebly against my palm, and I let out a sigh of relief. "Hey there, little sweetheart. Not doing so good this morning, huh?"

I stepped into reach of her tentacles, and she started to move with painful slowness. She wrapped around me as she had last night, seeking comfort. It never once occurred to me to be afraid, even though she was well over twice my length and could crush me without hardly trying. She was sad and alone, drowning in her own loss and grief, just like any other person would be in her situation. At the back of my mind I wondered, just a little, if I'd've been so quick to feel that way, back before I met Xandri. But now wasn't the time for a walk down retrospective lane.

"Holy shit, man! You space-fried or something?"

I twisted around enough to peer over my shoulder—and bit back a bitter retort when I saw Betancourt and her cameraman standing behind me. *Do they have no hearts at all?* No doubt the camera Dave held was rolling. I turned away again, sheltering Engineer behind my body as much as I could. Had no idea how much she understood about the concept of cameras—probably a lot, considering how intelligent she was—but I didn't want her even more upset than she was already.

"You're not scared?" Dave carried on. "It's huge! What if it decides to like, eat you or something?"

"Dave..." Betancourt began.

"*Her* name is Engineer," I corrected, in the low, growling warning tone you tended to learn on the streets, "and she wouldn't hurt me."

"But what if it—"

"Shut up, Dave," Betancourt snapped. I heard the swish of moving water behind me. "God...she looks awful."

"You would too, if you'd lost your entire symbiotic family in one go."

"I heard about that. They're...pretty amazing people, aren't they?"

To my shock, Betancourt reached over my shoulder and rested her fingertips on one of Engineer's tentacles. Engineer stirred, the gray of her skin changing to something brighter as curiosity got the better of grief. The end of her tentacle moved, probing Betancourt's fingers inquisitively. I expected Betancourt to pull back in disgust, but she let out a small laugh and poked at Engineer in turn. Surprised, I turned my head to look at her and found her smiling gently.

"Ugh! I can't believe you're letting it touch you, Ash."

"Dave, I thought I told you to shut up," she retorted. "And stop calling her 'it.'"

"But—"

"Do you *want* to be fired? Because I can operate that camera just fine if I need to. I won't have a crew that behaves like the LHFH, understood?"

"Fine." The answer sounded sulky.

"And turn the camera off."

"What? But Ash—"

"Turn it off," Betancourt repeated firmly. She continued to play her fingers along Engineer's tentacle filaments, like they were a pair of children playing some hand game. "Give her some peace."

I was right. Captain Chui is up to something with this one. Of course, Betancourt could be up to something too, and I'd damn well be keeping an eye on her. But for the moment, the novelty and curiosity of the reporter was taking Engineer's mind off her grief, and that was enough reason for me to let the woman hang around. Though I'd knock Dave into next standard if he called Engineer 'it' one more fucking time.

Chapter Twenty-Six

Xandri

I ended up going with a fire team for 'clean up duty,' as they called it. Combing through the jungle to make sure there were no LHFH stragglers left behind. I'd hardly call it my dream job; most of what we found was bodies, and many of them were horribly mutilated by the traps they'd fallen prey to. But the only other option was to stay behind while the bodies of our own were incinerated so they could easily be brought back with us, and I hated that. The smell of burning flesh and the knowledge that what once was a person was being reduced to nothing more than ashes always left me feeling sick.

By midmorning we were ready to head back. *At least this time we don't have to move so fast,* I thought, as I trudged along at the back of the group. I ached all over. Despite my armor, I'd acquired plenty of bruises and scrapes, and my back was sore from dozing against a tree. And dull, throbbing aches still pulsed up the arm that the LHFH soldier had twisted so badly.

"That was impressive, by the way," Jae said at one point.

I looked up from rubbing my arm and glanced at vir. "What?"

"You didn't let go of your weapon. A lot of people wouldn't have been able to hold on."

"Oh. That." I didn't mention that I was somewhat used to people grabbing and twisting me in excruciating ways. Even if I hadn't been exhausted as fuck, it wasn't a conversation I wanted to get into.

We continued to trudge along, mostly silent. Somewhere around halfway back to town, a platoon of AFC soldiers joined up with us. A good thing, considering how twitchy we were. Even I kept glancing at the sky, wondering what the LHFH would throw at us next. They'd already been after the Hands and Voices, too. That bit of gossip had trickled back to me and Jae sometime after lunch.

Hands and Voices were dying, and I couldn't stop it. I kept trying to tell myself that we'd *helped*, driving off all those LHFH soldiers, but my tired brain just wouldn't cooperate. It all felt like this was all my fault.

It was getting close to sunset by the time we staggered back up to base. I blinked to find so many AFC soldiers there. They directed us across the beach, showing us where the traps were that we needed to avoid. *Almost there. Just keep it up a little longer... one foot in front of the other.* Soon I'd be inside and I could take a hot shower and sleep in a real bed and—

"Xan!"

I almost collapsed. Diver pushed his way through the stream of soldiers filing into the building, fighting to reach me. Jae grabbed my elbow and held me up until Diver could reach my side.

"I've got her," he said, as he wrapped an arm around me. "Jesus, Jae! Your shoulder."

"You should help Jae," I mumbled, even as I leaned into him. "Vi needs help more than I do."

Jae snorted. "Don't be ridiculous. This is barely more than a flesh wound at this point." Blatant lie. "Besides, *I* am a soldier. I'm used to this shit."

That I couldn't argue with; Jae was far better equipped to deal with this than I was. There was so much going on around me and it all seemed to hit me at once, like I'd been caught beneath an enormous pile of toppled books. But in my exhaustion, I couldn't stop hating myself for my weakness. Surely if the other soldiers could deal with this, I ought to be able to, as well. I wasn't the only one who'd lost a friend.

"Hey, Diver," Jae said, "what's going on out there? The Voices having a meeting or something?"

I glanced out to sea. In the distance were Voices, about a dozen of them gathered in a semi-circle around the Grand Matriarch. I frowned. Although they were mere shadows in the water, I could make out a difference in their silhouette, a shape I'd seen before but, I was pretty sure, only in my studies. I tried to find the information in my fuzzy, exhausted brain, but it wouldn't come.

"Sort of," Diver answered. "Something uh... happened. Yesterday. Look, the end result is, the Voices brought in these 'Lone

Verses.' That's who's out there now. They've been in and out all day, reporting in to the Grand Matriarch on their work. They're—"

"Destroying the canisters!" I exclaimed, the sudden rush of memory shaking me from my stupor. "Of course! That makes so much sense!"

Diver sent a crooked smile my way. "Glad someone gets it. I've been a bit busy today, haven't had a chance to figure out what's even going on."

"I read a bit about the Lone Verses while I was studying up on Song."

"Shocker."

"Hush, you, or I won't tell you what's going on," I teased, feeling better for the first time in what felt like an eternity. "As I was *trying* to say, smartass, the Lone Verses are…well, kind of what they sound like. They're a sub-species of Voice that doesn't travel in a pod, and tends to have only one, maybe two Hands, regardless of size. They're mainly deep water, and have a few things in common with Ancient Earth sperm whales."

"The spermaceti organ! Of course!" Diver exclaimed, and I wanted to kiss him right then, he was so sexy. "They have something like it?"

I nodded. "Except even more advanced. Their power and range is phenomenal, definitely enough to take out the canisters from a safe distance, I'd think. I had no idea you knew about that, Mr. Inorganics."

"Yeah, well, you know me. Organics are useful models for a lot of things, and I've studied a lot of Ancient Earth species, among others, to find designs for my work. Still ain't got a good idea for something like a spermaceti organ, but—"

"Okay," Jae interrupted, "this conversation is getting way too nerdy for me. I'm going to head inside and—"

"But Captain Chui, you've *got* to understand! This is important."

All the joy of our nerdy conversation drained away as I recognized Ashley Betancourt's voice. Diver tightened his grip on my waist as we stepped into the antechamber. Betancourt and Captain Chui stood near the pool, with Dave the Cameraman hanging back as if he was terrified of them both. Betancourt stood tall, leaning into the argument, her body language aggressive and open, despite the fact that Captain Chui's own body language was practically blaring a desire to punch the reporter square in her defiant face.

I shrank against Diver's side. They were both so *loud*, the sheer volume of them poking me with sharply-tipped spikes.

"It's out of the question, Ms. Betancourt. You're lucky I'm letting you record this at all."

"What good does it do anyone if no one sees it until it's too late? Captain Chui, my ship has the technology to broadcast this footage almost live. People will know about this practically as it's happening."

"There are people dying out there!" Captain Chui snapped. "I will not allow you to exploit that."

"It's not about exploitation!" Betancourt looked ready to stomp her foot in frustration. "These LHFH bastards still have free run of the universe because they keep getting away with their shit! Because no one sees the atrocities they commit *while* they're happening. It all becomes something that happened weeks or months ago, so why does it matter now, anyway? We have a chance to expose what they're really up to *right now*. We have to take it!"

"She's right," I blurted out.

If I'd been less tired, I might've held it in. Certainly, I didn't much care for the incredulous stares aimed in my direction. And last time I'd trusted my instincts about a person, Marco Antilles kidnapped me and nearly ruined all my efforts on Cochinga. But I saw something in Ashley Betancourt right then that I recognized.

"She is?" Diver demanded.

"I am?" Betancourt stared at me.

"Ms. Corelel," Captain Chui said, regarding me blandly, "I was not made aware that you had suffered a head injury on the field."

I sighed. "Captain, you were there the day I convinced the Anmerilli to sign. Do you remember what I did?"

"Aside from threaten to shoot Nish mar'Odrea?"

"I showed them footage of the things the Zechak had done," I said, choosing to ignore that. "A move the press criticized as exploitive and crude, but it worked. The reason I did it was because— because words weren't enough. And I'm not sure it would've worked at all if I hadn't shocked them so much. Ms. Betancourt is right. People need to see this now, not when the dust has cleared and the LHFH has had time to put some spin on it."

"Finally!" Betancourt exclaimed. "Someone with some sense."

"This doesn't mean I like you."

She grinned.

"Or even that I like *this*," I went on. "Under most circumstances, I would have to agree with Captain Chui. But this isn't most circumstances. We need to catch the LHFH in the act, in a way no one can possibly deny later."

"You're certain, Ms Corelel?" Captain Chui asked, more gently this time.

"Positive. There are a lot of sapients who need an entire two-by-four of truth right to face to get it." I smiled wanly. "Humans especially. So let's give them one."

"Very well," Captain Chui conceded. She glanced at Diver then. "Mr. Diver, I know you're the one who's been caring for Engineer, and I understand that you might not care for this, but—"

"Wait," I cut in, "what happened to Engineer?"

I took a step back as they all turned to me and my stomach clenched. Aside from Jae, who merely looked puzzled, every face in the room wore a similar expression. And if I was reading it right, that expression was dread.

Diver

Captain Chui managed to order Jae to the temp medbay, but Xandri sat down on the floor and refused to move until someone explained. Technically, Captain Chui could have overrode her, but for some space-fried reason, she didn't. And since I was the one who'd been there, I got the fucking joy of explaining. I sat on the floor next to Xandri and recounted what had happened in as broad terms as I could.

She must've been hella exhausted. I'd seen Xan lock her emotions down like money in a vault, but she couldn't this time. Her eyes grew large and her nose grew red, and a few tears tracked slowly down her dirty cheeks.

"Darksong's gone?" she whispered.

I caught her hands in mine. "I'm sorry, fireball."

"She did it for all of Song," Captain Chui put in. "They were able to pinpoint how close they could get to those explosive canisters before they'd go off. That's how they knew to make use of the

Lone Verses. According to the Grand Matriarch, Lone Verses all across the globe are successfully nullifying the canisters. They've got enough range that there hasn't been a single casualty since they started."

Damn. That was impressive, no question. It sounded like these Lone Verses had a true sonic cannon if they could get that much range. All that sound, traveling through the water at a volume loud enough to set off an explosive…fucking scary thought. The canisters might go by motion detection, but I had to figure it was a certain kind of motion, a certain level of force, or the movement of the ocean—or hell, just their landing—that would set them off immediately.

"This is such a mess," Xandri moaned, rubbing a hand across her face and smearing the tears through the dirt. "It wasn't supposed to be like this."

"We're gonna stop them, Xan," I said. "We are. You guys cleaned up at the jungle, right? And now we can neutralize their explosives, and it won't be much longer before Alliance ships show up to help. It's gonna be okay."

"What about Engineer? She's not going to be okay."

Couldn't argue with that. I'd been with her a lot of the day, but she wasn't improving much. And at the times when I couldn't be with her, Betancourt, of all people, had volunteered to keep her company. Voices showed up throughout the day with their Hands to visit her, and she perked up a little at those times, but as soon as they were gone she turned gray again.

"I don't know what to do," I said quietly. "About Engineer, I mean."

"We'll figure it out," Captain Chui said. "We always do. I'm sure if you and Xandri work together you'll—"

Xandri straightened suddenly. "That's it!"

"Could I please finish just *one* sentence today?"

"Captain, that's what Engineer needs!" Xandri said. "Where's Bright? I need to talk to him."

When Xandri got her mind around something, she could be stubborn as hell, so Captain Chui didn't even ask. She contacted Marla and Kirrick, and no surprise, it was Marla who showed up to run down to the dock and find Bright. She'd been like that all day, finding ways to keep on the move, probably to keep her mind off last night.

We all waited, me and Xandri still on the floor, Dave and Betancourt in the corner, murmuring as they made plans. Captain Chui paced, keeping an eye on us. I could see her gunnery sergeant training was making her twitchy, and I thought she might just toss Xandri over her shoulder and carry our exhausted fireball off to bed herself, if Bright didn't show up soon. Fortunately, he *did* show up soon, popping up in the pool in the middle of the room with a small splash.

"Bright!"

"Hello, Xandri Corelel." His tongue lolled in good cheer. "Marla Thomas informed us you'd like to speak with us, and that it concerns Engineer."

"Yes. The Lone Verses… are there any who are only carrying a single Hand, who might be willing to carry another?"

Bright dropped beneath the water for a moment and air exploded from his blowhole in a way that reminded me of a surprised splutter. He came back up, bobbing as much out of the water as he could to lean against the side of the pool. One of his smaller, more octopodal Hands raised a tentacle in greeting.

"Yes," Bright said at last. "Yes, we think there might be, indeed. Xandri Corelel, are you thinking what we think you're thinking?"

"Probably. You'll have to fib a little to make it work. The Grand Matriarch should tell Engineer—tell her she was picked specifically for this job. To—to examine the wreckage of these things, to help us better understand how they work."

"We are not certain we will believe that."

"She'll believe it enough, right now," Xandri said with surprising confidence. "It doesn't matter if it occurs to her later that it was a ruse. Right now—she needs to be needed. To be part of the togetherness. The song. She needs company, and work will help, too."

I let out a small laugh and threw my arms around Xan, drawing her in to give her a big, sloppy kiss on the cheek, dirt and dried tears and all. Company and curiosity—those were the two things that had seemed to pull Engineer out of her funk. *Trust Xandri to put those pieces together.* In a lot of ways, she wasn't much different from Engineer. Having a puzzle to put her mind to seemed to have perked her up, as well.

"It is an unorthodox idea," Bright said, "but those are often the best kind. We like it. We will go present it to the Grand Matriarch immediately."

"And *you*," Captain Chui said, pointing at Xandri, "are going to get some rest. *Now.*"

"Yes, ma'am."

"C'mon, fireball." I pulled her to her feet. "Let's get you out of that armor. *Not* in a fun way, Captain, stop giving me that look."

Xandri let out a small laugh, and that tiny, trilling sound meant the entire damn world to me. I kept an arm wrapped around her as I helped her down the hall to her room. A door opened as we approached, and Anton peeked out long enough to see that Xandri was in good hands before nodding and disappearing back into his room. Holding Xan against my side, I pushed open the door to her bedroom.

She grumbled only a little when I made her stand still while I removed her armor. And she didn't protest at all when I sent her marching into the bathroom. I just hoped she remembered to take off those fatigues before getting in the shower.

Once again I found myself sitting on her bed, waiting. Someone had left a nutrient-bar on her bedside stand for her, but I wouldn't make her eat it; not until morning, at least. I did get up once, to glance out at the beach. In the slowly falling dusk, I made out a sperm whale-like shape in the water, and a group of Hands swimming towards it. *Go, Engineer. Being with your people will make you feel better.* God knew I wasn't the praying kind, but I sent up a tiny one just in case there was something out there to hear, that Engineer would recover from this.

I started at a faint knock on the door. Figuring I knew who it was, I got up to answer, and sure enough, there stood Kiri.

"Come to check on our fireball?"

She smiled wanly. "That, and Captain Chui came by and ordered me to rest, or she'd have me dragged off to my room and put guards on my doors and windows." Kiri stepped inside and started pacing. "I'm feeling a bit…jittery. Don't think I can sleep, so…"

"What've you even been up to? I thought you and *Carpathia* were finished with the sneaks-works."

"We are. But I've got my own little project going. I've been hacking deeper into their systems."

I stared.

She gave her head a defiant toss. "What? I've made decent progress. Enough to mess with some of their stuff, mix up rosters and supply lists and the like. Small fish. But by the time I'm done, I'm going to take control of their ships and wreak complete havoc."

"Have I ever mentioned that you're really fucking vicious?"

Kiri glowered.

"And that I like that about you?"

She broke into another wan smile. *She looks as tired as Xandri.* Guess that was what came of waging war, and no mistake, Kiri was waging war as much as any of the rest of us. I hadn't seen her like this before, stripped of her usual cheer and flirtatiousness. She'd had the sort of childhood, loving family and everything, that I'd never dared dream of, and I'd always envied her that. Seeing her so unprepared for this sort of thing, and so depleted by it, I kinda felt like a heel for ever envying her anything.

"Maybe I should go," Kiri said, as the shower turned off.

"Nah. She's falling-down tired. Might need some help getting her all the way to the bed."

Xandri came stumbling out a moment later, hair still soaked, T-shirt clinging to her where her skin was damp. She tripped, and I caught her before she fell. She pressed her face against my chest, mumbling something utterly incomprehensible—wasn't even sure it was in Trade Common.

"Oh dear," Kiri said, stifling a giggle. "Let me help."

She caught one of Xandri's arms. Xandri regarded her blearily, and managed a small, very tired smile. Together, Kiri and I maneuvered Xandri towards the bed. I climbed onto it and caught her around the waist; Kiri got her feet, hoisting them onto the mattress. *Good thing she's tiny, because she's about as moveable as lead right now.* As soon as we had her settled on the bed, she curled into a ball against me, pinning me between her and the wall.

"Uh...Xan..."

Kiri laughed. "I think you're invited to stay."

"You too," Xandri mumbled, turning her head enough to look up at Kiri. "Need sleep too."

"Don't worry, I'll go back to my room and—"

"Do work. You have a spare computer in there. Pretty sure," a yawn punctuated her words, "not what Captain Chui told you to do."

"You know, starshine," Kiri complained as she climbed into the bed next to Xandri, "sometimes you're far too perceptive for anyone's good."

"Things on the inside get easy to see," Xandri murmured, snuggling contentedly between us, "when you're always on the outside."

Kiri and I exchanged a glance at those words, but if Xandri was still awake, I couldn't tell. Besides, bugging her about it at a time like this seemed cruel.

She'll probably be embarrassed about being so forward once she's gotten some sleep, I realized. But it seemed to be what they both needed. Kiri settled down with Xandri's head nestled under her chin, and it wasn't long before her breathing evened out with sleep. I grinned, wrapping my arms around both of them, and in a way I wished I'd known them back in the old days, on the streets. A man could survive the end of the world with a pair like these two at his side.

Chapter Twenty-Seven

Xandri

I woke disoriented and sore. Really sore.

Sore didn't do much for shaking off the disoriented. I groaned and rolled over, and it was the empty space I rolled into that shook off some of the vestiges of sleep. Some part of my brain recalled, in a vague, foggy sort of way, that my bed shouldn't be so empty. I didn't quite know *why* but... yes, it definitely hadn't been so empty when I'd gone to sleep. I could recall the scent that I always associated with Diver and—and something else...

Oh, Sweet Mother Universe! I tried to sit up and promptly landed on my face as my tired arms gave out. Where I stayed, horrified by the memory of pulling Kiri into bed with us. It had been *so* nice, curling up with her like that, but god, what must she think? *I don't want to lead her on. I mean, it's not that I'm not interested, but I can't even untangle my feelings for one person, let alone two!*

I gripped the satiny lining of my blanket, running my fingers across it and forcing myself to take several deep breaths. There was no time for relationship stuff at the moment, anyway, so why get all stirred up over it?

I had no idea what time it was or what was going on, either. At least I could rest assured that if shit had hit the fan, I'd have heard about it. I climbed out of bed, trying to ignore the ache in my body. Now that I was paying attention, I could smell coffee, the good stuff that Captain Chui had given me. It sat on the table in a thermo-mug, next to a covered dish and a nutrient-bar. Naturally, I went for the coffee first.

Since nothing seemed to be on fire or in any other way urgent, I took my time over my coffee and breakfast, and even longer getting my hair into some semblance of behavior. Going through such a normal routine relaxed me, leaving me feeling more at ease than I had in—*Is it two days now? Three?* I didn't have a clue. It felt like we'd been at war down here for months, maybe years. Hard to believe there were people willing to do this sort of thing as a career.

Finally there was little left to do but see what was going on outside. A peek out my window showed the usual soldiers patrolling the beach, so I headed out of my room and down the hall. Voices and the roar of waves filled my ears as I strolled through the coral garden and down to the beach.

I found Kiri first. She sat in a clear space on the beach, beneath the shade of a large umbrella, working at a holo-slate. Captain Eira Rhees had crouched beneath the umbrella next to her and appeared to be inspecting her work, though I wondered if Rhees had any clue what she was looking at. For a moment I considered trying to sneak past, but if Kiri was upset in some way, I ought to face the music. So I stopped by her workstation.

She glanced up from the holo-slate and grinned. "Morning, starshine. Sleep okay?"

"Yeah." I shuffled by toes against the ground. "You?"

"Better than I have in a while. Captain Chui barely even glared at me when I sat down to get back to work."

"She's hacking the systems of the LHFH ships," Captain Rhees put in, her eyes on Kiri. "Is there anything in the universe better than a smart woman?"

"Oh, don't ask her that!" Kiri's eyes widened. "She's liable to answer, and then I'll have to feel inferior to coffee."

"No one would ever think you're inferior to coffee," I said without thinking.

Then of course I turned red, because I always did. Kiri's lips curved in a gentle smile, and Captain Rhees regarded me with raised eyebrows and narrowed eyes. Considering she'd been there to see me my rather thorough kiss with Diver, she must be wondering why I was flirting—however accidentally—with Kiri. On the other hand, if she was interested in Kiri, she'd need to get used to the fact that Kiri was polyamorous. I wasn't the violent sort, but I might just have to shoot someone who tried to make Kiri change who she was.

"You always brighten my day, starshine," Kiri said, her tone gently teasing. "Diver's down on the dock, by the way. With that reporter woman, of all people. She wants to interview Engineer."

"How is she? Engineer, I mean."

"Why don't you go see for yourself? She and the Voice she's working with are at the dock, too."

I couldn't resist that. Leaving Captain Rhees to flirt with Kiri—not an easy task when she was working—I began making my way down the beach, carefully. As I picked my way through traps, I noticed the Psittacans out on the dock, too. *What are they doing out there? Not harassing Betancourt, I hope.* The last thing we needed was for the rest of the universe to get the wrong idea about Psittacans, who were still rarely seen anywhere but their homeworld.

As I stepped onto the dock, I got a better look at what they were up to. Voices swam up to the docks in turns and the Psittacans stretched their legs down to the water, scratching wet, blubbery bodies with their flexible toes. I paused and stared.

"What are you guys doing?"

Dawn looked up. "There isn't much else we can do to help."

"And this is nice," the Voice she was scratching said. "Very nice. We are not so well equipped for taking care of our own itches."

"Well, I...I guess that makes sense," I said uncertainly. "How's the wing this morning, Lightning?"

"Much better." He flapped the wing in question. "It would be all healed, but the doc said it was too minor for military nanos. But I don't need it right now, anyway."

Which reminded me, I needed to check on Jae later. Vi'd put vir life at risk to save me, and I wanted to know vi was all right. *And no doubt Anton will pop in to check on me at some point.* With all the soldiers around I didn't really need a bodyguard, but he'd find some excuse, no doubt.

I left the Psittacans to scratching duty, glad they had something more restful to do today, and headed down the dock to where Diver, Betancourt and Dave the Cameraman had gathered. Betancourt was doing something, but I couldn't begin to make out what her gesticulating might mean. She was talking, yes, but...

"Right, I think we've got it," I heard her say. "Now, Dave, I just need you to—Dave! Pay attention!"

"I am paying attention, Ash. I just don't get this. Why would you want to interview it, it can't even talk."

"Don't push him in," Betancourt said, her eyes flicking to me. "That camera he's holding is valuable."

"Fine. I'll do it later." I sat down next to Diver.

"Morning, fireball."

"You didn't hit him for that. Why not?"

"Hit who?"

"Diver's pretending Dave doesn't exist," Betancourt explained. "Not that I blame him. I've had smarter tripods."

"Hey!" Dave protested, but we all ignored him.

"All right, Engineer, are you ready?" Betancourt asked, turning to the water.

The dark shape that was drifting in the water at the end of the dock rose. Water slooshed off dark gray skin. The Lone Verses didn't have armor like other Voices, which made me think their spermaceti organs had evolved very early on, growing more and more powerful since they were the only means of defense the Lone Verses had. Two Hands—one of them I recognized as Engineer—clung behind the Voice's dorsal fin. Engineer, I noticed with relief, had gone back to her normal coloration.

And now she lifted a tentacle and gave the thumbs-up Diver had taught her. To my surprise, Betancourt laughed.

"I'll take that as a yes. Dave, roll film."

As soon as Dave was filming, Betancourt's entire persona changed. She tossed her hair back, letting it blow in the ocean breeze, and spoke in a tone both slightly grim and strangely compelling. As she outlined the scenario on Song and recapped what had happened to Darksong and the others, I scooted closer to Diver. He reached out and caught my hand in both of his, rubbing his thumb across my palm.

"And now," Betancourt carried on, "I stand here with Great Warrior Of The Depths, who has graciously allowed us to call him Warrior, and Engineer herself. Which reminds me, Engineer, is that your full name?"

Engineer turned slightly pink, and something passed between her and Warrior. "It is not," Warrior spoke, "but we would not be comfortable sharing our full name. It would feel too much like bragging."

Betancourt chuckled. "I had a feeling you weren't called Engineer for nothing. All right, I won't push."

The pink tinge faded. As Betancourt asked questions—most of them about Engineer's job—the Hand herself changed color frequently. Sometimes her tentacles moved quite a bit, but I couldn't even begin to make out the sign language. Fortunately, Warrior translated everything as quickly and as clearly as he could. *The audience will still be confused by how he speaks, though.* Not *all* of them—some sapients adjusted to other syntax very well—but humans especially would struggle to comprehend it. Especially since they could be stuck up about that sort of thing.

"I hope you don't mind me asking, Engineer," and Betancourt's tone switched to a much gentler one, "and I'll understand if you don't want to answer, but…how have you been holding up since you lost your family?"

Engineer's tentacles moved in a slow, solemn dance, and Warrior translated. "We miss us a very great deal. It will hurt for a long time. But we cannot believe our family wished us only ill. We must have had good reason to leave us alive."

"I heard that what your family did was very brave. They were strong and courageous, so you must be too."

Engineer went pinkish again. "We try to be."

"Oh, I'm certain you are. That must be part of why they chose you. And look, they weren't wrong. You're already out there, working for the cause."

Engineer's tentacles fairly flew, then, and Warrior ended up blowing a snorting sound through his blowhole. Engineer made a motion that appeared sheepish and slowed herself down a bit, giving Warrior a chance to keep up with her. I leaned against Diver's shoulder, fighting a grin. His arm wrapped around my shoulders, and when I glanced at his face, I saw he looked far less upset than he'd been yesterday.

"It's proven to be very important work," Warrior translated. "It has given us an opportunity to examine these explosives and how they are put together. We have been studying the Alliance regulations, and these devices are, to our reckoning, clearly illegal. They resemble to exactness a device the Alliance declared illegal even for military use."

Betancourt and Diver looked startled, but I wasn't surprised. I pinged Diver on his private channel and explained—sub-vocalized, so it wouldn't end up on film—about the device the LHFH had used in the forest. His expression grew grim as I talked. The LHFH having *one* piece of Alliance tech was ugly enough, but them having two implied that someone on the inside had helped them acquire it. *I need to remember to tell Captain Chui about this later.* I'd been a bit too caught up in other things to remember, last night.

"Well," Betancourt was saying, "I won't keep you two any longer. I know you've been working most of the night. You've earned some rest."

"We would be willing to talk more later, if you want," Engineer offered. "We would like to talk to Diver now, though."

"Hear that, Mr. Diver? Willing to step in front of the camera?"

If she thought she was going to get any sort of shyness out of him, she was wrong. He gave my hand a squeeze, raising it to kiss my palm, before releasing me and rising to his feet. He paused to give the camera his most charming smile, then knelt at the end of the dock and extended a hand to Engineer. *She's doing better, but she still needs his reassurance,* I realized, as Engineer wrapped a tentacle around Diver's arm. Not that I couldn't understand where she was coming from.

Diver leaned over and murmured to her in low tones. Whatever he was saying, and however Engineer was replying, Warrior didn't translate.

Suddenly both Warrior and Engineer went very still. I looked up, my gaze moving quickly across the water, and I noticed a small form shooting towards us. Soon I heard it, the stream of song that must have alerted Warrior and Engineer. *Please, please let me be imagining it...*It sounded so mournful, so full of distress and urgency. I glanced around me at my companions, who all looked so concerned, I couldn't mistake it for a bad reading of their body language.

"Xandri Corelel!" the Voice called as she neared.

"It's Tides!" Diver exclaimed.

"Xandri Corelel!"

I stood up and, in three short steps, flung myself into the water to meet Tides. She was one of their fastest swimmers, fast enough that she had paralleled Marla's place as a message runner. Yet even though she was coming in fast, she was able to slow herself. She cut a tight circle, then another, letting the drag of the water slow her. She was still moving when she reached me, enough to bump into me and send me back against the docks. A hand shot down, grabbing my shoulder to steady me. I looked up at Diver, tried to give him a grateful smile, though I didn't quite manage.

"We bring bad tidings, Xandri Corelel, very bad indeed," Tides chattered. "These people we fight, they have brought new technology down on us."

"Easy, Tides." I reached out a hand, but she wouldn't settle. She kept swimming in small circles, as if she was pacing. "What is it? I'm sure we can stop it, too."

"We have tried! It is—it is like a cage, but it is not a cage. It came down from the sky like the canisters. We thought that's what it was, four more canisters, but far apart, quite far apart. We prepared to destroy them as we have the others, but they did not explode. There is—some kind of field between them, and it activated. It hurts to touch. Our people outside it cannot get in, and the ones caught inside cannot get out. We have even tried going deep under the water, but eventually we come up against the field and can go no farther.

"And they are watching! They drop their canisters on us when we try to get close. And they—they..." In her distress, Tides blew a great spout of air and water through her blowhole. "They are also dropping meat in the water, bloody and raw."

"To attract the Disharmonies," I murmured, horrified.

"It's gonna be okay, Tides," Diver said, and I admired him so much, that he could sound so calm and soothing. "We stopped their last shenanigans, yeah? We'll stop this too. We got lotsa smart heads on our side."

"Diver—Diver's right," I managed around the lump in my throat. "At the height they're at, they're probably using some sort of heat seeking to tell where you are, and with a little time we can jam that. Then we can—"

Boots pounded on the dock. My heart plummeted as I swiveled in the water to look. Captain Chui, Captain Rhees and, to my surprise, Major Douglas, led the way. Magellan and several lieutenants followed on their heels. They moved at a fast walk, what I recognized as the "shit has gone horribly wrong but we don't want to panic anyone" walk. Naturally, that made me panic.

"Get her out of the water, Mr. Diver," Captain Chui called. "Now."

Oh, because that *doesn't scare the piss right out of me.* I reached up towards the dock. Diver caught me and hauled me bodily out of the water, setting me on my feet. A moment later the entire group—

trailed by the Psittacans—reached us. I wrapped my arms around myself, shivering in spite of the warmth of Song. I didn't like the look on Captain Chui's face, not one bit. Whenever her expression grew easier to read, it was usually because the news was bad. Really fucking bad.

"Captain, Tides brought us news—" Diver began.

"I know. We've had…news of our own. Contact from a man called Nafar Santino. He is the one responsible for the captured Hands and Voices."

"We suspect he's responsible for this entire attack," Major Douglas said, scowling. "The bastard had the nerve to send us an ultimatum."

"A hostage price, in fact."

Diver slipped an arm around me and I leaned into him. "What does he want?"

Captain Chui gazed levelly at me. "He wants you, Ms. Corelel."

Chapter Twenty-Eight

Diver

Awful lotta people crowded into Captain Chui's office. Xandri huddled between me and Kiri, shifting and twitching any time someone else bumped into her. The Psittacans were there, Anton, Emin and Jae had joined, every higher-up we had had squeezed in, and several more *Carpathia* and AFC soldiers had stuffed themselves in at the edges. Even had people peeking in the door and the goddamn window.

Murmurs and whispers bounced through the room. Then Captain Chui raised a hand, and everything went still and silent. Damn, I wished I knew that trick.

"Half an hour ago we received transmission of a holo-mail," Captain Chui said quietly, "from a man calling himself Nafar Santino. Though he does not state his position in the LHFH, we suspect he's leading this mission himself."

Using a holo-projector, she produced an image of our beach and its surrounds, and zoomed in on a spot in the ocean about a kilometer south and maybe another kilometer outwards. "They dropped a specialized containment trap here. This is Alliance tech *usually* reserved for holding wildlife for study, but it's been heavily modified for use in water, and touching the field causes pain. The Lone Verses cannot break it, and they are attacked when they try.

"Under normal circumstances we would take the time to solve each problem one at a time, but Nafar Santino is one step ahead of us in that respect."

With a quick flick of her fingers, she drew out a second holo-projection. *Shit. You can practically* see *his gene-jumping.* Hulking brute of a fellow appeared in miniature. He wore fatigues and more ammo than a goddamned weapons locker, and he had one of those big, sharky grins that he flashed straight at the holo-recorder. Something small and boxy was clenched in one hand.

"Captain Chui Shan Fung," he said, in a gravelly sort of voice. "It's a pleasure. I've heard a great deal about you and your ship of alien-loving misfits. Unfortunately, I doubt you've heard of me, but I intend to change that very soon.

"I am Nafar Santino, a member of Last Hope for Humanity, which I'm sure you've already guessed. But I bet you wonder why I'm contacting you now. Yes, I bet you do."

"Likes the sound of his own voice a wee much, don't he?" I muttered.

Captain Chui shot me a warning look. Joke was on her, though; I saw the little bit of smile she tried to hide.

"Your little fish friends are pretty fast—"

"But they're not fish!" Xandri protested, a bit predictably, truth be told.

"—so maybe you've already heard about our trap. It's a clever little thing. All the Alliance does to ensure the protection of filthy aliens, and now we're turning it against you. We've got some of the overgrown fish in a containment field not far from where you've set up camp. And it won't be so easy to stop us this time.

"Now, maybe the predators will arrive first. We've heard they have very efficient noses. In which case we'll just wait until the containment field is surrounded and lower it, and see what happens." He shrugged, as if he was talking about the weather. "Or you could do as I ask, and we can stop the whole thing. It's not even a big request, Captain. All I ask is that you give me the girl called Xandri Corelel."

A murmur rippled through the room. I clenched my hands into fists; if the fucker had been standing in front of me when he said that, I'd have punched him right in his smug, shark-smiling face. And I doubted I was the only one. Even those *Carpathia* members who didn't know Xandri wouldn't care for the idea of handing over one of their own. But when I glanced at Xandri herself, the look on her face surprised me. She stared at the image of Nafar Santino with intense concentration. Had to wonder at the gears turning behind those eyes of hers.

"Now, I've heard about you, Chui Shan Fung. You're a wily one. So, just in case you were getting any ideas about stalling, allow me to show you this," Santino said, opening his clenched fingers. A small, black box sat on his palm. "This controls the destruct device on the containment field. That's an addition of ours, by the way. You're not the only one with clever crew members, Captain. If we don't have Ms. Corelel in front of us by, let's say, fourteen-hundred hours, I turn your friends into a dinner delicacy.

"I'll even let you bring your paltry army along. But I warn you, one twitch, one funny look, one finger on the trigger, and that's the end of your friends." He started to turn away and paused. Ugh, fuckers like him were all about the show and the drama. I'd known people back on the streets who pulled shit like this. I wasn't surprised when he opened his mouth to speak, as if he'd suddenly remembered something. "And I know you think the local sushi is so much more clever than we are, but we've reinforced the containment field. You won't be destroying it this time."

As if we would. Destroying it ourselves would still get the Voices and Hands trapped inside it very, very dead.

"Well," I said into the silence as the recording faded out, "don't know about the rest of you, but I wanna punch that fucker in the nuts."

Babble broke out all around us. Everyone seemed to want to speak at once, though Anton did a damn bang-up job of raising his big, booming voice above everyone else's. Captain Chui stood, an island of calm amidst all the chaos, letting everyone pour out their initial surge of outrage. Xandri was still and quiet too, her gaze fixed on the spot where Nafar Santino's image had been. I tightened my arm around her, but she didn't respond.

Finally, Captain Chui raised a hand and the noise began to quiet down. She waited until everyone had gone completely silent, and I had to grit my teeth against frustration. We didn't fucking have *time* to wait for anything.

"This isn't good," Captain Rhees murmured. "If we had more time to plan a strategy, but," she paused a second, checking her HUD, "we barely have an hour."

"The question is," Captain Chui returned, "do we *need* an hour?"

"I'm good, Captain, but I don't know if I'm *that* good."

"Then I have to go," Xandri spoke up suddenly.

"No!" Anton exploded. "Hell no! We ain't handing you over to those monsters!"

"Then what do we do? Let innocent people die? No. I won't let that happen." Xandri shook her head vigorously. "Kiri, you need to get to work *now*. Take out their heat-seeking software. *Everything* else can wait."

Kiri glanced at Captain Chui, who gave a small nod. Without another word she pushed through the crowd, grabbing her holo-slate on the way. *What's cooking in that head of yours, fireball?* For once, I couldn't read her very well; all I could guess was that Xandri had a plan, and, knowing her, it was probably a pretty space-fried one. Then again, if we were gonna stop this, space-fried was what we'd need.

"I'll need two volunteers, and one of them needs to be good with technical stuff. If we can't disable the containment field from a distance, we'll need to do it manually."

"If it involves tech, I'm your man," I said.

She glanced at me. "It'll be very, very dangerous."

"Pretty sure everything you're planning right now will be. And your part in it no less so."

She looked away, and I knew I was right. *Got a feeling I ain't gonna like this.* Fuck, I didn't like any of it. I wanted to get my hands around the neck of this Nafar Santino and squeeze until his eyes popped outta his goddamn skull. And if he wasn't threatening to blow innocent people to kingdom come, I'd do it in a heartbeat, too.

"Ms. Corelel," Captain Chui cut in, "I need to know what you're planning."

"It's simple, Captain." Xandri looked up, her eyes glittering with dark promises. "If the LHFH wants me, then that's what they'll get."

"You sure about this, man?" I asked Hans. "Ain't no dig site out there."

I pulled the HP suit up over my shoulders and popped my arms through the sleeves, keeping an eye on Hans. For an anthropologist he was in decent shape; good enough, at least, to get his HP suit on with ease.

"I'm aware of that, Mr. Diver," Hans responded. "But it only makes sense. All the soldiers are needed elsewhere, as are the civvies. Casaria's work studying the biology of the life here is too important to risk, as well. And I may not know that much about tech, but I'm an anthropologist with nearly a century of experience behind me." He smiled gently. "You won't find a keener pair of eyes or a steadier set of hands. Except for maybe your own."

I grinned. "Fair enough. As good an argument as any, that."

I supposed there was always Leev, but he wasn't that useful in a pinch. At least, not most pinches. Give him a pinch in space and he could emergency land a real clunk-fest of a shuttle on the tippy-top of a rock spire, but anything to do with anything but piloting set him to wild, headless-chicken type flailing. Plus, he'd joined up with the med team, offering his hands—as steady as Hans'—to people treating any wounds the Hands and Voices came by, and a few on the other species, as well.

"As long as you're sure about this…" Xandri's voice, uncertain but carrying, reached me on the dock.

I looked up, hands still working on getting every bit of the suit in place. Xandri came towards us, already in fatigues and armor, her pistols within easy reach at her thighs. Only she and Captain Chui knew the extent of her plan; everyone else had only the pieces that were absolutely necessary to make it work. Which made sense, sure, but it terrified the fuck outta me, not knowing precisely what she was up to.

"Of course we're sure," Christa's voice came back, indignant. "Are you kidding me? I just hope I can get close enough to punch one of these bastards in the face."

"It'll be dangerous. Very dangerous."

"We're *all* in danger right now, Xandri. *Song* is in danger. If we can help you get it out of danger, that's what we'll do."

A small, relieved smile broke out on Xandri's face. "Good. I'm glad to hear that. I'll give you the signal when it's time."

Time for what? I wondered. The Beta Team had two platoons of *Carpathia* soldiers and two of AFC soldiers, so I wasn't sure how much they could even do. We had our own two platoons, plus Major Douglas had moved in three extra platoons of AFC soldiers aside from the first two he'd sent, giving us seven platoons to work with. Not terrible, but not fantastic. Hoped it would be enough.

"Will do. Christa out."

Xandri deactivated the comm on her wristlet and came to a stop in front of me. She was trying to put on a brave face, no doubt about it; one corner of her mouth twisted in an effort at a reassuring smile. I reached out, settled my hands on her armored shoulders, wishing I could do more to comfort her.

"It's gonna be all right, fireball," I told her, leaning my forehead against hers. "We're gonna stop this, I promise."

"I hope you're right," she murmured. "Listen... Kiri will give you word when it's time, okay? Until then, don't get too close."

The words "unless you have no other choice" hung unspoken in the air between us. We both knew I wasn't gonna leave the Hands and Voices to die. And me, well, I'd gotten used to the idea of kicking the bucket a long time ago. You had to, 'cause on the streets it could happen at any time. Sure, in this day and age you were less likely to croak of disease or starvation, but a knife to the back or a gunshot to the head would kill you just as fucking dead.

"You be careful too, got me? I wanna come back to you in one piece."

"This Nafar Santino... I think he wants me alive. He won't kill me unless he has to."

"Don't care. He touches a hair on your head and I'll be treating him to a good ol' fashioned street-meet."

Xandri pulled back a little and raised an eyebrow. "Do I even want to know what that is?"

Instead of answering, I drew her back to me and kissed her. To my surprise, she wrapped her arms around me and kissed me back, with such ferocity and desperation that it almost hurt. Damnit all, I wished things could be different. Wished I could swoop her up in my arms and take her somewhere, somewhere I could kiss and caress away any hurts she'd ever known. Instead I was putting myself in danger of being fish food.

"C'mon, Corelel! We're moving out!"

She drew back with a sigh. "The gunnery sergeant doth bellow. I'd best get going."

"Us too. Be safe, fireball."

I gave her shoulders a squeeze and released her. She turned, her body language blaring reluctance, and trotted down the dock. I watched her just a moment longer, then turned—to find Hans watching me, a pensive expression on his face. I raised my eyebrows and he gave his head a shake.

"Sorry, it's just…well, I feel as though I've judged Ms. Corelel ill for a long time."

He sat on the edge of the dock and slipped into the water to join the waiting Voices. Warrior and Engineer had insisted on coming with us, so I slid into the water near them. Engineer extended a tentacle, wrapping it around me as I clambered onto Warrior's back. He didn't have a prominent dorsal fin, so I had to lean real low and let the Hands help keep me in place.

"I always resented her," Hans went on. "Here she is, so young and without any sort of experience or even a real education, and she has one of the most important jobs on the *Carpathia*. But watching her on this mission, I'm starting to see why Captain Chui chose her."

"Yeah, she can have that effect on people, given the chance."

"I still can't say I quite approve. She really is so very young. But…well, I'm glad the job is in the hands of someone who cares as much as she does."

"Sometimes that *is* the most important thing," I agreed. "You might wanna hold on."

Hans looked puzzled—until the Voice underneath him shot off through the water. With the urgency of the situation, they didn't even try to hold themselves back, skimming through the ocean at top speed. Water slooshed over me in great waves, so much of it that I activated the suit's helmet to protect my eyes and nose. Hans caught sight of this and did the same. He clung to the Voice's dorsal fin; me, if it wasn't for Engineer and her fellow Hand holding me down, I'd have been swept off Warrior's back right from the get-go.

Moving at that pace, it didn't take long before we were in position. As Warrior slowed, I flicked my attention to my HUD and the feedback from the gorilla. *Looks like it's in position…* Good. I'd be able to get to it as soon as we hit shore.

"We are going under now," Warrior warned.

I slipped the oxygen tube into place and twisted around, giving Engineer the thumbs-up. A second later Warrior submerged. I focused my HUD instead on zooming in on the distance, where the containment field held over a dozen assorted sizes and types of Voices. Each corner of the field had to be at least a hundred and fifty meters apart if not more. *Damn. I can't zoom in enough to get a look at them.* Which meant I'd have to figure out how to shut them down real fucking quick.

"*Please do not take this the wrong way, Mr. Diver,*" Hans said, "*but I sincerely hope this plan of Ms. Corelel's is going to work.*"

"*It'll work,*" I said, with more confidence than I felt.

It *had* to work. Failure could spell the death of an entire sapient species, and that simply wasn't an option.

Chapter Twenty-Nine

Xandri

Considering how much of my plan was wrapped up in assumptions and generalizations, I was kind of surprised Captain Chui had approved of it. But she had, and now here I was, marching straight into the arms of the LHFH.

We had to move quickly to reach the rendezvous point in time, and much of the land between us and them sloped upward. Nafar Santino had chosen to plant himself on a cliff overlooking the sea. Suitably melodramatic for a man that full of himself, but not a great spot for us. The area was too open, with no cover for combat or sniping. The only sheltered places nearby were a small cove and the beach next to the cliff, but neither would provide a good strategic position, according to Captain Rhees.

I marched at the head of the group, with Anton, Jae and Emin just behind me, and the Psittacans behind them, marching next to Captains Chui and Rhees. So many soldiers, but how could it possibly be enough? *Don't think about it too hard, Xan. It'll only make you sick.* And I had to get through this, for all our sakes.

"*How're you holding up, boss?*" Jae sub-vocalized at me.

"*Well enough that I still don't want you calling me 'boss.'*"

I could hear a smile in vir voice. "*Good. You hold onto that attitude and don't let it go, understand?*"

I managed a small nod that I knew vi could see from vir position and kept moving forward, one foot in front of the other. Sunlight beat down from overhead, but my EC kept me from overheating too much. As the terrain sloped farther upwards, I noticed small figures on the horizon. And as we climbed and climbed, those figures grew bigger, coming more and more into focus. I swallowed hard. We had to be outnumbered at least two-to-one if not more.

Spotting Nafar Santino was easy. He stood apart from his soldiers, out towards the edge of the cliff, gazing out over the ocean.

Even as we approached, he kept his back to us. So arrogant, so sure none of us would just shoot him in the back and be done. *He thinks because we care about other sapients, it means we're weak and unwilling to do what's necessary.* With any luck, that would be his fatal flaw.

We came to a halt, our soldiers falling into parade rest as if this was nothing more than a ceremonial meeting of two armies. Finally, Santino turned to face us. Sweet Mother Universe, he really was a big guy. If I hadn't known it was impossible, I'd have thought there was Zechak in his ancestry.

"So here she is at last," Santino said, spreading his arms—the detonator still held in his hand—in greeting. "The famous—or perhaps infamous—Xandri Corelel."

"You did ask for me specifically," I pointed out.

"Indeed. And you came." He gave his head a slow, sad shake. "It pains me to see it, Xandri—may I call you Xandri? You remind me so much of Antilles when I met him. Both so desperate for a place in the world that you were willing to do anything for it. Willing, even, to work for an Alliance that doesn't care about you."

"And *you* do?"

"Of course I do!" He feigned a look of surprise. "I consider myself a humanist, Xandri. Your wellbeing is just as important to me as my own."

I fought to control my facial expression, but couldn't quite keep my eyebrows from creeping upwards in skepticism. Did he think I was so shortsighted that I'd forget that the LHFH had left Marco behind to take the fall for the entire operation on Cochinga? That, thanks to his neurodivergence, he wasn't human enough for them to even try to rescue him? *Yeah, pretty sure your wellbeing means a whole fuck-ton more to you than that.* And so help me God, those thoughts better not be showing on my face.

"What do you want from me, Santino?" I demanded, folding my arms like I was impatient rather than terrified. "If you've got ransom demands, I'm not the one to negotiate with."

"You've got me all wrong, my dear. There are no ransom demands. What I want is simple. Give it to me, and we'll leave."

Something caught the edges of my perception and I flicked my eyes—gratefully, because it hurt like hell to look at Santino—in that direction. Santino followed my gaze and gave his soldiers a sharp look, but not before I'd caught sight of their confused shifting. *I—I might actually be right!* My pulse sped up and I had to take a deep breath to calm myself. I'd never get through this if I broke apart now.

"There's nothing I could give you."

"That's where you're wrong. All I ask is that you come with us when we leave." Santino smiled his shark's smile, and I fought the urge to wince. "Come away from these people who use you and spend a little time with us. Then you'll see the truth."

I pressed my fingertips to my temples as if I was developing a headache. "Do *not* tell me you started a war with an *entire planet* just for a chance to lure me to the dark side of the Force."

I turned my head slightly and sub-vocalized at my wristlet, sending the signal to Christa. A very slight vibration was all the acknowledgement I got that she'd received it. *Now it begins in earnest.* Even if Kiri got their heat-seeking software down, it wouldn't do us much good if they noticed it right away. No, we needed something that would draw their attention elsewhere. I just prayed I wasn't sending Beta Team and all those soldiers to their deaths.

"No, Xandri, listen to me," Santino said, his voice soft and persuasive. "We want to *help* you. These people have convinced you they're the good guys, but *they* are the ones who abandoned you only six standard months ago.

"Yet here you are, working for them again. Why? All you're doing is giving them what they want, with no benefit to yourself. They'll get the alliance they seek, and you'll be lucky if they even thank you for all your hard work. Why do you do it? Why do you give them what they want?"

"I'm not doing it for them. I'm doing it for the Hands and Voices."

"But *why?*"

I shrugged. "I guess you could say I consider myself a sophontist."

I flicked my gaze towards the sand as his expression twisted, growing ugly. It already hurt so much to look at him, but the darkness that crawled across his mien was sharp-edged and rough, and I could feel it right through my armor. Santino quickly schooled his expression—a skill a lot of LHFHers had to learn—but I'd seen the truth. Of course he didn't care about me, not one whit. Bad enough that my brain was different from those of my fellow humans, but I also cared too much about non-humans. I disgusted him.

Another stirring in the crowd of soldiers, and then one of them broke away, trotting up to Santino. I tried to school my features into something resembling bemusement, even though I knew *exactly* what this soldier would report. Santino leaned over, listening to the whispered words of his comrade. After a moment he straightened and a broad grin broke across his face. He started to laugh, a big, booming gut laugh that didn't sound very mirthful.

"Really, Captain Chui?" He swiped at his eyes even though there were no tears in them. "*That's* the best you can come up with? A last, pathetic rally from your tiny band of misfits? My soldiers will crush them in no time."

"Perhaps," Captain Chui answered. "Though no one said it was *my* idea."

Santino's eyes flickered to me. "You?"

"You're not the only one who can makes plans," I said. "I mean, that *is* who you are, right? Their strategy guy? Because I'm pretty sure that's what this is all about. What is it about me that makes LHFHers so willing to defy their orders?"

"I have no idea what you mean."

"Of course you do!" I said, widening my eyes. "Santino, let's not play games here. The LHFH didn't plan this mission just to get their hands on me. That's *your* idea. You're still mad that I foiled all your work on the Cochinga mission, aren't you?"

Something twisted in his expression, something he brought quickly under control, but I'd already seen it. It didn't matter now how he smoothed his features, how he raised his eyebrows slightly. It didn't matter how he spread his hands, opening up his posture in an expression of bewilderment. No, I'd been right, and now I had him exactly where I wanted him.

Diver

The waiting *seemed* to take forever, though I'd be surprised if it was more than twenty minutes. I kept watch through my HUD as the Voices trapped in the containment field swam back and forth. Despite already knowing how it worked, a few of them nosed the field occasionally. Trying to understand it better, Engineer explained to me via Warrior. *Typical scientists. Stick 'em in a cage of death and they* still *can't resist experimenting.*

"*Diver?*" came Kiri's voice in my ear.

Would've straightened abruptly, only it was a bit hard under water. "*Here.*"

"*I've almost got it. Just a few more minutes...*"

"*My goodness, Ms. Ayabara,*" Hans remarked. "*That's some impressive work, taking their software down so quickly.*"

"*I'm not taking it down. I'm manipulating it, which is better,*" she explained, her tone distracted. "*They'll continue to see exactly what they're seeing now. With any luck, they won't realize anything is wrong until it's far too late.*"

I grinned. *Always said she's a genius.* She had to be, to pull that kinda trickery so damn fast. It was finesse, not the ham-handedness of smacking something down completely. Smashing things to bits was useful in a pinch, but finesse almost always bought more time. *And we're gonna need it.* Just wished I knew how things were going with Xandri. We were trying to keep contact to a minimum, so I couldn't even ask.

A long, low note of song vibrated through the water. Behind me, Engineer's tentacles lifted. Something went between her and Warrior and the other Voice, so quickly I doubted I'd have been able to follow it even if I did know the language.

"We must go soon," Warrior said after a moment. "Disharmonies approach, many of them. The smell of blood has attracted them, in many sizes and great numbers. Our people can't stop them all."

"We just need a few more minutes," I said, trying not to let fear seize me. "Once we break your people out, the Disharmonies will be nothing more than the filling in an ugly reptile-thing sandwich."

"If we don't get out soon, we will not be prepared for the fight."

"I know, I know, but—"

"*Got it!*" Kiri cut in. "*All right, they can't see you. Go!*"

"That's our cue," I said aloud. "Time to take this thing out."

I'd barely finished speaking before the Voices started moving, heading full speed towards the containment field. Quickly I pressed myself low, plastering myself to Warrior's back so I wouldn't interrupt his hydrodynamics too much. The water rushed by in great sluices, too fast for me to focus on the containment field's pylons even with my HUD, so I just braced myself, waiting.

"*Join me at the first one,*" I called to Hans, "*and watch what I do. Then get to the next one and disable it.*"

"*Understood.*"

Warrior slowed just a little as we reached the first pylon, and Engineer and her fellow Hand released their hold on me. As Warrior plunged deeper into the ocean beneath me, I flung myself towards the pylon, using the momentum of Warrior's speed to propel me forward. The impact with it hurt a bit, and I came within centimeters of fetching up against the field itself, but managed to reel myself back in. Hans collided with the pylon a moment later, and I got to work the second he recovered.

As I'd predicted, the controls weren't on the surface. I ran my palms over the metal, my eyes closed as I searched for—there! They were hard to find, and the HP suit didn't help, but those were definitely rivets under my fingers.

"*Here, Hans, look,*" I said, raising a fingertip. "*This is what you'll need to find. If you have to, close your eyes and feel for them. Now watch.*"

I reached for the omni-tool at my belt and flipped the settings so I could release the rivets. The tool made quick work of them, and I grabbed the panel and sent it shunting through the water. The inside looked like a city, a network of switches and connections and god only fucking knew what. *Looks like it's been slapped together by someone who didn't quite know what they were doing...* So the LHFH had probably built these themselves, then, which meant I couldn't get by on just my knowledge of how they were *supposed* to work.

"*Mr. Diver?*" Hans queried.

"*They're a bit different from Alliance standard, s'all. Might take a moment...Damnit, man, think!*"

All right, even if it was different, it had to follow some kinda logic. Possibly a space-fried one, but it would still be logic of a sort. I followed connections with my fingertips, trying to get a sense for what to do and wishing I could smash the damn thing and be done. But doing that might set off the self-destruct. Some tech was twitchy like that.

"They're coming!" Warrior warned. "Diver, we have very little time left."

"I know, I know! I just...wait a minute!" Would've slapped my forehead if I wasn't so busy. *"Right, Hans, look. See this? This is what we want."*

I flipped a couple switches and the city began to darken. Whoever'd put these together, they'd wired them pretty good, actually. Made it so all four had to be shut off completely to get the containment field down. Normally these were made to go down if even a single pylon went down, so that any animals contained within them could escape in an emergency. Occasionally, if the wildlife in particular was *really* dangerous, it'd take two pylons before the field would go down.

I flicked the last switch, and the pylon shut down. Only then did I realize I'd barely been breathing the entire time.

"You got all that, Hans?"

He raised a hand, tapped the side of his head. *"Recorded it all on my HUD. And a good thing, because I didn't understand a damn thing you did."*

"All right. Warrior, we need transportation," I said. *"I'll head right. Hans, you go across and start working on the pylons there, got it?"*

"Right away, Mr. Diver."

Warrior swam up towards us. As he passed, tentacles shot out and caught me around the waist, dragging me along. I glanced back to see Hans clinging to the dorsal fin of his Voice—the one called Stars who'd brought me home the other day—who swam for the pylon across the way. I took a quick look with my HUD zoomed in, and thought I saw dark shapes out in the water. *C'mon, we only need a few more minutes. That's all.*

"We are doing our best to hold them off," Warrior said, as if he knew what I was thinking, "but some of them are slipping past us. We must hurry, Diver."

"On it," I said. "Drop me off...now!"

The tentacles released, and I glided through the water to the pylon, omni-tool first. This time I found the rivets faster, though I still had to close my eyes and feel for them. I focused all my energy into getting the cover off and working through the sequence of switches, instead of worrying about the damn sea monsters headed our way. *Almost got it...almost there...* I hit the last switch and—

"They come!" Warrior sang. "They have arrived."

Looking up from the pylon, I saw a huge Disharmony arrowing through the water, aiming at the containment field. It wouldn't be able to get through, of course, not yet—but it might notice that not every morsel was out of its reach. *Shit! Shit, shit, shit!*

"*Hans!*"

"*I've got the third pylon down. Now, if Stars will just escort me to the fourth...*"

"*There isn't time! We've failed!*"

"*Of course there's time,*" Hans said. "*Warrior, Engineer, please get Mr. Diver out of here and back to shore.*"

"*Wait, what? Hans, what are you doing?*"

"*Finishing the job we came here to do.*"

Tentacles wrapped around my waist, drawing me away from the pylon, and I had a horrible moment of flashback to the night Engineer's family died. *Fuck! It's happening again! Fuck!* I reached for my Barracuda, but what the fuck could it even do from this distance? A whole lotta nothing.

"*Hans, come on! We need to get out of here.*"

"*You go,*" Hans said placidly. "*Listen to me, Mr. Diver. There are thousands—hundreds of thousands—of anthropologists just like me in the universe. But there aren't many minds as brilliant as yours. And there are even fewer sapient species as wondrous as the Hands and Voices. You must get to safety, lad.*"

Not that Engineer was giving me a choice. She hauled me bodily onto Warrior's back and she and her fellow Hand pinned me there, tentacles wrapped firmly around my legs. Not that I'd go back. I fucking hated it, but I understood. This was Hans' choice to make. Just like it had been Darksong's choice. *Xandri was right. No matter how much we might care, we can't take people's choices away from them.* Especially when those choices saved lives.

"*You take care of that girl, you hear?*" Hans said, as Warrior swam farther and farther away. "*She cares, but she cares almost too much, and that leads to pain.*"

"*Tell me about it,*" I muttered.

"*Now, let's see here...this switch...and then this one...almost got it...*"

I held my breath. Maybe there was enough time for him to finish and get out of there. I glanced back, but Warrior was moving too fast for me to get a good look. Tried adjusting my HUD, but all I saw was the blur of water streaking past. I felt like I was torn in two, half of me back with Hans, urging him to finish so he could get out of there, half of me already back on shore, desperate to get to Xandri and the others.

"*And there's the last one,*" Hans declared. "*The field is—*"

His words cut off abruptly, and a scream came through the channel, slicing through my eardrums. It cut off almost as quickly as it had begun. I held very still on Warrior's back, hoping, hoping… but there was simply no way he'd survived.

"We are free," Warrior said. "We are sorry, Diver, that your friend did not make it. But the Disharmonies will not get a chance to enjoy their meal."

I pressed my face to Warrior's back and let out a heavy breath. The Voices and Hands would obliterate the Disharmonies to avenge Hans, but at the moment, that was cold fucking comfort.

Chapter Thirty

Xandri

"Perhaps the reporters were right about your state of mind after all, Ms. Corelel."

Oh, not Xandri anymore, am I? Santino's words stung only a little; after all, he wasn't the first one to sling them at me recently. And they were clearly a defensive reaction. I set my hands on my hips and tried for one of those cool, unimpressed expressions Captain Chui did so well. I had to goad him, had to keep his attention long enough for Diver and Hans to finish the job.

"Maybe they are," I said, with what I hoped was a nonchalant shrug. "But I don't think I'm wrong about this. It's the only answer that makes sense."

"Nothing you're saying makes any sense, my dear. Marco Antilles was in charge of the Cochinga operation."

"Antilles was the man on the ground, yes, but I no longer think the entire operation was his idea. You see, because even the LHFH isn't foolish enough to start a war simply to get their hands on me. And," I tipped my head to the side, "it's pretty clear why they started this war. An opportunity to scare other sapient species, to show them the Alliance can't protect them. Not a bad idea, all told. Had you succeeded, it might have sown a fair bit of dissidence among the sapients of the universe.

"But you—you must have invested *years* into your work on Cochinga. And like it or not, I'm the one who foiled that work. That must piss you off something fierce, huh?"

A coldness had settled on me, one I recognized well. It had come over me on Cochinga too, after I'd been rescued from Marco's clutches, after Katya had died to save me from Cochingan dissidents with enormous guns. I didn't know if I liked the person it turned me into, but whoever she was, she had a quick, sharp tongue and seemed to know all the right words to say. Which was much better than the flustered combination of anger and frustration I usually experienced.

Santino shifted from one foot to the other, a very slight movement that could have meant anything. Then he threw back his head and laughed, long and loud, until a number of his soldiers began chuckling along. It didn't sound as confident as his previous laughter, not to my ears, and when he cut himself off, a few last nervous titters emerged from the crowd of soldiers.

"You ridiculous little girl," Santino said. "If I hated you that much, why not let you die down here with everyone else?"

"That's not winning, though, is it? I mean, if all you wanted was to kill me, you had six standard months to find me and get the job done." Not that he'd likely have been able to get to Karrckchak. "And there's been opportunities since you arrived on Song, as well. Yet for some reason, LHFH soldiers just keep trying to kidnap me instead."

"You're imagining things."

"Well, not really," Jae put in. "There's an awful lot of soldiers here who saw that your people weren't willing to shoot her, and she would've been dragged off if I hadn't put a stop to it."

"I guess I'll have to talk to them about that." Santino flashed his shark's grin. "Orders among the LHFH are always shoot to kill."

"But sir," one of the LHFHers piped up, "you said to—"

He pitched forward as the soldier next to him struck him hard on the back, and ended up on his face with a mouthful of sandy turf. *That's the problem with having zealots rather than soldiers. They don't know when to keep their damn mouths shut.* I regarded Santino with raised eyebrows, wondering how he'd try to dodge that one. Because he *would* try to dodge it. This was a man who couldn't stand to acknowledge when his work was falling apart.

"All right, you got me," he said. "I wanted a chance to kill you myself."

"No, you didn't. You wanted exactly what you said just a little while ago. A chance to turn me to your cause."

"Would you listen to yourself? You're not making any sense. First you say I hate you because you ruined my plans—plans, I might add, which were *not* mine—and now you say I want you on my side. That's a complete contradiction."

I smiled. "Keep your friends close, and your enemies closer. You don't want me 'on your side,' you want me under your control. Dead, people might make a martyr out of me. If I'm under your thumb, doing exactly what you say, I'll never ruin your plans again *and* you get access to all the things I know." I pursed my lips for a moment, as if in deep thought. "I suppose you could even make an effort to turn me into a spy, though I'm not sure you're clever enough for that."

Santino let out a low chuckle and reached for his sidearm with the hand not holding the detonator. I heard the shuffle of *Carpathia* soldiers behind me and held up a hand, stalling their movement. Much as I wished we could just blow this guy's face off, we couldn't risk that he'd set off the containment field first.

"Maybe we should test your theory," Santino said, raising the gun and pointing it at me.

"Hypothesis."

"What?"

"I'm enough of a scientist to confess that I don't have enough evidence to call it a theory just yet." *Holy shit, Xan, don't taunt him! Shut your big mouth!*

Behind me, laughter rippled through the combined *Carpathia/* AFC crowd. The Psittacans clacked their beaks in delighted approval. No surprise, Nafar Santino looked far less amused. His sharky grin twisted into a scowl, bringing his thick, dark eyebrows close and low over his eyes, giving him a vaguely Neanderthal-like cast. When a few of his own soldiers chuckled, he aimed the gun low and shot at the sand near my feet.

"Shut up," he growled. "Or have you forgotten that I can turn your friends into sashimi with just a little tap of the button?"

"You keep mentioning food," I said. "You know, if you're that hungry, we can take a break, come back to this later."

It was the terror talking; it had to be. I was *not* this space-fried normally. Santino fired another shot near my feet, and somehow I managed not to run screaming. Because I really had him now. He was too angry to consider that we might have found a way to slip under his radar and stop him. *And surely the containment field is almost down by now...* I glanced out towards the sea, but saw nothing but waves.

And then, as it was wont to do, everything started going to Hell in a top-of-the-line hand-basket.

Santino froze, tilting his head in an evident listening posture. Along the line, his soldiers followed suit. As he listened, his face twisted in such fury that I thought he might shoot me after all.

"Ships?" he roared. "There weren't supposed to be any ships! Who are they? Where did they come from?"

All good questions. I dared to take my eyes off him, to glance at Captain Chui. She had her eyes down and her expression revealed absolutely nothing. Talking to Lieutenant Zubairi, if I had to guess. *Did the Alliance get here early?* My heart sped up. What would happen if they had? How would things change? And Sweet Mother Universe, where were Diver and Hans? I knew it hadn't been very long, but it *felt* like it had.

"How can you not know?" Santino was practically apoplectic. "What do you—hello? Come in. *Come in!*"

"We've lost them, sir," one of his lieutenants said. "I think the ship is—"

"Shut up!" He turned his red-faced fury on me. "This is the last time. *The last!* I will not having you snatching victory from me ever again."

I thought for certain he'd shoot me then, but it was the hand holding the detonator that he lifted. My breath caught. I took a step towards him without thinking.

"We did what you asked!"

"Naive little girl," he said. "Did you think coming out here and giving me what I wanted would ever be enough to protect that alien scum? You think you can run around the universe with these freaks you call a crew and protect these tentacled horrors, but you'll never stop *us*. We will never give up, not while monsters roam the—"

A scream of fury tore up my throat and suddenly I was running straight at him, with no thought but to stop him. All I could see was his sneering face, which quickly transformed, his disdain turning to shock and fear. He raised his gun with a shaking hand and took aim. Something crashed into my shoulder, almost throwing me to the ground, tearing through me and leaving behind a wake of searing pain. I gritted my teeth, put my head down, and barreled onwards.

I thought someone was screaming my name, but my focus was only for Nafar Santino.

The thing about people was, when they already were half-convinced you were space-fried, getting them the rest of the way wasn't hard.

Santino fumbled with his pistol, in a show of real fear, as I charged towards him. He lost his grip on it and it hit the sand, mere seconds before I collided with him.

I threw myself at him with everything I had, screaming, my hands clawing at the arm still holding the detonator. Santino staggered, lost his balance—and then we were both falling.

The ocean came rushing up at me, a blur of pure blue. The fall lasted an eternity; it lasted no longer than the blink of the eye. I hit the water with such force that I could've sworn it was passing right through me, its molecules tearing through my own as if I was made of nothing more than tissue paper. Pain exploded through my entire body and the air was slammed right out of my lungs. I opened my mouth in a gasp and took in liquid, what felt like liters and liters of it. And I plummeted down, down, down.

Some part of my brain urged me to fight back. I clawed at the water ineffectively, unable to see with eyes full of salt. Yet no matter how I fought I seemed to continue only to move down, ever down, and I couldn't breathe at all, and darkness squeezed in on me, clouding my mind like a fog.

Fight, a voice whispered at the back of my mind, and it sounded like Diver. *You have to fight.*

I tried. I tried so desperately, but I felt so heavy, so tired. It didn't matter how hard I tried, I couldn't hold off the darkness anymore. It came up from beneath me, jaws open to swallow me whole. Just before it caught me, it seemed like something else had arrived, had grabbed me to pull me away, but I doubted I'd ever know what.

Diver

Warrior took me about halfway before passing me off to Bright. With only a wave from Engineer, Warrior made a huge, swooping turn in the water and shot back towards the deactivated containment field, where the battle was still raging. Swearing a little, I grabbed Bright's dorsal fin. Nothing I could do about it, and at least Bright was fast. I had to get to my gorilla, now.

"*Kiri?*" I tried through the comm, and got no response. "*Damnit, Kiri, what's going on up there?*"

"*Busy,*" came a terse reply. "*Gotta—holy shit!*"

"*What? What? Kiri!*"

"*Get to shore, Diver! Now!*"

"Fuck! Fucking hell! Bright, I think there's trouble on shore!" I shouted over the roar of water rushing past us.

"We are almost there," Bright told me. "If you would just have a little patience, we—"

A shrill, long note of song carried through the ocean to us and Bright came to a halt as abruptly as a kick to the gut. Didn't have much time to prepare for the fact that his Hands released me; I scrabbled at Bright's dorsal fin, but ended up slinging off his back and going under. Thank fuck for the HP suit. Instead of getting water up my nose and down my gullet, I was able to resurface quickly—in time to catch sight of Bright's tail as he started swimming away.

"Hey! What the hell, Bright!" I called after him.

"We must go," was the only response I got.

"At least tell me what's going on! Bright!" But he kept swimming, pulling farther and farther away. *Fuck me.* "For the record, I don't care for this new 'leave Diver out of the loop' strategy!"

Of course, no one answered. And I had to get to shore. I saved breath I could've been using to swear up a blue streak and started swimming for the cove where the gorilla sat. Good damn thing Captain Chui'd had a rule that all her crew members had to learn to swim. Street-kids weren't usually much for swimmers, but we were great sinkers, and I'd been no exception. Now I was good, good enough to make it onto shore in the little cove in minutes. *Thank fuck we were so close.*

And also that, even with the smart-fab covering it, making it blend into the cliff wall, I knew where the gorilla was. I grabbed hold of the smart-fab tarp and yanked, freeing the great metal beast and the pack with my guns and armor. My heart hammered, especially when I noticed the sound of gunfire somewhere high above me, a short way in the distance. I quickly stripped off the HP suit and traded it for fatigues and armor, and as much ammo as I could carry and still fit in the gorilla.

In moments I had myself—and the gorilla—ready to go. I positioned myself in the back, sliding my arms down into its arms, my legs into its legs. As I started up the steep, winding path to the top of the cliff, I integrated my HUD with the gorilla's system, allowing me to fire whatever guns I wanted with little more than a flicker of my eyelashes.

As I reached the top of the cliff, the sound of gunfire grew louder. *Over that way.* I curled my hands into fists, slamming the gorilla's hands against the sand, and off I went, using the machine's fast-building momentum to carry me along. Seeing through my HUD, combined with the gorilla's vision grid, I soon made out fighting in the distance. Utterly chaotic, space-fried fighting, the kind you only got in a desperate situation that involved no cover. *Fuck. Can't use my guns in this clusterfuck.* Good thing the ol' gorilla didn't need guns to do damage.

As I charged at the edge of the fray, I tapped into Captain Chui's private comm. *"Captain, Diver here. What the shit is going on here? Where's Xan?"*

Figured it might take her time to reply, so I waded into the fight. Our people knew the gorilla, knew the hand signal that told me to pass them on, even if I couldn't tell who was who. There was more hand-to-hand combat going down than you usually saw these days, on account of the chaos, and the fact that LHFHers were ding-brained. Which suited me and the 'rilla just fine. I grabbed hold of the nearest LHFH soldier—knew he wasn't AFC cause there was no blue trim on his fatigues—and slammed him into the ground with all of the gorilla's hulking metal strength.

"Mr. Diver?"

"Here, Captain. What the fuck happened here?" A brave—though perhaps not very smart—LHFHer came at me, guns blazing. I waited until he was close, bounded forward, and knocked him flat with a blow to the chest.

"Help arrived."

"The Alliance? Weren't they gonna be at least a few more hours yet?"

"Not the Alliance, Mr. Diver. Have you ever heard of the mercs known as Alueyn's Drifters?"

I whistled through the comm channel. Who *hadn't* heard of the Drifters? One of the youngest merc companies in existence—and one of the largest and most successful, too. They had their own damn fleet, high class ships with more illegal weapons than even I could finagle, and they did so much work cutting down pirates and bringing in the worst scum crime had ever seen that the Alliance looked the other way for them, too.

"*How'd they know? Didn't we send a narrow with the distress call?*"

"*We did. But we—hang on.*" The sound of impacts and a loud "oof" echoed through the channel. "*There. We did not send out Ms. Betancourt's footage on the narrow. Since it was headed straight to news stations, we didn't think anyone would bother with it.*"

"*Leave it to mercs. Anything for a job. How much they gonna take out of our hide?*"

"*Even if Tenna Alueyn wasn't an old friend, and even if she didn't owe me a couple,*" Captain Chui said, "*they're not big fans of the LHFH. Got a lot of non-human crew. They're more than happy to help.*"

"*Well, that's—*" I grabbed two LHFHers by their fatigues and crashed them into each other, "*—great. They know the hand signal?*"

"*Yes.*"

"*Good. Where's Xan?*"

"*Diver...*"

The hesitation in Captain Chui's voice filled me with dread. I looked around, setting my HUD to home in on Xandri's wristlet, but got nothing.

And then it started, a loud, wailing keen of song from multiple Voices. The sound came off strange, not like it usually sounded. I turned the gorilla in that direction and took off, trying not to mow down any of our own. Most of them were smart enough and fast enough to move out of the way, anyhow.

The song kept on, meshing oddly with the ring of gunfire and the pinging of bullets as they bounced off the gorilla. I punched my way through a line of LHFHers trying to hold their ground, scattering them like bowling pins. Then I was heading down, leaning back as the gorilla half-slid down the hill towards the beach. I could already see them, at least a dozen shallow water Voices. They'd beached themselves and continued to sing—which sounded odd, outside of the water—even as a line of soldiers advanced on them.

Or tried to. The Psittacans were on the beach too, defending the Voices. They were moving so damn fast, it seemed like there were more than five of them. *Fuck me. There* are *more than five!* There had to be more than a dozen of them, which meant the Drifters had picked some up too. Scary thought, that. And then I realized it wasn't just the Voices they were defending, and my heart started doing fucking jumping jacks in terror.

One of the Voices was Bright; I recognized his dorsal stripe. And laying next to him in the sand was a still form, a *very* still form. *Oh God. Xandri.* It *had* to be her.

"*Many,*" I called into our channel, "*I'm coming through. Might wanna get out of the way.*"

A loud cry went up from one of the Psittacans and all of them scattered. I planted the gorilla's fists and swung into action, barreling through the line of soldiers. Something lodged in my armor, sending a flare of pain down my back. I swung around, slamming a metal fist into the nearest LHFHer, hard enough that the soldier collided with several of his fellows and took them down. But I was on the other side of their line now and they were distracted with me, which proved a good way to end up getting their throats torn open by Psittacans.

Hold on, Xan. I stopped the gorilla and jumped out, scrambled across the sand to where she lay. So still, so terrifyingly still. Bright caught sight of me and keened, low and sad. He twisted in the surf and nudged Xandri as gently as he could. She didn't respond, not even a twitch. I slipped in the wet sand and landed on my knees beside her. Reached out, placed a hand over her nose and mouth. Felt nothing.

"*Captain! Captain, I've found her, she's not breathing, oh God!*"

What did I do? Fuck, I had no idea what to do. I set my hands gently on her chest and pressed, worried about what injuries she might've taken. *And what does that matter if she dies!?* With modern nanotech, a person could stop breathing for something like half an hour before there was risk of brain damage, but I had no idea how long she'd been like this.

"*Captain!*"

"*We're on our way. Just stay with her.*"

How can she be so damn calm? I gave Xandri's chest another gentle press, but nothing happened. "C'mon, fireball! Fight this! I know you can do it, just—just don't give up."

"We found her in the water," Bright said. "She had fallen a great distance. We also found the man who was threatening us. He did not survive the fall."

"Oh, Xan, what did you do? Damnit, wake up, would you?" Nothing.

"Please!"

I bowed my head. Why this, why now? I could fix anything in the universe, but I couldn't fix this.

All of a sudden a tentacle lashed out and slapped Xandri's hard across the chest. I straightened, reaching instinctively for my guns—and froze as she jerked and started to cough. Holding down my wave of emotions, I reached out and carefully helped her onto her side as she hacked and spat up water. The coughing carried on for a while, and as soon as it stopped she let out a low, pitiful moan.

"It's all right," I murmured, turning her onto her back and cradling her in my arms. "It's gonna be fine, little darling, I promise. Help is on the way."

"Dive—er?"

"Yeah, it's me. I got'cha, yeah? Just hang in there."

"Hurts," she gasped out, tears leaking down her cheeks.

"I know. But it'll be fine." Didn't know who I was trying to reassure, her or me. I leaned over her, shielding her body with mine. "We been giving them the ol' roust-up down here, y'know? Get 'em bruised up but good."

I was rapidly lapsing into street-cant, something I hadn't done in years, but I didn't care. *She's all right, she's gonna be fine, I know it.* I curled over her farther, kissed her forehead, then her temple, then her eyelid, everywhere I could reach. And all that time, no one reached us. No one got past the Psittacans. They fought like feathered demons, from what I could tell when I glanced in their direction.

And then suddenly our people were pouring down the hill by the dozen, *Carpathia* soldiers and AFC soldiers, and people in motley but expensive bits of armor who were clearly mercs. They crashed down on the LHFHers like a wave, overwhelming them. I noticed Anton, Emin and Jae at the front, three different kinds of heavily armed and armored terror, turning the LHFHers into a very squishy sandwich between themselves and the Psittacans. I turned my attention back to Xandri.

"You know, fireball, you have a knack for drawing a most impressive cavalry."

She snorted. "Lucky—me."

Chapter Thirty-One

Xandri

I hurt like hell, and honestly, I was pretty sure I deserved it.

My parents were right. There's something fundamentally wrong with me. How else could I explain the way I'd lost control like that? My rage had gotten the better of me and I'd nearly died for it. What must everyone else think of me? What would Diver think, when he learned the truth? *What if—what if Captain Chui sends me back?* Panic seized my already aching chest and I forced myself to drag in a deep, painful breath. No. She'd promised me, *sworn* on her ship that she'd never send me back.

The noise was dying down, first to bursts of gunfire, then to almost nothing. I looked up at Diver, who was still bent over me, stroking my hair back from my face. An extra ache started in my chest. *He deserves someone who isn't going to go completely space-fried and throw herself off a cliff.*

"Mr. Diver!" Captain Chui's voice.

"S'all right, Cap'n," Diver called back, with that heavy drawl I'd heard in his voice a few minutes ago. "Her puffers are running a'right now, far's I can tell. What did?"

"What *happened,*" Captain Chui said firmly, "was that Nafar Santino decided to blow the containment field after all when Tenna's mercs showed up, and Xandri, ah, took umbrage at that."

"She threw herself at him," Jae put in wryly. "Sent them both off the cliff. How's her shoulder?"

Diver blinked and looked down at me again. "Damn. Didn't even notice that. He shot her?"

"And she still wouldn't go down," Anton said, his voice ringing with pride. There was a loud thump as he set down his Gabe and then he was kneeling next to me, gazing down at me too. "How're you holding up, kiddo?"

I opened my mouth, but all I managed was a wheeze. Must've been an eloquent one, because Anton chuckled.

And then suddenly there were even more people around me, Captain Chui and Emin and Jae, and Doctor Marsten, who pushed her way through all of them to crouch by my side. And then Betancourt and her damn camera showed up, and next to her a tall, dark-skinned woman with a bright pink puff of curls surrounding her face. *Oh yeah. Definitely wishing the ground would open me up and swallow me about now.*

"All right, Xandri, can you hear me?" Doctor Marsten asked.

I managed a small nod.

"I'm giving you an injection of short term military-grade nanobots," she said, holding up a hypospray where I could see it. "They'll take care of the worst of the physical damage without danger of healing anything serious too fast. Captain?"

"Yes, Doctor?"

"We need to get her back to the *Carpathia*. I don't have the equipment down here for a brain scan and we need to know if there was any damage and what kind, if we're going to be able to treat it."

Brain damage? Would a scanner even be able to tell? I did *throw myself off a cliff, after all.* I lay still as Doctor Marsten applied the hypospray, and then drew out another, probably one with painkillers. The kind of painkillers that started working as soon as they hit your bloodstream. The hypospray stung only very slightly, and then sweet, sweet relief began coursing through my veins.

"Tenna," Captain Chui said, "can you get us to the *Carpathia*?"

"Should be doable," the pink-haired woman replied. "It's chaos up there. Something like four or five of their command ships just self-destructed—"

"Kiri," Diver said with a grin.

"—and as it turned out, they don't actually *know* how to deal with a space battle. And our dropships are made to evacuate under any circumstances."

"Good, tell your pilot to stand by. Doctor Marsten, can we move her?"

Marsten drew a long, paddle-shaped wand from her bag and flicked it on. Purplish light lit up along its length. Starting at my neck, she moved the wand slowly down my body, studying the readings that scrolled across the screen at the back of it. Already the painkillers were working, chasing away the very worst of the aches

I'd picked up. My legs felt the worst of all, wobbly and weak and barely there.

"You can move her," Marsten said at last, "but *gently*. Bring her to Zahran, she'll know what to do."

"I'm coming with you," Diver said, already beginning to scoop me up with care.

"I figured as much. P'yo, Mulroney, Nazaryan, stay down here and help with cleanup. I think the Voices could use a bit of help, as well."

A few notes of meek, embarrassed song met her words. As Diver lifted me, I finally caught sight of the state of the beach, in particular all the beached Voices. I recognized Bright's dorsal stripe, and suddenly I remembered those moments under the water, when the darkness had been coming for me. Something had grabbed me and hauled me away from it. *It was them. They brought me here.*

"So *that's* why you abandoned me like that," Diver said.

"We are sorry, but we had to. We could not leave Xandri Corelel to drown after everything she has done for us."

"Saved me," I managed. "Thank you."

Bright let out a small trill. "We did nothing you would not have done for us, if you could have. But uh...we *could* use a little help getting back in the water. It is not terribly comfortable out here."

I rested my head against Diver's shoulder, comfortable in the knowledge that our people would take care of them. Already Emin, Anton and Jae were crouching in the sand to get a good look at the problem, and other soldiers were coming forward to join in. No doubt Doctor Marsten would stay down here to search out injured soldiers. Betancourt had already disappeared too, probably getting some footage of the battlefield. It would just be me, Diver and Captain Chui, and whoever Tenna sent along with us.

Diver, cradling me with great care, fell into step next to Captain Chui. When I tried to roll my head to get a better look at everything, he cleared his throat and gave me a look. *But...I want to know everyone is okay...* Everyone wouldn't be okay, of course. Not in a battle like this. There were always casualties in battles like this. But I wanted—needed—to know that my plan had saved some lives.

"Sure you can come along, Captain?" Diver asked.

"There are more than a dozen reporters on my ship, Mr. Diver. You are damn right I'm going to be there. Magellan can handle things down here. Besides," and I could hear the scowl in her voice. "When I reported in to Major Douglas about what I was doing, he insisted he come with us. To 'protect' Xandri from the press, he said."

"Wants—to make sure," I struggled out, "I—don't say—wrong things."

Diver grinned. "Something tells me her brain is just fine."

We started up a slightly sloping terrain—and soon paused again. I turned my head and found—*whoa. That's* way *too many Psittacans. Maybe I have got brain damage after all.* Except... I didn't recognize most of them. One was clearly Silence In The Night, since none of the others were as dark in color. One was Swifter Than Lightning with his slightly forward bending crest, and one was naturally Shadows Beneath Sunlight, because she was so beautiful. Many Kills and Day Dawns Red might have blended in with the others, except they were standing amongst their fellows.

"We're going with you," Many Kills declared.

"That won't be necessary," Captain Chui said.

"It is a good idea, Captain," Dawn spoke up. "There is no better defense against the press."

"Much as I appreciate the offer, I'm pretty sure allowing you to eviscerate the press will cause something of a universal uproar."

The Psittacans—*all* of them—clacked their beaks in amusement. I let out a coughing laugh. "No, Captain. They—offer themselves—as bait."

"Yes," Dawn agreed. "Bait for nosy monkeys."

Humans weren't the only sapients who had reporters; ours were just the worst behaved. Which, as I understood it, continued a long and hallowed tradition that had begun millennia ago on Ancient Earth. Some claimed they weren't as bad as they'd once been. Others said that modern technology allowed them to be far worse. When the Psittacans had first joined the *Carpathia*, we'd had a hell of a time with reporters—usually humans—trying to sneak aboard to get a look at them every time we swung by a space station.

"Well," Captain Chui said, "I can't disagree with that. You can come. And Ms. Corelel? Next time we recruit Psittacans, please don't teach them that humans evolved from apes."

The painkillers must've been getting to me. For some reason I found that hysterical.

When I asked the pilot of the Drifters' dropship for the ship's specs, Captain Chui had no choice but to agree with Diver that I'd probably escaped brain damage. Which was funny, because I felt rather lightheaded and loopy, like I hadn't been getting enough oxygen. Of course, I hadn't been, a thought that sent me into a spate of random-seeming giggles despite not really being funny. *Pull yourself together, Xan. You're not helping your case here as far as mental stability goes.*

The dropship was one impressive space-faring vehicle. It handled atmosphere like a fighter jet, carrying us across Song and launching us into orbit much closer to the *Carpathia* and decently far from the battle. I'd managed to convince Diver to let me sit at the window and lean my head against it, watching as we rose through the atmosphere. When we broke out amongst the stars, I let out a small, contented sigh. For now at least no one was going to send me anywhere.

Soon the *Carpathia's* great opaline hull appeared, and before long we were easing into the docking bay. Most of the pain had gone, and I could move my limbs with relative ease. Hell, I could *feel* all of them again, which was a relief.

"Think you can walk?" Diver asked, as he helped me out of the harness.

"I need to try," I said. "This is going to be bad enough without looking like a damsel in distress."

"Not many damsels in distress have your aim, fireball."

I sighed. "I don't think my guns are in any shape for firing after that fall. My wristlet is definitely broken, too."

"Well, then," and Diver wrapped an arm around my waist to help me up, "I'll just have to fix 'em. C'mon."

I wish someone could fix me. Thanks to the painkillers, my mood was bouncing all over the place, and now it had slid into melancholy. Something was wrong with me, very wrong with me, and what if the reporters already knew? What would they do if they knew I'd kind of thrown myself off a cliff? Betancourt had been there to film it all, and they probably knew by now that we were broadcasting footage from Song. *Oh Sweet Mother Universe...*

"It's gonna be all right," Diver murmured in my ear. "Just hold onto me. We'll get you through this."

The Psittacans paraded off first, their crests up and their chests puffed out, and that's when the noise began. Excited chattering reached my ears, then shouted questions. I held tight to Diver as we followed Captain Chui and Major Douglas onto the ramp. As we descended, I caught sight of the crowd in the docking bay and wished I felt well enough to bolt back into the dropship.

Thanks to things like sound and camera crew, there were far more than a dozen members of the press here. At least three dozen, perhaps more, all of them crowding excitedly around the Psittacans. I huddled against Diver, trying to make myself small and invisible. And we might have gotten through it, if it wasn't for Major Douglas puffing out his chest, making himself rather large and *definitely* visible.

"Major Douglas!" a reporter called. "I've seen the footage taken by Ashley Betancourt on Song. What is the Alliance going to do about this?"

Major Douglas cleared his throat. "I'll answer any questions you have later," he said, his tone unctuous. "Right now, I have business to attend to."

Please don't let them notice me, oh please, please...

"Is that Xandri Corelel?" someone else asked. "The girl who threw herself off a cliff?"

Good news travels fast.

"Is she all right?"

"Why'd she do it?"

And oh, curse my betraying tongue, because I blurted out, "Didn't you just say you saw the footage? Isn't it obvious why I did it?"

Which was a damn foolish thing to say, since even *I* wasn't clear on what had possessed me. But it also brought all those curious noses in my direction, and honestly, it was a bit like being stared down by a pack of overeager monkeys. All of those nosy, curious gazes burned on my skin. *Huh. Guess the Psittacans have reasons for calling us monkeys.* The Psittacans hurried closer, making a small circle around us, but the damage was done.

"Xandri! Xandri! A question for you!"

"Ms. Corelel, over here!"

"Ms. Corelel, if you had to jump off that cliff again—"

"Xandri, what would you say if—"

Oh God, this is my own personal hell. I tightened my grip on Diver. Didn't they have eyes? Couldn't they see that I was damp and wearing armor and there was a hole in my shoulder that only didn't hurt because of the painkillers I'd been given? I'd never understand people, how they could look at someone and yet see nothing, could look through a person and catch none of the details of their physical state. Just a glance showed me all kinds of things: a woman wearing shoes a size too big; a cameraman who struggled to hold his camera straight despite its tiny size; another reporter whose shirt had stains leftover from his last meal; someone towards the back of the crowd who kept fiddling with their hair.

"All right, all right," Major Douglas boomed genially. "That's quite enough. I understand the excitement of meeting a true Alliance hero face-to-face, but Ms. Corelel has had a long day and she needs her rest."

A hero? Now that's *a change.*

A man pushed his way through the crowd, coming to stand at the front of the reporters despite a number of vehement protests. He was sharply dressed for a man who seemed to make his living chasing gossip, and he stood tall enough to see over the Psittacans. I disliked him on sight. He had the sort of oily smile that clung to your skin, but never reached *his* eyes.

"Please, Major, just a single question. Just the one, and I'm sure myself and my fellow reporters can agree to give Ms. Corelel her space."

I glanced at Major Douglas. He continued to smile broadly, but shook his head faintly at me. *Wait just a minute here. Isn't it* my *decision whether or not I answer any questions?* A sudden spark of defiance lit inside me. Probably those damn painkillers. I turned to the crowd of reporters, making an effort at a gracious smile. It slipped a little as they began taking holo-stills. *They're sharks, yes, but get some blood in the water and sharks will attack other sharks without reservation.*

"I'd be happy to answer a single question," I said, tilting my head in what I hoped was a charming and inviting manner.

"Xandri," the reporter began. "May I call you Xandri?"

"Well, you can," I said. "Though I should warn you, I pushed the last man who asked me that question off a cliff."

His smile became more forced. "So we saw. That was quite some stunt you pulled."

"He was going to blow up my friends. I guess I got a little mad." Pray God it never got out that the containment field had gone down just before I did that.

"That's one way of putting it." His smile turned patronizing. "I have to be honest with you, Xandri. I'm a little surprised to see you, after what happened on Cochinga and the way you were dismissed from the *Carpathia*. Now suddenly you're an Alliance hero. How do you feel about all this?"

"Yesterday a scapegoat, today a hero." I shrugged. "I don't know how I feel about it. I *am* a little curious what I'll be tomorrow."

"If you felt like a scapegoat, why come back at all? Why not refuse?"

"That's two questions," I pointed out. I paused, then added, "Actually, technically it's three."

The reporter forced out a chuckle. "Very cute, Ms. Corelel. But really, why *did* you agree to this mission?"

"Was I supposed to refuse? The Hands and Voices asked specifically for my help. Sure, refusing might have salved my ego a bit, but it wouldn't have done *them* any good. I had to help."

"That's surprising," he said. "I mean, after the way you were treated, for someone of your nature especially to show such empathy..."

"I know. But I try to look on the bright side," I said cheerfully. "It could always be worse; I *could* be a reporter."

Major Douglas cleared his throat. "I think that's quite enough. We have orders from the ship's head doctor to get Ms. Corelel to medbay immediately."

"One last thing, Xandri," the reporter said, striding to keep up with us as Captain Chui led us away. "What you said about being a scapegoat and having to come to the aid of the Hands and Voices... does that mean you feel the Alliance isn't doing their job properly?"

I knew I shouldn't, but this guy was an asshole, and I'd had a horrible last few days and the painkillers were messing with my head, which I was pretty sure was already messed up beyond redemption anyway. So I just let fly. "If you need me to answer that, you can't be very good at *your* job."

The reporter halted, staring at me in fury. I let Diver and the others sweep me away from the crowd, who seemed a little at a loss. Tears of exhaustion started to prickle in my eyes, exhaustion and fear and confusion. For a terrifying moment I thought I'd start to cry where all those reporters could see me. And then Diver leaned over and whispered in my ear.

"Have I ever told you how much I love it when you just say whatever's on your mind?"

And the world righted itself just a little bit.

Chapter Thirty-Two

Xandri

Information reached me in the medbay in a slow trickle.

The first trickle came when Doctor Zahran visited me to tell me there was no sign of brain damage. I thought she'd be on her way to visit with other patients—the worst of the *Carpathia* injuries had been sent up shortly after me—but she sat by my bed, exclaiming over the differences in my brain as compared to a neurotypical one. Eventually I got it into my head to pretend that the painkillers were making me drowsy and she left off, thank god. Like I really needed *another* reminder, just then, that I was abnormal.

Next I learned about my injuries. I had hundreds of small hairline fractures all over my body. The short-term military 'bots had healed them enough that I'd been able to walk, but I was going to be fragile for a while. Too much activity could do massive harm, and with the slower 'bots I had in my system now, that meant a lot of bed rest. When I complained about being stuck in the medbay, Captain Chui had reminded me—gently, for her—that it was a good excuse to keep the reporters away. I still wasn't thrilled about it, but Diver showed up a little later with a holo-slate full of books and games, so at least I had something to do.

I learned about the casualties, too. They were far less than they would have been if the Drifters hadn't shown up, and the Hands and Voices had lost very few, to my relief. In a strange twist of fate, Beta Team had come out with nothing more serious than some injuries. Knowing my team was safe from the LHFH, I'd sent along orders for them to stay down on Song, and *not* to return to base. I wanted them safe from the reporters, too.

The worst of it was when Captain Chui sat down with me, on the third day, and in quiet tones related the fate of Hans Klee.

I sat for a long while in silence, staring at the cool white walls of medbay. They'd never looked more unwelcoming. My eyes remained dry, and I couldn't tell if I was just an awful, heartless person, or if I even had a right to cry. After all, Hans would never have been on Song if it weren't for me. He would never have gone out with Diver and gotten killed by Disharmonies if it wasn't for my plan.

"It can be hard, being a leader," Captain Chui said into the silence. "You have to make decisions, and those decisions can end badly for a lot of people. And it becomes very easy to forget that you're not the only person who made decisions in a situation.

"When Hans Klee joined the *Carpathia*, he'd already been a field anthropologist for a century. He'd explored a number of planets long colonized by humans and he was bored. He thought a change of pace, studying other sapient cultures, would reinvigorate his interest in anthropology. I warned him that any field assignments he drew would be *very* different from what he'd done before, that they could be dangerous. He joined anyway."

I turned my head slowly, hardly seeming to see what was right in front of me. When my gaze reached Captain Chui, she smiled faintly.

"Hans Klee was a man who loved science, and he had a good heart, too. He didn't have to agree to go down to Song; if he hadn't wanted to, we have other anthropologists who could have done the job," Captain Chui said. "And there were others who could have taken his place on that last mission, too. He could have escaped. He chose not to because he was a good man who believed very strongly in the rights of people.

"As a leader, you will always need to remember that the people you lead make choices too. When you take all the blame for what happens onto yourself, all you really do is deny people their autonomy. You need to remember that they are their own people, capable of making their own decisions."

She reached over and patted my arm, an almost motherly gesture. Then she rose from the chair beside my bed and headed towards the door of my private—but tiny—room.

"Does that make you feel any better?"

She paused and glanced back at me.

"What you just said," I clarified. "Does it make you feel any better?"

"Not often," she answered, and I valued her honesty more than ever. "But sometimes, when I think about all the times over the years I've spoken with Hans, how happy he was, how much he loved his work again…sometimes that makes me feel a little less worse."

I sat for a while remembering Hans playing volleyball with us, how excited he'd been by the very prospect of a game with a sapient species entirely new to him. Captain Chui was right: I didn't feel better, precisely, but the weight of his death dragged on me a little less.

Diver brought me news all the time. He told me first about how Kiri had indeed hacked into the systems of a number of the LHFH command ships and set them to self-destruct. After the first four, she couldn't access the systems anymore; they had, as she apparently put it, 'shut down harder than an Ancient Earth Catholic nun.' Between that and the Drifters' ships, the chaos and confusion had made the LHFH sitting ducks.

The arrival of the Alliance had been the final nail in the coffin. Now it was down to chasing out pockets of LHFH soldiers still on Song, hunting down their remaining ships, and mostly importantly, helping the Hands and Voices. Of course, the Hands and Voices had wreaked a lot of havoc for ocean-bound creatures, and their med tech was, in places, almost as good as ours, but they didn't say no to the extra help. And, Diver told me with great pleasure, Engineer was doing quite well as a heroine of her people.

On my fifth day of confinement, I got several new visitors. The first surprised me. She stalked into the room without knocking and stood at the foot of my bed, grinning down at me. Even though I'd been a mess when I first saw her, I recognized Tenna Alueyn's bright pink hair. Her casual dress—jeans and a fitted, slashed tank top—didn't make her look less like a merc. It was the way she stood, straight and tall, absolutely blasting confidence and competence.

"Um…hi?"

"Hello, kiddo," she said. "Figured I'd come check on you."

I gazed back at her, bewildered. "Why?"

"Got some time on my hands. Came in for a tune up, but I'm

kinda low on the priority list at the moment." She raised a hand and wiggled her fingers. They responded stiffly and slowly.

"Didn't bond with the regrowth treatment, I take it."

Her eyebrows went up slightly. "What gave it away? Most people see I've got that much chroming and they freak out."

"Advantage chroming is high-class stuff. It never stiffens like that. Who'd pay for an advantage that needs to be oiled once a month?"

She broke into another grin, and I decided she reminded me of Anton in all the best ways. *People must think because she's a merc, she went out and bought herself advantage chroming.* People who lost limbs or other body parts weren't always compatible with regrowth treatments, and most of the time others would give you the benefit of the doubt before assuming you'd gotten chromed for selfish reasons. But most people also wouldn't hesitate to judge a mercenary.

"You know," Tenna said, "I saw the footage of you taking that bastard down."

I sighed. "You and everyone else in the universe by now." Including my parents, a thought that made me want to find the nearest black hole and hide in it.

"You got a lot of guts for such a tiny thing. You didn't even flinch when he shot you. That's the kinda spirit I like in my mercs, and I was thinking, if things ever get too boring for you around here, I could find some use for you. Especially if your aim is as legendary as people keep telling me."

I stared at her. The idea of me as a mercenary was so ridiculous, I wanted to laugh. But I swallowed it down, because I didn't want her to think I was laughing at *her*. She'd saved our tail feathers but good, after all.

"I think," I said carefully, "that anything more exciting than falling off a cliff is well above my pay grade."

She tossed her head back and let out a roar of a laugh, reminding me more than ever of Anton. An answering smile touched the corners of my mouth; her mirth was absolutely irresistible. *I wonder why the Drifters and* Carpathia *don't work together...* The LHFH might not have made a move if we'd had our own personal merc company with us.

"Well, the offer stands if you ever change your mind, though Shannie'd never forgive me for poaching you."

"Shannie? Oh." My eyes widened. "You mean Captain Chui. I'm not sure she'd forgive you for calling her 'Shannie' in front of me, either." I waited until Tenna had finished another laugh, then added, "You know... if you really don't want to wait around here for too long, you could head down to R&D and find Diver. If you tell him I sent you, he'll get you fixed up first thing."

"The mad genius kid, right? You know, I think I'll do that. Thanks, Xannie."

So I'd acquired a new nickname and maybe even a new friend, which carried me through the rest of my morning in a pretty decent mood. I even ate the nutrient-bar that came with my lunch with minimal complaint, to the relief of Doctor Zahran. Thus it came as a really nasty surprise when, shortly after lunch, the door to my private room opened and Ashley Betancourt walked in.

"Space-faring is bad for the human race," I remarked, refusing to look up from my holo-slate. "No one knocks anymore."

"I don't see why you're complaining, Ms. Hero," Betancourt said, dropping uninvited into the chair next to my bed. "No one else in medbay gets the luxury of a private room."

I looked up sharply. "No one else in medbay is autistic, either."

I couldn't deal with medbay very well. It was a bit like being shoved in a box made out of pain and fear, especially at a time like this. And then there were all the machines and the noises they made, the whirring and beeping that ground on my nerves. I couldn't rest in medbay with all that stimulation around me, and I was under very strict orders to rest.

"Must be nice, having an excuse to get so many perks."

"Oh yeah, it's real stellar," I snapped. "I just love being thought incompetent and emotionless, losing my job because I make a perfect scapegoat, and having people who don't even know me write terrible things about me for the entire universe to read. You know, if you came here just to antagonize me, the door is back the way you came."

Betancourt held up her hands. "All right, sorry. I didn't come here to start a fight."

"Could've fooled me."

"I just... wanted to ask some questions, that's all. Find out how you're feeling about this. The Alliance's current projection has the LHFH in tatters. They might never recover."

"Good."

"People know more about your role in things this time, thanks in part to my reporting," Betancourt pointed out. "You won't be losing your job. There'd be riots if you did. Right now, people are thinking of you as a hero, a selfless young woman who nearly died to save an entire race of sapient beings. But the public is fickle. A few months down the line and they might forget everything they've seen. Shouldn't you take advantage of how things are now to try to sway public opinion?"

"Public opinion that *you* helped contribute to?" I asked with false sweetness, and she had the good grace to look ashamed. "Who are you to call other people fickle? Six standard months ago you were more than happy to hang me out to dry, but now you want to talk about what a hero I am? You know, you don't have to chase the big story anymore. You've got your career back."

Betancourt glowered. "I don't know what you're talking about. I'm a journalist and I—"

"You're better than this. You know how I know? I did some reading about you recently. Because I always wondered what Captain Chui was up to, allowing you to report on our mission on Song. That's not like her. What *is* like her, though, is giving people second chances. Captain Chui specializes in misfits, outcasts, and lost causes.

"After your parents were killed by the LHFH, you made it your mission to discredit them. And I get that, I do, but you faked evidence, and you were caught. It ruined your career. That you even got a job at all is something of a miracle. Now you're the star reporter in all this and you don't have to chase the obvious story anymore.

"But if you want to write about heroes, write about heroes." I sighed. "Write about Amelia and all the soldiers like her who died. Write about Darksong, who gave her life to protect her people, or Engineer, who kept living in spite of losing everything she'd ever known. Write about Hans Klee, who was an *anthropologist,* not a soldier. Leave me out of it. I'm just a space-fried girl who lost control and acted without thinking. If I'd had a clear mind at all, I'd never have done what I did. And you can quote me on that."

She stared at me, stunned, and I stared back, equally shocked. *New rule: No talking to reporters while I'm on painkillers.* I was definitely not the sort of person who should be allowed to speak without thinking it through first. Where had all of that even come from? I dropped my gaze to the thin blanket that covered me, suddenly exhausted. *I don't want to answer any more questions for reporters ever again.*

"Ms. Betancourt," came *Carpathia's* familiar voice, "Ms. Corelel is under very strict orders to get her rest. I must ask that you leave now, or I will be forced to call security to escort you out."

"Yeah, fine, whatever," Betancourt muttered. "I didn't feel like staying, anyway."

She rose and stomped out the door. I wanted to say thank you to *Carpathia*, but all my words got stuck behind my teeth. Instead I buried my face in my hands and squeezed my eyes shut hard. Maybe I ought to cry. After everything I'd been through, I probably needed to. But even the thought of it was so tiring, I just couldn't let myself.

Diver

Damn near got run over by a pissed off Ashley Betancourt on my way in to see Xan. Had to dodge out of the way, which earned a couple of annoyed squawks from Cake and Marbles, who sat in a small carrying cage. And that got me no shortage of annoyed looks from everyone else in the medbay. *Like it's my fault she's raging through here like a mama hippo with an axe to grind.* She even glared at me, and I'd thought we were kinda starting to get along, or at least to stop hating each other.

I shook my head and made my way to the small, private room Xandri was in. Knocked, but got no response. I hesitated outside the door, wondering what I should do. Things seemed a little weird between us lately, kinda strained. Seemed like Xan was holding a lot back from me, and it frustrated me that I couldn't comfort her. If I just upset her even more...

"You should go in," *Carpathia* said, startling me somewhat. "A visit from you and her birds is exactly what Xandri needs."

Wasn't so sure about the me part, but Xan always seemed to feel better with her birds near, so I opened the door carefully. She was awake, sitting propped up against her many pillows, her hands pressed against her face. *Shit. What do I even do?*

Marbles solved the problem for me by squawking out, "Mommy!"

Xandri looked up, astonished. "Marbles! Cake! Oh, Diver, how'd you get them in here?"

"I uh, *might* have told Doctor Zahran that you were likely to stop complaining about being stuck in bed, at least for a little while, if you were allowed to see your birds," I said. "Think you can make good on that?"

She held her hands out eagerly, which I took for a yes. Grinning, I set the cage down on the end of the bed and opened it. Marbles and Cake were out like a shot, crawling expertly over the covers and Xandri's legs. They clambered up her arms and took a perch, one to each shoulder, and she didn't scold them for it. Cake, however, scolded the state of her hair and promptly began preening it. And Marbles rubbed her entire feathery head against Xandri's cheek.

And Xan, well, she gazed at me with big, glowing eyes, and things started to feel a bit like normal for the first time in days.

"Thank you," she said. "Thank you *so* much."

"Eh, think nothing of it, fireball. Just glad to put a smile on your face."

"There isn't a lot to smile about lately," she said quietly.

"What're you talking about? The LHFH is scattered to all corners of the universe—well, what's left of the bastards, anyway. Song is safe now, and," I flashed a grin, "I've almost got your wristlet fixed. It held up pretty well. Better than you did, I might add."

She managed a tiny smile. "But so much went wrong…"

I could just imagine the load of guilt and anguish going on in her head at the moment. I set the cage aside and dropped into the chair next to her bed, watching her reach up to scritch Marbles' head. Lotta people would've blown sunshine up her ass, but that shit didn't work with Xan. She was too damned keen, that was the problem. Or maybe too wary. I was beginning to wonder about that. She reacted to positivity with the sort of distrust I knew—from personal experience—tended to come from abuse.

"Yeah, shit does tend to go wrong when there are bastards like the LHFH in the world," I agreed. "But don't you think it'd go more wrong without people like us?"

"I don't know…"

"The Hands and Voices did a bang up job protecting themselves overall, but they had some disadvantages. We helped them overcome that. I didn't get it at first, you know, why they'd even want to join the Alliance. But I get it now. Really, I've understood it ever since joining the *Carpathia*. Having allies is real damn useful."

That wasn't entirely bullshit, either. I'd been wary when I first came aboard the *Carpathia* about the whole working-as-a-team thing. It hadn't gone so great for me the last time I'd tried it. But the more I thought about it lately, the more I realized how good it was for me. Maybe that's what the Hands and Voices were thinking too. They'd shown no signs of wanting to withdraw from the Alliance. If anything, they were more eager to join than ever before. Pretty sure they wanted to stick it in the LHFH's collective face.

"I guess," Xandri murmured.

"And I'll have you know," I said, deciding to change the subject, "that I don't appreciate having the life scared out of me by the sudden appearance of a dangerous merc. That woman is almost as tall as I am, and she walks like a cat. Scared a decade off me at least."

Xandri's eyes widened in surprise and a hint of amusement. Seeing I had her attention, I launched into every funny story I could think of, and there were quite a few to be found. She laughed an awful lot when I described the reporters' attempts at a covert break-in to R&D for an under the radar investigation. It was only 'cause we knew what we were doing down in R&D that no one had gotten killed or even lost a limb.

And she almost choked when I explained how, after that, Captain Chui had 'borrowed' the Drifters' Psittacan members, and the reporters ended up chasing them all over the ship in desperation for an interview. They never managed to catch a single Psittacan, and *Carpathia* kept them from wandering anywhere they shouldn't be, so it was amusing rather than horrifying.

Before I could launch into tales of Private Jensen's unsuccessful flirting escapades, the door opened again. Xandri turned to it with an annoyed expression—and broke into an enormous, delighted grin as Aki trundled in.

"Aki!" she cried. "I was beginning to think I'd never get to see you!"

"*I* was beginning to think I'd never get a break. I'm a starship pilot, not a taxi pilot." She gave her great body a shake and approached the bed. "Hello, Xandri-pup. Feeling any better today?"

"Diver brought Marbles and Cake to see me."

"Good thing Diver is cleverer than he looks."

"Hey!" I protested.

Aki settled on the floor next to the bed, propping her front limbs on the mattress for support. "Now, what's this I hear about you jumping off a cliff?"

Xandri sighed. "I'll never live that down, will I?"

Aki chuffed softly, and even Xandri smiled a little. Cautiously, while Aki talked about her job shuttling injured soldiers and other personnel from Song to the *Carpathia*, I reached over and lay a hand over one of Xandri's. She shifted her hand under mine, turning it to wind her fingers through mine and hold on tight. *See, old boy? You were getting all worked up for nothing. Things are gonna be fine between us.*

Chapter Thirty-Three

Diver

It took almost two weeks for Xandri to heal enough that Doctor Zahran was willing to let military nanos finish the job. I stayed on *Carpathia* the entire time, even though I was a little curious how Engineer and everyone planetside was doing. Seemed to me Xandri needed me most of all. Things still seemed a little odd between us, but she was loosening up as the days went by and she healed more. And getting her wristlet back seemed to perk her up immensely.

Once she was well enough for small trips out of bed, I went with her for short walks. Together we contacted Kiri to find out how she was doing—pretty well, all told, according to her—and I always managed to get Xan back to medbay just before she got too tired. Probably helped, too, that I made an ally of myself, convincing Doctor Zahran to give her a break on the nutrient-bars and keeping her in a supply of new books to read.

Finally, after a few days on military nanos, Doctor Zahran declared Xandri fully healed, and it was time to head planetside again. The Hands and Voices had a small ceremony planned to thank us for our aid, apparently. *Well, maybe not small,* I thought, glancing out the window at the other ships in the docking bay, all of which were getting ready to launch. Every single person who had helped would be there.

Xandri jittered the entire way, and as soon as we touched down, she fled to find Kiri, to get some help tidying herself up. I just ran my fingers through my hair, shrugged, and went to see if I could find Engineer.

No real surprise that she and Warrior were there, amid all the other Hands and Voices—including the Grand Matriarch—who were there for the ceremony. I whistled, long and loud, then took a seat on the edge of the dock. A short time later Warrior came swimming over and paused near my dangling feet. Engineer crawled up along Warrior's back until she was close enough to reach out a tentacle to me.

"Hey, little darling," I crooned. "How's it been going down here?"

"It is…unusual," Warrior said for her. "Working together has caused us to bond, and it makes for a strange situation. Engineer must continue our job, and we must go with us when we work. A Lone Verse has never done that before."

"Well, there's a first time for everything, right? And hey, you get to experience a whole new world."

"We are…not sure we care for it, but Engineer assures us we are happy to be together. We agree, so we will learn to adapt to this new situation."

I reached down and stroked Warrior's head. He was so different from Darksong, more serious and reserved, but if Engineer was happy, everything was stellar as far as I was concerned. And she sure seemed in a much better mood.

I hung out there for a while, enjoying the soft lap of the water against the dock, until Warrior pointed out that everyone—all several hundred plus of us—was lining up on the beach. I rose and went to join them, searching out *Carpathia's* crew among all the rest. Captain Chui hadn't forced us to wear uniforms, so everyone was dressed casually. The AFC folks were all dressed to the nines, of course, and the mercs, well, they were mercs.

Found Xandri next to Kiri, and I kinda wanted to kiss her, but figured an audience this big might be too much for her. But she looked nice, wearing a short tunic dress in a nice blue that matched her eyes, her hair pulled into a loose French braid that coiled over her shoulder. Kiri was a stunner as usual, her long dress cut simply but alive with an array of colors, but truth to tell, I couldn't much tear my eyes away from Xandri. As I took my place next to her, I leaned in close to whisper in her ear.

"You clean up good, Corelel."

She let out a huff of mock indignation. "This is *supposed* to be a serious occasion, Mr. Diver."

"They shouldn't have invited me, then."

"By that reckoning," Kiri said from Xandri's other side, "*none* of us should've been invited."

"There's still plenty of time for them to regret it," I pointed out.

"There's also plenty of time for Captain Chui to space us," Xandri said. "And I don't know about you, but I've taken enough of a beating for a while."

"Well, then hush," came Jae's voice from behind us. "I'd like to hear this."

Only it turned out, there wasn't much to hear. Normally I couldn't take the pomp and circumstance of ceremonies. They always seemed to drag out needlessly, and people loved to give speeches at the damn things. Long, boring speeches. One time I'd damn near fallen asleep on my feet. The Grand Matriarch though, she knew how to do a ceremony right. Her short but sweet thank you speech was broadcasted across the beach and that was that.

Well, almost that. There were boxes, rectangular and made of coral, each one about thirty centimeters long and around fifteen centimeters high. Major Douglas had brought a few AFC personnel down to hand them out. I reached out to take mine, and was surprised to find it fairly heavy. Almost opened it immediately out of curiosity, until Jae poked me in the back. Had to wait until everyone had theirs, and then there was the whole saluting business that always seemed to come in any ceremony with military people in it. Not being a trained soldier myself, I found it a bit tough, figuring out how to hang onto the box and salute at the same time.

"What's this even for?" I hissed through my teeth. "Ain't like the Hands and Voices can see it."

"The press can," Xandri said, her tone distinctly bitter. "Got to put on a good show for the paparazzi, right?"

"Let me guess. This was Major Douglas' idea. Man, this thing is heavy."

And no wonder, too. As the ceremony broke up, a lot of people headed up the beach a short ways, where food was being prepared. But some of us—me included, it was the street-rat in me—couldn't contain their curiosity. I dropped to the sand, Kiri and Xandri besides me, and opened the box.

"Holy shit!" I yelped, and heard an echo of similar sentiments around me.

"Wow," Xandri murmured, staring down into her own box.

"Well, if nothing else, we can retire now," Kiri joked.

No fucking kidding. The box was filled—completely filled, from one corner to the next —with nebula pearls. A small fortune of nebula pearls, and everyone had gotten a box like it. A glance over Xandri's shoulder showed that hers indeed held the same reward. She stared down at the pearls, an expression of wonder and—and something I didn't recognize on her face. Then she shut the box and hugged it against her chest with clear possessiveness. Not the possessiveness of greed, either. I knew that one well. No, she wore a look on her face like someone had just handed her all her dreams in that one box.

"Well, damn," I said. "They sure know how to say a proper thank you, don't they?"

"We *did* kinda save their entire planet," Kiri pointed out, setting her box in her lap and stretching. "Besides, I have a hunch that these are far less valuable to them than they are to the rest of the universe."

"Ain't that always the way, though? We find something shiny and we think it's special, but the locals, they're just like 'well, okay, we'll sell it to you, I guess, but it's more common than dirt here.' "

"We *are* talking about a mollusk's solidified defense mechanism against parasites. I mean, that's basically all it is, a parasite covered in calcium carbonate. I can see why someone would find it weird that we think they're valuable," Xandri said. "So, anyone else hungry?"

"I *was* about five seconds ago," Kiri muttered.

Xandri let out a soft trill of laughter, the freest, most relaxed sound I'd heard out of her in a good long while. It was the best ceremony I'd ever been to.

Xandri

"Xandri Corelel," came the Grand Matriarch's voice from my wristlet as Diver, Kiri and I started up the beach. "Might we talk to you in private for a moment?"

"Oh, uh… of course," I stammered, staring at Diver and Kiri in confusion. "Um, where would…?"

"Come to the end of the dock, please."

"I'll be there in just a moment." I made sure the comm channel was completely closed before speaking again. "I have *no* idea what this is about."

"No worries, starshine."

"Yeah," Diver said. "We'll hold some food for you. Want me to keep an eye on the box there?"

I had to fight hard against the instinct to clutch it against my chest and turn away, protecting it with my body. I knew *exactly* what I'd do with the contents of the box, something I'd been dreaming of for a very long time now. *With this, I'll truly be free.* No one *will ever hold me against my will again.* But Diver wasn't going to steal it from me, and I knew that. Everything he'd done the last few weeks had been to comfort me and make me feel better, even when I wasn't being as open with him as I once was.

"Thanks," I said, relinquishing the box. "I doubt I'll be long."

"Take all the time you need, yeah? I won't let anyone finish off your favorites before you get back."

He leaned over and gently kissed the corner of my mouth, then headed up the beach. Kiri grinned at me, waggling her eyebrows lasciviously before following him. Torches were being lit as the sun began to set, and the smell of food made my stomach rumble. There were so many people there, spread out across the beach, and somewhere music was playing. Normally all of it would make me want to hide, but just then, I wanted the comfort of all that company and laughter. I wanted to be one of my fellows more than I had in a very long time.

And if I kept standing here, all I'd do was think about how that might not even be possible, and it would ruin my night, so I headed for the dock.

The Grand Matriarch awaited me, an enormous dark shape in the water at the end of the pier. Considering we'd probably be here at least another month or so before we felt ready to hand the operation over to the AFC, I wondered what it was that couldn't wait. *What if… what if they want to cancel the Alliance after all?* But there'd been no sign of that. The LHFH had tried to wipe them out or, barring that, scare them away from the Alliance. The Hands and Voices seemed determined to not let anyone scare them away from anything they had set their minds to.

I sat at the end of the dock, folding my legs and leaning over to run my fingers through the water, announcing my presence. The Grand Matriarch surfaced.

"Greetings, Xandri Corelel."

"Greetings, Grand Matriarch. You wished to speak with me?"

"Yes. More precisely, we wished to give you something."

"Oh." I blinked. "But you already gave me something. And it's wonderful, truly. You can't imagine the gift you've given me, it's beyond valuable—"

"And what is more valuable than our home?" the Grand Matriarch asked. "A few nebula pearls are a paltry sum for a young woman who nearly died to save us."

"But I *didn't*," I protested. "Well, I nearly died, but the containment field was already down. I did it for nothing."

"You did it for *us*. We are not part of your song, and yet still you gave everything for us. We have been in contact with the rest of the universe long enough to know there are few hearts as big and welcoming as yours, Xandri Corelel. Please, allow us to give you this gift."

I swallowed. Tears—tears I probably should have already cried sometime during these past couple of weeks—prickled my eyes, and one escaped down my cheek. It wasn't true. I was a cold person, someone who had never told her parents she loved them, who hadn't attended a single funeral for those that had died on Song, who hadn't shed any tears for them. I couldn't even stop myself from drawing away from Diver, who was my best friend and who I was, I was pretty sure, quite madly in love with.

But all I said, in a tear-roughened voice, was, "Okay."

The Grand Matriarch let out a short whistle of song. One of her Voices moved, crawling up along her length with fast shifts of its tentacles. It paused near her head and reached out two tentacles, clearly wrapped around something, to me. I held out my hands. The tentacles unfurled, and the largest nebula pearl I'd ever seen— nearly the size of my fist—fell into my cupped palms.

I nearly fell off the dock.

"Oh, Grand Matriarch, I can't! It's too valuable, I can't just—"

"Of course you can. It is a gift. And it is only valuable because your song gives it such value," she said.

"But surely one this size must be really rare!"

Water and air erupted from her blowhole in what I thought was a chuckle. "None of them are rare. It is no effort at all for us to cultivate them, and there are many large species of mollusk within our song. We could make them by the thousands if we desired, but they benefit us more like this. Your song thinks they are of great value and pays us large sums, allowing us to continue improving our song, and we control how resources leave our planet. It all works to the best."

The smugness in her tone surprised me so much, I let out a soft laugh. No, 'innocent' was far from a good descriptor for the Hands and Voices. They knew *exactly* what they were getting into.

"Besides, it seems very little in return for all your help. We knew your compassion and honesty would be of value to us."

"Oh, Sweet Mother Irony," I gasped out. "Grand Matriarch, I—if this is meant to be about my *honesty*, I could never accept it. I shouldn't. I might not lie with words, but everything I *am* is a lie." The words came tumbling out, along with a sudden rain of tears. "I'm not who you think I am, not at all. I'm not—not—"

"Not what... Alexandria Corelellia?"

I *would* have fallen off that dock that time, had the Matriarch's Hand not reached out and caught me around the waist with its tentacle. A mixture of shock and panic filled me, and the tentacle around my waist felt like a binding, cutting off my air. I struggled, gasping for breath as the Hand moved me gently back from the edge of the dock so I wouldn't fall. Though I was starting to think another header off that cliff would be a good idea. *What do I do? Once it comes out, everything will fall apart. I'll lose everything!* I could *not* let my friends find out who I really was, who my *family* really was.

"Oh dear," the Grand Matriarch said. "Forgive us, Alexandria Corelellia, we did not mean to startle you so."

"How—how do you—"

"Think you that because we are ocean-bound we can learn nothing? No, we have known who you were for some time. After we heard your name mentioned four years ago, when the trade deal was first struck, we set out to learn more about you." She lolled in the water, turning an eye up to me. "If it is any comfort, it was not *easy* to discover who you truly were, and we were not completely certain until now."

"I... why haven't you... I mean... you never mentioned..."

"Many creatures on Song hide, and they have good reason to do so. We assumed you had good reason as well. Were we wrong?"

"No," I said emphatically, "you weren't wrong. If anyone else finds out, they might send me back. I'd rather jump off that cliff for good this time than ever go back."

"Then your secret is safe with us, Alexandria Corelellia. We would not send you back to a place that fills you with such terror." Her voice was such a gentle, reassuring croon that I relaxed. "So, will you accept our gift?"

"I will," I said, pressing the nebula pearl to my chest, over my heart. "Thank you, Grand Matriarch. I'll keep it always. I'll never sell it, no matter how valuable my song thinks it is."

"Make no promises. It is yours to do with as you wish. And besides, might there not come a time when you have great need of its value?" she pointed out. "You have been a good friend to us, and it is our feeling that you will be so again sometime in the future. If you must eventually sell the pearl to do so, then it will only be more of your kindness."

"What kind of friend lies to everyone she cares about?"

The tentacle moved from my waist up to my tear-streaked cheek. "Would you like our advice, Alexandria Corelellia?"

"Please," I sniffled.

"Worry less about the person you hide, and spend more time being the person you are. In time you will find you are never truly lying to anyone. A name is only a name, after all. There is nothing truer than a heart."

Cynical voices began clamoring in my head, but I clutched the nebula pearl and found the strength to push them away. The Grand Matriarch was a being far older and wiser than me. I didn't know if I could always succeed, but I would try. At the very least, I'd put all my will into following her advice tonight. The music and laughter and the smell of cooking food still called to me, and I didn't want to miss any more of it.

I stumbled back to my room sometime in the wee hours of the morning, exhausted but feeling the best I had in weeks. I'd already stashed the larger nebula pearl here earlier, tucked away with my clothes; now I set the box of smaller pearls on the table beside my bed and dropped to the mattress with a sigh.

I smelled of salt and sand and smoke from the cook fires, and I was so full I felt a little sick, but I didn't care. Everyone was right to celebrate. We'd saved the mission, stopped the LHFH, maybe even destroyed them for good. We'd protected the Hands and Voices, who had done nothing to deserve the LHFH's ire. *Captain Chui is right. We do good work.* For all some sapients—humans came to mind—could be ungrateful, helping others when they needed it, that was a worthwhile life.

My wristlet buzzed. *Who's contacting me now?* With effort, I lifted my arm to check my messages. But this wasn't from someone I knew. I sat up, my eyes glued to the message, a mixture of fear and confusion and excitement cutting through my sluggishness.

> *You aren't alone. We're here too. We know of you. If you need us, really need us, we can find you, or show you the way. You never have to go back to Wraith ever again.*

The Quiet Hands

Quiet Hands. Those words drew me more than any other with their familiarity. No, I'd never heard of a group of any kind called The Quiet Hands, but... *Quiet your hands, Alexandria. You're a young lady, not a bird. Stop fluttering.* Mother's voice. And the message said *You aren't alone. We're here too.* We. I knew there had been others born with neurodivergences during that thin slice of years, others like Marco and me. I'd always been too scared to wonder what had happened to them.

"But what if they're out there even now," I whispered.

I rose from the bed and headed to the window. The last few partiers were clearing off the beach, and the stars were out, hundreds of thousands of tiny silver specks in the sky. We'd found so much amongst those stars. So many worlds, so many species, so many sapients. *Is it possible that others like me are out there too, waiting to be found?* Except it sounded as if *they* had found *me*, not the other way around. Suddenly questions, hundreds of them, crowded my mind.

"Who are you?" I murmured. "*Where* are you?"

A chill walked down my spine. I'd always known that the universe was huge, unfathomably so. Now my own personal universe was expanding far faster than I could deal with. What did I do? Should I try to contact them, try to find them? What would I even do if I did? *No, no, calm down, Xandri.* I forced myself to take a deep breath, draw in the fresh air and relax my tensing shoulders. I'd gotten through everything else that was thrown at me without breaking, and I'd get through this too.

But only if I took things one day at a time.

Starsystems Alliance Planet Classification System

As updated by Xandri Corelel in the year 4273 AE by human reckoning

Habitability

U	Uninhabitable
H	Habitable
T	Habitable with Terraforming
I	Habitable, Already Inhabited

Indigenous Lifeforms

NL	No Life (only used on class H and T planets)
BL	Basal Life
CL	Complex Life
SL	Sapient Life

Resources

NR	No Useful Resources
RU	Resources Unknown
AR	Available Resources
RD	Collection of Resources May Present Danger to Lifeforms (applies to native lifeforms or potential workers)
TR	Trade for Resources Available

Alliance Status

AM	Alliance Member
AM-1	Tier 1 (involved in government, military, technological and social development, trade, etc.)
AM-2	Tier 2 (involved in trade, possibly in government, military OR technological and social development, but not all of them)
AM-3	Tier 3 (under protection of/ward of Alliance, not yet involved in Alliance society)
NM	Non-Member
NM-1	Tier 1 (receives full protection/benefits from the Alliance with the goal of advancing sufficiently to join)
NM-2	Tier 2 (may receive protection/benefits from the Alliance, may even trade some, but limits the amount of Alliance involvement to varying degrees)
NM-3	Tier 3 (desires no involvement/interference from the Alliance)
NM-4	Tier 4 (actively antagonistic/dangerous to the Alliance)
NM-SC	Special Class (non-member worlds that for some reason or another are under Alliance watch and protection)

Special Classifications

DL	Inhabited by Dangerous/Hostile Lifeforms (i.e. dangerous predators, not hostile sapients)
FE	Fragile Ecosystems
C	Classified

Example of full planet classification as applied to celestial body known as Stillness: I-SL-RU, NM-SC, Special Classifications: All

Planet classifications are often shortened for ease of use. Example: Song is referred to as an ISTN-2 planet. Its full classification string is: I-SL-TR NM-2

About the Author

Kaia Sønderby is an American currently residing in Sweden with her Danish husband. She hopes to eventually escape to a warmer country that actually sees the sun for more than one month out of every year. Her hobbies include reading, playing video games, various and sundry art projects—usually involving far too much glitter—and being a feminist killjoy, and her interests vary from history to the paranormal to maritime disasters. She is also the proud momma of a continually expanding array of rodents (expanding in numbers, not just expanding outwards, though they're doing that too).

Want More?

At The Kraken Collective, we know how frustrating it can be to reach the end of a book and want more. Within the following pages, you'll find books with a similar feel to help you scratch that reading itch and why we're recommending them.

We hope our suggestions will help you find your next favourite read!

A Promise Broken

If you're looking for rich worldbuilding with unique cultures and ocean themes, check out *A Promise Broken*, by Lynn E. O'Connacht. When four-year-old Eiryn tries to call rain at her mother's funeral, others worry she might have upset the balance of the world. As her new guardian, her uncle Arèn must learn the ropes of parenting while trying to protect her from harm. Yet all Eiryn wants is to make everyone happy even as grief and fear tear at them. *A Promise Broken* is a beautiful tale of kindness and grief that will slip into your heart quietly and stay with you.

Moon-Bright Tides

The *Xandri Corelel* series aren't the only Kraken book with a queer autistic protagonist and a wonderful ocean vibe. If you want more, check out *Moon-Bright Tides* from RoAnna Sylver, in which a witch goes out every night to call back the tides while the moon is gone—a lonely endeavor, until she meets a lost, starved mermaid. *Moon-Bright Tides* is a delightfully sweet and gorgeous f/f novelette.